# VACANT STEPPES

Balestier Press
Centurion House, London TW18 4AX
www.balestier.com

*Vacant Steppes*
Copyright © Steven Sy, 2021

A CIP catalogue record for this book
is available from the British Library.

ISBN 978 1 913891 07 7

# VACANT STEPPES

A NOVEL BY

STEVEN SY

BALESTIER PRESS
LONDON · SINGAPORE

"The question is not whether you will love, hurt, dream, and die. It is what you will love, why you will hurt, when you will dream, and how you will die. This is your choice. You cannot pick the destination, only the path."

—Brandon Sanderson, *Oathbringer*

"It may feel impossible, but sometimes you just have to take the first step, even before you're ready."

—Sisu, *Raya and the Last Dragon*

*For my favorite little sister, Kaitlyn.*
*I can't wait to watch you take on the world.*
*I'm already so proud of you.*

# Content Notes

This page contains details about this novel that some readers might consider 'spoilers'. I include it as a way for readers to inform themselves about potentially disturbing or triggering scenes.

- There is no swearing or explicit language in this novel.
- There is no sexual content in this novel.
- There are frequent references and depictions of war, violence, and death.
- Certain characters display symptoms of mental illnesses such as post-traumatic stress disorder, anxiety, and depression. There are also frequent descriptions of grief and loss after the death of loved ones.
- Depictions of physical injuries, blood, and other bodily fluids are present, but not gratuitous.
- Certain characters infrequently make racist and/or imperialist remarks.
- Most of the novel takes place in military and/or militaristic settings.
- Violence against animals such as deer or horses in the form of hunting and butchering are infrequently described.
- Damage to the environment is frequently described or referenced.

I am open to the possibility that this list of content notes might be incomplete or insufficient. Let me know if there is something you think I should include.

# I

# Wide Open Sky

# 1

# Sara

War was brewing, but all Sara could worry about was whether her brother's robes fit him correctly. The two weeks that followed Sara's father passing into the wind were a blur: the funeral, the smoke rising into the sky above the Great Steppe, and her father's eagle letting out a final cry, flying into the horizon.

"Remember, Od, these people are vicious," Sara said. "They're the most powerful men in our tribe, and all this while, they'll be looking for ways to manipulate you."

She couldn't get over how strange the chieftain's robes looked on her brother. Od had broader shoulders than their father, so the robes seemed to strain against his chest.

"You know, we're all part of one tribe, Sara. That means something, doesn't it?"

"It does, but you should still be careful. Have you forgotten that there's news of war?"

Od raised his eyebrow as he mounted his horse, but Sara didn't budge.

"Okay, okay," he said, holding up his hands. "I'll keep my wits about me. You know Sara, I'm the older brother, but I always feel like I'm just trying to catch up to you."

Sara gave him a laugh. "Now you're really going crazy, Od."

"Are you sure you don't want to come?"

She looked up at him, taking a step back. When her brother was mounted on his horse, the ill-fitting robe somehow looked a lot better. She could almost imagine him galloping into council in her father's place.

"I'm sure the camp will manage without us for two days," he said.

Sara smiled at her brother. Mounted on his horse and dressed in their father's regalia, he really did seem like a chieftain. "Come on. You need to do this alone—it's what Father would have wanted."

"Right. You're right," Od said. "It's just... I wish he were with us now. There's so much I want to ask him."

"I do too," Sara said. "Saenor's scales, we haven't had any time but...Father and mother are both gone. It's just us left."

"I know. But we'll stick together, won't we?"

"Of course I know that. But I didn't expect it to hurt this much."

"Me neither," Od said. "Gaeon saved me—I think I'm going to be sick."

"You'll be fine."

"Will I though? I'd pledge my soul to Gaeon if I could be half the chief he was."

"Well, I don't think you ever will be," Sara said.

Od laughed, and as he did, Sara felt like her brother was finally coming back to her. "I thought you were supposed to be comforting me."

"I am comforting you. Father never wanted you to be the same leader like he was. He was the strong, silent type. But Od, you're not like that. You can be better than him."

Od thought for a moment, then he smiled. "I like the way that sounds. You know, I'm surprised Father didn't declare you to be the chieftain after him."

"Me? Come on, Od. You know that I'd never survive a council meeting. Too many voices. I'd have forgotten what my own sounded like."

"You know, Sara, whenever I have doubts about my own maturity, all I need to do is look to my little sister."

Sara laughed again—it was the most she had laughed since their father passed. "But he was right, you know? Don't worry, Od. You'll do fine. I'll be right beside you all the way."

Od grinned as he sat up straighter in the saddle. For a moment, just as the sunlight crested over the nearby hill, Sara thought she could see Od sitting right alongside the other tribe chieftains at their meeting.

"Thanks little sister. I'll see you in two days," Od said, patting his horse on the neck. But the creature didn't need any more guidance than that, since it had been bonded to Od when he was a child. Within a few moments, Od was cantering off into the horizon, becoming a speck in the distance that Sara could barely make out.

"Gaeon ride with you," Sara muttered.


Sara pulled a saddle onto her horse and buckled the straps. She ran her hand across its mane, trying to get a feel for what the animal was thinking. The horse let out a breath and thumped its hooves on the ground. Sara laughed and gave it a pat, placed one foot into the stirrups and with one fluid motion, mounted her horse.

Elsewhere in the stables, one of Sara's other hunters, Kara, was having more trouble. She pulled tight on her horse's bridle, but it wouldn't even allow her to get a saddle on, much less be mounted.

Sara let Kara try her luck for a few more moments, then she called out, "Just use manna, for Gaeon's sake."

Kara released her horse. "Fine, fine! By Saenor, that beast's never going to let me near him."

"He just needs some time to trust you," Sara said, throwing Kara a pouch of manna. "Give it time."

Kara scoffed and reached into the pouch, pulling out a handful of azure powder. She approached the horse, this time going slowly so as to not startle it, and sprinkled the powder on the horse's mane. The powder glowed and Sara saw Kara whisper to the horse, which seemed to calm it down. She noticed Kara's shoulders relaxing, with her voice becoming less agitated as the manna brought her and her horse's spirits closer together.

After a few moments, Kara finally managed to saddle and mount her horse, much to her relief.

"Come on, Kara, you can't manage to mount a horse without using manna?" Khulan said, hopping onto her horse without so much as a whine from the creature. "At this rate, we'll need to make an extra trip to the Temple to stock up."

"Yeah, but unfortunately I need my neck," Kara said.

"Good hunters don't break their necks."

Sara laughed while Kara made it a point to ignore Khulan by checking her equipment. Sara did the same, busying herself by making sure that she had extra binding for any game they got that day. Her hand found the longsword that she kept in her saddle pack, though she knew she wouldn't need it. Then she took out her bow and strung it, which took less than a second.

"Are we all ready?" Sara muttered to herself, glancing around the stable, where their group of hunters, seven in total, were in varying states of preparedness. She shrugged. "Guess not."

The only other hunter who was ready to move was Ganbold, a grizzly old warrior who had weathered a thousand hunts.

"Come on! Any longer and the deer will be gone when we get there," Ganbold said, spit flying from his mouth as he barked. Then he turned to Sara. "Where do we ride today, Sara?"

Sara considered for a moment. "We'll ride around the hills to the north, then survey the plains beyond. Yesterday's party told me that they found tracks going there."

Ganbold nodded. "We will be right behind you, then."

Within a few minutes, the rest of the riders had mounted up and were ready to hunt. They watched Sara with expectant eyes. Their gaze made her shudder.

She took a deep breath, then addressed them in an even tone. "We ride north today, to the plains beyond the hills. Got it?"

They nodded. Khulan managed a half smile. "Nothing else to say, Sara?"

"Well, what else is there to say?"

Khulan waved her hand dismissively. "Never mind. Inspiring speech, as always."

Sara rolled her eyes and patted her horse on the neck. She clucked, and thankfully, the creature followed along, turning and leading her horse out of the stable and into the open air. The wind was merciless today, but Sara was thankful for it—the wind made the sun easier to bear. Her horse turned north and her hair whipped back in the wind.

Before long, Khulan was galloping alongside her, while Ganbold and the rest were struggling to keep up. Sara was glad to finally be free of the tent and the camp. The wind whipped past her with increasing speed, and her horse's hooves clomped on the grass like the pounding of a rainstorm. The wind howled and the hooves pounded, yet Sara had never felt such peace before.

She was free—the village disappeared behind them and there was nothing but the huge sky above them. The world never seemed so big as when she was out on the plains. Out here, there was no cover, no shade, no sanctuary in the sea of grass, save for the occasional mound of dirt and lonesome tree.

They rode like this for half an hour before Sara could feel the terrain changing. Her horse began to pant with the effort of going uphill, and soon she could see their destination. The hills towered over them, but Sara knew their crags and curves—she had weathered them so many times before. She wished she could climb one of those hills and watch the plains from above, but she couldn't do it today. They rounded the hills, and Sara could feel her horse begin to pant with the effort. She sprinkled more manna on its neck, watching the blue powder glow and dissolve into the wind.

Only when they emerged on the far side of the hills did Sara slow her pace and allow the group to rest. She looked behind her and was glad to find that all her hunters were still with her—some looked the worse for wear, but she needed to take a break in the greenhorns somehow.

"All good?" she asked, getting off her horse. Some of the newer hunters were uneasy on their feet after dismounting, but Sara was relieved that none of them toppled to the ground. She closed her eyes and summoned Altan, her soul-bonded hunting eagle. It took no more than a thought, and within a few moments, she saw the creature's shape emerging from the clouds.

Altan perched himself on her shoulder and spread his wings, startling some of the newer hunters. She stroked his feathers, and as she did, the creature's wings glowed a bright blue. For a moment, she saw the world as he did. She felt the wind in her hair and the sunlight on her back.

She felt the wind under her wings and the entire world below her. She felt every wind current, every change in moisture, every spot of turbulence. It was so easy to get lost in the vision, but Sara had to discipline herself to stay in the moment. Her eyes were sharp as a blade, and she could pick out each herd of deer, each tree, and each mound of dirt. That was all she needed.

With a heavy sigh, Sara slipped out of the vision and let Altan fly off. She knew that he was hungry, and there were rabbits in the grass that he had his eye on. He deserved it, especially after the morning of scouting work she'd put him through.

"Okay, here's the plan," she said, addressing her hunters, who watched her in awe. Only Ganbold and Yargai had their own eagles, but still both of them were floored. "We split into three groups. Kara and Khulan, you're with me. Ganbold, take Orda. Yargai, take Mide. I'll ride straight north and get the herd of deer there. That's probably the biggest one, so I'll need two riders with me. Ganbold, I want you to follow the foothills west until you reach the stream. There's a herd there. Yargai, ride east for five hundred meters, then turn north until you reach a patch of trees—the deer are hiding amongst them. Got it?"

Without question, the hunters nodded and began to mount their horses.

"I've seen your eagle-eye so many times before, but to this day,

I'm still impressed with the way you handle him," Ganbold told her, approaching her as she settled into her saddle.

"What?" Sara said. "Oh, uh, it's nothing. My father taught me all he knew. And I don't think of my eagle as something I wield—he's my partner."

Ganbold nodded. "There's no need to be humble, Sara. You must be the best eagle-eye our tribe has seen in a hundred years."

"Thank you, Ganbold. That means a lot coming from you."

Sara made sure her bow was in order, then she looked around, making sure that all the hunters were mounted. She whistled. A moment later, the storm of hooves moved off, and the hunt was on.

"You're really going to the range on our off day?" Khulan said as Sara passed her tent three days after their hunting trip, bow in hand.

"If I don't shoot every day, I get rusty. You should come with me, it might do your aim some good."

Khulan considered for a moment. "Nah, I'm good right here," she said, leaning back in her seat. "You get enough practice for the both of us."

"Suit yourself," Sara said. She had hoped that Khulan would refuse. Sara's daily trips to the range were the only time she had to herself, and despite her fondness for Khulan, she was not quite ready to give up her alone time.

She made her way to the archery range, keeping her eyes to the ground for fear of meeting someone's eyes by accident. But that was unavoidable—before she reached the range, a voice called her from behind.

"Sara! Wait up, I need to ask you something."

She turned, and saw that the voice was coming from Bataar.

"What do you need?" she said.

"It's just—shouldn't Od be back by today? We expected him early this morning."

Sara stopped in her tracks. "You mean he isn't back yet? I thought he was resting in his tent or something."

Bataar shook his head. "I looked out for him this morning while watching the herds. But there was no sign of him."

"Maybe he got delayed. I guess… I suspect the council might have had more to talk about."

"Hmm, perhaps. I'll send you a messenger as soon as Od gets back. I think we'll have a lot to talk about."

"Yes, thank you Bataar. The moment he gets back." Sara heaved a sigh and headed for the archery range.

Sara resolved that if Od wasn't back by that evening, she'd ride to Chinua's camp right away. She should have gone with him in the first place.

Sara drew back her bow and loosed the arrow, but the point missed its mark entirely.

"Saenor's scales, why can't I get this right?" she whispered to herself, pulling another arrow from her quiver.

Her ears pricked up at a sound, though she couldn't tell what it was at first. Then she pinpointed the source—a single set of hooves pounding against the dirt. But a lone rider didn't make sense. Hunters always went in twos or threes. Something was wrong.

There was a hill next to the range that shrouded part of the field, but it was also their camp's first watchtower in case of trouble.

Sara was at the top within minutes, but she wasn't winded. Anxiety pumped through her veins as she scanned the landscape, before seeing a black speck approaching at a full gallop. She would recognize Od's horse anywhere, and she breathed a sigh of relief.

Then her breath caught in her throat. The stallion's back was empty—there wasn't even a saddle fastened. That only meant one thing. A bonded animal never strays too far from its master.

"Od…" Sara whispered, tears building in her eyes. "Oh no, Od."

# 2
# Batu

The thunder of hooves echoed on the horizon. From Batu's spot on the hill, he could see the chieftains approach from every direction. He took a deep breath and stood. Now was his time to prove himself, and he'd finally show his father that he was worth something. Since the First War, the Omnu had become the most powerful tribe in the Steppe, rising higher than the cowardly Asjare who hid in the Arban Valley or the Qhurin who secluded themselves in their marshlands. As the son of the head chieftain, Batu carried that proud Omnu legacy on his shoulders.

"Feet on the ground, eyes to the sky," Batu whispered to himself as he moved to the camp's central clearing, where he would welcome the incoming riders.

The clearing was filled with Chinua's hunters, all dressed in formal regalia, complete with gold lace and dyes from the east.

Batu spotted Nugai, who gave him a wink. His friend looked different in his formal dress—Batu was used to seeing him in a simple dishevelled shirt and trousers. There was a longsword at his friend's belt, which Batu found odd, since Nugai was most comfortable wielding two war axes in battle.

"Can't wait to get out of these things," Nugai said, stretching his collar. Batu could see beads of sweat forming along his neck. "It's roasting me from the inside."

"You look better this way," Batu said. "We need to look our best for the council."

Nugai rolled his eyes. "I'd rather stab all the chieftains in their sleep."

"Nugai, don't let anyone hear you say that."

"Relax, no one's near enough to eavesdrop. For Gaeon's sake, you're always playing politics, Batu. When are you ever going to loosen up?"

Batu shook his head. "It's what's the tribe needs."

"If you say so."

The first chieftain entered the camp, galloping in like a thunderstorm. His huge, bushy beard swayed in the wind almost as much as his horse's mane did, and he looked like he could take on a thousand horses with his bare hands. Batu recognized him—his name was Khasar, but everyone called him the Bull.

The Bull was followed by two chieftains who Batu recognized in an instant—one was young with an auburn goatee, carrying a herder's staff, and the other was old and uneasy on his horse. Dagun and Yegu.

Last to arrive was Odgerel, the newly-minted chieftain. His face was clean-shaven, but his chest and shoulders were built like an ox's and he wore the tribe's formal wear well. Batu didn't know what to make of him. They hadn't gotten along, mostly because when they were younger, Od and his sister preferred to run with the horses, but Batu preferred to listen to the elders tell stories.

The chieftains gathered in the clearing before dismounting and approaching Batu in a neat line. Batu noticed a moment of hesitation in Odgerel's stride—but he hid it well enough. They stood in silence for a few moments, then Batu bowed.

"Praise to Gaeon," he said. "Welcome."

"Praise," the chieftains said, nodding. They then relaxed their pose.

Batu gave them a polite smile. "Good afternoon, chieftains. I trust that your ride was pleasant."

"As pleasant as riding for four hours in a day can be," the Bull muttered. He shook Batu's hand and turned to the council tent.

"Good to see you, Batu," said Yegu. "I see that Chinua's letting you handle the welcoming ceremony. It's about time he started entrusting you with more responsibility."

"Wise man, that Chinua," Dagun said. "Soon, you'll be presiding over these meetings as well."

Batu bit his lip. "I hope so, if my father can find it in him to let someone else tell him what to do."

Yegu and Dagun laughed and followed Batu's direction towards the tent, but Batu bit his lip.

The last to approach him was Odgerel. The man was the perfect politician, and he extended his hand to shake Batu's with a smile that could charm the world twice over.

"Batu, good to see you. I hope your father is well?"

"He is."

"Good to hear. I'm sure his work keeps him busy—so busy that he couldn't find the time to attend the funeral of one of his chieftains."

Batu flinched. "You have our deepest condolences for your father's passing. He was a good man."

Odgerel smiled, but it was so slight that Batu barely noticed it. "Yes, sure, thank you."

Without another word, Odgerel pushed past Batu and entered the tent, leaving Batu to fume in silence.

"That boy's got a mouth on him," Nugai said. "I like him."

"Let's see him use that mouth on my father," Batu said, turning away from Nugai and entering the tent.

"Wow," Nugai said as they entered. "Looks like old Chinua's really made a show out of it."

Instead of the simple set up that Chinua had for his regular council meetings, he prepared the full spectacle for the chieftains. Gold-laced embroidery decorated the walls of the tent and the symbol of the Omnu tribe, a galloping stallion on a snowy peak, was displayed on flags spread throughout the room. Torches kept the tent lighted, crackling as they bathed the tent in a sombre crimson glow.

"It's a show of strength," Batu muttered so that only Nugai could hear. "He wants them to know that he still has control."

The chieftains of the Omnu tribe sat themselves in a ring—this time, Chinua sat on the same level as them. Chinua was wearing his usual ceremonial robes; they were huge and embroidered with gold, made from the skin of wolves that roamed the Steppe. Everything about him, from the way he sat to the way he spoke, commanded authority and respect.

Years ago, Batu's mother, Oyuun, would have sat next to Chinua during these meetings. When things were good, she would have been the one to calm her husband's fiery temper. In the years following her death during the plague, the space beside Chinua remained empty, and Oyuun's absence loomed large. The memory of Batu's mother sitting there brought back nothing but pain for Batu, and he had to bite his lip to distract himself.

The rest of them—Batu, Jochi the master hunters, and Nekhii the master herder—sat in an outer ring around the chieftains. Some of the other chiefs had brought guards or advisers, but Odgerel came alone. He showed no weakness when Chinua began the council—his head did not bow and neither did his eyes flinch, even when Chinua addressed the group in his booming voice.

"Good afternoon, chiefs of Omnu," his father said. "Gaeon's blessings have brought you safely to my tent today—I pray that our council will be just as fruitful."

The chiefs nodded. The Bull looked like he had something to say, but the huge man kept it to himself. The chief that hosted the council spoke first—that was the way things worked.

"Welcome," Chinua continued. "My friends, I bring you grave news—I told you in my message to remember the Fulgar. After the last war, we swore that if war were to haunt our lands again, we would remember those words."

The chieftains weren't surprised—they knew what the message meant. Batu could see the unease and anticipation in their faces.

"Then what are we waiting for?" the Bull roared. "Let's ride out and meet them!"

"In time we will, Khasar," Chinua said, his voice even. "But we cannot be hasty—the Empire knows that they cannot attempt another hasty invasion. They will be cunning this time. Craftier too."

"But we'll beat them again—same way we did last time," the Bull said, crossing his arms.

"We will," Chinua told him. Then he addressed the entire council. "Jochi, why don't you tell everyone what your scouts found?"

"Certainly," Jochi said. "There are outposts being constructed on both sides of Gaeon's Pass."

Dagun interrupted, stroking his beard. "What fortifications do they have? How do we know they aren't just scouting posts?"

Jochi shook his head. "It's far more than that. We didn't get a close enough look to see their numbers, but we saw walls four times the height of a man, and the empress's flag was hoisted up. This is no mere scouting post—they're preparing for war."

"What do they want?"

"Same thing they've always wanted," Chinua said. "They want control of the Temple of Gaeon, and our manna. We won't let them have it."

"We must call for aid then," Dagun said without pause. "Bring the other tribes together. The Omnu cannot weather this storm on its own."

Batu raised his head in surprise.

"Agreed," Odgerel said. "Do as we did twenty years ago."

"Things aren't the same was twenty years ago," Yegu said. "It would be wise to consider other options."

"What other options do we have? It's the same as twenty years ago—our way of life is threatened, so we must go to war together. Isn't this the same?"

"You don't know what you're talking about, kid," the Bull roared. "I've been in war tents since before your balls dropped."

Before Odgerel could reply, Chinua raised a hand, bringing the tent to silence. "That's enough. We are one tribe. I will not abide a fight between chiefs." He took a deep breath. "Chief Yegu is right. Things are different now. Do not forget that Omnu controls the passage to the Temple of Gaeon and the manna spring, and the other tribes, especially the Asjare, will be looking to steal that from us. There is also the issue of the Qhurin's control of the Spring of Gaeon."

The Bull nodded vigorously. "I will not beg the Asjare or Harnda swine for anything. They'll sooner have us slaughtered at the Empire's feet."

"My people were slaughtered by the Asjare on the Serpent's River two years ago," Yegu said. "We will not fight with them."

"Thank you, friends," Chinua said. "Does this mean we are in agreement?"

Dagun thought for a long moment, then said, "If the tribes cannot trust each other, we have no business fighting together. A horse must stand on all four legs."

All eyes turned to Odgerel, whose fists were visibly shaking. He then got to his feet with such force that the chair beneath him fell over. "This is ridiculous, and you all know it. If we try to stand against the Empire alone, we will die. No two ways about it."

"What would you propose we do then?" Chinua said.

"We must call for aid. We can offer them free passage to the Temple if we need to. It's the only way."

Chinua leaned back in his seat. "We cannot do that."

"Then you're all fools," Odgerel said, turning to leave without so much as a second glance. "I won't take part in this suicide mission."

The hunters at the entrance tried to stop him, but Odgerel pushed past. He exited the tent without another word, leaving them all speechless.

The Bull was the first to break the silence. "Good riddance," he scoffed.

"The boy's got fire," Yegu said.

"Let me speak to him," Chinua said, getting to his feet. "We'll convene again tomorrow. In the meantime, I'll have my hunters take you to your tents."

The chiefs looked unhappy with having to stay another day, but none of them seemed keen on handling Odgerel, so they consented. Tradition dictated that all chiefs were to be in agreement before a tribe moved forward on decisions related to war.

"To give him credit," Dagun said as he passed Chinua on his way out. "He's his father's son. "

"That's what I was worried about," Chinua muttered.

Batu watched the stars rise slowly from the hilltop, but he still couldn't get Odgerel's words out of his head. He had said the same things that Batu told his father nights before, but Odgerel did not falter. Batu wondered what sort of courage that took.

He looked into the sky, and noticed that the moon was at its zenith. Nugai had gone with his father to speak with Odgerel, as if the sight of the former bandit would terrify him into submission. He hoped that Odgerel would stand firm, and perhaps Batu and him could convince his father to walk a different path.

Batu got up and made his way to Odgerel's tent and began to rehearse what he'd say to his father.

Batu turned his words over and over in his head until he was sure they were perfect. He had been so lost in thought that he didn't realize that he was standing in front of Odgerel's tent.

He took a deep breath and pushed through the canvas flaps. When he entered, he was immediately struck with a strange smell of metal. Then he realized what it was. He looked down and found Odgerel's body lying spread-eagled on the floor, bathed in his own blood.

He took a closer look, trying to push the dark thoughts from his mind, then recognized the nature of Odgerel's wounds. There were two huge cuts on his back, one of which cleaved deep to reveal bone. The size and depth of the cuts told Batu that the damage was done with a war axe.

Batu knew only one man in this camp who could make those wounds with that weapon.

# 3

# Erroll

Erroll stared at the blank piece of paper in front of him, pen in hand, wondering what in the world he was going to tell his mother.

"Dear Mother," he wrote.

*"I left Ruson two months ago to enlist in the Empire's Second Expedition to the Great Steppe. I'm following in Father's footsteps. We leave for the Steppe in a week, so this is my last chance to write to you. I guess I owe you some kind of explanation. The truth is..."*

"No, that's stupid," he muttered to himself, crumpling up the sheet of paper. "She already knows that."

He started again.

*"Dear Mother,*

*I'm sorry that I left Ruson without telling you why. You must have been so worried. I was so sure that you wouldn't let me, and I didn't want to worry you, so I..."*

"Now I'm making excuses," Erroll muttered. "That's not good either."

He crumpled the piece of paper before retrieving another sheet.

*"Dear Mother,*

*I want you to know that I plan on coming back. I enlisted in the army, but only for the Steppe expedition. I won't be gone forever. I promise that when the expedition's over, I'll be back to see you."*

"So I'm lying to her now?" Erroll said, putting his head in his hands. "For Galele's sake, I should just be honest."

"Dear Mother," Erroll wrote for what felt like the hundredth time.

*"I left Ruson without telling you because I knew that you wouldn't
let me. But I'm a grown adult, and it's time for me to start making my
own decisions. I wasn't going to spend the rest of my life in the smithing
district."*

Erroll sighed and returned his pen to its holder, reading over the
words he'd written. There was no way in hell he'd actually send that
letter to his mother, but it felt good to finally commit the words he'd
carried in his chest to paper. He set the letter aside, drew out another
sheet and was about to start again, but then the door burst open.

"Erroll," Manvel said. "Oh. I'm sorry. Are you busy?"

"No, not at the moment," Erroll said.

"Good. Praxis is about to give everyone their assignments. Dining
hall. Be there in ten minutes."

"Got it, thanks."

The door closed again, and Erroll was left with yet another bank
page. The words escaped him, and he knew that he wouldn't find
them again no matter how hard he tried. He put away the pens and
paper and got up from his seat, heading for the door.

Erroll took a seat next to Manvel right as Praxis ascended the stage in
the front of the dining hall. The marks of the festivities from the week
before had been cleaned away, and everything was back to bare wood
and old cutlery.

"You ready?" Manvel asked.

"We're about to be sent to fight horse-riding, axe-carrying savages
for a year or more," Erroll said. "How ready do you think I am?"

"Okay, forget I asked."

Praxis cleared his throat and the dining hall fell silent immediately.

"Attention, recruits. Orders just came in from the capital. We're to
be assigned to the front line in the Second Expedition to the Great
Steppe."

Erroll could feel the room growing uneasy, but of course, Manvel had discovered their assignment the week before, so it was no surprise.

"These orders come directly from Empress Tomyris herself. She has decreed that it is now a matter of utmost priority for the nomads to be swiftly brought under the Empire's rule. She will therefore be committing two entire legions to the expedition: General Sandulf's legion and General Asghar's legion. Most of you will be assigned to General Sandulf's force."

"You know who Sandulf is, right?" Manvel muttered. "Didn't your father serve with him on the First Expedition?"

"Yeah," Erroll muttered, fists tightening underneath the table. "I know him."

"Remember that all of you will carry the banner of the Jusordian Empire on your backs as you march to battle," Praxis continued. "The nomads know how to fight, but they have no awareness of honor, righteousness, or discipline. They worship false gods and work unnatural magic, which we will bring under the peace of Empress Tomyris. Carry those virtues with you, and the Steppe will be under the Jusordian flag by the end of the year."

The assembled recruits began to pound their tables and cheer at Praxis's words as he stepped down from the stage. Erroll, however, noticed that some of the other recruits were silent, either with their heads in their hands or staring blankly at their laps. He wondered what was going through their heads. He wondered if they had the same doubts, worries, and anxieties that he did.

By the time the cheers died down, some recruits had already begun to leave the dining hall. They were saying their own goodbyes or enjoying the last bit of time they had left in civilized territory. Erroll noticed that Manvel stayed in place.

"Why aren't you leaving?" Erroll asked him.

"What? Oh, nothing. Just thinking," Manvel said.

"Manvel! Drinks tonight? My place?" Quince shouted right as he was about to leave the dining hall.

"Sure," Manvel answered, staring blankly ahead.

Erroll sat across from Manvel in silence until the dining hall was completely empty.

"You're thinking about your father, aren't you?" Erroll said.

"What?"

"I don't think you ever really thought he'd send you off to war. You thought this was just to teach you a lesson and that he'd bring you back with full honors when training was over. But now you're worried because we'll be deployed next week, even though he hasn't written to you. You…"

"For Jarnis' sake, Erroll, shut up."

"What? I'm just trying to understand what you're thinking."

"Yeah, well, you don't know everything about me. Stop pretending like you do," Manvel said. "And for the record, you're wrong. My father wrote to me today to tell me that my older brother died in an accident. He wants me to return home."

"Oh," Erroll said. "I'm sorry about your brother. Will you be going home?"

"I don't know. I'll have to figure it out. On my own," Manvel said. He got up to leave, but before he did, he said, "You should come for drinks tonight. Quince managed to find some whiskey."

He left Erroll alone in the dining hall. Erroll scanned the empty seats, remembering when they used to be filled with laughter and conversation. They were empty now, but soon they would be filled with another group of recruits.

He noticed that some of the other recruits had carved their names into the wood underneath the table, as though they couldn't bear to leave without making some mark on the space. Erroll was unbothered by such concerns. It was just another place he was passing through.

# 4

# Sara

Sara ran her hand through the mane of Od's horse. She did it slowly, wishing to prolong the moment with her touch. She sprinkled some mana on its mane, and even though she knew how much of a waste it was, feeling the horse's pain and its grief allowed her to imagine that she was closer to Od. For a moment, it seemed as though Od was sitting next to her.

She sat next to the horse in the empty stable. The darkness made her feel as though her brother sitting next to her, as he always did. But then moonlight shone through the windows again, and she was alone.

She put her face in her hands and allowed herself to cry. She had managed to keep it together when announcing the news to the camp. Such incidents were unheard of. A murder at council was considered a great blasphemy. They would wage war, pray to the gods, and destroy those who were responsible. But nothing they said would bring Od back to her.

She heard footsteps and immediately pulled herself together, straightening her shirt and turning away so they wouldn't see her bloodshot eyes.

"Sara," called Khulan. Her hair fell in a mess around her shoulders and her face was haggard. Behind her was Bataar, who looked no better. "I told you she'd be here. Where else?"

Before Sara could stand, both of them sat next to her on the ground. Sara breathed a long sigh, then leaned back, bumping her head against one of the pillars. She winced in pain. Khulan managed a weak chuckle, but Bataar stayed silent.

"What are you thinking?" Sara asked him.

"I didn't see him off," he said.

"What?"

"I was out in the fields and I forgot that he was leaving that day. I didn't get to say goodbye." A tear rolled down Bataar's cheek, but he wiped it away as quickly as it came.

Sara reached out to place a hand on his shoulder, her hands trembling. "He knew that you were with him."

Bataar didn't seem satisfied, but he said nothing more.

Khulan sat down next to Sara, and placed her arms around her. Sara crumbled like a broken tree swept away by the wind. Khulan buried her head in her hands and sobbed, her tears dripping to the ground like drops of blood. Sara had never even seen her cry before.

"He deserved so much better," Khulan said in between gasps for breath. "It should've been me instead."

Sara looked at her two friends. She could see her anguish reflected in their twisted faces. As the pain churned in her stomach, she realized what she needed to do.

"No more tears," she said, sitting up, her eyes finally clear.

"What?" Bataar said.

"We can't sit here any longer. The camp needs us."

"They'll come after us," Bataar said. "They won't stop with Od. They know we won't accept his death. They'll think that they'd have to destroy us. It's hopeless."

"Then we'll fight back," Sara said. "If Chinua thinks we'll just roll over and accept defeat, he's mistaken."

"How do we even know it was Chinua?" Khulan asked, finally wiping away the tears on her sleeve. "It might have been the act of a jealous chief. Chinua could help us get justice."

Bataar shook his head. "All chiefs go to council unaccompanied by their hunters except for the host. That's tradition. No one else would have had the means to kill him except for Chinua himself."

"Bataar's right. We can't trust anyone. As far as I'm concerned, every other Omnu chieftain is an enemy," Sara said.

"What's the use of it? We haven't the strength to stand against Chinua and the other chiefs. They'll crush us underfoot. And if they don't, the Empire will. We're at war, remember?"

"We won't be alone. Don't you remember who my father was? What he did during the First War? We'll do it again—bring the tribes together and stand against the Empire. Against Chinua too, if need be."

Khulan nodded without hesitation. "If that's what you think, I'm with you. Whatever you need from me."

"Thank you."

Bataar frowned. "And how do you propose we do that? The tribes are divided as ever—they're fighting over the Fulgar's old land, and everyone hates the Omnu because of what Chinua did with the Temple. Sara, your father brought the tribes together during a better time. And…you're not your father."

"Bataar, now's not the time for questions," Khulan snapped. "Sara can do it. She's just as good as her father."

"You and I both know that's not true. Od was the one he trained to be the leader. Not Sara."

Khulan raised a fist, but Sara interrupted her.

"Stop it!" she said, shifting between Khulan and Bataar. "He's right. I'll never be as good of a leader as Od or my father."

"I'm sorry, I didn't mean to…" Bataar began.

"But we have to try," Sara said. "I need some way to make it up to Od. Will you help me, Bataar?"

Bataar paused, his face unreadable in the low moonlight. Then he nodded. "For Od."

Sara's order went swiftly through the camp. Bataar made sure of that. "Collapse your tents, collect your possessions, mount your horses. We ride tomorrow."

The sun shone bright on her herding camp as she walked through the rows of tents, watching families and children pack up their entire lives with the huge leather straps that they used only twice a year.

"We need to make sure the herds are ready to move. If you need any extra manna, you've got it," she told Bataar as they walked through the tents, watching families pack their belongings and dismantle their homes. "Cull the herd. Any yak or ox that can't pull its weight must be left behind. Make sure that Ergene gets the venison. I'll send Sain and Ergene along to help you get them loaded."

"Got it," Bataar said. He left them then, heading for the pens.

Sara turned to Khulan, but before she could tell her what she needed, someone tapped her on the shoulder. She turned and saw Orda, one of the hunters in her group.

"Sara," he said, his eyes watery. "I'm sorry for your loss. Od was a good man. He would have been an excellent chief."

She nodded, biting back the tears that threatened to gush from her eyes. She still flinched whenever Od's name came up in conversation. "Thank you, Orda. I'll miss him dearly."

"We all do. But I need to speak with you about putting the camp on the move."

Sara gulped. "What about it?"

"We grieving for both Od and Julian. It feels wrong to do this so soon after we've lost them. Can't we have a few days, to grieve? Why must we move so urgently? The winter winds haven't arrived yet."

"I'm sorry, Orda. But there's no time. We need to move quickly or else we'll be overrun."

Orda's eyes flashed with fear. "Overrun? By whom? Od told us that the Empire was far away."

"No, I, uh, I misspoke. It's not the Empire that's after us."

"You mean to say there's someone else?"

Fortunately, before Sara could do any more damage, Khulan spoke.

"It's Chinua," Khulan said. "We think that Od was murdered by him and that he might be coming after us."

"But why?" Orda said. He looked uneasy, but Khulan's authoritative tone calmed him a little.

"We don't know," Khulan said. "It might be that with the war, Chinua needed something to establish his authority. So he's coming after the newly-minted chief to set an example."

"That's barbaric," Orda said, stroking his beard. "In any case, we stand with you, Sara."

"Thank you," Khulan said before Orda headed back to his tent to continue packing.

Sara sighed. "I messed that up completely, didn't I?"

"Just a little bit. It was cute, though." Khulan chuckled.

"I'm not much of a leader, am I? Gaeon save me—I miss Od."

Khulan exhaled. "You'll get used to it, Sara. Like it or not, you're chief now. Come on, we have things to do."

The mess where Ergene served the camp food every night was little more than a few campfires surrounded by wool blankets and a mat at the front where she served the food. Sain did the cooking a short distance from the field on coals and spits. At this time of the morning, he would usually be busy preparing lunch for the returning hunters.

"I need you to gather the hunters," Sara said to Khulan while they were still some distance away. "Divide them into three groups. I need outriders—you know the drill, except the best ones should scout behind us. We need to make sure we know where Chinua's riders are at every moment. Three shifts—they'll need to keep themselves energized around the clock. We'll also need a group to watch the livestock, and a final group to guard the non-fighters. Two shifts each. Got it?"

Khulan nodded. "Wait, if you're chief now, what happens to the master of hunters?"

"Do I even need to tell you? You lead the hunters now. I wouldn't trust anyone else."

"You mean you're finally giving me permission to force everyone to ride backwards?"

Sara laughed. "Okay, don't make me take it back."

"No no, I'm just kidding. Thank you, Sara. I'll do my best."

Sara entered the mess alone. In the spot where Sain would normally attending to some grilled meat, she saw him binding huge cuts of meat and supplies into bundles. Zhims was busy hefting more stacks of food into the mess, while Ergene followed behind him.

"Faster, boy, faster!" she barked. "We only have a day to get all our food loaded onto the oxen. Hurry up or I'll make you wish we left you behind."

Zhims was already panting with the effort, but he managed to heft his load into the center before collapsing onto the grass.

"Come on, get up," Ergene said, poking him with her cane. "We've still got lots to load."

Sara chuckled. "Give him a break, Ergene. The boy's exhausted. I'll have Bataar send some of his people over to help you. Then Zhims can have a rest."

"Thank you!" Zhims called, lifting his head slightly from the ground and then collapsing again.

"Sara," Sain said, not looking up at her. He was busy noting each package that Zhims and Ergene brought, making sure that the meat was packed tightly enough, and that there were no signs of mould. They could only bring so much of their stock as they rode, so each package had to be well-maintained.

"All good here, Sain?"

"Well as it should be. The short notice kind of shocked me, but I'll do what I'm told. Don't worry about it."

"Appreciate it," Sara said. She'd been worried about troubling Sain and Ergene, though they seemed cooperative enough. She turned and took a deep breath of the fresh air. She wondered what it was like in the cities of the Empire, with no wind to flow through the streets and no horse to ride into the horizon.

"Sara," a voice came from behind her.

"Ganbold," she said when she saw who it was, relaxing a little. There was something different about the old lion today—his eyes were crestfallen and shadowed, and his posture, while it remained strong-willed, betrayed a certain air of fragility. It seemed like he was about to collapse under his own weight.

"I'm so sorry about your brother," he said. "I didn't know him well, but he was a good man. A good leader too. He would've served us well."

"Thank you, Ganbold," Sara said, then began to turn away from him. She could no longer bear listening to condolences.

"I haven't finished."

"What is it?"

"Since you're chief now, that means that the master of hunters post is vacant, correct?"

Sara's fists tightened, but she said nothing. Ganbold took her silence as affirmation.

"Well, I want you to make me master of hunters. I'm the camp's oldest hunter, and certainly the best among them."

Sara nodded slowly, the words catching in her mouth even as she said them. "I...you're right, Ganbold."

"I can start whipping those youngsters into shape..."

"I've already made Khulan master of hunters. She's the best hunter in the tribe, and I trust her with my life. I hope you will, too."

Ganbold's eyes flashed with anger. "Khulan? I've been hunting for twice as long as she's been alive..."

"Enough, Ganbold. I'm putting you in charge of the outriders. I need you there during the move to watch our backs. Can you do it?"

But the old hunter was already leaving, barely giving her a second glance before he left the mess. Ergene, who had been watching the exchange silently until then, approached her.

"Did your father ever tell you that he had a fight over a girl with Ganbold once? Watch out for that one."

Sara nodded and took a deep breath. No use worrying about Ganbold now. She had more important things to worry about.

"I hate politics," she whispered to herself as she headed to the stables to inspect the horses.

# 5

# Batu

"You did it, didn't you?" Batu asked. He was sitting opposite Nugai on some benches near the council tent. The other chiefs hadn't liked it, but after watching Chinua kill one of their own, they had to be ready for him to do it again. They fell in line within moments, and the council was over before anyone could have second thoughts.

"Did what?" Nugai answered.

"You know what I mean."

"No, I don't. I do lots of things, Batu. You'll have to be more specific than that."

Batu breathed a long sigh. "You killed him, didn't you?"

"Killed who? Ah, forget it. Yes, I killed the boy chief because your father told me to. Are you happy now?"

"Not particularly."

"I figured. You never are."

Batu averted his gaze, unable to meet the eyes of his best friend.

"What do you want me to say, Batu?" Nugai said. "That I didn't want to do it? That your father bullied me into it?"

"I just thought you had changed from… from the old days."

"From the old days? Why don't you just say it out loud—yes, I was a bandit. Yes, I killed innocent people. And I owe your father a debt for getting me out of that life, one that I'll never be able to repay. So I do things for him. Is that what you wanted to hear?"

Batu made eye contact with Nugai, and he saw that the youth's eyes were filled with anger. Sometimes, he forgot that Nugai was so young; he was barely older than Batu, but he had been through much more. He had the eyes of a veteran, and he had the same look in his eyes that Batu sometimes saw in the older hunters that had fought in the First War.

"I'm sorry," Batu said. "It's not your fault. I'm just...confused."

"No sense in being confused now. There's a war coming. We all need to be ready for it; that means swallowing our pride for a little bit. You get me?"

"Somewhat. But do you think that what you did was right? For Gaeon's sake, Nugai, you killed a man in cold blood. Don't you feel anything?"

Nugai considered the question for a long while. "I don't think much about right or wrong these days. I was like that three years ago, but after everything that's happened, I don't do it anymore. It just gets in the way of things. Point is, I made a choice and it was the right one, because your father would've killed me if I didn't."

"Is that what you really believe?"

Nugai folded his arms. "Yes."

Batu didn't know what to make of it—Nugai's words made sense, but they did nothing to convince him. His thoughts were interrupted by Chinua himself, who approached Nugai and Batu alone.

"Son," Chinua said.

"Father," Batu said without looking up at him.

"I have a task for you."

"To Saenor with your task," Batu said, meeting his father's eyes.

"Batu," he said, then he glared at Nugai, which made the younger man leave without a word. "You know that it will not end well for you if you refuse."

"What are you going to do, Father? Murder me in my sleep? Banish me to the plains?"

Batu braced himself for his father's wrath, but instead, he got silence. Wordlessly, Chinua sat opposite his son, where Nugai had just been sitting.

"I need you to know that whatever I did was for the tribe. Do you understand?"

Batu paused for a long moment, during which he searched his father's expression for any hints.

"You've never listened to what I think, so why start now?" Batu said. "I've never been a good enough son for you."

Chinua sighed. "Batu, if you won't do it for me, then do it for the tribe."

Batu stayed silent.

"I need you to go to Odgerel's camp in my name. Offer to bring them under our protection, so long as they agree to fight with us in the coming battles."

Batu laughed. "You know that they won't agree, Father. They'll hate you for what you did to Odgerel. They're probably riding here as we speak, in search of revenge."

"I know they won't forgive me—the Omnu have long memories. But they will not ride against us. The new chief will be Odgerel's sister, Saragerel. I know enough about that girl to know that she's too meek to wage war against her own people. Most likely, they'll flee. I need you to follow them and track them down."

"And what if I refuse?"

"Then I'll find someone else and I'll have you piling meat for the rest of your days."

Batu met his father's stare for a long moment. "Fine. I'll do it. But I won't kill them. I'll convince them to side with us, and then you'll see my worth, Father."

"I suppose I should have expected this," Chinua said, folding his arms. "Do what you want, but it will be on all of us if you fail. We will need all the hunters we can gather for the coming battle."

Batu nodded then stood to leave. Before he did, Chinua caught him on the shoulder.

"What?" he asked.

"Be safe, son," his father said.

Batu freed himself from his father's grasp and left, ignoring the doubts clawing at his insides. He couldn't afford to worry about his father's opinions now.

Batu led his hunters in silence until they came upon a cliff. If the scout reports were to be trusted, this was where Saragerel's camp would be hiding. There was an outcrop that overlooked a huge clearing, ringed on both sides by hills so that the area only had one entrance. The grass was trampled and Batu could see large patches of soil peeking out. The area was a common camping ground for Omnu hunters who were far from home. It made sense that Saragerel would seek it out.

Batu tried to get a better look, but he could only glimpse a few figures gathered around some fires. None of them appeared to be moving, and it seemed like most were in their tents.

"I can't see anything," he said, turning back to his hunters.

"Saenor's scales, you need to get better eyes," Nugai said, pushing past him. He surveyed the camp for a few moments, then turned to the group. "Okay, so there's about a hundred of them, based on the tents. Most are inside, though a few are out by the fires."

Nugai looked like he was about to continue, but Batu cut him off. "If we split into two groups, we should be able to cut off their escape. Once we've done that, I should be able to get Saragerel to talk to us."

The hunters looked at each other nervously.

"What? Is there a problem?" Batu asked them.

"No disrespect here," one of the hunters said, eyeing Nugai, whose hand had fallen to the hilt of his axe. "But the chief's orders were to bring them under our control. Most of the time, we'll need to burn a few tents to make that happen. Maybe kill a few of them."

"These people aren't going to bend easy, you're right about that," another said. "Especially that Saragerel. She'll be out for blood—it's

Gaeon's will, after all."

"There will be no killing until I say so," Batu said. "I just want to talk. That's an order. You will not raise your weapons against the people of this camp until I give an explicit order instructing you to do so. Is that clear?"

The hunters exchanged another look.

"You got it?" Nugai asked.

"Yes," they replied, though they avoided his gaze.

"Good," Batu said. "Now, mount up. I don't want to give them any chance of getting away."

His hunters got on their horses, but some appeared reluctant to do so, as if they were contemplating whether or not to fight him over the order.

"Orders?" Nugai asked him.

"Let me think," Batu said. He turned around and scanned the terrain. He could feel his hunters getting restless behind him, their anxiety bearing down on his shoulders. He turned back. "Nugai, I want you to lead twenty-five hunters down the eastern slope. Surround the entrance to the camp, and don't let anyone in or out. I'll wait a few moments, then I'll take ten hunters and go down the western hill. Understand?"

Nugai nodded and growled at the rest of the hunters. They listened as well. Within moments, he led them down the eastern slope and around the mouth of the camp.

The people in the camp would had definitely noticed them by now, but they weren't moving. He mounted his horse and led it down the slope, taking the rest of their hunters with him. His horse buckled and whined as they descended, but he sprinkled more manna on its mane to keep it steady.

"Keep going. We can do it," he whispered, though he wasn't sure if he was talking to the horse or himself. The horse finally relented, and they trotted down the hill with the hunters following closely behind.

Batu looked up from his horse, finally managing to reclaim some control. He noticed a commotion going on at the mouth of the valley. Nugai was barking some orders, and the other hunters were shouting back at him. Some hunters were drawing weapons. Batu couldn't make out the conversation, but he could tell it wasn't good.

Another dose of manna fell onto his horse and they started galloping, the wind whipping past Batu's face. He drew out his bow, which he had strung on the way here.

He looked behind him and noticed that the rest of his hunters were following along, though their careful descent had disintegrated into a rushed scramble. Some of the quicker hunters had careened past him. The control that Batu had managed to hold onto was now gone.

As they neared the mouth, Batu began to make sense of the ongoing commotion.

"We're not going to wait any longer!" one of them said.

"The boy wants to talk. He can do that, but we won't listen," another said.

"Stay where you are," Nugai shouted, but his voice was barely audible.

"Those bastards are going to pay for trying to run from us," said one.

Some hunters pushed past Nugai, and it was as though a stone was dislodged from a hill's foundation. Everything came crashing down at once. The hunters charged past Nugai into the camp, lighting torches and brandishing swords. Only a few hunters had stayed behind with Nugai, but even they seemed apprehensive.

Batu finally caught up to Nugai, who was fingering the hilts of his axes.

"Well, the raid's started," Nugai said. "What now?"

"Wasn't supposed to go like this," Batu said. "They have the upper hand now that we're the ones charging in. Casualties will be high."

Batu glanced over his shoulder and saw his hunters had nearly reached the enemy camp.

"So? What do we do now?" Nugai asked.

"Only one thing we can do," Batu said, stringing his bow and checking his quiver. "Attack."

He spurred his horse into action and he took on the horse's mind. He could feel a familiar weight on his back and his hooves clattering against the rough soil. There was no longer any distinction between Batu and the beast, only one entity charging forward with a single goal.

When he arrived at the camp, he found that most of his hunters had already arrived. The tents were overturned and cut apart. Some of them were burning, and he thought he could see hints of fabric and burned flesh inside. He looked ahead of him and saw that his hunters had managed to cut their way through the entire camp without any resistance whatsoever. The camp burned and not a single soul raised a sword in defiance.

"Something's wrong," Batu said, getting off his horse just as Nugai came up beside him.

Nugai approached one of the tents and, using a knife from his belt, cut open the cloth until he could clearly see what was underneath.

"Saenor's scales," Nugai said when he saw what was underneath. The humanoid shape underneath the canvas was nothing more than a mass of straw arranged in the form of a person. The straw had been stuffed into what looked like a worn set of clothing, and it had been left upright so that it seemed like a person relaxing.

Nugai turned to Batu, and the look on his face was pure terror.

"What's wrong?" Batu asked.

"They tricked us," Nugai said, gesturing at the figure underneath.

"They knew we'd come looking for them here. And that we wouldn't be able to see them up close until we were in the actual camp."

Batu looked over at the rest of his hunters, who had nearly shredded their way through the entire camp. Then they stopped abruptly, and the shouts of anger turned to shouts of alarm.

"What's happening?" Nugai said, trying to look over the flood of horses.

There was a mass of whinnying and baying, reminding Batu of the time he'd gotten his horse stuck in a ditch with a broken leg. The horses had gone wild, losing their footing and abandoning the commands of their riders. They rose up on their hind legs and threw people off. Some even careened into the hill, breaking their own legs and collapsing in a heap.

In a panic, Batu looked over at his own horse. It looked distressed, but it did not balk. He thanked Gaeon for his soul bond with the creature. It was probably the only thing keeping it from going wild. Among the other hunters, the only ones that managed to keep their horses were the ones with soul bonds. Those who were bonded with eagles lost their horses.

Most of the hunters had been thrown off and were struggling to find their feet, while some others were still on their horses, struggling to maintain control. Batu heard curses and shouts. Some hunters tried to form defensive positions, but as far as Batu could tell, they weren't under attack.

Batu drew out his bow and nocked an arrow, glancing around the surrounding cliffs to check for rival hunters lurking in the distance.

"There has to be someone doing this," Batu said. "But how? And from where?"

Nugai had taken out both his axes and was chopping through the ruins of tents "Where?"

"Stop. Look closely. There's manna in the air," Batu said, as his eyes squinted to observe on a ray of sunlight that had pierced through the clouds. He saw the light catching on a thin sheet of azure powder dissipating in the air. "It was all a trap from the start. They're long gone by now."

Nugai stopped in his tracks and dropped his axes. It was then that he began to glimpse the fine mist in the air, nearly invisble if one did not look closely, and definitely impossible to notice when galloping on a horse.

"What can we do? Can we reverse it? We've got manna of our own, haven't we?"

"We don't have a herder with us," Batu said. "Even if we did, we don't have the speed to catch up with the horses."

He looked into the distance, watching his hunters desperately try to chase down their horses, only to find the beasts trampled and broken, their legs shattered by the rocky hillside.

"What do we do now, Batu?"

"We've lost. There's nothing we can do."

# 6
# Erroll

Erroll didn't think much of General Sandulf when he first saw him. The renowned warrior ascended the stage before the three new squadrons that were to be added to his legion. He took his time going up the steps, wearing nothing but plain steel plate armor. He did not have medals or decorations like some of the other generals.

Sandulf was balding except for a few patches on the sides of his head. He had a pronounced jawline and a face shaped like a bulldog's. He reminded Erroll of some of the older blacksmiths in the Ruson smithing district. If he had bumped into Sandulf on the street, he never would have guessed that he was one of the most decorated generals in the Jusoridan army.

He spoke quickly, though each word was perfectly enunciated. Erroll caught every syllable. "In my legion, I do not tolerate complaining, disloyalty, or incompetence. If you exhibit any of these three inclinations, you will be punished. But if you do your duty, you will be rewarded. In the coming weeks, we will be marching into the Steppe and occupying new territory. This is an important task, and if we succeed, we will win glory for the Empire. I expect great things from you."

Sandulf finished his address then left the stage. There were a few moments of silence as the assembly of six hundred waited for more orders. A captain whose name Erroll had yet to learn took Sandulf's place.

"You're all off duty for the next few hours. Get acquainted with your new quarters. That's all."

The men dispersed quickly and the clearing in which they were standing was soon empty. Erroll found Manvel and Quince afterwards, and together they headed to the barracks where their squadron had been assigned.

As they walked through the camp, Erroll noticed that it was full of activity. It was populated with old veterans and new recruits alike, but everything seemed ordered perfectly. The outpost had only been established a few months ago, but it appeared to be as well-run as any of the factories in Ruson.

"What did you think of him?" Manvel asked.

"Seems like an old geezer. Reminds me of my old man," Quince said, shrugging. "Nothing special about him."

"But I heard he's one of the best," Manvel said. "The senior soldiers seem really scared of him."

"Maybe they're just scared easily."

"There are stories about him," Erroll said. "He runs the camp the same way a conductor might run an orchestra. Every movement coordinated to the second. I've also heard about what he does to new soldiers that aren't up to his standards."

"Oh really?" Manvel said. "Do tell."

"He strings them up for two days in the dungeons," Erroll says. "Or he leaves them naked in the noontime sun."

"Galele's breath," Quince said. "Hope that doesn't happen to me."

Manvel frowned. "I don't think he's the type. A man like that? Seems like he's all talk but no bite. Reminds me of my father when he'd catch me in the craft guilds rather than the sparring grounds."

"And what were you doing in the guilds?" Erroll asked.

Manvel laughed. "I wanted to be a sculptor, of course. It's the reason my father decided to ship me off to war. Have I not told you that?"

"You're just full of surprises, aren't you, Manvel?"

Quince laughed. "And how about you, Erroll? Are you scared that he'll string you up in a dungeon?"

"You know where I'm from, right?" Erroll said. "In Ruson, getting chained up would be a nice evening. At least I wouldn't need to spend so much time running away."

They rounded a corner and entered the barracks, which was organized into a few sleeping rooms surrounding a common area. The common area was furnished with a few benches and tables for soldiers to gather around but for the most part, it was empty. Erroll glanced into the rooms and saw that most soldiers were sitting on their beds, either completely still or idly sharpening their weapons.

"It's a damn ghost town in here," Quince said.

"Works for me," Erroll said, taking the nearest bench and wrenching a boot off his foot. He undid the other boot then leaned back in the bench, finally allowing himself a few deep breaths.

"It's too quiet. I'm going to find something to do," Quince said. "Either of you coming?"

Manvel and Erroll shook their heads.

"Fine by me. See ya," Quince said, making for the doorway.

"Do you ever wonder what Sandulf's like in bed?" Manvel said after a long pause.

"What?"

Manvel laughed. "Sorry. Just a little thing of mine. Whenever I'm trying to judge someone's character, you know, what they're really like, I think about three things. What they're like when they're doing something they're not supposed to, when they're drunk, and when they're having sex. That's how you really know a person."

Erroll chuckled. "I'm not sure I want to picture what his bald head looks like in the throes of passion."

Manvel laughed even harder this time. "Fair enough," he said, then his face turned serious and he leaned forward. "There's something I have to ask you."

"What is it this time?"

"I heard you snuck out of the barracks last night. What were you doing?"

Erroll raised an eyebrow. "You were spying on me?"

"That's not what I meant. I just happened to notice that you were gone and got worried."

Erroll folded his arms. "Yeah, sure, you were 'worried'. I just needed to piss and wanted some privacy."

"Oh yeah, and it takes an hour to piss?"

"Well, maybe I wanted some time to think. It's none of your business."

Manvel was silent for a long time. "Fine, you can keep your secrets if you want."

"What happened to not needing to know everything about everyone?"

"I'm just trying to help. You know, it's okay if you're scared about going to war. All of us are."

"I'm not…" Erroll said, turning away from Manvel. "Are you saying that I'm not cut out to be a soldier?"

"That's not what I mean, Erroll. I'm looking out for you because I'm your friend."

Before Erroll could respond, the camp erupted into activity as horns sounded from the direction of the Steppe. Erroll shot to his feet, trying to listen past the scrambled noise of five thousand soldiers getting to their feet. After a few moments, he recognized the type of horn being blown.

"A raid," he said. Then he turned to Manvel, frowning. "By the nomads? We've only just arrived in the Steppe."

"They're anxious to get rid of us, I assume," Manvel said. "They don't want a long war like last time."

"I suppose not." Erroll moved to grab a sword and shield from the racks on the wall. The other soldiers in their squadron were swarming towards the same shelves. By the time he finished lacing up his boots, the squadron was already on the move, taking up defensive posts along the camp's borders.

# 7

# Sara

Sara sat atop the hill across the river, clutching Khulan's hand. The hill overlooked Harnda territory. From there, they could see the vast plain extending before them, but the sight did not bring Sara the solace she hoped for.

"Sara. Khulan," came a voice from behind them. Sara turned and found Bataar standing alongside them on the hilltop, out of breath.

"Yes, Bataar?" Khulan said.

"They're coming," Bataar said.

"Thank you. Return to the camp and help them set up for the night."

Sara turned back to observing the plain, where a small host of riders was approaching them with the haste of an eagle.

"That's them? The Harnda hunters?" Khulan asked. She squeezed Sara's hand tighter, though Sara wasn't sure whom she was trying to reassure.

"Seems like it," Sara said.

"Do you know what you're going to say to them?"

"Not really."

"I wonder if Od would've known what to do," Khulan said. Sara noticed that her eyes were filled with tears.

"Hey, what's going on?" Sara said, placing her hand on her friend's shoulder.

"It's…it's nothing," Khulan said. "I just…haven't really had time to miss him. I can't believe he's gone."

Sara lowered her head. All she could say was "I know." She wished she could reach out and take the pain from Khulan, but it was impossible. There was already so much pain inside her.

"This isn't the time," Khulan said, wiping the tears away. "So what are you going to do?"

"I'll figure it out. I'm good at that, right?"

"Are you trying to convince me or yourself?" Khulan said, finally cracking a smile.

"Okay, I'm going to stop talking to you now."

"Sure."

The hunters reached the bottom of the hill, and each of them began to encircle the base of the hill until there was no way for Sara and Khulan to escape except through the Serpent's River by the back.

Sara got to her feet and spread her arms so that the hunters could see that she was unarmed. Khulan did the same. When the Harnda seemed to be satisfied, three figures left the circle and began to ascend the hill. One of them was a huge, imposing man with a large, leather cloak draped over his shoulders. His hair flowed over his shoulders, and he seemed to make the grass he walked on cower in fear. Sara had never seen him before, but she immediately identified him as Zayaat, the Harnda's master of hunters.

The other two alongside him weren't nearly as imposing. As they approached, Sara could see that they were women barely older than she was.

Zayaat approached them while his two hunters stood a short distance behind him. Try as she did, Sara could not read the expression on his face.

"I am Zayaat, master of hunters of the Harnda," he said. "You are not one of us. Leave at once."

Sara noticed Khulan take a step back, an effect that she was sure Zayaat was used to. Sara, however, refused to be intimidated. Even though everything inside her screamed against it, she took a step forward to stand mere centimeters away from Zayaat.

"I am Saragerel, chief of the Omnu, daugher of Julian. My camp is pursued by Chinua. We have come to seek refuge with the Harnda."

Zayaat flinched at her words, but if they made him uneasy, he did not show it. "And how would I know that this is not a plot to invade our lands?"

"You don't. But by the custom of our people, you cannot turn away someone asking for refuge."

Zayaat frowned. "The customs are dead, girl. You will have to think of a better reason."

Sara hesitated for a moment, but she was determined to not let Zayaat control the exchange. "Then how about this? There's a war coming, and we need to stand together if we want to survive. Let me speak to your chief."

"Do not lecture me about war, child. I've been fighting in them since before you were born."

"My father taught me enough to know that you need us. If you care about your people at all, let me speak to your chief."

Zayaat considered for a long moment. Finally, he turned to one of the hunters. "Alaqa, send word ahead. Tell the chief that we have guests."

Alaqa nodded and began making her way down the hill. When Zayaat turned back to face Sara, she noticed that his expression was softer than it was before. There was even a hint of a smile on his lips.

"I fought beside your father in the first war," he said. "He was a great man, and I am glad to see that his fire lives on in his daughter."

Sara blinked in surprise. "Thank you. My father was very fond of you. He said it was a shame that you declined his offer to join our tribe."

Zayaat chuckled. Then he turned and started down the hill, gesturing them to follow. "Come. We will ride ahead to the camp, and my people will provide you with food and supplies. Gerelma, fetch these two cloaks. The winds in the Harnda lands, as you will soon find out, are sharper than any arrow."

Gerelma, the other hunter, left them to find cloaks and Sara and Khulan followed Zayaat from behind. Sara finally allowed herself to relax. Khulan noticed her relief and squeezed her hand.

"I knew you could do it," she muttered.

When they arrived at the Harnda camp, Dagasi, the Harnda master of herders, led them to a tent that stood at the center of the spiral. It stood taller than the others and was draped with banners depicting the symbol of the Harnda tribe: a three-horned bull. When Sara saw the banner, she found herself touching the Omnu symbol sewn into her shirt. They entered the tent and found even more hunters posted inside to keep watch. There were four in total. Sara could not see their faces because of the hoods they wore.

A woman sat cross-legged in the center of the tent, with long, flowing hair that ended at her chest. She did not seem much older than thirty, though the wrinkles around her eyes said much about the things she had seen. Still, she was beautiful. In Sara's eyes, the way her hair fell loosely around her shoulders without braids or ties made her seem perfectly in control amidst the chaos.

The woman was stroking a hunting eagle, which was seated beside her on the ground.

"Chief Ibakha," Dagasi said. "They're here."

Ibakha finally looked up at them. She met Sara's eyes for a few long moments without relinquishing her gaze. Sara felt her palms sweat as she couldn't read Ibakha's expression. Finally, she relented. Ibakha smiled freely, as if she was greeting an old friend. "Splendid. You must be Saragerel and Khulan. I've been looking forward to meeting you."

Sara stepped forward. By now, she was used to the routine. "Yes, Chief Ibakha…" she began. Before she could finish, Ibakha held up a hand.

"Before we get to business, could we get some privacy?" Ibakha said, gesturing at the hunters that have gathered around the edges of the tent. "Could I ask everyone to leave the tent?"

Zayaat stepped forward. "Ibakha, are you sure that's wise? Perhaps if I could stay, or at least one of my hunters…"

Ibakha held up her hand again, bringing the man to silence. "There's no need, Zayaat. Thank you for your concern, but they are not some backwater traders from K'harin. Our guests include a chief, so we will give them proper respect."

"Yes, Ibakha," Zayaat said. At his command, he, the hunters, and Dagasi left the tent without another word. Khulan hesitated to follow them, but left when Sara gave her a nod.

Ibakha winked at Sara as the hunters left and patted the rug beside her when they were alone. "Come. Sit. Zayaat and Dagasi mean well, though they're a bit too uptight sometimes. I'm glad that I finally get to speak to someone younger than sixty for a change."

Sara sat down, though she did so with care, making sure to keep the path to the exit clear in her mind. She was still unsure of what to make of Ibakha.

"It's good to meet you, Chief Ibakha," Sara said.

Ibakha raised an eyebrow. "You still don't trust me?"

Sara shrugged.

"I guess you have a point," Ibakha said, chuckling to herself. "There's more than enough reason to be on edge these days. But please, call me Ibakha. And Saragerel…that's too long. Can I call you Sara?"

Sara blinked. "Oh, yes, sure you can. If that makes things easier."

"Perfect, Sara it is, then," Ibakha said. "So, Sara, why have you come here today?"

Sara sighed and allowed some of the tension to escape her shoulders.

"My brother is dead," Sara said, and she found that it was more difficult to say than she had imagined. "Murdered by our head chieftain, Chinua. We were chased down by Batu, his son, who would have put our entire camp to the sword. We had nowhere else to go, so we came here to look for protection."

Ibakha was giving her a confused look.

"You don't believe me, do you?" Sara said. "I know it's hard to believe, but…"

Ibakha held up her hand, and Sara fell to silence, even though she didn't intend on it. "Of course I believe you, Sara. My scouts confirmed precisely the same things you told me."

Sara folded her arms. "I'm not surprised. I've heard great things about Ibakha of the Harnda tribe."

"Then the two of us should get along just fine," Ibakha said. "So, protection. You've got it. Our hunters can escort your people here, and we should have some food and supplies to spare. What else do you need?"

"Well, honestly, we also need your support in the war."

"Ah," Ibakha said. "Yes, I figured you might ask for that."

"The Empire is coming for us, Ibakha, probably stronger than before. If we have want any hope of standing against them, we have to fight together."

"I'm not sure you realize what you're asking of me. It's true that I'm head chief of the Harnda, but the other chiefs in our tribe are stubborn. They will be difficult to convince, especially with all the bad blood with Chinua since the First War. They still believe that he stole the Temple from underneath their noses, and that we've been starved for manna ever since."

Sara nodded. "My father was never happy with that decision either. But to Saenor with Chinua. If we win this war and hold the Temple of Gaeon, you'll have free passage to the manna spring."

"That's a big decision, Sara. One that you shouldn't take lightly."

"It's one I'm willing to make."

Ibakha considered Sara's words for a moment. "You're so young. I've forgotten how that feels like."

"You knew my father, didn't you? He taught me everything he knew. Trust me like you trusted him."

Ibakha sighed. "I don't know if your father ever told you this, but he's one of the few reasons the Harnda and Omnu never openly went to war in the last twenty years."

"He did tell me that. He said that he liked you better than the old head chieftain," Sara said, then she realized she was talking about Ibakha's father. "I mean, sorry, I didn't mean to…"

Ibakha laughed. "No, it's okay. My father was a piece of work. But by Saenor, I guess I've got no other options. Harnda will stand with you in the war."

Sara breathed a sigh of relief. A weight lifted from her shoulders, though she didn't know that she'd been carrying it. "Thank you. You don't know how much this means to me. Chinua refuses to cooperate with the rest of the tribes, but at least he could hold the Empire off for a little while…"

Ibakha raised her hand again. "Oh, Gaeon's wind, I thought you knew."

"Knew what?"

"I suppose you couldn't have known. We only received news from our scouts an hour ago."

"It's too late, isn't it?" she said, and Ibakha nodded.

"The Empire raided Chinua's camp. We don't know how many survivors there were, but from the smoke, it seems that it was a decisive raid. I don't think we can continue to rely on the Omnu to hold the Empire back. I'm so sorry, Sara."

# 8

# Batu

"I wonder what old Chinua's going to say," Nugai said as Batu's party neared the camp. "You've lost control of your hunters and didn't even manage to catch Saragerel."

"Yes, thank you, Nugai, for reminding me that I'm a complete failure," Batu said.

"I'm just kidding. Don't worry about Chinua, just be glad that all of us are home and relatively intact."

"I might not be intact after I speak to my father."

Nugai laughed. "Well, we'll see about that."

Batu looked towards their herding camp, but noticed something strange rising in the horizon. "Gaeon's staff... is that smoke?"

"What?" Nugai said, but he was busy fiddling with his horse's bridle. "Yes, Batu. It's a herding camp late at night. We light fires because it gets dark."

"No, Nugai, it's more than just a campfire. Will you just look up, for Saenor's sake?" Batu said, and he saw that the rest of the hunters were beginning to notice as well. There were several huge plumes of smoke rising into the sky along a dozen smaller pillars of smoke. They weren't close enough to see or hear what was happening yet, but Batu felt his throat fill with bile.

Batu exchanged a look with Nugai, who was beginning to realize the gravity of the situation.

"What are we...what do we do?" Batu said. He felt his breath shorten as he spoke. The hunters behind him began to whisper to each other.

"We need to see what's going on first," Nugai said. "Come on."

Nugai spurred his horse into a gallop, racing for the hill nearest to their camp. Batu watched him go for a few moments before kicking his horse into motion.

They ascended the hill within minutes. When Batu reached the hill's crest to overlook the camp, he stood alongside Nugai and watched as their camp burned.

Batu had never smelled burning flesh before. Neither had he ever heard screams of terror. He had seen battle before, but nothing like this. This was not an even match between two parties. It was slaughter. Slowly, the frayed strings in Batu's mind began to connect, and he gradually understood the gravity of the situation.

Chinua's herding camp had been invaded from three sides. Batu could see the Empire's soldiers, their polished silver armor colored by the orange flames. Most carried a shield and a longsword. Against the scattered resistance mounted by the hunters, it was more than enough.

Line after line of hunters armed with swords charged the tightly-packed groups of heavily-armored soldiers. Each time they tried, they were forced to retreat. Every broken cavalry charge allowed the soldiers to take more ground, burning and killing as they went. Neither Chinua nor Jochi, his master of hunters were anywhere to be found, which meant that Batu was in charge.

"How could this have happened?" Nugai said from a horse next to Batu.

"They...They must have been taken by surprise," Batu said, pointing at the ruined tents with bloodied corpses inside. "Otherwise, my father would have been able to evacuate those who couldn't fight."

"We need to do something," Nugai said. "Batu! Give us orders."

"Hold on," Batu said, glancing around him. Their group was mostly on foot, with only about a dozen hunters with soul-bonded their horses. But when Batu scanned the group, he noticed that they were a few heads short. A few hunters had seen the chaos, dropped their weapons, and fled the battlefield.

"Okay," Batu said finally. He turned his horse to face the hunters. "Here's what we need to do. Everyone on foot, approach the camp but do not engage the enemy directly. You have to try to confuse them with your bows, send them into disarray. Delay them as much as possible. Those of us on horses, we need to make for the center."

He pointed to the central tent, where the remaining hunters had formed a circle and were trying to fend off the Empire. Batu spotted Chinua himself directing them from behind their lines.

"The chief needs our help. Once we meet up with them, we get the chief and we get out of here. Got it?"

The hunters were silent for a few tense moments before a panicked voice rose up from the back of the group. "To Saenor with that! I need to make sure my family's okay."

A few voices murmured agreement, and some began to make their way down the hill.

Batu shook his head. "No! Stop! Can't you see? If they haven't made it to the central pavillion, they're dead. Our only hope is to save the chief."

"You only care about him because he's your father! You don't care about our families at all," came another voice. Before Batu could get another word in, half of the hunters dispersed and began making their own way into the chaos, calling out the names of loved ones that did not answer. As they did, some of the Empire's soldiers noticed and began dispatching small groups to deal with the newcomers.

"Stop! You'll die!" Batu shouted after them. He directed his horse to start down the hill, but Nugai caught his shoulder.

Nugai gave him a dark look, eyebrows arched and eyes full of cold steel. "They're goners. You'll have to make do with what you've got."

Batu gave the hunters one last look as they began to engage the Empire soldiers, and then he nodded. He turned back to the remaining group, who looked like they might flee any moment. "You know your orders, right?"

Some in the group nodded. That was good enough for Batu.

"That's it then. Let's go," he said, turning his horse and leading them down the hill. He glanced behind him and, thankfully, the hunters were following him. He turned back to the battlefield and, with hands quavering so intensely that he almost dropped his bow, Batu charged into the burning camp.

Batu led his forces through the blazing tents into the heart of the battle. They passed a few stragglers rummaging through the canvas. A few arrows were enough to dispose of them, but the main force was circling the central pavilion defended by Chinua and his hunters.

The Empire's soldiers were trying to break through Chinua's lines by charging down three paths between burning wreckages, advancing slowly with shield lines, though each advance was thwarted with a few well-placed cavalry charges and arrows. Still, each charge took down a few of Chinua's hunters, while the Empire seemed to have an endless supply of soldiers.

"It's only a matter of time before he falls," Batu said.

Nugai nodded. "We have to hurry."

Once they were a suitable distance from one of the groups, Batu turned to the men assembling behind him. A few of them were on horseback, but most were on foot with their bows drawn.

"For those of you without horses, I want you to begin harassing the enemy with your bows. Focus on the group nearest to us and clear a path."

The hunters nodded and took up positions behind the wrecked tents. They took aim at the soldiers and fired their arrows at a group of oblivious soldiers. They managed to fell a few, but the enemy ranks were still thick and impenetrable.

Still, their volley managed to get the group's attention. With a few orders from the officers, the group turned to face Batu's hunters. They began advancing on them, shifting their focus away from Chinua.

"Okay, we've got their attention," Batu said. "What was the next step?"

"We kill 'em," Nugai said, licking his lips and raising his war axe. Batu had seen him in battle once before. He was glad that he had Nugai on his side.

Batu turned to the archers and shouted, "Another volley!" just as the solders began to advance. They were slow compared to the hunters on their horses, but their tight ranks made them tough to crack for the nomads' mounted hunters.

Their volley felled a few more Empire soldiers, but the rest of them kept advancing.

"Fire at will!" Batu called to the archers when the soldiers were twenty meters away, then he turned to his hunters. "Let's go."

Nugai let off an animal-like screech and galloped off in the direction of the enemy, like a predator embarking on a wild chase. Batu shook his head and drew his sword.

When Nugai made contact with the enemy, it was as though a storm had struck a weakened tree. The soldiers crumpled beneath his blows, flying to the sides as he swept them away. Batu roared as he cut his way through the crowd, the enemy ranks buckling under his assault.

A few seconds later, Batu and his own hunters connected with the enemy. There was a thunderous crash as Batu's sword sliced through the armor of the man in front; he went down immediately, blood spurting from his wound.

The man behind him gave Batu no time to react as he advanced with his shield raised in front of him. Batu took stock of the man's fighting stance before using the added height of his horse to beat down on the man's shield. He struck the shield once and the vibrations went up his arms like an earthquake. He struck again and again and finally knocked the shield from the soldier's grasp, sending him off balance. Batu's ears were ringing and his arms felt like shattered logs. The soldier fell to his knees, and Batu cut his head off with a swing of his axe.

The next man began to advance, but Batu took a moment to look around him. The rest of his hunters had made some headway, even though their assault was going slower than Nugai's. Half of the enemy had fallen to them and the rest were backing away cautiously.

Batu engaged the next man. This time, he felt strength surging through his veins, compelling him to fight. He knocked aside the next man's sword. With his blade like a viper, he impaled the soldier's head.

As Batu pulled his sword out of his opponent, he noticed that the enemy was in full retreat, trying to regroup near the rest of their force.

"Let them go," he said to the rest of his hunters. They stopped in their tracks, and while a few enemy soldiers fell to their bows, the Empire soldiers got away without incident.

Nugai approached Batu, his axes dripping with blood. His armor was stained crimson, though Batu was sure that none of it was Nugai's own blood.

"Why did you make me stop?" Nugai said, his voice dripping with hunger. "We could have gotten 'em all!"

"I need to decide our next move," Batu said, taking stock of the hunters they had left. They had lost six hunters in their initial charge, which meant that their force was nearly in half.

Before Batu could clear his head, Nugai grabbed his shoulder and pointed. "While you decide your next move, your father is fighting for his life. No time to think, Batu. You've got to act."

Batu looked where Nugai was pointing and his eyes widened with fear. He had assumed that engaging one of the enemy groups would allow his father to regain control of the battle, but the opposite was true. The sight of more hunters had invigorated the Empire's soldiers, and they were desperately fighting to end the battle.

Most of Chinua's defensive line had fallen, and the rest of them were retreating into the wreckage of the central pavilion as it burned around them. The Empire had set fire to the grass around the clearing and the tent was now surrounded by a ring of fire. After making sure that the nomads had no way of escaping, the Empire's soldiers then began invading the clearing, cutting down any living defenders.

"We have to go help him," Batu said, his mind going blank. Suddenly, all his plans were crumbling away. The rest of the battlefield faded away while Batu drew his sword and charged, no longer caring if his hunters followed him.

He clashed with the Empire's soldiers. This time, his strikes were no longer careful and calculated. It seemed as though his blade was moving on its own, a hungry leopard unleashed from its cage. It swung to the left, then to the right; a trail of blood followed Batu as he spurred his horse onwards.

The next few moments were a blur as Batu's eyes lazily followed his sword, watching his blade draw blood. He fell into a stupor, only focusing on the path ahead of him, the enemies engaging him nothing more than obstacles before his goal.

Batu broke through the enemy lines in a flourish, galloping past them towards his father's pavilion. But when he reached the fire that had begun to encircle the clearing, his horse balked, unwilling to pass through the flames.

"Saenor's scales, this is useless," Batu said, leaping off his horse and charging through the flames himself. The heat scorched his skin, but fortunately the grass was short, the flames only as tall as his knees. Within a few moments, he was through. Although he saw that the cloth on his trousers had burned away, he barely felt anything more than a light throbbing on his calves.

Batu looked behind him, and the rest of his hunters were engaging the defensive line, but they were not going fast enough to join him. He would have to do this alone.

He saw his father and advanced towards him, brandishing a huge two-handed sword and felling attacker after attacker. But the hunters fighting with him were thinning, and it was only a matter of time before his father would be surrounded and outnumbered.

Sword in hand, he started towards the central pavilion, but not before a few attackers left the main group and started approaching him. Batu's sword was moving before he knew it, and five of them were struck down.

By then, the Empire's soldiers were backing away, regrouping until they could organize themselves again. The rational side of Batu told him to take a step back, take stock and gauge their strength, but he saw that his father was standing alone.

He growled and charged the enemy line. Two soldiers fell immediately. The next few were ready though, and they came at him with shields raised. He battered their shields desperately, his attacks becoming more animal than human, but they held up. When one defence faltered, two more came to take its place.

Finally, Batu felt something snap in his arm, and his sword dropped. He stepped backwards, and the soldiers, sensing his moment of weakness, came at him, bashing him in the shoulder and face with their shields. The sword fell out of his hand, and Batu was on his arms and knees.

"Father!" Batu shouted, and Chinua looked in Batu's direction. Their eyes met. Then Chinua's sword was knocked out of his hand and he was pushed to his knees. In front of Batu, two soldiers were approaching him, their spears drawn.

Batu rolled away before the soldiers could get him and managed to get to his feet. His sword was gone and his arm felt as though it had split in two. Batu extended his right arm, but the pain shot through him again. Right under his eyes, an Empire soldier put his sword through Chinua.

Batu screamed and collapsed to the ground, but there was nothing he could do. He looked up as the soldiers approached him, ready to dispose of him at any moment. He did not move.

The nearing soldiers were interrupted by the sound of crashing hooves, followed by shredding metal as Nugai's war axes cut into the soldiers' backs.

Nugai approached Batu and extended his arm. There were tears in

Nugai's eyes and he bit his lip so hard that it bled. "We have to go."

Nugai extended him a steady arm. He nodded and grasped it, allowing himself to be hoisted up and seated behind him on his horse. He noticed that Nugai was holding a war axe in one hand, and leading Batu's horse with the other.

Nugai screamed and his horse moved with him, galloping to the edge of the clearing and leaping over the flames entirely. Nugai met with a few of Batu's hunters that had survived. Together, they galloped down the burning pathways, passing scorched bodies and ruined homes.

They rode up the hill next to the camp and through the rolling plains. Only when the smoke was a distant pillar on the horizon did Nugai allow Batu to mount his own horse. Nugai sprinkled some manna on both of their horses to soothe their emotions and threw a pouch to the other hunters that rode with them.

When they did, Batu turned to look back in the direction of his camp, his cheeks stained from the tears. The burns on his legs began to sting.

"Gaeon save us," he whispered. "He's gone. He's actually gone."

# 9

# Erroll

Erroll entered the barracks and immediately fell into one of the benches, his body drenched in sweat. Manvel followed him, though his movements were careful as he nursed a sprained ankle. He winced when he took a seat and elevated his foot, pressing a wet cloth to the wound. His injury hadn't been serious enough to warrant a trip to the medical tent, so the medics had told him to come back later.

Slowly, the soldiers in their squadron without serious injuries began to trickle into the barracks. Erroll hadn't had much time to pay attention to them during the battle, but he managed to take a closer look as they entered the building,.

Many of them walked without really seeing, their eyes glassy and vacant. Others walked in with some resolve, as though their first taste of battle had reassured them that this was where they belonged.

Jarlen entered the room a few moments later. He scanned the common area before approaching Erroll and Manvel. Manvel looked like he wanted to get to his feet, but his injury didn't allow it.

"How is he?" Manvel asked.

"He'll live," Quince said, sitting down on the bench beside them. He had come away from the battle mostly uninjured except for a few scratches on his face and arms. But his eyes seemed unable to focus on anything and his hands were still shaking. "The arrow got him good, but it didn't hit any vital areas. Old Jarlen is made of tougher stuff than that."

"Thank Jarnis," Manvel said. "So we all got through our first battle alive, somehow."

"Well, there'll be plenty more where that came from. We haven't even managed to enter the damned Steppe."

"That's it," Erroll said, sitting up. "One hundred and seventy-three."

"What's that?" Manvel asked.

"Out of the two hundred in our squadron, there are a hundred and seventy-three of us left. Twenty-seven are either dead or seriously injured."

"How'd you figure that out?" Jarlen said. "Don't tell me you counted everyone as they came into the barracks."

"That's exactly what I did," Erroll said.

"Well, in any case," Manvel said. "That's a good thing, right? Most of us got off all right."

Erroll shook his head. "Did you see how well those nomads fought? That was Khasar the Bull we were up against. He was in the Battle of Tears in the First Expedition. Fought Sandulf's army to a stalemate despite being vastly outnumbered. Say what you will about the savages, but they fight like they're guarding the gates of hell."

"Well, he's dead now," Quince said. "Sandulf made sure of that. That's what matters, right?"

"No, Erroll has a point," Manvel said. "If Khasar was that good, there are sure to be more nomads out there as strong as him. Our squadron was helpless against them. If those other nomads hadn't turned up to help us, we would've been wiped out."

"That's the other thing I'm wondering about," Erroll said. "How did Sandulf convince the nomads to betray their own kind? Though I guess loyalty means nothing when you're uncivilized."

"They must not all be united," Manvel said. "My guess is, they're not like the Empire with one ruler. They're probably broken up into a bunch of groups."

"Or maybe Sandulf just paid them with ox hearts or whatever those savages use as money," Quince said. "Honestly, you two think too much about this stuff. We're infantrymen. All we need to do is follow orders."

"Even so, these things matter if we want to survive," Erroll said. "I don't know about you two, but I didn't come here to die."

Manvel chuckled and laid back in his seat; the movement made him wince with pain. "You make a very good point. Say, out of curiosity, did either of you kill any nomads today?"

Quince shook his head. "After the nomads charged us for the first time, the captain had me help brace the gate. Didn't get much to do after that."

"Same here," Manvel said, nodding. "After Jarlen took an arrow, I spent of the rest of the time making sure he didn't get trampled."

Quince barked a laugh. "That's your own damn fault, then."

Then they both turned to Erroll, who was doing his best to avoid their gaze.

"And you, Erroll?" Manvel asked.

Erroll paused for a long moment. Then, finally, he said, "Three."

"By Galele, Erroll," Quince said. "How did you manage it?"

Erroll shrugged. "I just followed what they taught us in training."

"Yeah, well, so did we," Manvel said. "And you can see how well that went for us. I beat you on the sparring ground a month ago, but I guess I'm out of my depth now."

Erroll shook his head and then got to his feet. "I don't want to talk about this anymore," he said.


When Erroll got back to his bunk, the entire sleeping quarters were empty, since most of the other soldiers were outside in the common area. He was glad for the privacy as he searched through his crate without having to worry about someone looking over his shoulder.

He pulled out his canteen and took a long drink, letting some of the water spill over his cheeks and onto his shirt. He noticed that there were still some drops of blood on it, so he stripped it off and tossed it to the side. He'd left his armor with the smiths, but the plate hadn't been enough to shield his body from the taint of war.

He ran his hands through his sweat-slicked hair and did his best to wipe some of the sweat away from his chest and face with a cloth tied around the bed frame. By the time he finished, the cloth was drenched and Erroll still felt drained. It was as though something had sucked the blood from his veins.

He felt like he was going to collapse any second, but somehow, he still kept himself together, like a glass pane about to shatter, with spiderweb cracks spreading across it. He took a few deep breaths then pulled out a few sheets of paper from his bag, but as he did, a chunk of metal came out and landed on the floor.

Erroll scooped it up quickly, but as he did, he looked at it for the first time in a few weeks. It was his father's medal, or rather the medal they sent to Erroll's mother after his father's death during the war.

Erroll ran his hands over the medal, his fingers tracing his father's name, "Erwan", and the words below it, "Died in service of Her Imperial Majesty Tomyris." There had been no body, nor an explanation of when and where he died. Erroll himself hadn't even found the medal until a year ago, when he was rummaging in the attic of his mother's jewelry shop.

"You didn't tell me Father served in the army," Erroll had said, dropping the medal on the table in front of his mother. "Why would you hide this from me?"

His mother didn't answer him immediately. She picked up the medal and examined it closely, then she finally said, "You were too young to understand."

"So when were you planning to tell me? I'm an adult now, probably almost as old as he was when he left."

"That's why I decided to wait," his mother said, setting the medal back on the table. "I didn't want you to go chasing after your father in the Steppe. You won't find him there."

Erroll gripped the table, but even then, he couldn't stop himself from shaking. Neither could he stop the tears from pouring down his face. Without another word to his mother, Erroll reached out and shoved the medal back into his pocket, then he climbed the steps back upstairs.

"Where are you going?" she called.

"To pack," Erroll said.

Even as he sat on the floor of the barracks, hundreds of miles away from home, Erroll could still remember the look his mother gave him that day. He hadn't known what to say to her then, and he still didn't now.

He pulled out the letter he must have rewritten over a hundred times at this point, and he scanned the words that he had at the moment.

*"Dear Mother,*

*You told me that you didn't want me to look for my father in the Steppe. You need to know that that's not what's happening. I just couldn't find what I'm looking for in the smithing district. You see, I'm looking for…"*

These words were all he had at the moment. They were the most honest ones he could find, but when he turned that last sentence over in his head, he found that they have left him yet again. He'd missed his chance to send the letter when they left the Empire, so the letter was more for him than his mother. Still, he wondered if they'd be able to send the letter to her if he died in battle. Maybe then he'd be able to give her the answers she deserved.

# II

# Empty Hills

# 10

# Sara

"Don't worry, Sara," Khulan said as they passed the tents where the hunters were preparing for the morning shift. "I can handle our hunters. You focus on the important stuff."

"You sure? Zayaat approached me yesterday to ask about running joint hunts with his own hunters. I think it's a good idea, especially if our hunters will be fighting together soon," Sara said. "And we still need to worry about supplies."

"Relax. We've been here two weeks and we're no longer relying on Ibakha's supplies for food. And I've spoken to Zayaat about working with his hunters. It's under control."

Sara took a deep breath. "I know. Of course it is. I'm sorry."

"It's fine," Khulan said. "It must be weird for you, not being master of hunters anymore. Probably can't help but stick your nose in. Even after handing it over to your very capable friend."

Sara laughed. "I'll try to keep my distance then. How are things going with Ganbold?"

"As good as I can make it, I guess. I've been assigning him to scout Asjare and Omnu territory to make sure that we're aware of enemy movements. I'd like him to pay special attention to the mountain pass that leads to the Temple of Gaeon. The way I see it, the more time he's away from camp, the less time he has to make trouble."

Sara knit her eyebrows in surprise. "That's…actually a really good idea."

"Can't take credit for it. It was Bataar's plan."

"Maybe Bataar should be chief, then."

"Yeah, maybe. Problem is, he doesn't have your charm."

Sara laughed again. "Speaking of, I should go check on Bataar."

"Sounds good," Khulan said, patting Sara on the shoulder. "It's good to see you laugh, Sara."

Sara left to find Bataar at the livestock pens. As she walked through the camp, she was surprised at how normal everything seemed. Apart from the switch to warmer clothing and the sharp winds that made fabric fly everywhere once in a while, she could have convinced herself that they were back in their camp in Omnu.

But when she looked closer, things couldn't have been more different. As she walked towards the livestock, Sara tightened her fists when she saw Sain and his wife comforting a sobbing child. She wished she knew what to tell them.

She began walking away. Before she got far, she heard Sain's voice call out to her from behind.

"We'll get through this, Chief."

Sara turned and saw that Sain was still kneeling to comfort his child, but his eyes were turned towards Sara.

"We'll get through this, but it's going to take all of us. We all look up to you. But you can't do everything yourself. I hope you know that, Sara."

The man turned back to his child before Sara could reply, so there was nothing left for her to do but to leave. She turned over the words as she walked to the livestock pens and approached Bataar.

"Good to see you, Sara," he said as she approached, though he didn't take his eyes off the yaks. "What do you need?"

"I need you to tell me about the tribes," Sara said. "Who they are, how they operate, and how we can get them on our side."

Bataar turned, a huge grin on his face. "I never thought you'd ask."


"Sorry we're late," Ibakha said, pushing open the tent flaps and entering the central pavillion. Zayaat trailed behind her, with his long hair tied into one large braid.

When they entered, Khulan and Sara began to rise to their feet, but

Zayaat waved at them to stay seated. "No need," he muttered as he and Ibakha took seats across from Sara.

"The meetings with the chiefs took longer than I thought they would," Ibakha said. "Turns out old men can be more stubborn than I thought."

"Don't worry about it," Sara said.

"Well, don't leave us in suspense," Khulan said, leaning forward. "How did the meetings go?"

Ibakha gave a long, exasperated sigh. "Well, they happened. And, fortunately, no one has threatened to oppose us. So I suppose that's a good sign."

"No one has threatened to oppouse us yet," Zayaat clarified. "Some of the chiefs were speaking together after the meeting. Might be cause for concern."

"None of that talk, now, Zayaat," Ibakha said. "We need unity, now more than ever. We can't afford to suspect our own allies of treachery."

"Fine, but I'll keep my eyes open," Zayaat said.

"Sure. But the Harnda chiefs are no longer our biggest problem." She turned to face Sara. "I hope you realize what you've started. The tribes haven't come together like this since twenty years ago. Many of them are at war with each other and may mistake our offer of alliance as conquest."

"I understand," Sara said. "It's what my father did, and I'm sure he would do the same if he was still around."

Ibakha nodded. "Good. I just wanted to be sure."

"We need to talk about the Asjare," Khulan said. "Are we completely sure that they've betrayed us?"

"As sure as I can be," Zayaat said. "We have met a few survivors from Khasar's raid on the Empire's outposts. They said that the Leopard of Asjare himself was at the battle and there were a few skirmishes involving the outriders we sent to the border. The Asjare will not stand with us."

"Saenor's scales," Sara said. "The Asjare have always been jealous and resentful of the Omnu, but I never thought they'd go so far as to betray us."

"It'd never have happened with their last head chieftain, but the new one, Dayir, I don't trust him," Ibakha said. "And of course, you can't forget that the Asjare struggled the most because of the Temple's closing. They need that manna more than anyone else in the Steppe."

Sara bit her lip. Every day was another reminder of the cost of Chinua's lust for power. She wished that she could go back and right his wrongs, but all she could do was clean up after him.

"We need to make sure that the Asjare don't get any further than their border," Khulan said. "I can spare some hunters, but we don't have the numbers for a full patrol."

"The other Harnda chiefs are providing us with reinforcements," Zayaat said. "With some adjustments, it should be enough."

"Luckily, it should be pretty easy to keep watch on the two remaining bridges after we destroyed the bridge across the Serpent's River."

"Speaking of," Sara said. "Has there been any luck with reaching out to Dagun and Yegu?"

Ibakha shook her head. "Not much. We don't even know where the remaining Omnu chieftains are. With the Asjare issue, we don't have many hunters to spare looking for them. My guess is that they're deliberately trying to hide. The Empire's started making their way into the Steppe, and they don't have the strength to challenge them directly."

"Chinua might have been able to," Zayaat said, then he saw how Sara's face changed when he mentioned his name. "I'm sorry. I did not mean to say that."

"No, don't worry about it," Sara said. No matter what Chinua did in the years following the war, he was still the leader that led them to victory against the Empire. "Anyway, the last thing we need to discuss is how we're going to get the other tribes on our side."

"Another alliance," Zayaat said. "And I was hoping I would not live to see another one."

"We still need to get them to agree to come," Sara said. "We can offer them aid, supplies, even free passage to the Temple when this is all over."

"It would be wise not to offer them everything at the beginning," Zayaat said. "You should instruct the envoy to only offer manna at first and dangle—not promise—the prospect of free passage to the Temple's manna spring only if they fully commit to the alliance."

"It was our control of the Temple that started this conflict to begin with," Sara said.

"I know, Sara," Ibakha said. "But right now, with the tribes as divided as they are, the Temple is our only bargaining chip. If we squander it, they'll walk all over us."

Sara didn't like it, but she didn't have a better idea, so she crossed her arms and leaned back in her seat. "So who's going to speak to the chiefs?"

"Ah, right," Ibakha said. "Our choice of envoy will matter greatly for each tribe. And there's also the Gur's hierarchy that we need to consider."

Zayaat groaned. "The less we need to deal with Thaube, the better."

Ibakha laughed. "Zayaat just can't wait for that old bastard to die."

"That is not the way I would've said it, but yes."

"In any case, I don't think Zayaat should be the one to approach the Gur. I have some proposals for the envoys."

Zayaat and Ibakha gave each other a quizzical look, as if a rug had just been pulled out from below them.

"Let's hear it, then," Ibakha said.

Sara tightened her fists, took a deep breath, and told them what she thought.

As Sara stood next to Khulan, ready to send off her best friend, she got the strange feeling that she had been here before.

"It's a long road to Delbeg's camp, isn't it?" Sara said. "You'll have to pass through the Eagle's Perch. Maybe it would be faster if you took the route along Arban's Peaks."

"Sara," Khulan said, placing a hand on her friend's shoulder, which seemed difficult to do from horeseback. "You're doing it again."

"Doing what again?"

"Sticking your nose where it doesn't belong. Which is what you always do when you're anxious."

"Right," Sara said. "You're right. I'll leave you to handle things."

"That's a good girl."

Sara looked behind her, scanning the camp for Khulan's companions. The sun had barely risen yet, so the winds were still deadly. A cold breeze struck them and Sara shivered, pulling her cloak tighter around herself. They'd been on Harnda land for a few weeks now, and she still couldn't get used to the cold. The less time she spent standing around, the better.

"They're not here yet," Sara said.

"I had Ganbold pick up a few extra supplies," Khulan said. "And you know how Kara is with punctuality."

Sara laughed. "I suppose you're right."

"You're absolutely sure that Ganbold is the right choice for this?" Khulan said. "He's done everything he could to oppose us since we fled. Why would you give him the task of appealing to the Gur for aid?"

"His heart's in the right place, Khulan. If he wanted to betray us, he'd have done it a long time ago. I just want to show him that we want what's best for the tribe as well, just like him."

"Whatever you say, Sara. But I'll keep my eyes on him."

"I expected you to say that. Still, remember what Ibakha said. We need unity, so don't do anything stupid unless you're absolutely sure."

"Don't worry. I'm an expert at not doing stupid things."

Behind them, Ganbold and Kara approached them, both mounted on horses that were burdened with a wealth of supplies. They needed enough to reach one of the Harnda herding camps along the border. From there, they would have to cross the entire Gur territory before arriving at Delbeg's camp. It would be tough and slow going, especially since their horses would have to bear so many supplies.

"Sara, Khulan," Kara said. "Sorry we're late."

"Yes, well, part of my job this morning was to wake Kara up," Ganbold said with a slight grin. Then he turned to Sara with an entirely unreadable look. "I didn't realize that the chief herself would come see us off."

"Ganbold," Sara said. "Thank you for coming. I just came to wish your group all the best. You're the first of our envoy parties to leave the camp. The Gur's support will be crucial."

Ganbold nodded. "We will do what we need to do for the good of the camp. As we've always done," he said.

"You'll be okay," Sara whispered to Khulan as Kara began inspecting the supplies, making sure they had enough.

"Who are you trying to convince? You or me?" Khulan asked.

"Don't know," Sara said. "I just can't help but remember the last time I sent someone off like this."

Khulan's face fell when she realized what Sara was talking about. "Oh. It won't be like that. Believe me."

"He asked me to go with him back then. Did I tell you that? Od wanted me with him at the council meeting. And I know I would've died if I went, but maybe there was something I could have done?" Sara wiped away a tear.

"Hey, hey," Khulan said, running her hand through Sara's hair. "What are your hunters going to say if they see you like this? What was it that you told me back in the stable? No more tears."

"I'm okay. It's just...I don't know what I'd do if I lost you, Khulan. You're..."

Khulan placed a finger on Sara's lips to silence her. "I'll be okay, Sara, I promise."

Sara took a few deep breaths and pulled herself together. Then she turned to address all three of them. Ganbold and Kara stood at attention, ready to leave. "You three carry the hopes of our tribe with you. Gaeon ride with you."

# 11
# Batu

Batu's days had been consumed by visions of red and black. When his sight did clear up, he saw his father. Usually, he would be sitting at a fireside cleaning a knife or skinning a deer. His father was never really doing anything of note and he would never speak, save for one moment that had been etched into Batu's memory.

He tried to speak to his father, to tell him that he did all he could, but he would never listen. Chinua's gaze alone was enough to sear a hole through Batu.

Periodically, Batu would wake up but his vision would blur. The stars above him looked red and the red would branch out to flood the entire sky above him. His entire body burned and the pain alone would be enough to make him fall back asleep.

"You're too spineless to be head chieftain. It seems that I've failed as a father," Chinua said without ever meeting Batu's eyes.

When he heard those words, Batu turned and ran, cursing his father, but the words would follow him. His father was dead, and despite everything Chinua taught him, Batu wasn't there for him when he needed him most. His father's voice grew louder and louder in his mind and there was nothing Batu could do but scream for mercy.

Batu woke in a cold sweat. There was a dull, throbbing pain in his side and in his legs and his head felt like it was on fire. But for the first time in a while, his vision was clear, and he looked up into the sky and saw stars.

Someone was at his side within moments, pressing a damp cloth to his forehead.

"Saenor's scales, calm down, you idiot," the voice said, and from its texture, Batu could tell that it was Nugai. "You'll give our position away if you keep screaming like that."

Batu rose shakily into a sitting position, but a wave of nausea struck him the moment he did.

"How long have I been asleep?" he asked.

"Two days, and you haven't given us the best time of it," Nugai said, scowling. "Your fever broke last night, and the burns on your legs are improving thanks to some herbs Cirina found on the riverside."

Batu lifted himself up by his arms and took a look at his feet that were still bound in tight bandages, but he could see hints of the skin around the wound. Even he could tell that the scars would never heal fully.

Batu got to his feet and stumbled once, but Nugai helped him to steady himself. His legs burned, but he forced himself to stay upright. He looked around, finding about half a dozen empty sleeping mats strewn about on the grass. There was a fire burning a few meters away, surrounded by five hunters, most of whom Batu recognized from the group he led to capture Saragerel.

"We're next to the River of the Serpent," Batu realized. "Why are we here?"

Nugai shrugged. "We couldn't think of anywhere else to hide. The Empire is in the Steppe now."

"What about Khasar's raid?"

"Broken. The Asjare stabbed them in the back."

Batu's eyes widened. "We can't stay here, then," Batu started to make for the campfire. "We need to make a plan."

Before Batu could get far, however, Nugai caught his shoulder. "Hold on a moment, Batu. There's something I need to talk to you about."

"What is it?" Batu said, frowning.

Nugai took a deep breath. "No easy way to say it. Batu, your father's dead. You know what that means?"

Batu averted his gaze, staring at the grass at his feet. "Why don't you tell me?"

"It means that you're chief now."

"Chief? Whose chief am I? They're all dead, Nugai. The Empire made sure of that."

"For Gaeon's sake," Nugai said. He pointed at the hunters sitting around the campfire. "You're their chief, so long as their hearts are still beating, you've got to start acting like one before I put an axe in your skull."

"What's the use? We've got nowhere to go."

"Maybe, but you owe it to them to be a damned leader for once. And not the pathetic excuse for a leader you normally are."

Batu's face fell as reality dawned on him. "Even if I wanted to be, I don't know how. My father told me as much."

"Old Chinua wasn't perfect either. They called him Gaeon's chosen, but it all felt like nonsense to me," Nugai said. "You know that as well as anyone, so stop trying to be him. Just look at them, Batu. They're scared, grieving, and exhausted. They need to know that someone is still looking out for them. Can you do that?"

Batu looked at the souls surrounding the campfire and looked into their faces for the first time. He saw in their eyes what Nugai was talking about. Then he looked back to Nugai. "I don't know."


Batu took a seat at the campfire between Nugai and a female hunter whose name he didn't know.

"So, the man who walked on fire finally rises from the dead," came a gruff voice from the other side of the campfire. Batu looked up and saw Jochi, his father's master of hunters.

"Jochi, you're alive," Batu said, barely able to hide the surprise in his voice.

Jochi laughed. "I'm made of tougher stuff than you think, kid. Imagine my displeasure at finding out that you're our chief now. Let's just hope you're better at being chief than I am at being the master of hunters."

"I'm glad you're here, Jochi. Really."

Jochi grunted and went back to devouring the piece of venison in his hands.

Batu looked around the campfire and saw, for the first time, the people with whom he was working. Whenever he'd worked with hunters from his camp, he'd always think of them as his father's men, not his. But as he looked into their eyes, he realized that he couldn't be his father at this moment.

"I'm sorry that I haven't been particularly helpful these past four days," he said, and even though he said the words quietly, his voice carried over the raging river and got their attention. "And I'm sorry for my recklessness during the battle. I could've gotten you all killed."

He saw a few nods around the campfire and knew that that was all he was going to get.

"I'm not very good at this sort of thing," Batu continued. "But I guess I'm your chief now. So, uh, that means I'll be looking after you. Does that work with everyone?"

Batu was looking straight into the fire as he said those words. For some reason, he couldn't find the strength to meet their eyes.

"You know, Batu actually expected an answer to his question," Nugai said.

A few chuckles and even a hearty laugh from Jochi erupted around the campfire. Batu sighed in relief as he felt the tension lift a little bit.

"Yes, Chief," said a woman who was idly sharpening her knife as she spoke. "We're with you."

"Look Batu in the eye," Nugai said, but Batu held up his hand.

"Thank you," Batu said. He shifted in his seat, and noticed that his fists had been clutching the grass at his side the entire time. "It occurs to me that I don't know any of your names. Well, except Jochi and Nugai, of course."

"I'm Cirina," said the woman with the knife. She met his eyes as she said her name, and Batu noticed that she wasn't much older than him, but her long hair and intense stare made her look much older.

"Cirina," Batu repeated.

"Bala," came a quiet voice from beside Cirina. The man to whom it belonged didn't match his voice. He was large and hulking and lying on the grass beside him was a longsword nearly as tall as Batu. His long hair came down in locks around his chin, but his face was clean-shaven save for some stubble.

"Khabichi's my name, Chief," came a voice. Batu's eyes found a man whose smile rested willingly on his lips, but didn't reach his eyes. He braided two strands of his hair that swayed around his ears as he spoke. He winked when Batu met his eyes. "Here's hoping you'll get us out of this mess."

"Suppose I'm the last one then. I'm Dorgene," said a woman from the other end of the circle. She was older than the rest, and it showed in her voice. Her hair was cut short so it didn't go past her ears, and she looked like she could strangle a deer with her bare hands.

Batu repeated each of their names and made a mental note to remember them.

"Thank you for telling me," Batu said. "Next thing—we need to figure out where we're going next."

"Why can't we just stay here?" Khabichi said. "Seems like we've got a pretty good set-up, anyway."

"Can't do that. Within a week or so, this place will be overrun with Empire soldiers. There won't be anywhere left to hide, especially since Khasar's raid didn't go as planned."

"What's this about the Bull?" Cirina said. "No one told me."

"We hoped to take the Empire by surprise," Jochi explained. "So we sent Khasar with most of the Omnu hunters to attack their outpost while their soldiers weren't battle-ready. The raid failed and as far as we can tell, it was because the Leopard of Asjare fought with the enemy."

"Damned Asjare," Dorgene said. "All those greedy bastards ever cared about was the manna. They know nothing of honor and loyalty."

"In any case," Batu said. "It means we can't stay here. The Harnda lands don't work either. Thanks to my father, we've made an enemy of Saragerel and her camp, who were always close allies with the Harnda. That leaves us with one option: we have to flee into Asjare territory."

"What did you just say?" Khabichi said. "Did you just suggest that we go deeper into enemy territory?"

"Gaeon's staff," Cirina said. "We should just strike out on our own. Maybe even join the Empire. Not like our chiefs did us much good, anyway."

"I can't believe you suggested that," Batu said, feeling his fists tighten. The next words that came out of his mouth was like blood spilling from an old scar. "My father would never…"

But Nugai cut him off. "What Chief Batu meant is that we won't survive on our own out there with empire soldiers crawling through the lands and enemies in every hill. Right now, they're busy securing the mountain pass to the Temple of Gaeon but soon they'll be hunting down every last nomad this side of the river."

"Of course," Batu said, taking a deep breath after Nugai placed a hand on his knee and squeezed. "We can't go into Harnda, since that means crossing the Serpent's River which they'll be watching closely. But the Asjare will have most of their hunters patrolling their border with Harnda, so the bridges from Omnu to Asjare will be unguarded."

"Even so," Khabichi said. "We'll still be in enemy territory. Did the fire burn your head, too?"

"It's not ideal, I know," Batu said. "But we'll have to be creative. That means some light raids on small hunting groups, a bit of misdirection to draw them out, and a lot of sneaking around. But we're a small group, so with some planning I think we can pull it off."

The muttering from the hunters fell silent as they turned to Jochi who was stroking his beard, deep in thought. After a long pause, he finally spoke. "I don't like it, but I can't think of anything better. The Flamewalker has it right. I'm glad to see he isn't a complete idiot."

Batu smiled and nodded. A week ago, the comment would have offended him. Now, he would take anything he could get. "We'll leave in the morning, then."

# 12
# Erroll

Erroll lowered his crossbow and prepared to fire again. As he did, their squadron's captain, whose name Erroll had learned was Fabio, was walking nearby.

"That's a good shot, soldier," Fabio said, peering at the target from behind a pair of half-rimmed spectacles. He reminded Erroll of the tax collectors the Empire always sent into the smithing district once a month. "Practice your reload time and you'll soon be one of our best marksmen."

Erroll rolled his eyes and loaded another bolt. He practiced the same way for an hour or so, until that he began to feel the strain on his muscles. At least he didn't need to exert effort to keep the bowstring locked. Eventually, he got quicker at locking the bowstring and loading a bolt, but each time he fired an arrow, his muscles grew tense and sore.

"Not good enough," he whispered to himself. If the stories were any indication, the nomads wouldn't wait patiently for him to reload each time. Each second in between shots from his crossbow felt like an eternity.

Finally, Fabio declared that training was over. Several of Erroll's companions collapsed to the ground in exhaustion. Erroll paid them no mind as he walked to the armory, where he returned the crossbow and his bolts.

As he passed the practice field's entrance, one of Fabio's assistants was standing there with a clipboard to watch each soldier as they passed and give them their assignments.

"Erroll, you're on dishwashing duty next. Get to it," the assistant said.

"Of course," Erroll said, then the moment he had some distance between himself and the training ground, he ducked into a space between two buildings.

There was a soldier waiting for him there. Erroll didn't know his name, but he had enlisted his help during breakfast.

"You're...you're Erroll, right?" the soldier said. "My name is..."

"I don't care," Erroll said, cutting him off. He brought out a handful of coins from his pocket and approached the man. "Five silvers to take my dishwashing duty. You can manage that, right?"

The soldier stared at the coins for a few moments, then scooped them up and put them in his pocket. "Yes, I can."

Erroll shoved the rest of the coins into his pocket. With every moment that passed, he was beginning to forget the soldier's face. "Good. Then we're done here. Make sure you sign my name into the logs as well. The captain loves his records."

"Wait," the soldier said as Erroll walked away, but he made no move to follow him. "What are you going to do now? If you do anything illegal, you won't bring me into it, right?"

Erroll peeked out from the alleyway and watched the guards patrol up and down the street. The change of guards would be happening in a few moments and it would give Erroll just enough time to break into the storehouse without anyone noticing.

He waited a few moments, then the two guards heard a bell chime in the distance. The guards nodded to each other and headed for the barracks.

Erroll sprinted across the street until he was at the door of a small wooden storehouse squeezed in between two smithies. When he got to the door, Erroll pulled a lockpick out of his pocket and started working the lock. One of his friends in Ruson had shown him how to do this a year ago, but Erroll hadn't had the chance to try it until now.

Erroll had been watching Sandulf's personal guard for a few weeks now. Whenever the final bell rang, they would always come to sweep this street first, as though they were preparing for something. It only took him a few more nights to figure out the storehouse Sandulf was keeping his records.

Erroll looked up from his work and noticed that the two new guards were about to round the corner, but they were talking to each other so neither of them noticed Erroll. He picked up the pace, and just when he thought they were about to spot him, he cracked the lock and slid open the door.

He entered the room, closing the door behind him and throwing himself into the pitch darkness. He didn't notice it just now, but when he rubbed his palms together, he realized that they were sweaty. He was panting and he could feel the anxiety right up to his throat.

The room had no windows. Even if there were any, the sunlight would be blocked by the buildings beside the tiny storeroom.

Erroll got on his knees and started running his hands over the floor. His hands touched something metallic and he discovered that it was a handle. He pulled on it, and dislodged the piece of floor it was attached to. Light shone through the hole, and Erroll saw that there was a ladder leading downwards into the earth.

"I knew it. Trapdoor," he muttered to himself, then he climbed into the earth below.

The room was tightly packed and there was only enough space between the bookshelves for one man to stand. The room was lit by a set of oil lanterns that had just been changed, probably in case Sandulf needed to find something in the middle of the day.

As Erroll descended down the ladder, he realized that there was someone waiting for him at the bottom.

"You're far too predictable, Erroll," Manvel said, arms crossed and leaning back in a chair in the middle of the basement.

"What the hell...Manvel, what are you doing here?" Erroll said.

"I should ask you the same question."

"There's just something I need to find out."

"From General Sandulf's secret records? Are you out of your mind?"

Manvel was on his feet and right in front of Erroll's face. The expression on his face was livid, like nothing Erroll had seen before, not even during the fiercest drills that Praxis had put them through.

"It's none of your damned business, Manvel," Erroll shot back. "How did you even get in here?"

"You think you're the only one with problems, Erroll?" Manvel said. "You think you're the only one that knows how to figure things? I came here because I didn't want you to get caught."

"Why do you care so much?"

"Because you're the only friend I've got, idiot," Manvel said. "But I guess you're too thick-headed to see that."

Erroll was silent for a long time before he responded. "I thought you didn't want me to get involved in other people's business. Just like with your brother."

Manvel shook his head. "No, Erroll. I told you about that because I wanted you to know. Even when you're being an insufferable idiot."

Erroll was quiet again, and he found that he couldn't meet Manvel's eyes. A part of him thought he should leave the storeroom and never speak to Manvel again, to run away like he's always done. But no one has ever gone to such lengths for him before. Not even his mother.

"You followed me here?" Erroll said.

Manvel rolled his eyes. "The guy you paid to take your dishwashing duty? He told me where you were headed, so I got here first."

"The guards?"

"Paid them off. Being rich has its perks."

"Of course you did."

"So," Manvel said, taking a seat again. "Are you finally going to tell me why you're here?"

Erroll sighed. "Fine. I'm looking for information about my father."

"Your father…the one who served with General Sandulf," Manvel said.

"He died twenty years ago in the First Expedition, but unlike everyone else whose relatives died, they didn't tell my mother why or how he died."

Manvel stroked his chin. "And why didn't they?"

"Well, I figured that since he served under General Sandulf, who's known for keeping detailed records, I might be able to find something in this camp. Getting assigned here was a stroke of luck, really."

"Is this the reason you enlisted in the first place?"

"Yes," Erroll said, shrugging. "Not really. I just needed to get away from home."

"I can understand that," Manvel said, then he gestured at the rows of bookshelves behind him. "So, how are we going to find the information we need in this mess?"

"What? You're offering to help me?"

"Of course," Manvel said, then he got up from his chair and began browsing the spines of Sandulf's journals. "There must be some kind of organizational system to this."

Erroll crouched next to Manvel. "You don't need to do this, you know."

Manvel met his eyes. "Erroll, it wouldn't be the end of the world if you trusted someone."

"Yeah, well, trust isn't exactly cheap in Ruson."

Manvel shrugged, then he began looking through the dates listed on the covers. Eventually, Erroll sighed and looked at the notebooks with him. The dates went back thirty years and included entries from the Uyammad Expedition and the K'harini Revolts. Erroll hadn't been alive to witness those events.

Before they could get so far, however, a door on the other side of the room swung open. Manvel and Erroll both stopped in their tracks and watched the door, but all they saw was a darkened corridor without any light bright enough for them to see.

A few moments passed. Then they heard a faint sound echoing through the corridor, sounding louder and closer each time it rang out. Erroll's ears took a few moments to recognize the sound.

A slow round of applause.

# 13
# Sara

Sara sat on top of a hill overlooking the Harnda camp, Altan on her arm. She stroked the hunting eagle's feathers tentatively, as thought it would break apart if her touch was too rough.

"It's too much," she said. "I'm not meant for this."

She took a few deep breaths, then turned to watch the camp. From afar, everything seemed to operate smoothly. Each person had their own task. But after she made her rounds today, she realized that things were more precarious than they seemed.

"They're barely holding it together," Sara said.

Her eagle placed its head near to her face and nuzzled her shoulder. She sprinkled some manna on its feathers. Seeing the blue powder glow allowed her to feel her eagle's worry, fear, and frustration. She felt it as if it were her own. She leaned her head against it and tried to soothe its emotions, even as her own roiled and raged inside of her. She wasn't sure how long she sat there, but the sun was low on the horizon when someone tapped her shoulder.

She turned to find Bataar standing behind her. It took all the strength she had to rise to her feet and temper her expression. "What is it, Bataar?"

"There's trouble," Bataar said. "The group you sent along with Khulan is back, but..."

"Is she safe?" Sara said.

Bataar placed his hand over hers. The gesture was small and almost entirely inconspicuous, but Sara's feet felt surer on the ground.

"Khulan is fine," Bataar said, and Sara breathed a sigh of relief. "Kara as well. But Ganbold...he was separated from them on the way back. He went to accompany one of the patrol groups along the border with Asjare."

"Why would he do that? He should've come back to report to me," Sara said.

Bataar shook his head. "I don't know, Sara, but listen. That same patrol group...we think it's under attack."

Sara blinked twice, then turned away and started down the hill. Bataar started behind her, and tried to get in front of her, but she didn't slow down.

"Sara, we just got the report from one of the scouts. We don't know how many there are."

"Get Orda and the rest," Sara said. "Tell them to meet at the northern gathering point."

Bataar grabbed Sara by the arm, and would not let go when she tried to shake herself free. "Sara, hold on a moment. You need to be cautious about this. You're not the master of hunters anymore, you can't just run off into battle whenever you want."

"Bataar, I'm tired of letting people die when there was something I could have done. Let me do this, Bataar. Don't you trust me?"

Sara waited a second, and then another. Right before she was about to speak again, Bataar took a deep breath and nodded. "Okay. I'll make sure Zayaat sends some hunters along with you."


Sara rode her horse through the northern clearing, taking stock of the hunters that had already assembled there. She was relieved to see that within such a short notice, they had nearly twenty hunters mounted and armed. The scouts had told her on the way that the Asjare patrol was pursuing them across Harnda territory and were trying to corner them along Arban's Peaks.

She looked around her, watching as her hunters strung their bows and examined their swords. There was little talk among them, and those that did spoke in hushed tones that faded into silence as she approached. She tried to give them a reassuring look, but she wasn't sure if she'd made a difference when she left them.

Sara tried to shake the feeling of dread seeping into her. She resolved to focus on assembling her forces. Altan leapt off her shoulder and soared into the sky.

When her eagle had reached a suitable height, she took its eyes and circled the camp from above, watching as the hunters trickled into the clearing from throughout the camp. Most of them she recognized as her own hunters from the way they pulled their cloaks tightly around them while riding, but she was surprised to see some of Zayaat's hunters entering the clearing. They did so in small groups of two or three and hovered among the edges, as if they were unsure of whether or not they were welcome there.

From the corner of Altan's eye, Sara spotted a figure entering the clearing and riding up next to where her body was. It took her only a moment to realize who the figure was, and she snapped back into her own body.

"Khulan!" Sara said, meeting her friend's eyes. She was different from how she remembered, but she couldn't put her finger on it. "You're meant to be resting."

Khulan shook her head. "I'm joining you. Don't try to stop me."

"For once in your life, won't you just listen?" Sara said. "I won't risk your life for a second time."

Khulan shook her head. "It's my life to risk, Sara."

Sara took a deep breath. "Fine. But I'm going to need your help with them," she said, gesturing at the assembling hunters. "They're all scared, and I don't know how to reassure them. Onoe's blood, I don't know how to reassure myself."

"Oh, Sara. If you keep thinking like that, we'll never beat the Empire."

"Then how am I supposed to think?" Sara snapped. "Everyone keeps telling me I've got to be a leader, that I've got to take charge, but I don't have any idea how to do it."

"Look, Sara, Gaeon knows we're in a rough spot. But if you go on believing that, you'll never get anywhere."

"So what am I supposed to do? Lead the tribe with nothing but a positive attitude?"

"Maybe. Or you could just smile every once in a while. You look like you've just been dragged through a river of salt."

Sara met Khulan's eyes for a few moments. She managed a small chuckle and brushed a few strands of hair away from her face. When she looked up at Khulan, she was smiling, if only for a fleeting moment.

"I suppose I could lighten up a little bit."

"That's the way I like it," Khulan said. "You're gonna do great."

Sara glanced behind her and found that the troops were almost ready. They were assembling into ranks and nearly all of them had their weapons ready. Sara rode to the front of the group so that everyone in their force could see her. She made eye contact with Khulan, who nodded and mouthed something that Sara couldn't make out.

She turned to the rest of the group. "Our people are out there," she began. She was shocked at how quickly the clearing fell into silence when she spoke. "And they're in trouble. You're one of the best hunters in the Steppe, so I don't need to tell you that we have to go help them."

"I'll just say this: feet on the ground, eyes to the sky. Gaeon ride with us all."


Sara watched the battle from the sky. Her body lingered on a hill near the battlefield with a small force of reserve hunters but she had taken the eyes of her eagle, watching from above as their strike force approached their tired and beleaguered patrol group, right as they were being surrounded by the Asjare force.

Even from this high up, she could pick out tiny animals like rabbits and mice scurrying around through the grass as her hunters charged through like a thunderstorm moving through their peaceful night.

With each gust of wind, the Steppe took a breath, and the grass swayed along with it.

Some of the grass had already been stained with blood. The Harnda patrol had managed to beat back most of the Asjare charges, but they couldn't do it for much longer. Another gust of wind rolled over the battlefield like a wave. She expected the hunters to move along with it, but they remained resolute.

She watched as the Omnu and Harnda hunters appraoched from two fronts, flanked by Khulan and Alaqa. Both rode at the head of their companies and Sara realized how similar they looked from so high up. Both of them had their hair tied into a single long braid that fell across their backs.

The Asjare hunters, having long since noticed the attackers, abandoned their attempts to break the weakened patrol group, instead dismounting from their horses and forming ranks. They began to form a defensive line, some taking out their swords and others preparing bows.

She saw Khulan's company move faster as the master of hunters shouted commands, probably looking to outpace the Asjare hunters while Alaqa's company slowed down, splitting their formation into three groups. After they had regrouped, Alaqa began the charge again, but Khulan was already far ahead of them.

A part of Sara was screaming at her to swoop down and intervene, but she knew that it was foolish. A single well-placed arrow would be enough to take Altan down, and her soul bond was too precious to her. Besides, she doubted that Khulan would understand. All she could do was watch as the two forces collided.

It was strange watching the first volley being launched as a storm of arrows cascaded over Khulan's group. Their speed meant that the vast majority missed their target, but Sara saw a few hunters fall. Another gust of wind blew, and it seemed to propel the arrows forward, guiding their path as they sunk into the skin of their hunters. Khulan's hunters fired a few arrows in response, but few hit their mark as it was too difficult to aim while charging at an enemy.

Before the enemy could let off another volley, Khulan led her hunters into the fray, crashing into the enemy with the shattered tension of a snapping bowstring. The Steppe erupted, and Sara forced herself to look away.

On the other side of the battlefield, Alaqa's hunters dispersed to avoid a volley of arrows. Almost none of them fell but they went slower, their formation careful and tentative even as they drew closer. Alaqa led the center group, while the hunters on her wings went before her, testing and weakening the enemy's defenses. The hunters would draw closer, trade blows with the enemy in front and shoot arrows into the crowd, carefully placing them to make sure the enemy couldn't fight back, before retreating and repeating the process.

Sara thought that the process looked more like a dance than a fight. Eventually, the Asjare hunters were weakened and frustrated, some even breaking formation to pursue the Harnda hunters. Alaqa led her central company, fresh and ready to fight, past the two other groups and into the fray.

This time, the enemy gave way easier, allowing Alaqa to break past their first line and cut into their reserves. The enemy fought desperately, but the Harnda gained the upper hand with almost childlike ease. It was like a wave breaking through a weakened dyke. Once the initial barrier was broken, there was nothing left in the way.

She heard a piercing scream and glanced towards Khulan's side of the battlefield. She cursed herself for not checking on them sooner and felt her limbs suddenly grow weak. For a moment, she was in between her eagle and her own body, and sensed her face go white with fear. She forced herself to focus and was soon back in Altan's eyes, watching from above as Saenor twisted around her limbs.

Khulan's forces were in full retreat, their cavalry charge broken. They had bloodied the enemy, but not broken them, Asjare mounted their horses and began to pursue them.

Sara snapped back into her body. She turned to Orda, who was standing at her side and watching the same spectacle from the ground. "We have to go," she said. Before he could answer, she led the reserve force down the hill towards the battlefield.

"Sara, there aren't enough of us to save them," Orda called after her. She ignored him.

They careened across the battlefield beyond an advisable speed, but Sara knew that Khulan was running out of time. Her hunters' horses would be weak, out of breath, and possibly injured, so they would not be able to get far in a retreat. She knew that if she was watching from above, she would order herself to fall back and link up with Alaqa's hunters to plan a counterattack. She hadn't even gotten a good enough look to see if Khulan was still alive.

But as she flew across the battlefield with gusts of wind blowing through her hair and  propeling her forward, she did not care about any of that. She took out her bow but she barely noticed what her hands were doing. Her eyes stared forward. As she did, she was surprised to hear the thunder of hooves. They were all right behind her.

"Feet on the ground, eyes to the sky," Sara repeated to herself as she nocked an arrow.

She led her forces directly into the gap between the pursuing Asjare hunters and Khulan's fleeing group. They charged into the fray and Sara turned her horse to face the enemy.


Sara pressed the damp cloth to her shoulder, wincing as pain sprouted from her wound. She wiped away the dried blood and bits of splintered wood that had lodged themselves around the cut.

Bataar saw what she had done and rushed over, a bandage in his hands. "By Saenor, Sara. I told you not to do anything on your own." He pushed aside Sara's cloth, which was slick with blood, then began wrapping the wound himself. His hands were still shaky, but he completed the task well enough.

"Others need the more help," Sara said, looking around her. She was impressed with how quickly the Harnda had managed to set up a field camp for their wounded hunters.

She got up, wincing from the pain of her sprained ankle. With Bataar's help, she managed to limp through the camp, watching the Harnda medical corps tend to each of the wounded in turn. Some of Sara's hunters had some training in medicine, but they mostly assisted the Harnda as they went about their business.

The herders were busy tending to the wounded horses, which tended to get skittish and shell-shocked after a battle. The already-sparse supplies of manna they had were passed between the herders to calm the animals, but without a supply of manna from the Temple of Gaeon, there was little they could do.

Whenever they passed one of Sara's wounded hunters, she had Bataar help her kneel beside them and whisper a few words of encouragement. Usually, she would have nothing more to say than "Thank you." From the looks the wounded gave her, it was enough. The voices that normally screamed at the back of Sara's head had dulled for once, and she was happy she could give them some reassurance.

Khulan was nursing a large scratch on her forehead that had taken her out of the fight near the end, but she was otherwise unscathed. When Sara had last seen her, she had been in a daze with blood still seeping from the wound, but now she was sitting up and chatting with Alaqa and Gerelma.

When Sara approached, all three ended their conversation and looked up at her. Alaqa tried to rise, but Sara shook her head.

"Sara," Khulan said, grinning. "The hunter of the hour."

Gerelma nodded. "That was a mighty thing you did. I'm sure even Zayaat would be impressed."

"It was only because Alaqa subdued their left flank," Sara said, unable to meet Gerelma's eyes. "I didn't do much."

"It won't kill you to take a compliment once in a while, Sara," Khulan said.

"Even so," Alaqa said, looking up at Sara. "We did it together."

"We did," Sara said, then she turned to Khulan. "How's the wound? I can get you more bandages if you need them."

Khulan laughed. "You really need to stop mothering me, Sara. I'll be fine. Go talk to the others."

"Khulan…" Sara began, but Khulan cut her off.

"For Gaeon's sake, Sara, go away."

Sara sighed, then got up and let Bataar bring her to the bodies lining the camp's edges. On her orders, their faces were still uncovered, laying there as if asleep. For a few moments, Sara could imagine that they were still alive, their eyes to the sky.

She made it a point to pass by each body, looking into their faces and saying their name if she knew who they were. She wished that there was a way she could make sure each's memory was preserved such that it would live on when their bodies did not. But even as she passed some of her own hunters, she found that the sound of their voices was beginning to fade from her memory. Soon, she would be left with only the ghost of those memories.

When they neared the end of the line, Sara noticed someone else kneeling beside one of the bodies. It took her only a few moments to realize who it was. She asked Bataar to let her stand on her own feet and leave her to help the medical corps. Sara staggered over to the figure. She winced from the pain in her foot but made sure that none of it showed on her face.

Ganbold noticed her first. "He believed in you more than anyone else," he said, gesturing to the body that lay before him. "Orda wanted so badly to believe that you could lead us as your father did."

Sara looked into Orda's face. Her father had told her long ago about guilt after a battle, and she tried to remember his words as she spoke.

"He was one of our best. May Gaeon ride with him," was all she could manage.

Ganbold rose to his feet, towering a few inches before Sara. From the look he gave her, he seemed pained more than anything else. "It was my fault we got ambushed by the enemy."

"It wasn't..." Sara began, but Ganbold held up a hand.

"It was my fault. I chose to accompany the patrol. I chose to keep going even after we spotted trouble. I chose to move forward despite not knowing their numbers."

"What are you trying to say?"

"I'm saying that this was entirely on me. But Bataar told me what you did after he told you I was in danger. No one would have blamed you for choosing to be cautious, and yet you came to help."

"You were in danger. It was the honorable thing to do."

Ganbold nodded. "You say it like it's the simplest thing in the world. But maybe I'm the one who's forgotten what honor means. Maybe it's time for me to remember. I had my reservations about you. I thought that Od was the leader and you were the hunter. Now I see that I was wrong. I hope that you can forgive me."

Ganbold bowed his head, his eyes on the ground. Sara motioned for him to meet her eyes.

"You did what you thought was right for the camp. There's nothing to forgive."

Before Sara could speak again, she spotted Bataar approaching them from behind.

"Is there trouble?" she asked. "What is it now?"

"Not exactly," Bataar said. He gave Ganbold a sidelong glance, raising an eyebrow.

"Go on, Bataar," Sara said.

Bataar nodded. "We just had a message from Ibakha back at the camps. They've taken a few rogue Omnu hunters prisoner, and Batu is among them. It seems like they were the reason behind the diversion of this Asjare force."

"Batu," Sara said, the name tasting like poison on her lips. "Bring him to me."

# 14

# Batu

"Same drill as always?" Cirina asked, mounting her horse and taking out her bow.

"Do you even have to ask?" Batu said, getting on his own horse. He drew his sword and nodded to Nugai, who had taken out his two war axes and was practically quivering with anticipation.

Batu saw the signal: the archers mounted atop the hills drew their bows and began firing into the small group of hunters passing in between them. The hunters were caught in the middle, and were sent into disarray after the first volley by Khabichi, Dorgene, Bala, and Jochi.

"Here we go," Batu said, his horse moving forward immediately as if it could sense his thoughts. He charged forward, feeling the wind whip past his horse's mane. For a few moments, he didn't pay attention to Cirina and Nugai following after him.

Cirina rode in an arc around the enemy, picking off the desperate hunters that tried to flee while Nugai and Batu crashed into the main group.

The skirmish was over in only a few minutes. Batu and Nugai cut through the enemy like lightning through a weakened tree. Those that survived their initial charge were quickly felled by the arrows.

When they were done, Nugai cleaned his axes on the fallen hunters' clothing. The four archers descended from their perch and began going through the bodies.

"How are we on arrows?" Batu said, approaching Khabichi, who was going through one of the hunters' equipment. He tossed the hunter's sword that had been bent when she fell off her horse, but pulled out a mostly-intact quiver of arrows.

"Enough to keep us going," Khabichi said. "Lucky that we got them before they had a chance to string their bows."

"And manna?" Batu asked.

"They weren't carrying any," Khabichi said. Batu sighed. They had run out of their last supply of manna a few days ago, and they could barely keep control of their horses as it was. They would need to find more soon or they would risk their horses abandoning them.

Batu nodded and turned back to the rest of the hunters, but then he found Nugai waiting to speak to him.

"Something the matter?" Batu asked.

"Packs are empty," Nugai said, and there was a pause as Batu waited for more.

"What did you say?"

Nugai gestured at the pile of saddle bags that Cirina and the others were assembling off to the side.

"They're all empty," Nugai explained. Though others added more to the pile, none of them had anything in them. When he saw the bags, Batu felt his stomach twist in fear, but he couldn't figure out why. "No food, no supplies, nothing. Except for some flint that they probably used to start a fire. Waste of a raid, I'd say."

"Yeah, same situation here," Khabichi said, pulling out an empty saddle bag from underneath a dead horse. "How could they ride this far from the camps without food? It's like they came out here to starve."

"Maybe there's another group nearby that they're meant to meet up with?" Nugai said. "In any case, we'll just have to plan another raid. Saenor's scales, all that effort for nothing."

"Could be," Batu said, but none of the explanations did anything to address the knot in his chest. Then his eyes widened. "Or they knew that we'd be here."

"What?" Nugai said, turning back to Batu. "If they knew we'd be here, why would they walk right into our trap?"

"Not good. The two of you, get on your horses. We need to get out of here," Batu said. He started walking to the rest of the group to warn them, but his ears perked up when he caught the whistle of an arrow on the wind.

He heard the arrow before he saw it. When he did, it was barely a wisp of brown that whizzed past his head and sunk into something soft behind him. Batu turned around just in time to see Khabichi fall to the ground, an arrow lodged in his throat,.

"They're here!" Batu shouted as he started sprinting back towards the main group. They all noticed Khabichi being struck by the arrow, but none of them were moving. They were all still in shock.

Batu looked behind him. To his relief, Nugai was springing into action, mounting his horse and taking out his axes.

"Three archers, spread out around us on the hills!" he shouted as arrows thudded into the ground around him. "By Saenor...we've allowed ourselves to be surrounded."

"We need to get out of here!" Batu repeated, but none of the others moved.

Batu saw one take aim at Cirina. He just managed to get there in time to tackle her to the ground. The arrow sank into the ground behind them.

"Move!" Batu screamed at his hunters. Finally, they sprang into action, picking up their weapons and going for their horses.

Batu heard the sickening sound of metal on flesh as he mounted his horse, and looked up to see that Nugai had killed the last archer. Batu was about to breathe a sigh of relief until Nugai rode down the hill and was alongside the group.

"There's more of them," he gasped in between heavy breaths. "Easily fifty riders, maybe more."

"The Asjare knew we'd be here, then," Batu said, glancing over the rest of the group and making sure that they were all mounted.

"What do we do?" Nugai asked, and Batu instinctively turned to Jochi, but the older man looked like he had yet to recover from the state of shock. Batu glanced back towards the clearing at Khabichi's corpse and he felt a twinge, like a knot inside of him was coming loose.

Batu froze and nearly dropped his bow, but Nugai reached out and patted him on the shoulder. "Batu. What do we do?"

The touch snapped Batu back into reality, and he shook his head and clenched his fist. He would have to wait before he could grieve.

"We ride south, into Harnda territory," he said after considering for a few moments.

"You sure about that, kid?" Jochi said, finally snapping back to reality. "I don't particularly like the cold. And in case you've forgotten, the girl is still there and she probably isn't happy that we killed her brother."

"Look, if you've got a better idea, I'm happy to hear it," Batu said. "But unless we want to be caught in between, we have to go. Now."

"Don't worry. We trust you, Batu," Cirina said, and without question, the rest of the hunters nodded their assent.


"May Gaeon ride with us, then," Batu said, and spurred his horse onwards. They rode up the hill to the south. Batu felt for the first time what it was like to ride at the head of an army.

He took a moment to get his bearings when they reached the top of the hill. He saw a mass of hunters moving towards them; the instinct his father had built inside him told him to face them and charge. He could almost hear his father's voice in his head, but he forced it away. "Coward," it whispered as he scanned the horizon and saw the Serpent's River in the distance.

"This way!" he shouted.

Nugai caught up to Batu eventually, but the others remained trailing behind. "The horses are tired, Batu. I'm not sure how far we can go before they're spent."

"They'll get there," Batu said.

"How do you know that?"

"By Saenor, I don't," Batu said. His bones were like water and his muscles were like burning grass. "But what choice do we have?"

"Come up with a plan, for Gaeon's sake," Nugai said. "Don't lead us blindly to our deaths. We deserve better than that."

Batu bit his lip and rode onwards, turning over Nugai's words in his head. As he led them across the hills, he could feel his horse growing tired beneath him. He took a moment to gaze into the horse's eyes, feeling his own weight upon its back and the strain in its limbs.

As he grew weaker, he heard his father's whispers at the back of his mind, but they passed into the wind as he galloped onward defiantly.

"You can leave them behind," his father's voice whispered in his head. "Have them divert the enemy and escape on your own. You are the son of the head chieftain. That is your birth right. You owe them nothing."

"They're my hunters," Batu answered. What he had to do next became clear.

He stopped in his tracks and his hunters followed suit, gathering around him as the Asjare hunters drew near. Batu didn't waste any time.

"Nugai, give me the flint you found," he said.

Without any hesitation, Nugai reached into his saddle bag and pulled the flint out, passing it to Batu.

"Cirina, Dorgene, I need you to take the eyes of your eagles."

The two of them nodded.

"What do you need us to do?" Cirina asked. By looking at her eyes, Batu could see her fears melt away for a moment.

"We're going to make a fire to drive them away," Batu said. "I need you to fan the flames in their direction."

He expected them to react poorly to the plan. They would think that he was insane, that he would only get them killed, or that he should never have been made their chieftain. Instead, all of them nodded and Cirina and Dorgene closed their eyes. Their eagles descended from the skies and prepared to make their move.

Batu took his knife from his belt, struck the piece of flint against it, and sent a few sparks into the grass below. He did this a few more times and started a small fire at his horse's feet.

"Go!" he shouted. His hunters' eagles began to beat their powerful wings against the air and the fire began to spread. He spurred his horse and led his hunters away from the fire.

He looked behind him for a moment and saw a massive inferno begin to take shape, the Asjare hunters barely specks of brown and red behind the fire. The fire consumed the dry grass in an instant, and the Asjare hunters saw the fire begin to spread and changed their course.

"We've bought ourselves a few minutes," he said as he found himself blinded for a moment from the ash. The billowing smoke meant that he couldn't see anything, and he had to hold his breath or else his lungs would burn as well. He covered his eyes with a piece of cloth he found and moved onward.

When he tried to spur his horse forward, the creature wouldn't budge. He tried again, but its feet stayed planted to the ground.

He took his horse's eyes, but the horse immediately ejected him from its perspective. Their minds were too out of sync, too weak to function together. Then the thoughts began to come. He would be left here to die. If not from smoke inhalation, the Asjare would find him sooner or later. They wouldn't give him a quick death. He knew their reputation. They would let him bleed for hours and hours.

Then he heard the sound of hooves beat in front of him, and one thought came through clearer than the others. He realized that his hunters would be safe.

The hooves thundered louder and an eagle burst through the smoke, its wings beating against it until a small pocket of air was created around Batu. Cirina burst into the smoke, coughing and hacking while extending her hand to him. She mouthed something at him but he didn't hear her properly. He took her hand. When she pulled him forward, his horse finally began to move. He felt its muscles finally pulse beneath him and its thoughts scream in its mind, suddenly desperate, clinging to its life. So did he.

Batu held his breath for a few moments as they exited the cloud of smoke that had erupted. While his horse seemed worse for wear, it plowed forward. Cirina guided him out of the smoke. Without a word, she released his grip and continued forwards before Batu could thank her.

After they were out of sight from the fire, they rode for a few more hours until they encountered the Harnda patrol.

# 15

# Erroll

"General Sandulf," Erroll muttered as their commanding officer stepped into the corridor. Two soldiers that Erroll recognized as part of Sandulf's personal guard followed him into the room. Their swords weren't drawn but their hands hovered near the pommel of their blades, daring Erroll and Manvel to make a move.

Sandulf stood in front of them, arms clasped behind his back. His expression was unreadable. He didn't speak, looking between Erroll and Manvel as though he was appraising vegetables at the market.

"What now?" Erroll said. Sandulf raised an eyebrow, but he didn't respond.

"What now?" Erroll repeated. "Are you going to throw us into the dungeons? Leave us as bait for the savages? Get it over with already. I'm tired of waiting."

Sandulf motioned to one of his personal guards, who then stepped forward to face Erroll. He raised his hand and struck Erroll with a blow that staggered him. He tried to maintain his footing, but the guard struck him again, this time with a punch to the gut. Erroll crumpled to his knees.

Erroll thought that the guard was about to take out his sword, but then Sandulf raised his hand and the guard backed away, returning to his earlier position.

"You are speaking to a general of the Jusordian Army," Sandulf said. "Know your place."

Erroll rose to his feet shakily, then he nodded. Every instinct in his body screamed at him to fight this man, but he knew better than that. This wasn't a petty skirmish in a Ruson alleyway that he could run away from.

"Good," Sandulf said. "I have no doubt you are aware of the position you are currently in. I could kill you here and no one would question it. You would turn into just another entry in my records."

"My father…" Manvel began.

"Is far away in K'harin surrounded by Jusordian officials loyal to the Empire. You are not the only one here that is well-connected." Sandulf grinned. "Besides, I am sure that Duke Marcel will not mind the loss of his least-favored son."

Manvel's eyes widened and his jaw slackened, losing its normal vigor. For once, he looked like he was at a loss for things to say. Sandulf leaned against one of the bookshelves, looking as though he was waiting for a carriage to pick him up—shoulders relaxed, arms hanging loosely at his side.

"I take it that means we're all aware of where we stand," he said.

Manvel and Erroll didn't respond. Sandulf seemed to enjoy their silence, dragging it out as long as he could.

Then he spoke. "Erroll. You want to know about your father."

Erroll took a moment to register Sandulf's sentence, then he nodded. "Yes. That's right."

"Splendid," Sandulf said, grinning and taking a seat in the chair that Manvel had been using. "As an act of good faith, I will tell you. Your father was a traitor. He was spying for the nomads, giving them key information about our movements and sabotaging our operations. We found out and sent him and the rest of his traitor friends to Ruson, where he was executed in custody by Empress Tomyris herself."

Erroll bit his lip. He should have known, and yet the news hit him like a lightning bolt. "Why didn't you tell my mother?"

Sandulf shrugged. "Now, that would just be cruel. And I am not a cruel man. We preferred to let you think that he lived and died as a man of the Empire. As luck would have it, that decision brought his son straight into my legion."

Erroll didn't speak for a long moment, but the news cut deep inside him. "If he's a traitor, then he's no father of mine," he finally said.

"Good," Sandulf said. "Back to business, then. I will give the both of you two options. Option one, I kill you for trespassing into my personal archives."

Erroll grit his teeth and he could see Manvel begin to sweat next to him.

"What's option two?" Erroll asked.

Sandulf's mouth curved in what Erroll thought was a grin. "That's for you to decide. Give me a reason I shouldn't kill you."

"Just let us go," Manvel said, and Erroll saw his fists begin to shake. "Please. We won't say anything about what we saw here."

"I'm afraid that groveling doesn't work on me, Manvel," Sandulf said. "You'll have to do better than that."

Manvel's face fell, while Erroll could felt the pressure mounting inside him. He had once been close to death on the streets of Ruson. All he had to do was solve this problem and he would get to live another day.

"Nothing? I have to admit I'm a little disappointed. I enjoy a little bit of banter," Sandulf said.

"Wait," Erroll said. "You can recruit us into your personal guard."

Sandulf raised an eyebrow, and even Manvel looked up in shock.

"I will admit that I didn't expect that suggestion," Sandulf said. "People normally offer me money. You may continue."

"Thank you," Erroll said. "By breaking into this storeroom, we have displayed the abilities you require in your personal guard. We also broke into the Imperial Archives in Ruson. If my guess is correct, your personal guard do much more than protect you. They serve as your eyes and ears throughout the Empire."

Sandulf chuckled. "You're not as dumb as you look. And of course, the detail which I think you've conveniently forgotten to mention is that my personal guard are the best paid soldiers in the army. The money may be of use to your mother in Ruson, Erroll."

Erroll froze, but he knew that the comment was meant to throw him off. He realized that he had absolutely no idea what kind of power he was dealing with here.

"So, what do you say?" Erroll said. "Let us pay back our debts by serving you."

Sandulf paced between the bookshelves for a few moments. Even the guards accompanying him appeared surprised. The entire time the general mulled over his decision, Erroll stood on the balls of his feet, ready to bolt if something went wrong. He wouldn't have much of a chance to get away, but at least he would die trying.

Then Sandulf turned back to face Manvel and Erroll.

"Very well then. You've made a convincing case. But you must understand that if you join my personal guard, I own you. I own your name, your actions, and your identity. Are we clear on that?"

He looked between Erroll and Manvel, his eyes searching for the hints of a reaction. Erroll tried to exchange a look with Manvel, but found that he couldn't figure out what his friend was thinking. As terrifying as the options were, Erroll already had his answer.


Erroll sat in the main area of the barracks across from Manvel. Jarlen and Quince were off drinking with some other friends they had made in the squad, but both Erroll and Manvel had declined their invitations.

"So we were wrong about him," Erroll said, breaking the silence.

"Yes, we were," Manvel said. "I don't think I've ever had a master-of-arms quite like that."

"Neither have I," Erroll said.

"So, what's our play?"

"What's our what?"

"You know," Manvel said, lightly patting Erroll on the shoulder. "What's the next scheme? How are we going to beat the old geezer?"

"Manvel, there is no scheme," Erroll said, looking around him. He eyed everyone sitting nearby with suspicion. Knowing Sandulf, any one of them could be one of his informants. "This is something much bigger than either of us. If we take one misstep, we're dead. Got that?"

"But there's more you want to know, isn't there?" Manvel said. "About your father."

"I know that he died a traitor. That's all I need."

"Erroll, you knew that already. You broke into Sandulf's storeroom because you wanted answers. The ones he gave you weren't enough, were they?"

"No. I got what I needed. I'm done. And even if I wanted to, there's nothing I can do about it."

"You can't be saying that we're just going to play by his game."

"That's exactly what I'm saying, Manvel. And you should watch your tongue. You never know when he might be listening."

"You're being paranoid. You can't honestly expect…" But Manvel's sentence was cut off by a man tapping him on the shoulder.

Manvel jolted like he'd been bitten by a snake. Erroll recognized the man at a glance—Adrius, one of Sandulf's personal guards. Today he was dressed in the uniform of a regular foot soldier.

"Follow me," Adrius said. Without waiting for their response, he walked out of the barracks and into the streets outside.

Erroll and Manvel exchanged a look. "I told you," Erroll said.

Adrius led them through the camp. As he did so, Erroll noticed the amount of detail that went into his disguise. The guard didn't only dress like a foot soldier, he also walked like one, full of over-emphasized confidence and exaggerated movements. Every foot soldier walked like that his first few months in the field, so no one paid him a second glance. To Erroll, it was masterful.

Adrius pulled the lever again and the stone door closed shut behind them. As hard as Erroll looked, he couldn't find any indication of a passageway behind where the door had been. It just looked like a wall.

"Now we can talk," Adrius said.

The room they were in was made of plain stones and lit by lanterns lining the wall. There were a few chests here and there and a table in the center, but otherwise it was empty. The flickering orange light gave everything an enchanted look; it was as though they had just walked into another dimension.

Adrius caught them looking around the room. He smiled, spreading his arms out as if he were showing them a castle. "Like it? It's so bare because we can either burn it all or take everything with us if the place is compromised,. The general never keeps too many things in one place."

"Are all your hideouts like this?" Erroll said, approaching the table.

"I couldn't tell you. I'm only familiar with this one. That way, if I get captured and tortured… no harm done."

"Sandulf really thought through a lot of this, didn't he?" Manvel said.

"You have no idea," Adrius said, taking out a few things from his satchel. He placed a large book and two envelopes on the desk. He slid one envelope over to Erroll and the other to Manvel. "These are your assignments. Read them, commit them to memory, then burn them. Both of you will leave immediately. You won't need to pack any of your belongings since you won't need them where you're going."

He pointed to a small metal box in the corner that was filled with ashes. "And Erroll, sorry about the beating I gave you the other day. The general likes to put on a show when he takes in new people."

"Don't worry about it," Erroll said, tearing open the envelope and reading his orders. "I'm to live among the Asjare?"

"Syra is already there. Meet him and discover what you can about the nomads and their magic. We control one of their temples right now and that seems to keep them loyal, but we're not sure why."

"I didn't know that the savages had politics," Erroll said.

Adrius laughed. "You have a lot to learn. It's not a problem. Syra will teach you."

Erroll nodded, realizing at that moment what he had gotten himself into. He was involved in things far deeper than he could have imagined.

"And Manvel will be accompanying me there?" Erroll said, eyeing his friend who was still poring over his own assignment.

"No," Manvel said quietly. "I'm to join General Asghar's camp and keep watch on his movements. And if necessary, I'm to take action if he becomes too dangerous."

"General Asghar?" Erroll said. As he did, he realized how much sense it made. Asghar was Sandulf's greatest political enemy. Since they would be marching into the Steppe soon, Sandulf would want to know everything happening in Asghar's camp.

"Praxis has already gotten himself a position as master-of-arms there. We'll send you along to be his assistant."

Manvel grinned despite himself. "So old Praxis is one of you then?"

"Of course," Adrius said. "He's one of the men in charge of looking for new recruits. Sandulf's had both of you on a short list for some time now."

Erroll raised an eyebrow.

"So the story is that Manvel was reassigned," Erroll said. That made sense. Manvel was one of the best swordsmen in the squad. With his father's status, it wasn't difficult to imagine Manvel asking his father to get him a position as an assistant master-of-arms. "What about me? People will wonder where I went."

"I'm glad you asked," Adrius said, leading Erroll to one of the chests pushed against the wall. It was large, about as wide as Erroll was and as tall as his knee.

He popped the chest open, and Erroll stumbled backwards in shock when saw what was inside. Adrius grinned. "That's the reaction I'm looking for," he said as Erroll got back to his feet and looked at the contents of the chest.

"It's…me," Erroll said. Inside the chest was a corpse with a large gash across its neck and blood still seeping from the wound. When Erroll took a closer look at the corpse's face, he realized that it looked exactly like him. The same nose, the same face shape, and even the same scars on his cheeks and upper lip. He didn't want to look closer, but he suspected that if he did, he would find familiar scars on the corpse's arms.

He turned to the side and gagged, but managed to keep himself from vomiting.

"What in Galele's name is that?" Erroll said.

"It's the body we're going to leave in your stead," Adrius said, snapping the chest shut. "We'll tell a story about how a nomad cut your throat while you were on scouting duty with Manvel. If both of you were reassigned at the same time, people might ask questions. But if you were killed, then it'd make more sense to send Manvel off. He'd be distraught and angry, so Sandulf would put him in a position where he can't do any damage."

"It also gives Manvel reason to be angry at Sandulf," Erroll realized. "Which will make Asghar trust him."

"Good," Adrius said. "You're catching on quickly. And of course, it entitles your mother to a large compensation package."

Erroll was about to complain, but he realized that he may as well be dead to his mother after what he did. He turned to Manvel.

Erroll exchanged a look again with Manvel.

"We won't see each other for a while, then," Manvel said.

"It seems like that'll be the case," Erroll said.

There was a pause between them as each man was trying to figure out what the other was thinking. Erroll reached out with his hand and Manvel grasped it.

"Don't die," Manvel said.

"I'm very good at that," Erroll said. Then he added, "You too."

Manvel pulled something out of his jacket. It was a small metal flask about the size of his palm, just like the one that he and Erroll had shared that night on guard duty. He handed it to Erroll.

"There's still some rum in here," Manvel said.

Erroll took it carefully, like Manvel was handing him some priceless treasure. "Thank you," he said.

"I've still got mine. We'll have a drink together again soon. Till then, this is something you can remember me by."

# 16
# Sara

Sara sat to the side of the tent as Ibakha and Zayaat examined the prisoner. He had been bound in ropes before, but they had allowed his hands to be free for this meeting. She knew his face well enough. She remembered the moment they shared in the tent after their mothers' funerals after the plague took them both. He had seemed so small then, so powerless as he sat in front of his mother's ashes. So was she.

The Batu that stood before her seemed different now. He was taller, obviously, and he had grown out his hair, letting strands of it frame his face. But the features were unmistakeably his. And for some reason, it seemed like his blue eyes had changed in color from that of a clear sky to one that resembled a stormy sea.

"Why did you come to us?" Ibakha asked.

Batu looked up. Sara saw his face and was surprised that she didn't see the eyes of a killer. He didn't seem cruel or vindictive. He just seemed tired.

"We had nowhere else to go," Batu said. "The Asjare were chasing us, and they would have sold us to the Empire in a heartbeat."

"What made you think that we'd accept you?" Zayaat said. "We could have let you die. Because of you, we lost many hunters to the Asjare patrol."

"When choosing between the sea and the river, I went for the familiar option," Batu said. "The Omnu and Harnda have always been friends. I hope that some of that friendship might still exist."

Sara noticed that Batu was avoiding her gaze.

"We have not spared your life yet," Zayaat said.

"Then? What is your judgement?" Batu said.

"That's not for us to decide," Ibakha said. There was a pause as all eyes in the room turned toward Sara.

Even Batu couldn't resist the urge to look at her. When she met his eyes, she found that she knew exactly what she wanted to say to him.

"Tell me the truth," she said. As she formed the words, she could feel the tears build behind her eyes. She forced them back. "Did you kill my brother?"

"No," Batu said immediately. "That was the work of my father."

"But you followed his orders anyway. You hunted us down."

"I did," Batu said. He fell to his knees. "But I was only doing what I needed to survive. My father would've killed me if I didn't do it. I never intended to hurt you."

"Get up," Sara snapped, and Batu was on his feet in an instant. "You're not the victim here."

"Of course," he said quickly.

"Nothing you do can bring my brother back. I've made my peace with that."

But as Sara spoke, another voice rose up from behind her. She looked behind her and saw Khulan rise to her feet.

"If you didn't kill him," she said, each word pronounced like a knife driven into Batu's gut. "Then who did?"

"That shouldn't…" Batu began, but Khulan cut him off.

"Don't lie," she said.

Batu's eyes fell to the ground. "The one who wielded the axe was Nugai. One of my hunters. But it was my father who gave the order."

"Then he's the one I want justice from," Khulan said, turning to Sara. "Sara, let me do it."

"Are you sure, Khulan?" Sara said, rising to face her friend. "I don't know if Od would want this."

"I don't give a damn what Od would have wanted," Khulan said. "In case you've forgotten, you're not the only one who loved him."

The words bit into Sara like salt on a wound. The woman that stood before her was no longer the best friend whom she'd grown up with. The icy winds seemed to build in the room, drawing out the silence.

"Please, spare him," Batu finally said quietly. Sara and Khulan turned to him, but Sara could still feel the glare in Khulan's face even though she wasn't looking directly at her.

"What did you say?" Sara asked.

"It was my fault for not stopping my father. So please, kill me instead. Just let my hunters live."

Sara looked into his eyes. For a moment, she saw a scared boy sitting next to his mother's ashes, his eyes pleading with Gaeon to bring her back. But that boy was dead, and in front of her, all she could see was a ruthless killer, someone who had taken her entire life away from her. Khulan's words echoed in her mind. At that moment, she didn't care that it wasn't Batu who swung the axe. He was as responsible as the rest of them.

She was about to give her order when a hand clutched at her shoulder.

She turned and found Ibakha whispering in her ear. "This decision will be a turning point in your time as a chief," she said. "Please, Sara, think about how you want to be remembered. Is a moment of revenge worth a legacy of violence?"

Then Ibakha released her and returned to her seat. Sara looked into Batu's eyes again, and the scared boy had returned. She didn't hate him anymore. She only pitied him, along with the monster his father had forced him to become.

"No one dies today," she finally said after a long pause. "Too much blood has already been spilled because of Chinua."

She heard Khulan leaving the tent behind her. Sara tried to say something to her, but Khulan was already out of earshot. She took a deep breath and then turned back to Batu.

"But I want you and your hunters out of the camp," she said.

"We have nowhere to go," Batu said. "Please."

"Don't make me repeat myself," she said.

Sara found Khulan where she expected to find her: sitting at the foot of a hill on the edges of camp. There she was, nestled into an alcove where no one could find her.

Khulan didn't look up at her when she approached.

"Hey," Sara said, and Khulan only gave her the barest hint of a nod. "I'm…sorry for what happened in there. I should've been more sensitive to what you were feeling. I guess I got caught up in what I was thinking that I forgot about you and Bataar. That was wrong."

Khulan didn't respond as Sara sat cross-legged across from her.

"You're not ready to talk, I guess," Sara said, moving backwards to give her friend some space. "It's okay. I'll be here."

Sara sat watching the early morning sun cross the sky. When she had heard that Batu had been captured, she had let her emotions get the better of her and rushed back to the Harnda camp before the field camp had been taken down. Khulan had followed her, but Ganbold had elected to stay with their hunters.

She saw Bataar emerge out of the Harnda camp's central tent. He walked through the streets until he reached them, kneeling down next to her.

"Batu and his hunters are under guard," Bataar whispered. "They're preparing to leave by dusk."

"Good, thanks," she said, then her eyes drifted over to Khulan, who hadn't spoken a word. "I'm sorry you all had to see that."

"It had to be said."

"And I'm sorry for not asking you before deciding what to do with Batu," Sara said.

Bataar smiled. "Sara, I don't think I've ever seen you like this. But… thank you. About Batu, I trust you to handle it."

"Thank you."

"Don't mention it. And I know you don't need to hear this now, but we've heard back from the Chenkah and Gur. Their eagles came in this morning."

"Good news?"

"We don't know yet."

"I'll speak with Ibakha about it later."

Bataar nodded and got to his feet. He walked over to Khulan, knelt beside her, and whispered a few words into her ear. Sara couldn't hear what he said, but Khulan's face seemed to soften as he spoke.

Khulan responded and clasped Bataar's hand in her own. She held it tight for a few moments before letting it go. He left without another word.

Sara met her eyes and realized that her friend had always felt this way about Od—she'd just been too caught up with her own problems to see it. Khulan was brave, probably braver than Sara was, but that didn't mean that she didn't get scared, too.

When Khulan spoke, her voice was no longer laden with accusations. It was wistful, as if she were somewhere else entirely. "Do you remember when I first tried to court your brother?"

"You asked me what his favorite types of flowers were."

"The purple ones that bloom only in the spring," Khulan said. "You even brought me to the right field."

Sara smiled. "I remember that. We skipped hunting exercises to make it there during the day. My father made us take extra cleaning shifts that week."

"But it was worth it. I got Od to take me to the eastern hills."

"He did, but I also remember that he politely rejected you after you tried to kiss him."

"Ah, well. That's not the part I like to mention."

Sara laughed, and so did Khulan. The sound of her friend's laugh was musical, like birds signaling the end of winter. Despite the biting winds, Sara felt like she was back in the Omnu camps, watching as the wind blew through the fields of flowers, petals flying off stems and swirling through the plains.

"I really wanted to do it, you know," Khulan said.

"Do what?"

"You know…kill him."

"Oh. That."

"I didn't want to tell you before. When we first got the news about Od, I tried to be strong because I knew you had it a thousand times worse. But it all just came rushing out just now."

"I didn't realize," Sara said, her voice quavering. She could feel tears building behind her eyes, but she forced them back.

"I still think Od deserves better than this," Khulan said. Instead of raising her voice, she spoke quietly, as if she were whispering to the grass she sat on. "Why do they get to live? They never gave Od that choice."

Sara considered for a long moment. She expected something like this, but she found that she lacked the strength in of her to argue.

"But…you're our chief," Khulan said slowly. "And my best friend. I trust you more than anyone else, so if you think this is what we should do, I'm with you."

"Thank you," Sara said.

Khulan pulled Sara into a tight hug. A few moments later, Sara felt her friend's tears drip onto her shoulders. She couldn't stop herself from crying either. They had not had the time to grieve properly when Od died. It had been far too much to bear. They sat there for a long time, holding each other and weeping for everything they'd lost.

Finally, Khulan released Sara, but her eyes stayed on Sara's face. It was wet with tears, but with fire burning beneath the salt.

"I don't want anyone to come between us," Khulan said firmly. "Least of all someone like that."

"Agreed," Sara said.

Khulan got to her feet and offered Sara her hand. Sara looked at it for a few moments, then she reached out and grasped it.

"From now on, nothing left unsaid, okay?" Khulan said.

"Of course," Sara replied.

"What's the news?" Sara said, striding into the central tent with Khulan trailing behind her.

Ibakha and Zayaat looked up from a set of letters arranged on a desk. Sara met Ibakha's eyes. She seemed like she had something to say, but saw Khulan behind Sara and seemed to relax.

"We have a response from Chief Chanar of the Chenkah," Zayaat said.

"And one from Chief Thaube of the Gur," Ibakha said.

"What did they say?" Sara said, she and Khulan taking positions at the table. These moments made Sara feel most out of place—she had always thought that war rooms and war councils were for her father and brother.

"Chanar is an old friend, so he was willing to listen," Zayaat said. "He will lend us his support, but he would rather station his hunters along the Chenkah side of the Eagle's Perch."

"Why doesn't he just have them join us?" Khulan asked. Zayaat flinched when Khulan spoke, most likely in response to her past outburst, but Khulan's voice was calm and rational.

"In his letter, he said that it'd be the most strategic location for their hunters to maximize their coverage," Zayaat said. "But I suspect it's because they do not want to leave their own territory unguarded. They are not at war with the Qhurin, but relations between them have never been friendly."

"That's nonsense," Sara said. "We're trying to unite against the Empire, not squabble among ourselves."

"Yes, but Sara, many of them are still in shock from the Asjare betrayal," Ibakha said. "They didn't believe us when we first told them. Trust is difficult to establish right now."

Sara shook her head, but she realized that there was nothing she could do about it. "How about the Gur?"

"We needed to push them," Khulan said. "At first, Delbeg wouldn't even let us move forward, especially when he found out that we'd also sent messengers to Qhurin."

"What convinced him?" Sara said.

"Land," Khulan said. "There are streams running along both sides of Arban's Peaks that the Asjare currently control. Anyone that holds those streams could nourish their livestock without having to graze too far out. We promised them the streams if we won."

"I don't like it," Ibakha said. "We're giving them too much, aren't we? If they have those lands, they'd be able to send hunters deep into Harnda territory."

"There was no other choice," Sara said. "It was either that or agreeing to help them against the Qhurin, and we can't do that if we want the Qhurin on our side."

"This isn't an alliance," Sara realized. "It's a transaction. They'll abandon us at the first sign of trouble."

Ibakha opened her mind to protest, but Zayaat spoke first.

"Sara is right," Zayaat said. "But this is the way it has always been. Your father said the same thing twenty years ago. We worked with what we had."

"Still," Sara said. "This isn't like last time. Last time, we had all the tribes together. I don't know if ties like these will hold, especially if the Empire starts getting the upper hand."

"Sara, you can't expect to change the way our tribes work," Ibakha said. "That's just the way things are."

"And why not?" Sara said. "We're all nomads aren't we? There's more that unites us than divides us. If we don't realize that, we'll lose."

Zayaat sighed and shook his head, but he didn't respond. Neither did Ibakha. No one ever seemed to have a good answer for her.

"In any case," Ibakha said, breaking the silence. "We still need to figure out the Qhurin."

"Dagasi returned yesterday," Zayaat said. "We thought that sending a holy woman would help. But they would not even let her in. It seems that when the Empire first invaded, they closed their borders to anyone except their own."

"Then we just have to keep trying, right?" Sara said. "We need the Qhurin. Since the Empire has the Temple of Gaeon, the Spring of Onoe remains the only source of manna in the entire Steppe."

"We might not have that luxury," Zayaat said. "Especially with the Gur placing more hunters on the bridges crossing Jarine's Tears. They have not threatened our messengers yet, but they might begin to do so if we continue sending more."

"And of course, there's the situation on the border," Khulan said. When she did, Ibakha and Zayaat nodded grimly, though Sara frowned.

"What situation?" she asked.

"That's right," Khulan said. "We forgot to tell you. We only just got the news before Batu was captured. The Asjare are setting up field camps along the border. The Empire as well, but on the Omnu side. We think they're preparing to invade soon."

"Saenor's scales, we're not ready," Sara said. "There's too few of us, and we're running out of manna."

"We aren't," Ibakha said. "But it's what we have."

Sara turned the words over in her head. She had spent so long running from the war that it almost did not seem real to her. But here was something she could not run from, and it was soaring towards her like an eagle, faster than she could ever have imagined.

# 17
# Batu

Batu led his hunters through the hills bordering the Harnda camp. He pulled the cloak they had given him tighter around him and took one last look at the camp behind him. His father had always admired the organized streets of the Harnda camps.

"The cold made them tough," his father had always told him. "That's more than the Omnu can say."

When he looked forward, he saw the vast expanse of the Steppe extending before him. It seemed to him a cold, unforgiving place. He knew these plains. He had lived on them his entire life, but they were foreign somehow; it was as though a simple change in temperature was enough for his image of the Steppe to break apart.

His hunters seemed to be even more out of place in the Harnda lands. Cirina, who rode next to him that morning, was given a cloak that was far too large. It fell around her like a cape past her feet and close to the ground.

"You have a plan, right?" she asked him.

"Of course I do," he said absently. He glanced behind her, noticing Zayaat and the other Harnda hunters that had been watching them as they left. They would probably watch them until Batu and his hunters were out of sight.

"Onoe's blood, Batu," she said. "You don't, do you?"

"Look, at least we're not dead," Nugai said, coming up beside them. "Batu got that for us at least."

"A meager reward for the price we paid," Bala said. "In case you have forgotten, we lost Khabichi."

"He's right," Dorgene said. "We're right back where we started, except now we've got to start raiding the Gur?"

"We're not going to raid the Gur," Batu said. "I listened in on their meeting just now. The Omnu, Harnda, Chenkah, and Gur are allies now. If we start raiding them, we'll invite the wrath of all four tribes."

"Excellent," Nugai said. "So we're just going to starve now?"

"No need," Batu said. "The Omnu aren't at war with the Gur, so we can move through their lands. We can hunt as we please as long as we don't interfere with Gur hunters. And my hunch is that the Gur will be focused on getting their hunters to the border anyway, leaving most of their lands unguarded."

"That still doesn't answer the question," Cirina said. "Where do we go now?"

"Easy," Batu said. "We go meet the Qhurin."

"What?" Dorgene said. "That's crazy."

"The Qhurin are not a welcoming people," Bala said. "This doesn't seem good."

Batu paused for a moment. He hadn't expected this kind of resistance, least of all from them, but he supposed it was rational. They were scared, and even though they'd followed him back in Asjare, he still needed to do more work to get them to trust him.

"Just order them," his father said in his head. "You're the chief. They should listen to you."

The thought remained in the back of Batu's mind, but he forced himself to ignore it.

"Think about it," he said. "The Gur and Chenkah lands will be emptied as they move to the war front—the safest place is to make ourselves their allies. Otherwise, we'll just get killed by bandits."

"Except Saragerel just threw you out," Jochi said. "So how's that figure in your grand plan?"

"They don't have the Qhurin's support right now even though it's what they need, especially since the Qhurin have the Spring as the only source of manna left in the Steppe. If we're the ones with the Qhurin's support, we'll be invaluable to them. They won't be able throw us out after that."

The group stopped to ponder on that for a moment.

"Still, you need to be able to get their support first," Jochi said. "How are you going to do that when Saragerel couldn't manage it?"

Batu looked to Nugai, who sighed. He knew that this would happen once the Qhurin were brought up.

"I might be able to help with that," Nugai said. "In case you didn't know, I used to be one of the Qhurin."

"But weren't you…" Cirina began, but then she stopped herself when she realized what he meant.

"Yes, I left my tribe to become a bandit," Nugai said. "Might be the worst thing I ever did. But anyway, yes. I'm Qhurin, so I can get them to talk to you. After that, it's up to Batu."

"Thank you," Batu said. "The Qhurin are a strange lot, but my father managed to get through to them. They'll remember that."

Batu could see the disbelief spring in his hunters' faces. Again, his father's voice echoed in his head but he pushed it back, letting the moment linger.

"Sounds good to me," Jochi said. "So long as you don't get us killed. You've managed thrice already, and I don't want to see you break that streak."

The rest of the hunters nodded or murmured their assent. Batu sighed with relief. Perhaps he wasn't as much of a failure as his father thought he was.


Nugai poked the fire with a stick and Batu was thankful that at least they could stoke a fire. He had grown so used to being on the run that he could not remember what it was like to have a roaring fire in front of him. The flames rose again,= and a wave of heat rushed over Batu.

"The woman… Khulan. She really wanted to kill me, didn't she?" Nugai said, his eyes still on the fire.

"She did," Batu said.

Nugai nodded. "You remember when you asked me if I regretted it the day after?"

"Yes. You told me that you didn't care about right and wrong anymore."

"That's what I said," Nugai said.

"Do you still think that?"

"I don't know, Batu. Do you regret following your father's orders to hunt her down?"

Batu shrugged. "Well, we ended up having to flee, so I think we're even."

"That's not what I meant."

"I know," Batu said, and Nugai got up to tend to the horses. Batu was left alone with the fire. As he stared into it, the crackling wood suddenly turned into his camp burning in the Empire's raid, soldiers storming through the tents and slaughtering his friends.

He wondered what his father would say to him if he saw him now. The great Chinua, the Leopard of Omnu, would not have groveled at Saragerel's feet. He would have stood his ground and fought until his dying breath. Because that was what chiefs do for their people, wasn't it?

Nugai arrived and dropped a few more sticks into the fire, causing the flames to surge and the image to disappear from Batu's vision. He managed to get his breathing under control and face Nugai, who was looking at him with a curious expression on his face. He seemed to be expecting an answer.

"Did you say something?" Batu asked.

"I said that Saragerel could have killed me. But she didn't. Why was that?" Nugai said.

"She said that it's not what her brother would have wanted," Batu said, tearing his gaze away from the fire. "That it wasn't right to have more pointless bloodshed."

"And you believed her?"

"I did. Saragerel is different from all the rest. I don't know what it is, but there's greatness in her."

"Are you just saying that because she outsmarted you with the fake camp gimmick?" Nugai said.

Batu laughed. "No, it's something more than that."

"You realize that we're still probably worth more to her alive than dead, right? Killing fellow Omnu hunters might have shaken the confidence of some people under her command. That's probably a good enough reason to leave us alive."

"I realized that," Batu said, waving his hand dismissively. "But that's not what she was thinking. She actually meant it."

Nugai scoffed, but he didn't argue further. He laid back onto the grass as he ate some of the meat they had hunted a few hours ago.

"In any case," Nugai said. "Your father's the one to blame for all this. If he hadn't sent us on that useless chase, we'd have been there to protect him. No sense in worrying about whether or not it was our fault."

Batu nodded. It seemed easier to let his father take the blame. After all, the man was dead and he had been nothing but horrible to Batu in the past few years. But the more he tried to relax, the louder his father's voice became in his head. It was as if his father's ghost was clinging to him like moisture on a humid day, refusing to give him respite.

Jochi returned to the fire with a few pouches of manna before Batu could sink too deep into his thoughts.

"Chief," he said, taking a seat next to Batu.

"How's the manna supply?" Batu asked.

"Not well. The Harnda were generous enough to give us what they could, but we only have enough to last a week's journey. We need to find a way to get more or we're going to lose our horses."

"That's another reason we need the Qhurin's help, then."

"You're gambling a lot on this trip. Are you absolutely sure it'll work?"

"It's the last chance we've got."

"Yeah, right," Jochi said. "Listen, Flamewalker, there's something I have to tell you before we make contact with the Qhurin. Your father had me swear never to tell you this, but, well, he's one with the wind now and I guess I'm not doing anyone any harm."

The mention of his father made Batu flinch.

"What is it?" he asked.

"Your mother…she wasn't from Yegu's herding camp like your father claimed."

"Where was she from, then?"

"She was Qhurin," Jochi said. "She and your father met during the war. They fought together in the Battle of Crimson Soil."

"But my father closed our camps after the war," Batu said. "He wouldn't even let travelers into Omnu lands without permission from a chief. He called Julian a traitor for marrying a Harnda woman."

"Which is why no one could know. Including his own son," Jochi said. "Chinua's ideals about our tribe were powerful, Batu, but they weren't absolute. He thought that our tribe was the finest in the Steppe, but even he went against that in the end."

"Why did he marry her then? If he cared so much about his ideals?" Nugai asked.

Jochi chuckled. "You should've seen Chinua and Oyuun when they first met. Everyone knew it was a bad idea. But love happened anyway."

"So he betrayed everything he stood for," Batu said. "Sounds like my father."

"Your father was a complicated man. But everyone who saw them afterwards knew that they were a perfect match. She was the water to your father's fire, and I've never seen him happier

Batu thought about his mother for the first time in years. It was a memory he did not like. He could only picture himself sitting next to her funeral pyre, watching the smoke rise into the sky and wishing that he didn't have smoke for a mother. All he wanted was to have her back.

But now, he could remember riding with her into the Steppe to pick flowers. He remembered the first time she taught him how to skin a deer and string a bow. He remembered falling asleep to the sweet sound of her voice, singing a tune that he could no longer place. There was a tear in his eye as these memories resurfaced, but after ten years without her, it felt like the scars had begun to heal on their own.

"Losing her was the worst thing that ever happened to him," Batu said. "Everything changed after she died."

Jochi didn't respond to him directly. "Perhaps. But I fought with Chinua for years, Batu. I'm sure of two things. He loved you, and he loved his people. He did what he thought was right for both."

Batu laughed. "That doesn't make it better. It's his fault we're in this mess."

Jochi grunted as though Batu had just punched him in the gut. "In any case, your mother's Qhurin identity is something we can use. They'll be more willing to speak to you if you point out that you're one of them."

"Right," Batu said, but he wasn't interested in talking strategy tonight. He got up from the fire and began walking away, taking his bow and a quiver of arrows with him.

"It's cold out there," Nugai called after him.

"That's the point," Batu said, walking until the camp was no longer in sight, the campfire's orange ring blocked from view by a hill. He drew a small target in the side of the hill with the bottom of his boot, then walked a hundred meters away. He strung the bow, nocked an arrow, took aim, and fired.

The arrow found the target, but it was far from the center. Batu cursed and tried again. Each attempt for him closer to the center, but he could never quite make hit the bullseye.

The Steppe was silent save for the occasional gust of wind and the sound of Batu's arrows lodging themselves into the dirt. The silence seemed to creep up on Batu, slowly enveloping him. He let himself ease into it, because he knew that if he dug too deep into his mind, he would find nothing but thoughts of his father.

# 18

# Erroll

Erroll's boots sank into the ground as he walked. With each step he took, it was clear that the soil could not support the heavy infantry sabatons that the Empire issued. He would have to find some replacements soon.

Syra walked next to him, wearing simple rubber boots that were well-suited to walking in the Arban Valley. The long march to the main Asjare camp had not been pleasant, but at least they had been able to ride in carriages. They were forced to abandon it a few kilometers back when its wheels began to sink into the soil.

"It rains frequently in the Valley," Syra explained. "And when it does, it floods. So the ground is often muddy in one way or another. Makes for some unpleasant marching."

"You could've explained that to me before we arrived. I can barely walk in these boots," Erroll muttered under his breath.

Syra laughed. "Then it wouldn't have been as fun. Lighten up, kid. In any case, we're almost there."

The Asjare outer lands were much like the rest of the Steppe: flat plains and rolling hills as far as the eye could see, with only the occasional tree or flower patch. But when they crossed Arban's Peaks, they found themselves in an entirely new world. The grass seemed greener here, as though the frequent showers meant that they were healthier. While it wasn't exactly a forest, there were far more trees than he expected.

"So why do they call it the Arban Valley?" Erroll asked as he brushed his hand against the bark of a tree.

Syra gave him an annoyed look. "The general assigned you to the

Asjare and you didn't bother reading anything about their history?"

Erroll shrugged. "I don't believe the savages have anything called 'history'."

Syra stopped in his tracks, holding up a fist to stop the squadron of soldiers. He leered at Erroll, who felt his breath catch as he saw the jovial man's face turn dark.

"You will not speak of the nomads this way, soldier," Syra said. "They are a proud people with a thriving culture. Our alliance with them is tenuous, dependent on the Empire supplying them with manna. If you offend them, however, there's every chance they'll switch to the other side. Do you understand?"

"Yes, sir," Erroll said. Syra had worked with the nomads since Tomyris began scouting for the first expedition. Erroll supposed it was understandable that he would have developed a soft spot for them.

"Good," Syra said.

They marched for some time in silence, then Syra finally spoke. "The Arban Valley is named after Arban the Carver, one of the nomads' heroes. They say that he was so strong that he managed to carve the entire valley out of the ground with his Warhammer. The stories say that he carved the valley in a single day so that when Jarine, goddess of the moon, woke for the night, she would be compelled to come down to see it on earth. The goddess was so impressed with Arban's handiwork that she lay with him for one night. That night, the moon was absent from the sky and the stars shone all the brighter without it. The nomads call it the 'Night of the Million Stars'. Arban and Jarine's union produced a son: Arlenn, who became a hero in his own right."

"Fascinating," Erroll said, though the story reminded him of the old folktales that his mother would tell him to put him to sleep. But one detail from the story nagged at him. "The goddess Jarine...is there any relationship between her and Jarnis, the K'harini goddess?"

Syra considered for a moment. "There may very well be. It wouldn't surprise me, since K'harin traded a lot with the nomads before Emperor Jurgen conquered them. Some even say that Ruson's goddess, Galele, is the same character as the nomads' deity, Gaeon."

Erroll nodded. Before the Jusordian Empire came to power and banned all religion, the Steppe was said to be the spiritual heartland of the continent. Pilgrims used to travel to the Steppe live among the nomads for years to seek enlightenment, though Erroll couldn't imagine what enlightenment could be found in these desolate plains.

Syra led them through a patch of trees and into a clearing. "Here we are," he said, gesturing at the space they had just stepped into.

They had passed a few scattered tents on the way, but this was the true center of the Asjare camp. Most of the main activities of the camp, it seemed, such as butchering, herding, and tanning took place in the central area, with each activity bleeding into the other. There was no order to the activities; butchers, herders, and hunters mingled together with the livestock and horses. Erroll even thought he could see children and parents playing amidst the chaos.

Several hunters gathered near a large central pavilion noticed when their contingent of soldiers entered the camp. They whispered among themselves, then one of them disappeared into the pavilion. Within a few moments, a young man that Erroll assumed was Dayir the chieftain emerged from the tent.

Dayir was no taller than Erroll, but somehow the man seemed older and larger than he was. He was dressed in a tight black cloak that wrapped seamlessly around his body and carried a large leopard-shaped headdress in his arm. Dayir had the stride of an old, seasoned warrior, and the face of one too—chiseled and square-jawed with a small scar running along his left cheek.

"Syra," he said as he approached, clasping Syra's hand in his own with the vigor of an old friend. "It's good to see that you've returned safely. Did your visits of the other camps go well?"

"They did," Syra said. "Your hunters are in good order, Dayir. You have much to be proud of."

Dayir barked a laugh. "And I'm sure you bondless would know a lot about that. Order and structure—we Asjare don't need such things. We fight with Gaeon's strength. That's all I require of my hunters."

Syra grinned. "I'd expect nothing less. I heard your men have had success against the Harnda recently?"

Dayir nodded vigorously. "Many have fallen to our raids. The other tribes are growing soft. By the time we launch our assault, they will fall like trees in a storm."

"Good to hear," Syra said, then he gestured to the soldiers standing behind him. Many of them had never been in a nomad camp before, so they were looking around the clearing with curiosity. "I have with me two hundred of our best men. They will supplement your forces on the border. We have five hundred more on the way for the other camps."

Dayir nodded, looking past Syra and Erroll to watch the assembly of Empire soldiers, who in their light mail and plate, seemed out of place among the leather-wearing nomad hunters.

"We will welcome them," Dayir said. "And before you ask, we should have enough supplies, but only if your men take some hunting shifts. Or would that be too difficult for these bondless?"

"Of course not," Syra said. "My soldiers are top-notch. They can handle some hunting."

"Excellent," Dayir said. "Temulun will find them assignments."

A woman stepped up from behind Dayir, and only then did Erroll notice her. She was taller than any woman he'd known and towered over Dayir.

Temulun nodded. "I can do that," she said, eyeing the soldiers. "Seems like you brought us a bunch of city boys. Probably never had a real day out on the plains. You're giving us the weak links, aren't you, Syra?"

Syra flinched, and Erroll thought his temper would flare like it did on the march, but Syra knew better than that. Even Erroll could tell that this woman Temulun was someone important, possibly just below Dayir in rank.

"I assure you," Syra said carefully. "These men are some of the best we have. True, many of them have more experience tackling robbers in the cities, but they will have no problem fighting nomads."

Temulun stared him down for a few more moments. Then she grinned for a second, but for long enough that they could see the delight in her eyes. "Good. Then I suppose we're all clear then."

Syra tried to hide the relief in his expression.

Temulun chuckled and patted him on the shoulder. "You should be used to this by now, Syra."

The captain grunted, but he said nothing more.

Erroll then noticed Temulun's gaze turn on him and he immediately stiffened, though he could not fathom why. Something about this woman that put him on edge.

"Who's the kid?" she asked after looking him up and down.

"A new soldier in the general's personal guard," Syra explained. "He'll be joining the camp along with these men."

"One of Sandulf's men, eh?" Temulun said. "He can join my hunting group. Can you ride a horse, kid?"

"Well enough," Erroll said. They had been taught basic horsemanship during their training, but since most infantrymen weren't given horses, it had only been the basics.

Temulun laughed. "Proud of yourself, are you? We'll see how you feel after we show you how an Asjare hunter rides."

Erroll nodded. "I can do it," he said.

Temulun personally led Erroll to his horse. When he reached their pen, he realized that all the other nomads he was to be riding with were already mounted, even hunters that were half his height and probably half his age. He swallowed hard, but he couldn't afford to back down now.

She pointed at a palomino horse with a sleek yellow coat that was on the smaller side when compared to the other horses in the pen. "You'll ride this one for today, Erroll. We've already saddled him up for you."

Erroll nodded, then he started to approach the horse.

"Sure you don't need any help?" Temulun said.

"Nope," Erroll said. The horse didn't pay him any attention as he got closer, so he actually thought he could do it before he put one foot into the stirrup. As soon as he did, the horse let out a high-pitched whiny and leapt forward, throwing Erroll off balance. He collapsed into a heap of grass. The next thing he knew, he was staring at the wide open sky above him.

Temulun started laughing, and so did the other hunters who were already mounted on their horses. She extended him a hand, but Erroll didn't take it. He staggered to his feet, rubbing his backside.

"Let me try again. I was just getting warmed up," he said, but he failed to get close to the horse without it running away from him again.

He scoffed, then he turned to Temulun. "Can I have a different horse? This one seems to be defective."

"The horse isn't the problem, city boy. It's you," she said, before tossing him a small pouch. He opened it and found that it was filled with an azure blue powder, as fine as sand but glowing bright like crystals.

"What's this?"

"It's manna, straight from the Temple of Gaeon," Temulun said. "Try to get close to the horse again, and do it slowly this time. Keep your stance firm and show no fear. He needs to know that you're the boss."

"And what do I do with the manna?"

Temulun chuckled. "I'll tell you if you get that far."

Erroll nodded, then he watched the horse again. He kept his feet firmly on the ground, and spread his arms wide, as if to keep the horse from running away just with his reach. Then he stepped closer, watching its every reaction. The horse's eyes were on him this time, and he could not tell if they were curious or scared.

He kept its attention, whispering so that only it could hear. "Hey, buddy. Don't worry, I'm not here to hurt you. I'm just an oddly-dressed soldier from far away. Nothing to worry about."

The horse tilted its head ever so slightly. For a moment, Erroll thought that it could understand him. Then he took a few steps forward until he was within an arm's reach from the horse. He got close enough that he could run a hand across its mane, and though it recoiled at first, he whispered again, soothing the beast.

"Don't worry, I'm a friend," Erroll said. The horse felt calmer, and its mane felt like soft grass. He felt its body rise and fall as it breathed, and he breathed along with it.

"Good," Temulun said from behind him. "Now, take out some manna and sprinkle it on his mane."

"And then what?" Erroll said, not taking his eyes off the horse.

"You'll see."

Erroll rolled his eyes, then he reached into his pouch and brought out a pinch of manna, which glowed in his hands as he brought it out. Then he took a deep breath and sprinkled it on the horse's mane. The moment he did, the manna glowed, and Erroll gasped.

All of a sudden, his eyes widened and he could feel a stream of new feelings flood into his brain, a wave of sensations that he had never felt before. He felt the wind in his hair and the sunlight on his back. He felt grass underneath his hooves and a calloused hand on his neck. It took him a few moments to realize that he was experiencing the horse's feelings.

Once he grew accustomed to the new sensations, he took out more manna from the pouch and sprinkled it on the horse. All of a sudden, he felt its emotions—its hunger, its curiosity, and its restlessness. The horse wanted nothing more than to bound out of this pen and race into the empty hills. For a moment, Erroll shared that feeling.

So this was what manna did. This was what the nomads were so jealously protecting, and why they needed the Temple of Gaeon.

Erroll ran his hand across the horse's beautiful mane once more. Keeping his movements slow and steady, he placed one foot into the stirrup. The horse gave a low whinny, which Erroll took as an invitation.

With some difficulty, Erroll hoisted himself up into the horse's saddle. He was a little unbalanced for a second, but the horse adjusted himself so that he fit comfortably into the seat. He gripped the saddle for a moment, and then he was secure. Erroll grinned widely when he felt himself settle onto the horse — he just couldn't help himself.

Temulun was standing in front of him, watching with a grin on her face and her arms crossed. He could hear some of the other hunters begin to applaud.

"Congratulations, Erroll," she said. "You're now a hunter of the Steppe."

Erroll staggered into the camp's main clearing, the entire lower half of his body in pain. Each time he tried to stretch his legs, his groin area flared in pain, so he had to take small steps that didn't put too much strain on that area. That meant that Erroll ended up staggering like an idiot—and he felt like one, too.

He drew laughter from some of the hunters that were gathered around the fires as he staggered through the camp. He did his best to avert his gaze. Then he felt a sharp strike on his back and he collapsed, legs folding underneath him like grass caught in a gale.

The circles around him erupted into laughter. Erroll thought he heard the words "city boy" and "bondless" get thrown around, but he was too dizzy to respond. He looked up and saw Temulun standing over him, having just slapped him on the back.

But unlike the others, she was not laughing. Erroll could not read her face—there was a small smirk that played on her lips, but the displeased look she gave him, complete with her crossed arms, reminded him of his mother. He almost expected her to help him up and get him some food to eat, but she did not.

He stumbled back to his own feet, wincing and cursing as he did.

"Well?" Temulun asked as soon as he stopped wobbling.

Erroll raised an eyebrow, but he didn't speak for fear that she would push him down again.

"How was your first day hunting?" she asked.

"Harder than expected," he said. "I think I'll be too sore to ride again tomorrow."

"Good," Temulun said, then she started walking again, gesturing for him to follow. "You'll do the same tomorrow. And the next day, and the one after that as well. It'll make you strong."

He followed her, slowly at first, but her pace was quick enough that he had to take larger steps. Eventually, he got used to the pain of his throbbing body. Just like that, without any argument. Erroll began to understand why Syra was so disarmed by her.

She led him past the central tent, where Erroll got a glimpse of Dayir speaking to a few older hunters. Despite their age, they were seated in a circle around him and it was clear that Dayir was in charge. He assumed that they would be the masters of hunters of other camps. Syra sat outside of the circle, listening to their discussion and chiming in from time to time. Erroll wondered why Temulun herself wasn't part of the meeting.

Temulun finally stopped when she came to a small circle of tents off the edges of the main clearing. There were a few hunters gathered around a fire trading food. He recognized some of their faces from his hunting exercises earlier that day, but he hadn't learned any of their names.

Temulun joined their circle and accepted a plate of food. Erroll tried to move to the side, but Temulun insisted that he join the circle. Erroll took a seat between two male hunters, but he sat down too abruptly and pain flared again in his legs. Although he tried to stifle his reaction, he ended up grunting in pain.

Both hunters next to him laughed and some of the other hunters in the circle chuckled. One of them patted Erroll on the shoulder.

"I remember my first day out on the Steppe," he said. "You'll get used to it."

"And when was that, Khalja?" his friend asked.

"I don't know, Geser," Khalja said. "Probably twenty, twenty-five years ago now."

Erroll's eyes widened in shock. Khalja didn't look much older than thirty. Either the man was older than he looked, or he had been riding since early childhood. His friend Geser was a little older—he seemed to be in his fifties, though the age did not show on him either. He seemed as full of life as any of them.

"So, you're one of those Jusordian soldiers, then?" Khalja said. "We've worked some of you, but none of them stay for very long."

Erroll wondered if all the savages were like this—did they always have to sit so uncomfortably close all the time? He looked at the rest of the hunters and noticed that they did the same. All were conversing together in smaller groups around the fire. Even Temulun was sitting with two of the youngest hunters in the group.

"I am," he said, staring at his food. "General Sandulf wants to improve relations between his army and our Asjare allies."

"Well in that case, shouldn't you try to get to know us better?" Geser said.

"Hey, Geser, don't be like that," Khalja said. "You're scaring him."

"Now what would be scary about me?" Geser said. "Saenor's scales, these Empire city boys have really got no spine."

"I'm not scared," Erroll said.

Geser and Khalja exchanged a look and burst out laughing again. Erroll wondered why these nomads enjoyed laughing so much.

"Sure thing, bondless," Khalja said, patting Erroll on the shoulder again. "Don't worry, Geser scared me too when Temulun put me into this group."

"That word, 'bondless'," Erroll said. "Why do you call me that?"

"What? Oh, I forget that you haven't been in the Steppe long," Khalja said. "That's what we call anyone that hasn't got a soul bond."

"And what is a soul bond?"

Khalja paused for a moment. He looked over at Geser, who just shook his head. "By Saenor, I don't know how to explain it. We've each got an animal. Mine's an eagle. Geser's is a horse."

Geser stroked his beard. "When we're kids, there's a ceremony. We pick an animal and it's with us for the rest of our lives. A companion."

Erroll nodded. Adrius had mentioned something about this before. He called the animals the nomads' servants. "Why is it called a soul bond, then?"

Geser frowned. "Because that's what it is."

Erroll considered asking further, but he got the sense that that was all he would get out of Geser. "Fascinating," he said, and left it at that.

Khalja turned to Geser. "How's your son getting along?"

"He sent us an eagle yesterday," Geser said. "They're sending more and more hunters to the river, so he's had less land to patrol. But my wife still isn't happy about it at all. She'd much rather we all be in the same place."

Khalja sighed. "I've got a feeling that soon enough, we'll all be sent south anyway."

"Gaeon's staff, if it comes to that…" Geser said. "We're hunters, not soldiers. This doesn't feel right."

"Dayir's doing the right thing, though," Khalja said, eyeing Erroll. "If not for the Empire, old Chinua would've probably taken all our land outside the Valley. We all knew another war was coming."

"I just wish that it didn't mean splitting our family apart."

Erroll frowned. "If you have a family, why are you having dinner here?"

The two of them turned to face Erroll suddenly.

"We spend half of the week with our hunting groups and the other half with our families," Geser said.

"And if a hunter is unmarried, he or she lives with their hunting group throughout the week," Khalja said. "Don't you do the same?"

"Normally, we would live with our families," Erroll said. "Unless we were out in the field or on an assignment."

"How strange," Khalja said.

"Is this something new because of the war?" Erroll asked. He knew that during the early days of Emperor Jurgen's wars with K'harin, young soldiers had been taken from their families and forced to live with their comrades for months, even years. But once Tomyris took power, she let the soldiers fight on rotations to improve morale.

Geser shook his head. "We've been doing this since the days of Arban the Carver."

"I see."

"You have a lot to learn, kid," Khalja said, grinning. "Fortunately, you have two excellent teachers."

"I don't understand why you're being so friendly," Erroll said. "Shouldn't you hate the Empire?"

Khalja and Geser exchanged a look. This time, when Geser broke the silence, he spoke slowly and carefully. "Kid, we don't hate anyone out here. That's not the Asjare way."

"Maybe the other tribes have grudges, like old Chinua, who still can't get over that little skirmish five years ago," Khalja said. "But most nomads in the Steppe are happy enough to get along with anyone. Even the Empire, if you give them the chance."

"Exactly. It's just our leaders that bear the grudges," Geser said. "But the way I see it, there's not that much different between the Empire and us. I'm just hoping that after the war, we can simply live and let live. That's all I'm asking for."

Erroll was quiet for a long time. He had been raised to hate the nomads all his life, to hate their culture, their way of life, and the land that they kept from Empress Tomyris's grasp. So of course he had expected that the nomads would hate him too, but clearly that was not true. Something was different here, but he could not quite understand what it was.

He was about to thank them, but Temulun caught their attention.

"Thank you," she said when they were all looking at her. "Dayir told me some news earlier and I wanted you to hear it from me first. He's mobilizing the hunters. All of us. The plan is to invade the Harnda camps within the next month. I don't know where we'll be stationed, but I've made sure that Dayir puts us all together."

"So we're really doing it, then," Geser said. "Invading the Harnda. By Gaeon, I used to ride with some hunters there before all this happened."

"I know that this will be difficult for many of you," Temulun said. "But as long as the Harnda continue to shelter the rest of the Omnu, they're our enemies. We need to put aside our feelings and do what's right."

"Never thought it'd come to this," Khalja muttered under his breath, so softly that Erroll thought he was the only one who heard it. Geser reached over and patted his friend on the knee.

"We'll get through this," Temulun said. "And you know why? Because this hunting group can do anything if we're together."

Geser nodded vigorously, muttering, "Yes," under his breath.

"Looks like we're going to be spending more time together," Khalja said, turning to Erroll. "Don't worry. It's going to be a long ride, but we'll protect you all the way."

# 19

# Sara

Sara emerged from the war meeting exhausted and drained. Thaube, Chanar, and Zayaat left the tent together, laughing and joking like old friends. Ibakha, who had only arrived at the tail end of the meeting, didn't leave with them.

Sara thought about the possibility of spending the night alone in her tent, waiting for Khulan and Bataar to finish their duties and return. Instead, she decided to follow Ibakha, who didn't seem to have a clear destination in mind. She wandered through the tents, speaking to a few of her people as she went, moving in the general direction of the hills.

Sara decided against announcing herself and decided to watch. She had never seen Ibakha outside of a leadership setting before. Ibakha eventually made her way up one of the hills and took a seat near the top. She sat there for a while, watching the sun set behind the clouds and gazing at the receding orange rays. Sara did her best to follow along, rounding the hill so that the chief wouldn't see.

When Sara reached the top of the hill, she had a good enough view so that she could see what Ibakha was doing. Her head was bent over, watching something intently in her lap. Her hands were moving, slowly but with purpose, though Sara could not quite see what she was doing.

Ibakha yelped and pulled her hand away from her lap, waving it like it was on fire. "Saenor's scales, that hurt like a bastard," she cursed.

When she heard Ibakha curse like that, Sara could not help but chuckle. Ibakha looked up at her, startled for a moment, but she did not seem angry when she saw Sara sitting there.

"Burned out, are you?" Ibakha said, and Sara gave a small nod, as if she was still reluctant to admit it herself. Ibakha patted the grass next to her. Without hesitation, Sara got up and sat next to her.

"What's troubling you?" Ibakha said. When Sara took a seat next to her, she could finally see what the woman was working on. Ibakha had been sewing a small handkerchief, but Sara could tell that the job was poorly done. The stiches were uneven and Ibakha had obviously pricked herself with the needle. Sara did her best to hide her curiosity.

"War meeting," Sara said simply, and Ibakha seemed to understand.

"Ah," Ibakha said, laughing. "That's why I try to avoid those as much as possible. Those old farts have no idea what they're talking about."

"They won't listen to me at all."

"Of course they won't. But they'll take your ideas anyway, won't they? Zayaat told me you gave a few suggestions today. But they made it seem like it was their own."

Sara nodded. "It's all a game to them, isn't it?"

"They've been at war for too long. Thaube would tell you that it makes you deadlier. But the way I see it, all it does is make you cruel."

"And that's why you're trying to stay away?"

"Most of the time," Ibakha said, then she eyed Sara. "But I guess that's not the path you want to take."

Sara shook her head. "It's not what my father would have done."

Ibakha laughed. "Then you're already a better leader than all of them."

Sara frowned. "But I'm not as smart as Chanar. Nor do I have Thaube's flair. I've heard the stories about what he's like on the battlefield."

"Sure, Chanar is a tactician. Thaube is a general. But it takes more than that to be a leader."

"So what does it take?"

Ibakha shrugged. "Don't know. I'm pretty sure I don't have it. But I think that you do."

"That wasn't very helpful."

"Like I said, I'm not very good at being a chief," Ibakha said, then she rummaged through a pouch at her side and brought out a needle and some thread. She handed both to Sara. "You know how to stitch?"

"My mother taught me a little."

"Great," Ibakha said. "Go ahead then."

Sara stared at the cloth in her hands. "I don't even know where to begin."

"Neither do I. You heard me shout earlier, right? But we have to start somewhere."

And so Sara did. As the sun set in the horizon and the camp prepared for war, Sara and Ibakha sat on a hill overlooking the herding camps, sewing badly and cursing as they pricked themselves.

Sara sat on her horse near the Serpent's River, watching as an army gathered on the other side. She had taken the eyes of her eagle and was soaring over the river, too high in the sky for any arrows to reach her.

On the Omnu side of the river to the east, she could see the Empire's soldiers begin to construct camps along the river. They were simple wooden structures that would probably fall to a storm, which meant that they were not meant to last long.

On the Asjare side of the river to the north, she saw hunters making their own field camps. These weren't permanent camps like the ones the nomads set for each season. Those camps would include long-term storage, manna tents, butchers' tents, and so on. The ones across the river had only the basics—stables, barracks, and sparring grounds.

One thing was clear. The enemy was preparing for an assault, and it was coming soon. In two weeks at most, she guessed.

She left her eagle's eyes and re-entered her own body again. She turned to Zayaat.

"Familiar?" she asked.

"Too familiar," Zayaat said, shaking his head. "I remember standing with your father all those years ago. We were on the banks of Jarine's Tears with the Fulgar chieftains."

"Right before the Battle of Tears?"

He nodded. "We were on the brink of defeat then too. Your father was so scared I thought he would fall off his horse."

Sara laughed. "I didn't think my father ever got scared."

"Oh, Julian was scared all the time. He was just better than most people at hiding it."

"And you won the battle," Sara said. "The elders still tell the story of Khasar and Chinua's combined pincer attack."

"They don't tell the story of the price we paid. So many died. Back then, the nomads were united behind your father and Chinua. We had unity and the best leaders. Now we have neither."

"Zayaat, tell me the truth," Sara said. "Are we going to survive?"

He raised an eyebrow. "Are you sure you want the truth?"

"Yes."

"Very well, then," Zayaat said. "Twenty years ago, the tribes were quarreling, yes. But our hunters were stronger. Our numbers had yet to be decimated by disease. The Omnu and Asjare, the tribes with the best hunters, were on our side. We had the likes of Chinua, your father, and The Bull commanding us. If you believe the stories, they were chosen by Gaeon to save us. And yet, we only barely won. This time, the Empire has returned stronger and smarter.

"The same cannot be said for us. The nomads spent the last twenty years ago quibbling over land and manna. If anything, we have only become more divided. And with the assault coming our way... I am afraid, Sara, that the odds are that we will not live to see the next month, let alone the end of the war."

Sara nodded slowly. She had expected something similar, though she had not expected Zayaat's predictions to be that bleak.

"I see," she said, and let out a sigh. "I don't know if I can do this, Zayaat. You knew my father. What would he think?"

"I think he'd be proud," Zayaat said. "You brought us all together, didn't you?"

"Not all of us."

"Well, as many of us as you could. I've stood on hills like this before with battle brewing on the horizon, and let me tell you, it never gets easier. All we can do is trust ourselves and have faith in our fellow hunters."

Sara nodded. "Do you trust me, then?"

Zayaat smirked. "Of course I do. You, Saragerel, are a leader like nobody I've ever seen before."

# 20

# Batu

The Qhurin lands were a different world. Batu sat outside one of the Qhurin buildings on a wooden bench, probably made from the mountain forests bordering the Steppe. All around him, he was given a strong sense that something was not right.

They had passed a few tents when they entered the camp, but they were mostly on the outskirts of the territory and belonged to hunters passing through the village. But the rest of the nomads, if they could be called that, were housed in small, one-storey wooden buildings. They weren't as large as the huge towers of stone that Batu had heard from merchants traveling from Ruson, but they had a sense of permanence to them. Each building was built to last, and the sprawling village around them would only grow larger and larger as time went on.

Even the air did not feel right here. It was thick with moisture, as if the winds themselves were sweating. It did not take long for both Batu and Nugai to be drenched from the heat. Each gust of wind was a blessing, though nothing could save them from the grounds they walked on, which were wet on good days and insufferable and muddy on bad days.

But the Qhurin didn't seem to mind. Many of them wore clothes well-suited to the temperature, complete with boots that didn't sink into the mud. Each house was raised a meter or so above the ground on wooden supports that were built into stone foundations in case of flooding.

Batu looked around as he tried to picture his mother walking in between the wooden buildings, collecting the flowers that grew along the paths or greeting to her neighbors. He found it nearly impossible to imagine. When he thought about his mother, all he could picture was her in the Omnu lands, riding a horse into the Steppe. The wind was in her hair and the sunlight was on her back. That was who his mother was, not someone from these strange wooden buildings.

Batu noticed that Nugai, who was sitting next to him, could not keep still. He kept glancing over his shoulder at the passing villagers.

"What's the matter?" Batu asked.

"There's a reason why I left," Nugai said. "I'm just lucky no one recognizes me."

"It can't have been that bad, Nugai," Batu said.

"They gave me everything. They raised me, trained me, and provided for me. Then I betrayed everything they taught," Nugai said.

"Well, when you put it like that, everything sounds bad," Batu said.

"Just…" Nugai did another look around them. "I still think I should've stayed with the others."

The rest of their group had stayed near the edges of the camp. Their gambit had worked—Batu's mother Qhurin had gotten them an audience with Galeren, but they still had no idea how it would go beyond that.

"Nugai, you're the only one that knows anything about Qhurin traditions," Batu said. "I need you here."

"Fine," Nugai groaned. "But that doesn't mean I have to like it."

The door to the wooden building opened and a large man dressed in a flowing robe stepped out. They had been taken to the largest building in the village, a round building with a porch encircling it.

The man that stepped out was the same man that had met them at the border. Instead of wearing typical hunting armor, he was instead dressed in a large, thick robe that was bright green and embroidered with silver. The robes seemed far too thick for the humidity, but it did not seem to bother the priest. Batu did not understand most of the robe's designs, but one of them stood out: the large silver eagle on the robe's front, stretching from right below the man's neck to his hip. The symbol of Galeren, Herald of Gaeon, Keeper of the Spring of Onoe, and leader of the Qhurin.

"The Herald has agreed to grant you an audience," the priest said, and he nodded to the guards that had been standing beside Batu and Nugai. They were wearing leather armor with metal plates on the shoulders and stomach. Their attire seemed far too heavy to wear while on a horse, and both of them carried spears instead of swords or bows. The guards saluted the priest and left.

Batu and Nugai got to their feet and followed the priest as he led them inside.

Galeren sat cross-legged in the center of the huge, circular room. She sat on a simple, elevated platform that was adorned with no more than a cloth and pillows. The rest of the room was similar. Other than the priests who sat on the edges of the circle in silence, the only other adornment came in the form of a few banners displaying Galeren's symbol. The rest was made of simple, dark brown wood.

At the back of the room was a small stone well that glowed blue. Two priests stood alongside it. Batu did not manage to get a good look at it, but he could guess what it was. The Spring of Onoe, the last source of manna in the Steppe that was nott controlled by the Empire.

The priest walked before Batu and Nugai, motioning for them to wait. He stepped forward.

"Lady Herald," the priest proclaimed in a loud voice. "As I have informed you earlier, I now present…"

Galeren raised a hand, stopping him. "No need to prattle on, boy. I know who they are. Let them in."

The priest bowed and stepped aside, letting Batu and Nugai step inside the room. Nugai had never been inside the Herald's chambers before, so he had not been able to tell Batu what to expect. They tried not to stare as they approached Galeren, who was younger than they thought she would be. Batu had pictured a tiny, wizened lady, but Galeren sat tall and straight, looking barely sixty. There were wrinkles on her face and her jet black hair was starting to gray; aside from that, however, Batu would not have found it odd to find her on the battlefield leading a company of hunters.

Batu and Nugai started to bow, but she interrupted them again. "Please. No need for the ritual. You aren't Qhurin, I know, so I won't impose our beliefs onto yours."

Batu frowned. "My mother…"

"Yes, yes, they told me," Galeren said, waving her hand again. "But children are not their parents, correct? Or do you mean to say that you are the same as your father?"

Batu thought he could hear his father's voice whispering in the back of his mind, but he shut it out. He shook his head. "No. You are correct."

"Good," Galeren said, leaning back in her seat in a languid manner. "Then we're on the same page. Pleased to meet you."

All of Batu's previous arguments fell out of his head. Galeren's opening words had wiped them all away. He had expected to meet a wizened, traditional old lady who would respond to his appeals for honor and family. It became clear to him that he needed to try something different.

"Pleased to meet you as well," Batu said. "We've come to ask for your support in the war."

Galeren raised an eyebrow. "Your father said the same thing to me twenty years ago."

"Then you know how dire our situation is," Batu said.

"That was before your father led us into ruin," Galeren said. She smiled when she saw Batu flinch. "He did do that, child. The Qhurin helped your father secure the Arban Valley and destroy the Empire's supply routes. We lost most of our hunters to secure Chinua a favorable position. Did Chinua thank us for our sacrifice? Of course not. He went on to win the Battle of Crimson Soil and claimed the glory for himself. 'Blessed by Gaeon', they called him, but he only managed it with the blood of the Qhurin. All we got in return was death and more war."

Batu did not know what to say.

Galeren folded her arms. "Here in Qhurin, each man and woman is their own person. Tell me, Batu. Why should I trust you?"

Batu hesitated. The way Galeren looked at him made him feel as though it was his words that were on trial.

"Well, I..." Batu began, but he knew he had nothing good to say. Then Nugai stepped forward and spoke.

"Most Holy Herald," Nugai said. "You don't know me or Chief Batu, but you can trust us. He is as capable a leader as any..."

Nugai was about to continue, but one of the priests stopped him. Before then, the priests seated in a circle had been silent with their heads bowed, but this priest's head jerked up suddenly. "Wait!" he shouted.

"What is this interruption?" Galeren said.

"I am sorry, Herald, but I recognize that voice," the priest said. He stood and raised an accusatory finger at Nugai.

"I don't know what you're talking about," Nugai said.

"He served in my camp's reserve force," the priest said. "I'd know that voice anywhere. We placed him on trial for blasphemy; he'd tried to steal manna from the Spring of Onoe without the Herald's blessing. He fled the tribe right after he was sentenced, and we thought he died on the plains. His name is Gaiun."

"That's not my name anymore," Nugai said. "I left it behind."

Galeren raised a hand to silence both of them. She pointed at Nugai. "You. Speak. Is this true?"

Nugai looked between Galeren and the priest who accused him.

"It is true," Nugai said slowly, and the priest made a small, vindicated gruny. Galeren shot him a look and silencing him. She motioned for Nugai to go on.

"I left the tribe three years ago because they told me I was a blasphemer. And I did make some mistakes, but the way I see it, I was just trying to keep my family from going hungry. I paid a hefty sum for that."

"You still have not suffered for your sins in front of Gaeon," the priest said.

Nugai spun on him. This time, there was nothing Galeren could do to quiet him down. "You think I haven't suffered enough? I've lost more than you will ever understand."

"I think that is quite enough," Galeren said, but Nugai refused to listen.

"You accuse me of treachery, but as you sit here in your wooden palaces, the rest of us fight for the scraps of manna you let us have. People are dying out there, and you never cared enough to listen."

"Nugai!" Batu said, catching his friend on the shoulder. Nugai finally stopped and looked his friend in the eye. "I think you should leave."

Nugai nodded slowly and began to leave the room. The priest stood speechless, his eyes on Nugai's back.

"Stop," Galeren said. "What you said would earn you a death sentence. But speaking in the presence of the Herald herself...such would earn you a most painful death," Galeren said.

Batu stepped forward to stand in between Galeren and Nugai, but he realized that he was unarmed and surrounded by priests, so it didn't matter where he stood.

Batu stood tall, looking Galeren straight in the eye. "I can't allow you to do that," Batu said. If he could take the woman hostage, then they might have a chance to get out alive.

The priests began moving in to protect Galeren, but she raised her hand to stop them. "That will not be necessary. I said before that I will not hold you to the laws of our tribe. I stand by what I said. You will not be punished, but I ask that you leave this place now."

Nugai looked into Galeren's face, as if trying to figure out if she was tricking him.

"Maybe I was wrong about you, Galeren," he said. "Thank you Herald. I hope you consider our request."

He left the room with the eyes of the priests staring into his back.

"I see you keep good company, Batu of the Omnu," Galeren said. "Tell me, what sort of person are you?"

Batu folded his arms. Galeren's stare terrified him. It seemed like no lies could pass her unnoticed, and he was too nervous to even try. But he could not afford to look uncertain, especially not after traveling this far away.

"I'm the best leader the Omnu tribe has right now. And the best hope the nomads have to win this war," Batu said. "I led my hunters out of the ruins of the Omnu camps through hostile Asjare territory and into the Harnda lands. I have as much battle experience as any veteran, and I have a mind for war tactics and strategies."

"Is that so?" Galeren said. The woman spoke slowly, drawing each word out. Batu's palms were sweaty. "To my knowledge, the Omnu commanded one of the largest armies of hunters in the Steppe. But my priests tell me that you came with five other hunters when you arrived here. What happened to the rest?"

Batu flinched. He was sure that Galeren knew the answer to this question, so she was trying to see how he'd react.

"They're in the Harnda territory."

"All of them?" Galeren said.

"We lost some of them in the raids against the Empire," Batu said slowly. "And more when our camps were burned and attacked."

"And the best leader the Omnu has let that happen?"

"I made mistakes," Batu said. "And many of those decisions weren't mine. My father had a certain…way of doing things. He refused to listen."

Galeren folded her arms, considering his words. Then she nodded, as if she had nothing else to say on the matter. A priest approached her and whispered into her ear. As he left to return to his place, she spoke again.

"The Harnda already sent us a delegation a month ago. We sent them away at the border. They tell me that it was that old crone Dagasi, which surprises me. Why would they try again a second time with you?"

"Plans change," Batu said quickly. "We realized that sending Dagasi first was the wrong move."

"You did not think to come on your own the first time? You honestly thought that it was a better option to send that woman?"

"Like I said, I've made mistakes," Batu said.

Galeren stood, taking a few steps forward so that her face was mere inches from Batu's.

"Tell me, Chief Batu," she said slowly. "Do I look like a fool to you?"

"What?" Batu stammered. He could barely get his words out as she faced him.

"I do not like to repeat myself," she said. "Do not make me say it again."

"N-no. No. You don't look like one," Batu said.

"Then why are you treating me like one?" Galeren said. "Do you honestly expect me to believe that sending Dagasi was a mistake? Not even your father, the blundering idiot that he was, would have made that error when he could have sent you instead. I will give you one more chance to tell me the truth. Do not waste it."

Batu took a moment to look around the room. The priests were supposed to be quietly praying to themselves, but even they could not help but stare. He took a deep breath.

"Okay. Here's the truth. I have no power over the Omnu. The ones that are alive are loyal to Saragerel, the daughter of Julian. The rest are either dead or scattered. Saragerel wouldn't allow me to join their alliance, so I had no other choice but to come here."

"I knew it," Galeren said, walking away and returning to her seat. "You sought an audience with me only to insult me, lie to me, and waste my time. And then you have the audacity to ask for an alliance?"

"Herald, please," Batu began, but she cut him off.

"My priests let you into the Qhurin lands because they sensed that you had a certain strength of character. I now know that they were wrong. We have nothing more to discuss. Leave before I regret my decision not to kill you."

Batu wanted to get another word in, but the way Galeren glared at him made him believe her threat. He began to leave. Without kowing it, his father spoke in his mind, reminding him that this was just another failure under his belt. The thought made his chest hurt and his palms bled from his nails digging into his palms.

He turned around, facing Galeren again. She raised an eyebrow, but did not order him to leave like he thought she would. He knew exactly what his father would do in this situation. He would march right up to Galeren and threaten to wipe her tribe off the Steppe if she refused to join. And if that failed, he would kill her. Batu had seen him do it dozens of times before.

Batu walked up until he was a few steps away from Galeren. Then he got on his knees, bowing his head so it was nearly touching the floor.

"Herald, I know that I have not given you much reason to listen to me, but please give me one last chance."

He took her silence to mean that he should continue. He raised his head from the floor but kept his body prostrate. Galeren raised an eyebrow.

"You are correct in saying that I don't have the wisdom nor the leadership to lead the Omnu. I'm not the best they have to offer. Not by a long shot. But, please, if you won't ally with me, then ally with Saragerel. She's the best hope we have."

"Saragerel is chief now?" Galeren said. "I thought that her brother, Odgerel, would inherit the place after Julian."

"Odgerel is dead," Batu said. "My father killed him, and my failure to stop him will haunt me for the rest of my life. But his sister is something else entirely. She bore the news of her brother's death on her shoulders and led her camp to safety. She brought together the Harnda, Omnu, Chenkah, and Gur into an alliance. All despite her youth and inexperience. The war ahead may destroy us, but if there is one who could save us, it's Saregerel. She's the leader I could never be."

Batu stepped forward. "But the Empire controls the Temple of Gaeon, and we're running out of manna. Saragerel needs the Spring. And the Steppe needs the Qhurin to defend it once again."

# 21

# Erroll

"Hey, bondless, hurry up," Geser called from the top of the ridge. "Khalja's about to finish scouting."

Erroll grunted and tugged at the straps of his pack, his shoulders straining from the effort. He pushed himself up the last twenty meters of the climb and emerged onto the ridge where the rest of the hunters had gathered.

He collapsed on the ground, falling to one knee and dropping his pack beside him. He let himself breathe for a few moments as his vision blurred. His limbs felt like they were burning. Then he caught his breath and managed to look in front of him, where he found Geser's hand outstretched.

Erroll stared at it for a few moments before taking his hand, letting Geser pull him to his feet.

"It isn't an easy climb, that's for sure," Geser said. He took Erroll by the shoulders and spun him about so that he faced the trail they had just climbed. "But the view is worth it."

Erroll gasped as he saw how far they had just climbed. The entire Arban Valley spread out before them. A mess of snaking rivers, sparse trees, and tiny nomad camps spread out like a few specks of dust on a vast sheet of green. From here, he could see eagles soaring through the sky, horses galloping through the wide open fields, and the trees swaying in the wind. It reminded him of the few times that his mother had taken him to his grandmother's house, out in the farmlands in Ruson's outskirts, but the scenery near her farm hadn't been nearly as grand as this. Every detail he saw was as intricate and sharp as if an expert blacksmith had carved it into stone, and yet it was all real.

Geser saw the look on Erroll's face and grinned. "What do you think, kid?"

"It's...beautiful," was all Erroll managed to say. Geser laughed and he left Erroll with the view.

"You can stay here for a little bit," Geser said. "Take a long, slow drink. It isn't going away anytime soon."

Erroll stared at the view for a long time. A flock of birds would move from one side of the valley to the other. A herd of deer stopped for a drink of water, then dispersed as a pack of hunters began approaching them. All this while, the trees hid entire ecosystems underneath their branches, too small for Erroll's eyes to notice. Everything was where it ought to be, not a hair out of place. Everything except for Erroll.

Finally, he turned away and he saw the rest of the hunters watching him patiently, sitting cross-legged in the grass.

"I'm sorry," Erroll said, approaching them. "I took too long."

"Nonsense," Geser said. "Everyone deserves a long look at the Arban Valley. No matter where you come from."

"Especially if you're from Ruson," Khalja said. "From what I hear, there isn't much to see there."

"Thank you," Erroll said. "But the city does have its own sights."

"You'll have to tell us about them," Khalja said.

"Another time, perhaps," Temulun said, who had already shouldered her pack. "Come. We need to reach the passage before dark. I don't want to risk climbing in the dark."

At her words, Khalja and Geser immediately hefted their packs. So did Erroll, despite the ache in his shoulder having not quite recovered yet.

"How much farther do we need to go?" Erroll asked as they started down another path. It led downwards this time, so it was easier going.

"Not far," Geser said. "The gathering point isn't far from here, but I bet Temulun just wants to be there early so she can check on our forces."

They arrived within an hour or so. If Temulun had not been leading them there, Erroll was sure that he would have missed it.

The entrance was nothing more than a small gap in the side of the mountain, obscured by a few trees. When Temulun led them through it, it opened up into a large clearing.

The mountain camp reminded Erroll of the nomads' camp in the plains, except that it appeared to be less permanent. There were no large scale fortifications and permanent tents. The only ones that Erroll could see were to house hunters and store weapons. The tents only filled up a third of the entire clearing, with groups of tents spaced sparsely throughout the space. He estimated that there were probably about thirty hunters in total.

"There are three other camps spread throughout the mountains," Geser explained as he led Erroll and Khalja to their place in the clearing. Temulun left them to speak with a group of hunting group leaders that were waiting for her. "All of them smaller than this one."

"To make sure we don't lose everyone if we get attacked?" Erroll asked.

"Exactly," Geser said. "You're catching on quick, kid."

There were a few wooden posts driven into the ground to mark where each new hunting group could set up their tents. He couldn't see any pattern behind their distribution, only that they seemed to avoid certain patches of earth that seemed more uneven than the rest of the ground.

He dropped his pack and began removing the contents inside. Erroll pulled out the poles and cloth and the packs of food that they had packed. He set the food aside and stared at the disassembled tent in his hands, having no clue how to put it together.

Geser left his spot to go speak to some of his friends from another group, but Khalja had already begun setting up his tent. Then he noticed Erroll sitting dumbfounded with the tent materials in his hands.

He laughed and set down his poles, walking over to Erroll's spot.

"Having trouble?" he said.

"Not at all," Erroll said, though he could not bring himself to meet Khalja's eyes.

"Okay, you're clearly out of your depth," Khalja said, taking the poles from Erroll's hands.

"Hey!" Erroll tried to grab them back, but Khalja had already begun to stick them into the earth.

"It's easy once you've got the hang of it, don't worry."

"Yes, but I can do it myself." Erroll was on his feet now, but Khalja wouldn't budge. He was about to push Khalja aside when the entire camp fell silent.

Erroll looked up and saw that hunters were getting up from what they were doing and gathering at the clearing's center. Khalja motioned for Erroll to follow, dropping the tent poles and leading Erroll to the gathering.

"What's happening?" Erroll asked Khalja.

Khalja didn't answer as they took their positions near the back of the crowd. Erroll realized that the camp had fallen completely silent. Without the sound of hunters sparring, tending their weapons, or chatting, the place felt as though something had sucked the life out of it.

Erroll tiptoed so that he could see above the crowd and saw that they had formed a semicircle around Temulun, who was standing alone. Temulun scanned the crowd until she was sure that everyone was there, and then she began.

"Today, we stand on the monument to those of us that we lost to the plague, more than ten years ago," she said.

He looked around and noticed that the strange patches of earth he'd noticed earlier looked roughly around the size of a person. They weren't standing on a secret campsite, but on a graveyard.

Temulun continued. "They have long passed into the wind, but they remain with us, in the grass, in the soil, in the empty hills. We have not forgotten."

"We have not forgotten," the hunters repeated.

"As I speak their names, we hope that Gaeon will grace the winds with their memory," Temulun said. "May they ride with us as we face our enemies in the coming days."

Temulun began reciting a long list of names that Erroll didn't recognize, but he noticed some of the other hunters in the crowd bow their heads when they heard certain names. Though the graves they stood on were old and covered with grass, the tears that the names spawned were still fresh.

Then Temulun came to the end of her recitation. Over two hundred names had been spoken, but none of the hunters made any noise throughout the ceremony. As she finished, one name caught Erroll's ear.

"...Qoribucha, Temujin, Chuluun, Erwan, Jegu, Kuyuk. May Gaeon ride with them all."

Erroll froze.

"Gaeon ride with you," the gathering repeated, but Erroll did not register it at all. He tried to steady his breathing and pushed his way to the front of the crowd as it began to disperse.

"What did you say?" he said as he arrived at the front of the crowd.

Temulun stopped her conversation with Geser and turned to him. "Yes?" she said. "Is there something you need?"

"That name you said," Erroll said. "Erwan. Did I hear that correctly?"

"Yes, you heard me," Temulun said, raising an eyebrow. "Why? Did you know Erwan?"

"I did," Erroll said. "He died twenty years ago by General Sandulf's order in Ruson."

"That can't be right," Temulun said. "I knew Erwan. He was a good friend, but he died of the plague ten years ago in this very camp."

"You knew him? Did he say where he was from?"

"Of course he did. He was from the Empire, but he defected during the war. Did you know him?"

"Erwan was my father," Erroll said.

Temulun's eyes widened. "Geser, why don't you handle that matter on your own? It seems that Erroll and I have much to discuss."

# 22

# Sara

Sara took reports from Ganbold and Khulan from the top of a hill overlooking the river. The Empire's legions and the Asjare hunters had mobilized in force across the river, and it was clear what their intentions were. The battle for Harnda was about to begin.

"Our hunters are nearly in position," Ganbold said. "We are meant to fight on the right flank and support the center of the army."

"Make sure that the hunters stay in their hunting groups. I don't want to leave any stragglers for the Empire to pick off," Sara said. "Does Bataar have his orders?"

"He's on standby," Khulan said. "I can send a rider to him at any moment and he'll begin the evacuation."

"Good," Sara said. "It's just a precaution, but the way things are going, I want to be absolutely sure."

Khulan nodded. Though she did not mean to, she glanced towards the central hill where the Chenkah and Gur forces formed the central bulk of their army.

"You sure we can trust those two? The only battle experience they've got is fighting each other," Khulan said.

"We've got no choice," Sara said. "They have the largest armies in the Steppe. If they decided to leave the alliance, we'd be destroyed in an instant."

With the Chenkah and Gur forces, they had put together a sizable army. Every hunter they could muster was on that plain. It was certainly larger than any nomad force that had gathered since the first war with the Empire. As Sara scanned the legions that the Empire had put together, she doubted that it would be enough.

line of hunters looked more like a quivering bowstring than a solid wall.

She would have to do this herself.

"Yargai, Mide, Kara," Sara called. "Come with me!"

Kara rode towards Sara immediately, but Yargai approached on foot, leading two horses: his own, and another one carrying a fallen Mide with an arrow in his neck.

"Saenor's scales," Sara said quietly, then she shook her head. "Get on your horse, Yargai. Now!"

Yargai's lip was quivering and Sara could see that his cheeks were slick with tears. Sara got off her horse and grabbed Yargai's shoulder.

"There's nothing you can do for him now," she said, shaking him. "But there are still people we can save. We need to go now."

Yargai nodded slowly and dropped the reins of Mide's horse. He got on his own, but Sara could see his hands shaking as he did. It would have to do. Sara got on her own horse and took her eagle's eyes. She could see Ganbold's reserve group putting up a valiant fight on the flank, but the Empire's soldiers were threatening to overwhelm them.

"Just in time," she said, and she called for her hunters to follow as she rode to Ganbold's rescue.


Sara and her hunters dove into the enemy ranks like a whirlwind. She heard Yargai and Kara crash into the enemy a few seconds after she did, but she was unable to pay them any mind. For a few moments, it was only her and the company of soldiers that she had leapt into.

Her horse bounded into the enemies, two of them falling to her sword the moment she did. They obviously had not expected a horse-mounted opponent to attack them so directly, so the rest of them backed off, raising their shields. Kara and Yargai arrived moments later, and they swept around themselves with their swords, felling soldier after soldier, until a pile of corpses grew at their feet.

Then the enemy ranks began to close. The scattered Empire soldiers finally stood at attention, raising their shields and getting into battle formation. Sara heard their captain barking orders at them from behind and they began to advance on the trio.

"Time's up," Sara said, giving Kara and Yargai the signal. As quickly as they came, they leapt out of range of the enemy infantry, breaking a half-formed shield line as they escaped.

Sara looked behind her to gauge how well they had done. They had managed to slay about twenty soldiers. It was barely a quarter of the square that they had assaulted, but they had managed to disrupt the enemy's formation for just long enough.

"Ganbold! Now!" Sara cried, and Ganbold's archers fired volley after volley into the enemy, who no longer had their shields ready to protect them from the barrage. About half of the enemy fell under the first barrage. Once they saw their comrades fall, including their captain, the soldiers were in full retreat, abandoning their posts and fleeing towards the river.

With the Omnu line secure, Ganbold's reserve forces and the remaining hunters reformed the line again, watching as two more infantry companies advanced towards them.

"What's the situation here?" Sara asked.

Ganbold pointed. "We've had heavy attacks from the Empire on this side. More than the rest of the army. I assume that they're trying to break our flank."

Sara cursed. "The main army isn't doing so well, either."

"We need Khulan's reserve forces," Ganbold said as the hunters engaged the companies. "I don't know how long we can survive out here."

"Can't do that," Sara said. "I've sent Khulan to help Chanar."

Ganbold did nothing more than nod, though Sara expected a stronger reaction. "We'll have to make do, then."

Then he rode back to his allies, taking out his sword as the companies crashed into their hunters. The Omnu fought like leopards leaping at

"Still," Ganbold said. "They ought to know that you're the most capable commander the Steppe has right now."

"They probably know that," Khulan said. "But those old farts would never listen. And they'll be the death of us."

"We could still refuse to follow their orders," Ganbold said. "I think we'll have a better chance of survival if we raid the Empire's forces instead of charging straight in."

"Enough," Sara said. "I don't like it either. But we agreed to these plans, so by Gaeon, we'll follow them. No more complaining."

Khulan and Ganbold looked at her in surprise. Even she had not realized that the past few months had made her into more of a leader than she'd ever expected.

"Of course, Sara," Khulan said.

"Apologies," Ganbold said, fingering the hilt of his sword.

"You have your orders," Sara said. "Go."

Khulan and Ganbold nodded. Without another word, they spurred their horses onwards to catch up to their soldiers, leaving Sara alone on the hilltop. The Omnu hunters gathered around the base of the hill, and Sara could see them staring expectantly at her. There were more of them than she was used to. Over the past few weeks, their numbers had swelled with refugees slowly trickling in from the Omnu lands, expanding to include any man or woman in the camp who could ride a horse and hold a sword.

Many of them were untested or had come fresh from defeat. They were waiting for their chieftain to lead them to victory. Truth be told, Sara felt more unqualified than ever. She had never fought a battle on this scale before. Hunting and tracking deer across the Steppe was much different from facing down the Empire. but she wasn't going to let them see her fear.

Today, she could no longer be Sara, the scared and uncertain hunter. She had to be Saragerel, daughter of Julian and their chieftain. At that moment, three hunters ascended the hill to join her.

Kara, Yargai, and Mide. The members of her original hunting

group. It was the same group that had trusted her as their leader for years. She didn't know if she could lead their entire tribe, but at the very least, she would keep this group alive. Perhaps that would be enough.

Yargai passed them each a pouch of manna. It was the last of their supply, but they had nothing left to lose. She took out some powder from the pouch and sprinkled it on her horse's mane. She felt its fear, its anger, and its anticipation. Running her hand over its mane, she whispered softly to it.

"We're going to be okay, pal," she said, trying to muster up enough bravery for the both of them. Then she turned to her hunters.

"Do you trust me?" she asked.

They appeared to be shocked at the question, but they did not hesitate.

"Of course, Sara," Mide said.

"Good. We'll get through today," she said. "I'll make sure of it."

With that, she closed her eyes and took to the skies, watching from the eyes of her eagle as two riders left the central hill where Chanar and Thaube were leading their armies. One headed to the Harnda side of the army and the other approached Sara's position. She already knew what the orders would be.

She cast her eyes towards the enemy as horns blared across the Serpent's River. Slowly, the soldiers on the banks of the river began to advance; the Asjare hunters were distributed in groups throughout the enemy ranks. And so the battle began, with the blaring of horns, the thumping of metal feet on grass, and the crashing of hooves across empty hills.

Sara crossed blades with an Asjare hunter. She could feel his strength as they locked blades. They traded blows for a few moments, and finally, Sara managed to get the upper hand. She swept aside his thrust and returned with her own blade, sinking deep into his chest.

He fell off his horse and died before he hit the ground.

Her instincts told her to charge further into the fray, but she held back, letting Yargai and Kara take care of the rest of the Asjare hunters that had broken past their lines. Soon, Khulan arrived with the reserve force, and the Asjare were forced to fall back.

A volley of arrows launched from the Omnu hunters, falling more of the Empire's soldiers before hunters swept in, swords flashing crimson before the Empire gained their footing and forced them backwards.

Sara called out a few commands and riders carried her orders down the line. They needed to make sure not to overexert themselves, lest they be trapped in the swarm of enemies.

"How's the rest of the line?" she asked Khulan as she drew out her bow and began taking aim at the ranks of Empire soldiers.

"Fine, mostly," Khulan said, taking out her own bow. Her face and hair were slick with sweat from riding up and down the Omnu line, and she was almost out of arrows. "Ganbold's group is managing to keep them from forming a shield line. But the Asjare hunters are holding up the main army and the Harnda are too busy securing the river to be of help."

Sara looked past the Omnu hunters to look over at the Chenkah and Gur, who had split their army equally between cavalry and infantry groups. The mounted soldiers crashed into the Empire's ranks and took down large swathes of enemies, but Asjare sent their own hunters to force their retreat before they could advance further. The enemy held their ground.

As Sara scanned the huge sea of Empire soldiers spread out before them, including the reserve forces and the walls of shields and pikes that began to form in front of the main army, she realized that the Empire would sacrifice however many of their soldiers they needed to win. The nomads, however, did not have any hunters to spare.

A rider wearing Chenkah armor approached Sara and Khulan. From the way he was panting, Sara assumed that he had come all the way from Chanar, who was commanding his army from a small hill in the middle of the carnage.

"The main army needs reinforcement," the rider said. "Our progress has stalled and our reserves are faltering."

"We don't have hunters to spare," Khulan said, gesturing at the thinning line of Omnu hunters.

"Hold on, Khulan," Sara said, stepping in front of her friend. "How many hunters did Chanar ask for?"

"Twenty-five should be enough," the rider said.

"I can give you fifteen," Sara said, then she turned to Khulan. "That's you, Khulan. Take the reserve group and help them."

But Khulan was already shaking her head. "I won't abandon you, Sara. Our hunters need us."

"Yes you will, Khulan," Sara said. "That's an order. We won't abandon our allies when they need it the most."

Khulan nodded, then called out a few commands. Soon, her hunters were following the Chenkah hunter back into the main army. Sara saw her reach into her pouch and sprinkle the last remnants of manna she had onto her horse. Khulan whispered a few words to her horse and they were off.

It was then that an Omnu hunter approached her, right as Sara managed to regain enough of her composure to survey the Omnu lines again.

"What is it now?" she asked, but then her irritation faded when she saw the hunter's face covered with blood and her quiver completely empty.

"A message from Ganbold," the hunter said. "The enemy managed to break through, and the rightmost flank is beginning to falter. We'll be surrounded before long."

Sara nodded and looked at the group of hunters surrounding her. Their steady advance had ground to a halt. Instead of moving in to break the enemy lines, the Omnu hunters had to retreat to prevent themselves from being overrun. From where she was standing, the line of hunters looked more like a quivering bowstring than a solid wall.

She would have to do this herself.

"Yargai, Mide, Kara," Sara called. "Come with me!"

Kara rode towards Sara immediately, but Yargai approached on foot, leading two horses: his own, and another one carrying a fallen Mide with an arrow in his neck.

"Saenor's scales," Sara said quietly, then she shook her head. "Get on your horse, Yargai. Now!"

Yargai's lip was quivering and Sara could see that his cheeks were slick with tears. Sara got off her horse and grabbed Yargai's shoulder.

"There's nothing you can do for him now," she said, shaking him. "But there are still people we can save. We need to go now."

Yargai nodded slowly and dropped the reins of Mide's horse. He got on his own, but Sara could see his hands shaking as he did. It would have to do. Sara got on her own horse and took her eagle's eyes. She could see Ganbold's reserve group putting up a valiant fight on the flank, but the Empire's soldiers were threatening to overwhelm them.

"Just in time," she said, and she called for her hunters to follow as she rode to Ganbold's rescue.


Sara and her hunters dove into the enemy ranks like a whirlwind. She heard Yargai and Kara crash into the enemy a few seconds after she did, but she was unable to pay them any mind. For a few moments, it was only her and the company of soldiers that she had leapt into.

Her horse bounded into the enemies, two of them falling to her sword the moment she did. They obviously had not expected a horse-mounted opponent to attack them so directly, so the rest of them backed off, raising their shields. Kara and Yargai arrived moments later, and they swept around themselves with their swords, felling soldier after soldier, until a pile of corpses grew at their feet.

Then the enemy ranks began to close. The scattered Empire soldiers finally stood at attention, raising their shields and getting into battle formation. Sara heard their captain barking orders at them from behind and they began to advance on the trio.

"Time's up," Sara said, giving Kara and Yargai the signal. As quickly as they came, they leapt out of range of the enemy infantry, breaking a half-formed shield line as they escaped.

Sara looked behind her to gauge how well they had done. They had managed to slay about twenty soldiers. It was barely a quarter of the square that they had assaulted, but they had managed to disrupt the enemy's formation for just long enough.

"Ganbold! Now!" Sara cried, and Ganbold's archers fired volley after volley into the enemy, who no longer had their shields ready to protect them from the barrage. About half of the enemy fell under the first barrage. Once they saw their comrades fall, including their captain, the soldiers were in full retreat, abandoning their posts and fleeing towards the river.

With the Omnu line secure, Ganbold's reserve forces and the remaining hunters reformed the line again, watching as two more infantry companies advanced towards them.

"What's the situation here?" Sara asked.

Ganbold pointed. "We've had heavy attacks from the Empire on this side. More than the rest of the army. I assume that they're trying to break our flank."

Sara cursed. "The main army isn't doing so well, either."

"We need Khulan's reserve forces," Ganbold said as the hunters engaged the companies. "I don't know how long we can survive out here."

"Can't do that," Sara said. "I've sent Khulan to help Chanar."

Ganbold did nothing more than nod, though Sara expected a stronger reaction. "We'll have to make do, then."

Then he rode back to his allies, taking out his sword as the companies crashed into their hunters. The Omnu fought like leopards leaping at prey, letting no mistake go unpunished; enemy soldiers fell as quickly as trees did in the storm. It would not be enough. Sara saw a few more companies split off from the main army to attack the nomads' flank.

She didn't even notice as two riders approached her, one from the Harnda and the other from the Chenkah. When she turned to face them, they both started speaking at once.

"Chief, Harnda forces are trapped…"

"A sudden new force of enemies…"

Sara raised a hand to silence them. Then she pointed at the Harnda messenger, taking a moment to recognize her.

"Alaqa. Speak first."

She nodded. "A sudden new group of enemies emerged from the mountains. They're Asjare hunters by the look of it, and it's a huge force, perhaps a hundred of them. We have no idea where they came from, but they've cut off the Harnda hunters from the rest of the army. Zayaat is trying to make his way through them, but he's abandoned his goal of securing the river."

Sara nodded. Then she pointed at the Gur rider.

"The Chenkah are in full retreat. The moment they saw the Asjare hunters, their flanks broke and Head Chieftain Chanar ordered them to fall back. Gur hunters are now facing enemies on two fronts, and they're falling fast. The Harnda can't do anything since they're surrounded themselves. Chief Thaube asks for the Omnu's support."

Sara looked around her, seeing the Omnu lines beginning to falter. Thaube probably didn't expect her to come at all.

"Please help us," the Gur rider said. "You're the only chance we've got."

His voice caught in his throat and there were tears in his eyes. She knew that Gur hunters have endured tough training since childhood, so she could not imagine what kind of horrors the Gur were facing at this moment, such that they would be brought to tears.

"What's your name?" she asked him.

"Osol," he said.

"Don't worry, Osol," Sara said. "I'm going to save your people."

She turned away then summoned Ganbold, Yargai, and Kara.

"Yargai, I need you to ride to Bataar. Tell him to get everyone out of the camps."

Yargai nodded, spreading manna on his horse's neck. Like a lightning bolt, he was gone.

"What about the rest of us, Sara?" Ganbold said.

Sara shook her head. "I'm sorry, Ganbold. But our allies asked for our help. And so we will answer."

Again, she expected him to protest, but he only nodded. "We're with you, then."

"Thank you," she said. "Give the order. I want every hunting group to ride with me to the Gur. Go!"

Ganbold left to spread the word and Sara watched him leave. He did not question her for a second, despite both of them knowing that she had just sealed the fates of every Omnu hunter they had.


Sara broke through the enemy lines and emerged into the clearing that the Gur were holding. Her sword was dripping with blood and her arm felt like it was about to fall off, but they made it.

Her hunters followed after her, leaping through the small gap they had created before the enemy ranks closed around them. They had managed to take the enemy by surprise, since they had assumed that the Asjare hunters would be enough to stop them.

The Gur hunters were arranged in a circle in the center of the clearing, mounted hunters with swords in front and hunters on foot with bows near the back. The Empire surrounded them on all sides, but they were beaten back each time they tried to advance on the Gur.

The Gur parted their ranks to make way for Sara's forces. She found Thaube commanding the remnants of his army from the center of their circle.

"Ganbold, make sure their defences are secure," Sara said, but then she looked around and realized that he wasn't there. "Where's Ganbold?"

"He fell," Kara said, pointing to a place past the enemy ranks where a few Omnu  hunters were caught by some Empire soldiers. Sara squinted but she could barely make out Ganbold's form lying underneath his horse. She couldn't tell if he was still breathing, but deep down, she hoped that he wasn't.

"No, oh, Ganbold, no," Sara said, soft enough that only she could hear.

She looked at the Omnu hunters that had gathered around her and wished that she could leave them behind and cut a path through the enemy to save Ganbold. She froze and her insides boiled with anger and pain. Everything inside her wanted to ride out and save him.

But instead, she took a deep breath and turned back to Kara.

"Kara, I guess you're in charge, then," Sara said slowly. "I need you to make sure the Gur defences are secure. Can you do that for me?"

"Of course," Kara said. "But...are you okay, Sara?"

"I'm fine," Sara said, though she could feel tears build behind her eyes. "There's nothing we can do for him. But there are still people we can save."

Kara nodded, then she began shouting commands at the rest of the Omnu hunters. The Gur seemed relieved to see the Omnu hunters join them, but their faces fell when they saw how few of them there were. Compared to the might of the Empire surrounding them, their support seemed like nothing

Thaube's eyes widened as Sara approached him. The old veteran was bleeding in several places on his arm His voice sounded raw from screaming, but he kept up the fight. A huge battle-axe was thrust into the ground next to him, covered with blood.

"You came," he said.

"Of course I did. You called, didn't you?" Sara said. She looked around and saw Khulan and a few more Omnu hunters holding the line to the south. Khulan met her eyes and left the frontline to approach the center.

Khulan grinned despite being covered in blood. "I knew you'd be here. Thaube didn't think so, but I did. And here you are."

"You have riders?" Sara asked.

"Some," Khulan said.

"Good. I'll need all of them." Then she turned to Thaube. "I'm going to get your hunters out of here, Chief Thaube."

Sara started to walk away to inspect their remaining forces, but Thaube caught her on the shoulder.

"Why are you doing this? Why are you helping me?" he asked. "I tried at every turn to take power away from you. If you left me to die here, you could take control of the rest of the alliance."

Sara frowned. "Because this is about more than just you or me, Thaube. We need to face this threat together, and every hunter we save is a step towards a stronger alliance."

Thaube nodded and took a deep breath. He picked up his axe. "Thank you, Saragerel. I had my doubts about you at first, but Julian couldn't have raised a better daughter. Tell me what you need."

Sara smiled. "First of all, call me Sara. Second, I want all of your best hunters to join Khulan's. You're going to use them to pierce through the enemy ranks. Anyone else who's too wounded or too tired should get on a horse and prepare to move."

Thaube nodded. "What will you do?"

"If you try to get out of here, you'll expose your backs to enemy archers. I'll stay here and hold the enemy back long enough for you to escape."

Thaube looked like he was about to protest, but he seemed to understand. "Gaeon ride with you."

He left to cordinate his hunters, and Kara approached Sara.

"This won't end well for us, will it?" Kara said.

"No it won't," Sara said. "Thaube's hunters are bent to the point of breaking. They won't last much longer. That means that our hunters will have to stay behind."

Kara sighed. "You should get out while you can, then. The tribe needs you."

Sara shook her head. "I could never do that. Not in a million years."

"But…"

"End of discussion, Kara," Sara said. "The tribe will survive without me. Khulan and Bataar are more than capable."

Kara nodded and left to organize the hunters.

Sara realized she was alone with a vortex of fighting that had erupted around her. She only had a few moments before she would need to act again. She watched as the seemingly endless sea of enemies spread out before her. She wanted to run and hide, but she knew that there was only one thing for her to do. Sara took a deep breath and drew her sword.

She ran her hand through her horse's mane, but she didn't have any manna left to soothe the fear running through both of them. It would have to do.

"This one's for you, Od," she whispered.

Then in the distance, horns began to blare. Sara recognized the sound. Sara listened as they sounded the arrival of a nomad army and breathed a deep sigh of relief.

# 23

# Batu

"You didn't tell us that we'd be arriving in the middle of a battle," Galeren said to Batu as they emerged on top of a hill overlooking the Harnda fields.

Cirina and Bala emerged next to Batu, both of them blowing their horns as loud as they could. Batu hoped that they were not too late.

Batu shrugged. "You knew a battle was coming. It just happened to take place sooner than later."

Galeren sighed. "I suppose you're right, kid." Then she called over a few of her captians. "Our first priority should be getting aid to the hunters trapped in the middle of the enemy's main army. Send the vanguard there immediately, then follow up with our reserves."

"Yes, Lady Herald," a captain answered and galloped off.

"I want the rest of our forces to split into two. One should take the enemy's main army head on. Send our strongest infantry units and some horse archers to harry their flanks. The second group should reinforce that group of Harnda hunters along the river. Secure the riverbank to make sure the enemy can't escape north to Asjare territory, but allow them to flee northeast to the Omnu lands."

The captains nodded and left immediately, sending riders to carry Galeren's commands across the army.

Batu found himself in awe whenever he watched Galeren take command. She exercised her sharp intellect even in times of chaos. It was no wonder her people thought she was an avatar of Gaeon. On the other hand, the Qhurin army comprised a mix of infantry and cavalry; instead of them doubling as hunters, the Qhurin troops were full-time soldiers. The horse-mounted fighters were the only ones allowed to carry manna, which was rationed strictly by Galeren's captains from a central supply.

Galeren left and Nugai approached from behind, looking around as he did to make sure none of her priests were still around.

"Finally," Nugai said. "I didn't think the old hag would ever leave you alone."

"That old hag just saved the Steppe," Batu said.

"She's just in the right place at the right time. Same as she's always done. You ask me, the real heroes are whoever's still fighting down there."

Nugai pointed at the battlefield where a small circle of nomads were keeping up a fight against a sea of Empire soldiers. There was another group still fighting along the river, but the fighting there was evenly matched. The rest of the nomad army was either dead or fleeing across the Steppe and the Harnda camps were burning, the Empire soldiers pillaging as they advanced on the nomads.

The scene reminded Batu of his own camp a few months ago during the Battle of Orange Sky—the battle where his father had fallen. Batu was about to order his hunters to ride into the burning camp, but then he realized that it was empty. All the nomads had already fled to the outskirts of Harnda territory, where the Chenkah and Gur tents were located.

"I wonder who those crazy bastards are," Nugai said, pointing to the outnumbered group of hunters.

"You know what?" Batu said. "I'd bet that it's Saragerel. She's the only one in this army with the balls to keep fighting even when it's clear that she'll lose."

Nugai laighed. "That's true. I can respect that. Can't see old Chanar or Thaube having that kind of courage."

Then the Qhurin horns blew. Just as Galeren had ordered, the soldiers began spilling into the plains, taking the pressure off the beleaguered nomads. The Empire itself seemed to forget about them and instead started to form ranks to face the advancing Qhurin forces. Galeren herself would be commanding her forces a little behind the front line with dozens of riders ready to send to any part of the army, while field captains would be leading their own sections of the army with their own groups of messengers.

Horns began to sound across the plain as the armies clashed. Batu looked around him and found his hunters gathered around him: Nugai, Cirina, Bala, Dorgene, and Jochi, all with their weapons drawn.

"I suppose we ought to join, too," Batu said, drawing his bow and adjusting his quiver.


Batu walked through the burnt ruins of the Harnda camps. He stepped on the charred canvas of what looked like a butcher's tent and found the equipment still lying underneath.

Butcher's knives, animal carcasses, and even a few crates that they would bury if they needed the meat to stay fresh for longer. It seemed as though he was walking through a memory of a camp, poorly rendered and about to fade. When he knelt and tried to pick up another tent, the canvas broke apart in his hands.

"What are you doing here?" a voice said from behind him.

When Batu looked behind him, he saw Saragerel. She was taller than she had been when they met at his mother's funeral. Instead of letting her hair flow around her shoulders, it hung in a ponytail across her back. He knew the stare she gave him well. It was the same one she had given him when he faced her a few weeks ago, and it made him wish he could sink into the ground.

Batu did his best to stand his ground. Her armor was bloody and torn from the battle. From the way she quivered like a tree worn thin by storms, it seemed as though she might collapse at any moment. And yet, she still terrified him.

"I could ask you the same question. Herald Galeren told me that you were overseeing the medical corps," he said.

Saragerel shrugged. "Zayaat and Khulan are overseeing them now. They told me to get some rest or else they'd drag me to my tent. So I don't have anything else to do at the moment."

Before he could speak again, she said, "I thought I told you to leave the camp. There are some that would have me kill you."

"I traveled across the Steppe to do what the Harnda couldn't. I got the Qhurin on our side and I've fixed your manna shortage problem. Wouldn't that have earned me at least some forgiveness?"

Saragerel paused for a few moments as Batu waited for her response with his fists clenched. Then, inexplicably, she smiled and gave a small chuckle.

"I'm sorry. I suppose you're right. It's just… I never thought I'd end up being saved by the man who was ordered to kill me a few months ago."

"Well, here I am. Now, will you finally accept my help?"

Sara scratched her chin. "I guess I was wrong about you, Batu. You risked your neck to save someone that threw you out. You're not your father's son at all."

"I used to be," Batu said. "I think I still am. But I'm trying to figure out what that means on my own terms."

He was not sure if he was making much sense, but Saragerel seemed to understand. She nodded. "Apology accepted. My father taught me that holding a grudge is like drinking poison and hoping someone else will die as a result. Your hunters can stay in the camps as long as they like."

Batu breathed a sigh of relief. "It appears that I'm in your debt again, Saragerel."

Saragerel walked over and patted him on the shoulder. "If you ever threaten me or anyone I love ever again, I can just as easily cast you out. Remember that."

Batu bit his lip he nodded. Saragerel seemed satisfied. She turned and walked away, leaving him in the middle of the burning camp.

But Batu was barely paying attention. "Not my father's son, eh?" he muttered to himself. He smiled. In his mind, his father's voice grew a little quieter.

# 24
# Erroll

Erroll sat on the edges of the mountain camp, watching as the last of the Asjare hunters returned from the battle. They were only a tiny fraction of those that had left the camp. He had never seen death on this scale before. Despite how much he told himself that he was prepared for it, he felt like he was hovering just outside of his body with a fog gathering around his vision.

They had been on the cusp of victory. They were just about to overrun the Harnda camps and send all the rest of them fleeing, but then the horns had sounded and the damned Qhurin had arrived. The Asjare had been caught right in the middle, with no place to run. But the Empire had managed to retreat just fine. Though Erroll was one of them, he couldn't help but be angry at their cowardice. If they had stayed and fought, maybe some of his friends would still be alive.

Khalja arrived with a group of hunters that Erroll did not recognize. Though he was without his horse or any of his weapons and tending a bruised shoulder, he otherwise was whole. He collapsed next to Erroll, who was unscathed save for the spear that he had lost while trying to flee the battlefield.

"Geser?" Khalja asked.

Erroll shook his head but he couldn't meet Khalja's eyes. Instead, his eyes followed the trail leading from the battlefield into the mountain camp.

"By Saenor," Khalja muttered to himself. "We shouldn't have allowed our group to be separated. How could Temulun let this happen?"

"It was the only thing to do," Erroll said. "She made a judgement call. She chose to save some of us rather than let all of us die. It's simple math."

Khalja grabbed Erroll by the collar of his shirt and forced Erroll to meet his eyes.

"Simple math?" he said, each word like an arrow. "She died to keep you alive and you call it mathematics?"

Erroll held up his hands. "I misspoke. I'm sorry."

Khalja released him. "I know. I'm sorry too. We're all just a little on edge, aren't we? I just... I've never lost so many people in one day. It's too much."

Khalja buried his head in his hands and wept quietly to himself, heaving as his sobs encompassed his entire body. Erroll didn't know what to do. Khalja had seemed like a giant when Erroll first met him, strong enough to crush stone and defeat an army of horses. But now, he looked no more imposing than a stray squirrel.

"What happens now?" Erroll finally asked when Khalja seemed to pull himself together.

"No clue," Khalja said. "But Dayir will have a lot to answer for. He told us that the Empire would protect us, but we were abandoned once things went sour."

"Damn cowards," Erroll said. He remembered the feeling of helplessness as the Empire retreated back across the river, leaving the remaining Asjare hunters to get surrounded by the enemy. And of course, Temulun had ordered them to fight their way out. Erroll was prepared to throw down his weapons immediately, but Temulun did not consider it for a second. She fought with the ferocity of a tiger till the very end.

Erroll still did not know what to feel about— he had looked up to Temulun. He had come to respect all the hunters he had fought with and even considered many of them friends, even though they were savages. But now, so many of them were dead.

"The only way out of this is to throw down our weapons and hope the Omnu let us into their alliance," Khalja said. "There's nothing else for us to do."

Erroll felt himself freeze. Losing the Asjare and the Arban Valley now would be disastrous for the Empire, who relied on the Asjare to scout ahead and alert them to enemy raids.

"Do you think that Dayir will actually do that?"

"Definitely not," Khalja said. "He's too proud of himself, and he hates the Omnu with a burning passion. Never mind that Chinua's dead and it's Saragerel in charge now."

"Why does that matter?"

"Chinua was the one who restricted passage to the Temple of Gaeon from the rest of the tribes. That was the main reason why Dayir chose to defect. But the rumors say that Saragerel is willing to grant the rest of the tribes safe passage to the Temple. Once it's retaken from the Empire, of course."

Erroll nodded. "So, there's no longer any point in this alliance."

"The way I see it, yes," Khalja said. "Well, the Empire still has the Temple, but if the Qhurin are on the Omnu's side now, they can just as easily get their manna from the Spring of Onoe. It's only a matter of time before the Asjare get caught in the middle."

"What are you going to do about it then?" Erroll said. He needed to figure out if Khalja was the only one feeling this way, or if they had an uprising in their hands. Sandulf had to be prepared for the nomads breaking their promises right underneath their noses.

"Nothing," Khalja said. "I'm just a common hunter, and if the head chief has got a problem with the Omnu, then we're fighting them instead. That's all we are, aren't we? Just minions that they're willing to sacrifice."

"No, Khalja," Erroll said, suddenly reaching out and gripping Khalja's arm. "We're more than that."

Khalja smirked as Erroll bit his lip. He still wasn't sure why he had said that, but Khalja chuckled. "Thanks for that, Erroll, but I've been a hunter long enough to know my place in this world. Maybe it's time for you to start learning that as well."

# III

# Howling Wind

# 25
# Sara

The war council felt different to Sara today. Since the Harnda war pavillion was destroyed in the battle, the chiefs and masters of hunters met on one of the hills between Harnda and Gur territory, far enough for the smoke burning on the battlefield could be ignored.

But the plumes of smoke still rose into the sky far in the distance. Instead of a bustling camp, the plain had rudimentary field camps filled with displaced nomads and wounded hunters.

"The first thing we have to figure out is how to rebuild the camps," Ibakha said immediately.

"How much supplies do you have?" Galeren said. The fierce old Herald of Qhurin was a new face at their meetings. Instead of attending with her masters of hunters, she brought two men dressed in long cloaks. Priests, she called them.

"Enough for about half of our people," Ibakha said. "Then we also have the Omnu to worry about."

"I can spare some extra tents and supplies, though it will take time to bring them from Qhurin. Manna as well, before anyone asks," Galeren said.

"I can send a group of hunters to bring them here," Sara said.

Galeren eyed her. Sara still was not quite sure what to make of the woman. She still wondered what Batu said that convinced her to bring her entire army to battle.

"That's very generous of you," Galeren said. "Though perhaps it would be more convenient if the tribes that own land bordering the Harnda could provide their own supplies."

She glared at Chanar and Thaube, who up till then were both sitting on the outer edges of the circle and staring at the ground.

"We should have some supplies to spare," Thaube said.

"So do we," Chanar said.

"How long will it take to bring them here?" Ibakha said.

Chanar exchanged a look with his master of hunters. "About four days," he said.

"Do it in two," Galeren snapped. Chanar flinched. "It's the least you can do, after all you've done. And don't think I've forgotten about you, Thaube. I've agreed to a truce between the Qhurin and Gur, but I'll think about breaking it if the Gur show even the slightest inclination that they're not committed to this alliance."

Chanar opened his mouth to protest, but Thaube cut him off.

"Of course, Lady Herald," Thaube said. "We're grateful for all you've done for us. The peace between us will be upheld. You'll have the supplies in two days. I guarantee it."

Chanar folded his arms. When he looked around, however, he realized that he no longer had a leg to stand on in these meetings. He nodded and whispered to his master of hunters.

"It'll be done," he said quietly.

"I'll send a message detailing the supplies we need," Sara said.

"Splendid," Ibakha said, giving Sara and Galeren a sly smile, as though the three of them were sharing an inside joke. "The next order of business will be our follow-up. If our scouts can be trusted, about three quarters of the Empire's army is still standing, though they're busy licking their wounds."

"We should hit them hard," Thaube said. "Attack them while they're weak and put an end to this."

"In case you haven't noticed, we took heavy losses in the battle as well," Zayaat said. "What have we decided to call it? The Battle of the Rivers?"

"That's what the hunters are starting to call it. And we'll take more losses if we don't strike now," Thaube said.

"Our hunters are tired," Sara said. "They've fought too many battles and they've lost many of their friends. How could you put them through another battle, Thaube?"

When Sara spoke, the entire council seemed to fall silent. Zayaat nodded, and even Chanar seemed to agree.

"That's reasonable," Galeren said. "But there must be something we can do."

"We can send hunters into the Omnu lands," Chanar said. "Disrupt their supply lines. Raid their camps."

"We've already been doing that, for all the good it's done us," Zayaat said. "The Empire's caught on, and now their convoys are heavily guarded. It'll take more than a small hunting group to crack those open."

"The Temple," Sara said, and again, all eyes turned on her. She took a deep breath, but she refused to let them intimidate her again. Not after everything she has been through. "The Empire still controls it, and as long as they have the Temple, they have the Asjare in their pocket. We can send a scouting party there and plan to retake it."

"I like the way you think," Galeren said, grinning. One of her priests leaned forward to whisper in her ear, but she waved him away. "Whenever our people faced their greatest hardships, they sought the guidance of Gaeon, and he showed them the way forward. Plus, the extra manna will be of help."

Galeren winked at Sara. Sara noticed Khulan roll her eyes beside her, but she did her best to ignore her. "Of course, Lady Herald."

"I can support that," Zayaat said. "With the Empire's forces in disarray, we should be able to send a small group across Omnu territory to visit the Temple. If we have the Asjare on our side, the Empire will think twice about challenging us again."

"The question is, who will go?" Ibakha said.

"Neither of those two, that's for sure," Galeren said, pointing at Chanar and Thaube.

"I can do it," Sara said.

"Don't be absurd," Galeren said. "You're needed here."

"I'm Julian's daughter. It makes sense for me to go."

Galeren shook her head. "I'm sorry, child, but this place would fall apart without you. No offense intended to the rest, of course."

"She's right, you know," Khulan said.

Sara looked between Khulan and Galeren, then she nodded. "Fine. But then who else can make the journey?"

"As far as I remember, two Omnu chiefs traveled there during the First War, didn't they?" Ibakha said.

"They did," Zayaat said. "And Chinua's kid is here too, isn't he?"

"It's settled, then," Galeren said. "We'll send Batu to the Temple, then the rest of us will figure out how to find the Harnda and Omnu a place to sleep."

On that, Galeren got up from her seat and left, even though no one else making any moves to leave. One of her priests followed her, but the other one stayed behind.

"Apologies. But the Lady Herald despises long meetings," the priest said, then he left to catch up with Galeren.

Ibakha laughed. "Honestly, I can understand that. I guess that ends the war council."


"I wonder what Ganbold would say if he knew what we were doing," Sara said as she and Khulan rode side-by-side along the Serpent's River, past the place where the Asjare camped before the Battle of the Rivers. The campsites were now empty. Only the occasional patrol passed by; they did not look eager at all for a fight.

"Now that he's gone, why would you suddenly care about what he'd think?" Khulan said.

Sara didn't laugh. Instead, she gave Khulan a dark look.

"Sorry, bad joke," Khulan said, turning away and gripping her horse's reins tighter. Sara looked at her friend as they rode in silence.

The sun was low on the horizon. It slowly dipped below the Eagle's Perch in the distance, casting huge shadows on Arban's Peaks to their right. A cold wind blew across the Steppe. Despite having spent months in the Harnda lands, Sara still shivered.

"You never really get used to it, do you?" Sara said after a long while. "To losing people."

Khulan shook her head. "I thought that after Od, it'd make a little more sense to me."

"But each time feels new," Sara said. "Like you're being ripped apart in a new place."

"And just when you feel like you're about to heal, the wound gets opened again, and it feels just as terrible as the first time. But after losing so many people, it doesn't feel like you have the right to feel sad anymore."

Sara nodded. She wished that there were things she could do to take her pain away. She wished that Khulan could do the same for her. But there was nothing else to say, and the two of them continued riding together in the fading sunlight, their pain at once united and distant.

"I think he'd trust you," Khulan said after a long while.

"What?"

"I think if Ganbold were here, he'd support you all the way. Might have something to say about your choice to send Batu to the Temple, but I'm sure he'd be right beside you if he could. Maybe he still is."

Sara smiled. "Yeah. Yeah, I think you're right."

"They're all with you, you know," Khulan said. "The chiefs. They see you as their leader now. Well, except Chanar, but there's not much that coward can do anyway."

"I'm not sure I want them to," Sara said. "I'd much rather let them handle the politics and just do my job."

Khulan laughed. "You're doing it again. Thinking like a master of hunters when you should be thinking like a chief. It was a slick move, you know. Deciding to go to the Temple of Gaeon."

Sara shrugged. "Galeren is the newest member of our alliance, and she played the role of savior during the battle. She's also our only source of manna right now, which is good, but I don't want to depend on her. That's all."

"You know, as much as you say you don't like politics, you're actually pretty good at it."

By then, they had arrived where the hills of the Eagle's Perch merged into Arban's Peaks. Instead of the gradual slopes of the hills, the land moved sharply upwards, covered with endless trees and trails to form a series of mountains that looked like a giant's teeth piercing the sky.

"This looks like the right place?" Sara said. "This is where Galeren's scouts said it would be."

Khulan got off her horse, sprinkling some manna on its mane. She knelt on the ground and ran her hand lightly over the grass. Sara followed a few moments after, though she wasn't sure if there was anything she could do to help.

"Looks like it," Khulan said, then she moved forward slowly, feeling the ground as she went. "The ground is trampled here, you see?"

She pointed, and only then did Sara notice that the grass was dirty and crooked, as though someone had just driven a boot into it. When Khulan investigated further, she found what appeared to be footprints.

"No doubt," Khulan said. "This is where that surprise Asjare force came from. We used to assume that Arban's Peaks were impassable, but they must have found a secret trail."

"Can you find that trail?" Sara asked.

Khulan did not answer her immediately. Instead, she got up and walked to the base of the mountain where the trees began. It was a steep slope, and their horses would not have been able to climb without assistance.

"I can, but it'll take time," Khulan said. "Trails are harder to follow in the forest. Too much activity. And it looks like the Asjare did some work to cover their tracks as they retreated. They thought ahead."

"So, not tonight."

Khulan shook her head. "Not tonight, sorry. I'll need to bring an entire hunting group here, maybe two since this forest is so damn big."

"Good. You'll have them, then. Just take some of our hunters off of their patrols."

Khulan frowned. "Then who will replace them?"

Sara considered for a moment. "I'm sure the Chenkah will be able to provide some hunters. I'll approach Chanar about it tomorrow."

"Won't he oppose the idea? He's always kept his hunters close to his chest."

"That was before the battle," Sara said. "But if I spin it right, I can make him think that it's his way to redeem himself, and maybe secure a couple of battle victories."

"As he should. The damn coward would have been the death of us if not for Galeren."

"Make sure you don't mention this to anyone outside the tribe. I don't want Chanar or Thaube knowing that there's a secret passage. I'm not sure what to make of Galeren yet. I need a little more time to figure her out."

"I'll only bring hunters we can trust."

"That reminds me, I need you to put some people in charge of training new hunters. Ibakha just gave us permission to recruit from some of the other Harnda camps, so I've sent people to do that…"

Sara started to ramble on, but she stopped when she noticed that Khulan was grinning.

"What?" Sara asked.

"What did I tell you, Sara?" Khulan said. "You had what it takes to be a leader after all. All it took was a war."

Sara laughed. "You know, I think the Sara from a year ago would be horrified at what I now have to do."

"Well, everything was different a year ago," Khulan said, putting her arm around Sara. "You're doing good, kiddo. I think Od would be proud of you."

# 26
# Batu

"She's not actually coming to see us off, is she?" Nugai said to Batu as their group waited at the northern gathering point. Cirina still hadn't arrived with the last of their supplies. Instead of coming alone, she came with Sara and one of her hunters that Batu did not recognize.

"It looks like she is," Batu said. "Maybe you should hide."

"We're at the gathering point, Batu," Nugai said, gesturing at the empty space around them. "There's nowhere to hide."

"Oh. Never mind, then," Batu said.

Nugai shrugged. "Well, guess I'll die."

Nugai and Batu stiffened when Sara approached them, but Cirina looked unfazed. She waved to both of them and immediately started loading their horses, including a horse that Sara's hunter was leading.

"Relax, I'm not here to throw you out again," Sara said. "We're past that point."

"Good," Batu said. He sighed in relief, but he noticed that Sara didn't spare Nugai a glance. Even when they had met to discuss his assignment to the Temple, she had refused to acknowledge Nugai's existence. "I'm all out of ways to apologize at this point."

"No problem. Just make sure you don't have anything else to apologize for from now on."

"So, why are you here, then?" Batu asked.

"Yargai will accompany you," Sara said, pointing to the hunter who was with her.

"Batu," he said, bowing. "It's an honor. Sara told me that it was you who convinced the Qhurin to come to our aid. It was also you who chased us out of the Omnu lands."

Batu bit his lip. He was not sure how to respond. Luckily, Sara spoke first.

"Yargai will only be with you until you reach the river. He has his own mission," Sara said. "After that, you're on your own. Remember, be careful on the mountain pass. We don't know how heavily-guarded it is and we only need you to scout ahead."

Batu nodded. "I'll do my best not to stir up trouble."

"Please see to it that you don't. And... don't get killed either, Batu. It would be a shame."

Sara turned to leave, leaving the four hunters at the northern gathering point. After a few moments, Yargai left to inspect his horse.

Batu heard Nugai sigh in relief after he left.

"That woman scares me," Nugai said.

"She is quite scary, isn't she?" Batu said, laughing. He started moving towards his own horse. "You two would make a good pair."

Nugai shook his head vigorously. "I'd rather be dragged through the bottom of a salt-filled sea."

"I'll bet there are worse things than being involved with Sara," Batu said as he got on his horse. He looked in the direction where Sara had left, but she was already out of sight.

Nugai scoffed. "Maybe you two should be together, then."

Batu laughed. He checked to make sure that Yargai and Cirina were ready, then he took one last look at the Harnda camp, which was beginning to recover from being burnt to a crisp. "Seems like we're always leaving this place, aren't we?"

"True," Nugai said. "They're sending us away every opportunity they get."

Batu nodded. "But this time, we aren't running away anymore. We're going home."

"What did you say your assignment was, again?" Batu asked Yargai as they rode through the hills. After about a day of riding, the Omnu side of the Serpent's River was finally in sight.

"I didn't," Yargai said. "But I guess there's no harm in telling you. Sara is having me and several others go into the Omnu lands to find other hunters that may still be hiding there. We're leaving one by one so we don't arouse suspicion among the other chiefs."

"That's a good plan," Batu said. He had not considered that yet. His impression had been that they had lost all of the Omnu hunters during Khasar's raid on the Empire's outposts, but it made sense that many of them would have escaped.

As they crossed the next hill, Batu realized that the Omnu lands were within sight. Omnu territory awaited them just across one of the two remaining bridges. The cold winds did not blow as sharply anymore and Batu recognized the familiar hills and slopes. It even seemed as though the flowers and bushes were different in the Omnu lands. Still, something terrified Batu about returning. It felt too familiar, like an old wound being burst open.

"Hey," Cirina said, stopping to wait for Batu. He realized that he had been lagging behind as the three of them had already reached the bridge. "What's the matter?"

"Nothing," Batu said, trying to move forward, but Cirina caught him on his arm. She looked straight into his eyes. The stare she gave him made him want to turn and run.

"Doesn't seem like it's nothing," Cirina said. "What's the matter?"

Batu didn't answer immediately. Instead, his eyes shifted towards the Omnu lands. Cirina saw where his eyes were and seemed to understand.

"You're scared about going back," she said.

Batu nodded slowly. "It's a place where I did a lot of things that I don't like to think about. All in my father's name."

She put her hand on his shoulder. "You're not your father. You've proven that time and time again."

"Have I, though?" Batu said. "My father did some horrible things, but everyone tells me that he was amazing. Who knows what I'd do if I thought it was for the good of our people?"

Cirina sighed. "I don't know, Batu. That's a decision you might have to make somewhere down the line. But… I trust you to make the right choice."

"How do you know that?"

Cirina shrugged. "Well, you saved my life, didn't you? No chief or hunting group leader has ever put their life on the line for me, but you did. I think you'll figure something out."

She winked at him and continued onwards. Batu stared after her for a few moments, then followed her. She was right. Worrying about the future was not going to help him with the here and now. Batu took a deep breath. Together with his hunters, he crossed the bridge and arrived home.

# 27

# Erroll

Dayir stood in front of the Asjare camp, standing on a wooden stool so that he could see everyone in attendance. A few days earlier, a call had gone out through the camps to signal that the head chieftain was preparing to give an address to the entire tribe. No one was required to join, but that did not stop them from filling the entire clearing.

Even Erroll had been persuaded to come. As they stood off to the side of the stage, he spotted a group of Jusordian soldiers standing close to the Dayir. Some even stood behind him alongside the Asjare's elite hunters, watching the crowd for any signs of danger.

"He's really making use of Syra's soldiers, isn't he?" Erroll said.

"Well, with our losses from the last battle, he had to find some way to protect the camps, didn't he?" Khalja said. "He doesn't have much of a choice."

The sound of drums brought the crowd to silence. For a moment, it was so quiet that Erroll could hear birds chirping in the trees above them.

"My fellow Asjare," Dayir began. The crowd was so massive that his voice could not be heard at the back, so he had positioned hunters throughout the crowd to repeat his words to the people in the back. "We are living in difficult times. I will be the first one to admit that the past series of battles have not been in our favor."

There was an earnestness in Dayir's voice that Erroll had not expected. But when Dayir spoke next, Erroll swore that he could hear his voice catch in his throat.

"We have lost people dear to us, and we will ache for their loss as they pass into the wind. The only way we can honor them is to move forward with the same strength that they have endowed us through their sacrifice."

"Have you ever seen him like this before?" Erroll whispered to Khalja. He heard whispers erupting throughout the crowd, who seemed unable to contain themselves.

"Losing Temulun shook him up quite badly," Khalja said. "He just isn't the same anymore. Patrols haven't even resumed yet, and there's no talk at all about launching a new assault."

"His wife is still alive though, isn't she? The master of herders?"

"Yes, but everyone knew about Dayir and Temulun," Khalja said, then when he noticed Erroll raise his eyebrow, he added, "Oh, except for you. Well, now you do."

Erroll looked back at Dayir, who was still talking despite the commotion.

"The Empire has agreed to give us their protection at the mouth of Arban's Valley, so we will be safe for now. They have also sent us fresh shipments of manna from the Temple of Gaeon. I ask that you all give them the same respect you would one of our own hunters. They have proven themselves to be trustworthy allies, and they will see us through to the end."

Erroll could see Syra among the soldiers that were standing behind Dayir. The head chieftain's newfound respect for the Empire was Sandulf's doing. Erroll was sure of it.

More whispering erupted in the crowd as Dayir started talking about the new adjustments each camp would have to make for the Empire's soldiers.

"They won't forgive him for this," Erroll whispered.

Khalja shrugged. "This war might be the end of Asjare."

In front of them, Dayir was finally wrapping up his speech.

"The coming days hold much uncertainty for us. We will face challenges that the Asjare have not faced in recent memory, not since the days of Siban and the War of White Soil. I ask only two things from all of you. Keep your feet on the ground and eyes to the sky. I will be with you the entire way."

He stepped off the stool and walked back into the tent without waiting for the crowd's response. They watched in stunned silence for a few moments before dispersing, some heading back to their work and others preparing to make the journey back to their own camps.

Khalja and Erroll headed back to their campsite. It felt wrong for them to be there since most of the places were empty. They still had not been reassigned or given any other work since returning from the mountain camps, so they spent their days sparring.

"Hey, I've been meaning to ask," Khalja said as they settled in around the campfire. Erroll began to cook dinner, but they lacked the usual cookware, so he had to do it slowly and carefully. "What did Temulun tell you about your father?"

Erroll raised his eyebrow, but he did not take his eyes off of the roasting meat. "What makes you ask that now?"

Khalja shrugged. "I've been meaning to ask for a while, but it never seemed like the right time."

Erroll sat back as he finished setting up the fire.

"No, I don't mind. I won't bore you with the long version of the story. The gist was that my father didn't die in the Empire like I thought. He escaped and ended up in the Asjare camps. Then he lived here for the next ten years until the plague got him."

"What did you say his name was again?"

"Erwan."

"I've heard the name, but I was not a hunter yet at that point. Our paths must not have crossed. But I think he was a good man."

Erroll nodded. "Temulun told me as much."

"You know what this means, right?"

Erroll looked up from the pot, and he saw that Khalja was looking at him intently.

"What?" he asked.

Khalja smiled. "If your father was one of the Asjare, that means that you are, too."

"That's not how it works."

"Of course it is. Back in the day, before things got bad, there used to be plenty of kids born from Jusordians and nomads. So, the chiefs decided that whoever had nomad blood in their veins was a nomad. Maybe they didn't live here, but they were nomads all the same. Same with you. So, where do you think you belong? Here or back in Ruson?"

"Well," Erroll said after a long pause. "I don't think I've ever belonged anywhere."

Syra had agreed to meet Erroll on the outskirts of the Asjare camp at midnight, but as Erroll was still alone as he stood in the moonlight.

Erroll thought about leaving. After all, he was not sure he trusted Syra to stick with him if things got hairy, but he banished the thought from his mind. They needed to act on this new information, and quickly.

Erroll looked around him. In the distance, he could see signs of the camp beginning to settle down for the night. There were much less hunters around. Erroll and Khalja, the only survivors of Temulun's hunting group, were one of the few that had been sent back to support the camp after the Battle of Harnda. Erroll suspected that had been Syra's doing, but the camp's activity remained. Families gathered around campfires to eat dinner and children played in the central clearing.

Erroll did not understand how they could remain so cheerful despite it all. Their entire way of life as they knew it might collapse soon, and yet they still carried on. He remembered the mood in Ruson's smithing district every time they received news that the army had suffered a defeat. The armorers would gather in the district's only pub and worry about whether or not their sons had survived, while their wives would stay at home with the curtains shut and offer prayers to Galele.

There did not seem to be any of that in the camps tonight, apart from the solemn ceremony earlier in the day. But the nomads had stood together even then.

"All right, what's this new information you have for me?" came Syra's voice.

Syra looked different from the last time Erroll had seen him. Instead of wearing his customary Empire-issued plate armor, Syra was wearing a suit of leather riding armor, the kind the hunters wore into battle. Erroll himself had worn a similar set during the battle.

"I think I know where the enemy will go next," Erroll said. "The Temple of Gaeon."

"That place is deep in Empire-controlled territory," Syra said, scratching his chin. "And the nomads are allied with the Qhurin now, so I can't see a reason for them to need the Temple of Gaeon."

"They've just won a great victory," Erroll said. Syra had a pained expression on his face. "It was a victory for them, no matter how you spin it. They must understand by now that the Empire has been controlling the Asjare by controlling their manna supply. Seizing the Temple of Gaeon would be a strong argument for the Asjare to defect to their side."

Syra scratched his chin. Then he grinned. "I see your point. Never thought I'd see you thinking like a nomad so quickly."

Erroll suddenly felt ashamed. He looked away. "It's just research, sir. These…nomads have a very strange manner of thinking. But it has a logic to it, one that we can manipulate."

Syra nodded. "See that you don't become one of them. This is good work, Erroll. I want you to visit the Temple and meet with our soldiers already stationed there. Inspect the defences and make sure that they can resist the upcoming assault. But keep this quiet. I don't want General Asghar hearing about it and trying to station his own troops there."

Syra started to leave, but Erroll stopped him.

"That won't be enough, sir," Erroll said. "No matter how many defences we put up, the nomads are relentless. I say that we strike decisively and make sure that they will never try to retake the Temple again."

"What do you propose, then?"

Erroll grinned, then he handed Syra a piece of paper.

"What is this?" Syra asked, looking over the paper. "A request for inventory supplies..."

Then he looked at what Erroll was requesting, and his eyes widened.

"You don't seriously mean that you want to..." Syra said.

"It will be the greatest blow to the nomads ever struck by the Empire. Also, we have enough manna supplies to last us until the end of the war. If we do this, we'll ensure that the Asjare's loyalty," Erroll said.

Syra raised an eyebrow. He clearly was not expecting something like this from Erroll. Syra studied him, but Erroll made sure to keep his stance firm. Then Syra sighed.

"I don't have the authority to approve a mission like this," Syra said, rolling up the inventory request. "I'll speak to the general about this. You are not to speak of this plan to anyone else until you receive further instructions."

"Of course, sir," Erroll said, and he watched Syra walk away. Erroll was tired of being told where he belonged, both by the Empire and the nomads. He would carve his own path, through flames if need be, and he would show them. He would show them all.

# 28
# Sara

Sara watched as Khulan's team sifted through the forest, leaving no stone or leaf unturned in their search. They had been working for an hour or so before Sara had arrived to take their reports. Within a few minutes of her arriving, Bataar emerged from the forest, his face and hair covered in sweat. He and Khulan were overseeing the tracking in shifts; Bataar had taken surprisngly well to the task, even though he was the master of herders.

"Anything?" Sara asked.

Bataar took a moment to take a long drink of water from his waterskin, then wiped off some of the sweat with the hem of his shirt.

"Nothing yet," Bataar said. "We have a few promising trails to follow, but so far, we've only turned up dead ends. It looks like the Asjare were rather meticulous when covering their tracks."

Sara nodded. She had originally hoped to find the trail quickly so she could present her findings to the war council, but two weeks had passed and they still had nothing.

"Hey," Bataar said, jolting Sara out of her train of thought.

"What?"

"You're doing it again. You start thinking too hard and you get this stupid far-off expression on your face."

Sara laughed. "And why can't I?"

Bataar grinned, and Sara thought she could see his cheeks flush. "Well, whenever you get lost in your thoughts, your mood tends to take a dip."

Sara smiled, then she took a deep breath. "Okay, fine, I'll try to give it a rest. But while we're giving each other comments on our looks, you should go wash your hair."

Bataar ran his hand through his hair, like it was the first time he'd noticed all day. "You know what? I'll do that."

He started to walk towards the river. It was then that Kara emerged from the forest, and she was not alone. Two Omnu hunters followed her. In between them was a man that Sara didn't recognize.

"Kara, who's this?" Bataar asked as the group approached. "You know that we're not supposed to let other tribes know what we're doing."

"He's Asjare," Kara said, and when they got closer, Sara realized that the man was bound.

"Asjare?" Bataar said. "Bring him here."

The hunters left the prisoner on his knees in front of Sara and Bataar and returned to the forest. Kara, however, remained. She looked down on the captive hunter with her hand on her sword hilt, though the prisoner himself made no moves to escape. He simply looked down at the floor, his expression downtrodden and defeated.

"We found him trying to sneak through the forest," Kara said. "He was probably trying to capture one of us and take us back to the Asjare camps."

"I wasn't trying to capture anyone," the prisoner said.

"He's lying," Kara said, moving to strike him, but Sara caught her hand.

Sara turned to the prisoner. "Continue," she said.

"I was only trying to return to my tribe. I got separated from my friends during the battle and only managed to get past the patrols today. Please, let me go."

Sara nodded. "And what is your name?"

"Why does it matter to you?" he said, looking up to glare at Sara. They locked eyes for a moment, then he relented. "Geser," he said quietly.

"Geser," Sara said. "Nice to meet you. My name is Sara. I'm a chief of the Omnu."

"I know who you are," Geser said. "Everyone in our tribe knows about the daughter of Julian. We were told to watch out for her on the battlefield."

"Good. So you know that I don't mess around when it comes to protecting my people. I want you to tell me how to get to the Asjare camps."

"How weak do you think my loyalty is?" Geser said. "You'll have to kill me."

"Good," Kara said. "Then we're on the same page."

"Kara, no one is going to kill anyone," Sara said. "What's wrong with you? Am I going to have to send you away?"

"I recognize this one," Kara said. She released her weapon, but her fist was still clenched tight. "He faced us on the battlefield right as we were about to pierce the Empire's ranks."

"And why does that matter?" Sara asked.

"He's the one who killed Ganbold," Kara said, and as she spoke, Sara saw the tears build in her eyes, but she refused to let them fall to the ground. The next few words she said pained her greatly. "She shot him in the back as we were about to advance. I think I was the only one who saw it happen."

Kara's face hardened, and she thrust her finger into his face. "It's because of traitors like him that Ganbold had to die. All of these Asjare scum."

"That was the chief. It was never my decision to make," Geser whispered.

Sara looked at Geser again. She had thought her thoughts of Ganbold would have faded to a minimum after two weeks, but looking at Geser's greying hair and defiant expression brought her memories came back like a storm. A part of her wanted so badly to do it. At least it would allow the boiling anger in her to subside.

Sara took a deep breath and imagined she was back on the plains with her hunters, with the wind in her hair, sunlight on her back, and a wide open sky above her. Those days were long gone, but the memory brought her solace.

She opened her eyes and was relieved to see that her hands were nowhere near her sword. Bataar stood there, his face unreadable. Sara knelt next to Geser and used her knife to undo his bonds. She was done with holding grudges.

"Sara, you couldn't possibly be considering…" Kara began, but Sara held up her hand.

Sara ignored Kara for now, and only spoke to Geser. "I won't fault you for killing my friend. We do what we must to survive on the battlefield. I hope you'll do the same for me."

Geser averted his eyes, but he didn't answer immediately. Sara decided to let him have some time to think. She got up and walked over to Kara, whose eyes were still fixed on the ground.

Sara placed her hand on Kara's shoulder. "Killing him won't solve anything. Trust me, I know."

Kara shook her head. "That's not…I can't…"

Sara pulled Kara into an embrace, letting her sob into her shirt.

"It should've been me," Kara said. "He should've killed me instead."

"Don't say that," Sara whispered. "You're still alive for a reason. It's up to us to live up to their memories."

"And how do you know that's what Ganbold would've wanted?" Kara said. "You're the one that let him die."

Kara took a few deep breaths and pulled herself free from Sara's embrace. There was a wide-eyed look in Kara's face, as though she was watching a horse being put down in front of her.

"I'm sorry…I didn't mean that," she muttered, but she couldn't meet Sara's eyes. Sara took a deep breath, feeling her insides twist up inside her. She shook off the feeling.

"Take all the time you need, Kara," Sara said. "But give yourself permission to let go."

Kara nodded and walked away to sit next to the river, sinking her feet into the water.

Sara turned back to Geser. He was on his feet now, but showed no indication of wanting to move.

"I'm going to let you leave, Geser," Sara said. "You can go back to the Asjare camps and we won't follow you."

Geser frowned. "And why should I trust you?"

"You don't have to," Sara said, shrugging. "But it's the offer you've got. We will find the secret passage, Geser, with or without your help. So, it's your choice where you want to be when that happens."

"I still have a family back in the camps. And many of my friends. I can't abandon them," Geser said.

Sara nodded.

"If you help us, I promise you, Geser, we will spare all the lives we can. Including your family. We don't want more nomads killing nomads. It's exactly what the Empire wants us to do. You can trust me."

Geser paused, then he nodded. "I'll show you where it is."

"Thank you.'

Geser turned and started walking towards the forest. The two hunters that had brought him there looked a little surprised to see him free from his bonds. Sara gestured for them to follow him.

Sara moved to follow them as well, but turned to Bataar first.

"You've been awfully quiet. What do you think about all this?" she asked him.

"You did beautifully, Sara," Bataar said.

Sara wrung her hands. "I didn't realize that this was part of becoming chief."

"Being a chief isn't just about being a leader or a general. Sometimes, one has to be a shoulder to cry on, or a gentle breeze on a warm day. Some chiefs have forgotten it, but it's always been true."

"I suppose. My father would've said the same," she said, turning towards the forest. A messenger eagle descended on them as she did, a piece of paper clenched between its claws.

"I know that animal," Bataar said. "That's Cirina's messenger eagle. Maybe they've already gotten the blessing."

Sara shook her head. "They wouldn't send us a message if that was the case. Something's wrong."

The eagle landed on Sara's arm. She took the message from its claws and unrolled it. Reading through its contents, Sara felt herself grow heavy again.

"What is it?" Bataar asked.

Sara looked up from the paper. She took a deep breath. "You're right, it's a message from Batu. We need to go. Now. Bring all the hunters you can find to the northern gathering point. He needs our help."

# 29

# Batu

When they arrived at the foot of the mountain leading to the Temple of Gaeon, Batu could nor believe how easy it was for them to begin their ascent.

"There are seriously no guards around?" Batu said, looking around. They had had to avoid a few Empire patrols on the way here and Yargai had left them a few days earlier to go deeper into the Omnu lands, but there was no one waiting for them when they reached the mountain itself.

"Something about this feels wrong," Cirina said, getting off her horse and securing it to a tree near the foot of the mountain. Their horses would draw too much attention as they climbed, so they decided to ascend on foot.

"They should know how important the Temple and its springs are to the nomads," Batu said. "I can't believe they would leave it unguarded."

"Maybe they don't think we're crazy enough to do this," Nugai said. "Or maybe they're too busy licking their wounds. Whatever the case, we're supposed to check the place out, so we need to get up there anyway."

"And if it's a trap?" Batu said.

"Then we'll fight our way out, same as always," Nugai said, grinning.

"Easy, Nugai," Batu said. "It's just a scouting mission. We need to figure out what their defences are and then get out."

"Sure, sure," Nugai said. "If you want to do it the boring way."

The climb to the Temple of Gaeon was as exhausting as Batu had last remembered it. They hadn't been able to bring their horses, so the ascent was slow and grueling, filled with steep trails and places where the path was so worn that they could only walk through in single file.

Finally, the peak was nearly in sight, and Batu's failing legs managed a final burst of energy to get there. They had not seen any Empire soldiers on the way up. Batu could feel the fear dancing constantly on the edge of his mind.

"Almost there," Batu said quietly to himself. He looked behind him to make sure that Nugai and Cirina were still following him. Whough they were lagging behind, they still remained in sight.

Batu decided to sit on an even piece of rock to wait for them. He placed his huge pack on the ground next to him and rubbed his shoulders. He then faced the Steppe and took a drink from his waterskin. Batu took a deep breath and allowed himself to enjoy the view.

The view was spectacular as always. It was as if the entire Steppe spread out before him. He could see the Empire's camps near the Serpent's River. The war camps were well organized with neat rows of tents and even some rudimentary wooden buildings. Further in the distance, Batu could see one of the Harnda herding camps that was near the Serpent's River; it was spread out without any recognizable pattern. The lands were so familiar to Batu, and yet he was still filled with awe whenever he got to look at them from this distance,.

"I won't let them take it away," he muttered to himself.

"Saenor's scales, this is a long hike," Nugai said, collapsing onto the rock next to Batu.

"I warned you, didn't I?" Batu said, handing him the waterskin. Nugai took a long drink, then poured some of the water over his face and neck.

"It's scorching hot too. We really couldn't have come on a worse day."

Batu laughed. "Whenever my father brought me here, it was always snowing, which made things a little easier. It was like going to another part of the world, even though it was just a three-day ride away from our camp."

"I forgot about that. This won't be your first time here, will it?" Nugai said.

"Not at all. We came here every year. Sometimes twice a year if my father felt like it. I think he thought of it as his chance to get away."

"Yeah, and he left the camp to us," Nugai said. "He never told us in advance when he was planning a trip, so the camp would always fall into chaos for a few days after you were gone."

"I'm sorry?" Batu said. Nugai was smiling as Batu glanced at his face, and he looked almost wistful.

"It's all right," Nugai said. "A lot has changed since then. Too much. I think I'd be happy to take a second hunting shift if it meant everything would go back to normal."

"But it won't ever be normal again, will it?"

"Won't it?" Nugai said. "After the Empire is gone, we'll go back to the way things were. Just with you as the chief."

Batu shook his head. "I think that nothing's going to be the same ever again. Isn't it hard to imagine going back to who you were before the war?"

"Not really. Things were so much easier back then. I didn't have so much responsibility. I just did what I was told."

"Well, did you wish you had never become a bandit?" Batu asked suddenly. "When we were in the Qhurin camps?"

Nugai thought for a long time. "Truth be told? No. I think I just got reminded of why I left. The place just wasn't right for me. If they had their way, I'd have died a long time ago in one of their stupid schemes."

Batu raised an eyebrow. "And you don't think that my father would have done the same?"

"That was different," Nugai said. "Chinua saved my life, I was just paying back a debt. But now that you mention it, I suppose I'd rather live in a world where I can make my own choices."

"Fine by me," Batu said. "So long as you're by my side while you're doing it."

Nugai chuckled. "Don't get too cocky, Flamewalker. I might change my mind one of these days."

At that moment, Cirina approached them, though she didn't collapse onto the rock. She didn't stop to catch her breath.

"Are you boys done confessing your love to each other?" she said.

"How are you not even winded?" Nugai said.

"I paced myself," Cirina said. "Didn't feel the need to show off like you two. Now let's get a move on. I don't want to have to spend the night in the Temple."

"Yeah, well, we got here first," Nugai said, staggering to his feet and grabbing onto a rock to keep himself from falling over.

"Exactly. I don't know how you two idiots managed to do anything without me," Cirina said, rolling her eyes at him. Then she offered her hand to Batu, who let her help him to his feet.

"Are you ready?" she asked.

"Of course," Batu said.


The Temple of Gaeon was exactly as Batu remembered it, if only a little more run down than before. As far as he could tell, no one had been here in more than a year, so the stone building had deteriorated slightly. The temple it was still standing, which was an encouraging sign. One of the best memories Batu had was when his father had brought him and his mother up here for Gaeon's blessing. That was so long ago, before his family had been torn apart.

The temple was on the other side of the clearing, built into the side of the mountain. In his mind, Batu had always pictured the Temple bigger than it actually was, soaring high into the coming up here every year reminded him of just how small the Temple was. It was barely as tall as three men standing on each other's shoulders, and about as wide as a herd of five oxen.

He started walking towards the Temple, taking in everything

around him. He noticed that something was off with the clearing around the Temple.

"The grass is thinner than last time," he said, getting on his knees and running his hand through the soil. "It started two years ago, but it's only gotten worse."

"What does it mean?" Cirina said. She had stopped right behind him, while Nugai was catching his breath near the clearing's edge.

"Probably nothing. But the last time my father was here, he said the last time this happened was during the War of White Soil. The temple is…wilting, and so is everything around it."

Cirina nodded. "The last great war of the tribes. I wonder if he thought of it as an omen."

Batu shrugged. "Might be why he got so damn paranoid during the last year. I never thought much of it, but it does feel eerie."

He looked up and the Temple seemed almost out of place in the dying grass, like the last remaining relic of a forgotten time. If anything, it only gave Batu a greater sense that time was running out.

"Be careful. At the first sign of trouble, we should get out of here," Batu said, starting to move towards the Temple. A sense of unease made his stomach drop, and he knew that he would not be calm again until they were away from this place.

"Nugai, get a move on," Cirina said before both she and Nugai caught up with him. Together, they entered the Temple.

They followed Batu into the Temple. He lingered for a moment at the doorway to admire the stone that held it in place. Then he scanned the rest of the building, which was not much more than a few stone slabs for people to sit on and a statue of Gaeon holding up a staff. Gaeon's beloved eagle, Onoe, perched proudly on his shoulder with its eyes turned to the sun. There were some rooms that had been dug into the mountain for when there used to be nomad caretakers that would live there, but those rooms were long vacant now.

At Gaeon's feet was a small pool of azure that was filled by a spring deep inside the mountain. The manna spring. From afar, the pool looked like water, but it was in a deeper shade of blue and seemed to have its own glow. Apart from the Spring of Onoe in the west, the spring in the Temple of Gaeon was the only source of manna in the entire Steppe. They needed to win it back.

In better times, the chiefs would gather here in the Temple once every three months to gather the water produced by the spring and extract the manna powder from it. As a child, Batu used to wonder whether the Temple or the spring had been there first.

"Something's wrong," Batu said the moment they stepped into the room.

"What?" Nugai said. "The Temple is empty. This is great news. We can send a hunting party to secure it within a week!"

"No, we have to get out. Now. Look there," Batu said, pointing to the back of the room where a stone door led into the mountain and the Temple's back rooms.

Whenever Batu came here, the door had always been shut tight since the back rooms were empty. But today, the door was open, and Batu could see the flicker of a torch from within.

"Someone's already here," Batu said. There was something in his tone that let Nugai and Cirina know that he was serious. He darted out of the room and they followed immediately.

When they emerged into the clearing, they found themselves no longer along. The field, which had been empty until a few moments ago, was now swarming with soldiers dressed in the armor of the Empire.

"Saenor's scales," he said. "I knew this was a trap."

The three of them took out their weapons. By Batu's count, there were nearly twenty of them. They did not stand a chance. Each soldier was armed with a spear and shield. Without horses, their defences would be nearly impossible to break.

"How did we miss them?" Batu said. "We were so careful."

"They must have known we were coming," Nugai said. His axes were already drawn, and his eyes were darting between the soldiers, trying to figure out which one would charge him first.

"Drop your weapons!" they shouted. "No one needs to die today."

Batu turned to Cirina. "Your eagle. We need to get a message to Sara. It's our only chance," he said, watching as the soldiers surrounded them, some of them darting into the Temple. Cirina nodded and closed her eyes, summoning her eagle.

"No, Batu," Nugai said, grabbing him by the shoulder. "You need to get out of here. Let us hold them off so that you can escape. You're the most important one here."

"I'm not leaving you behind," Batu said, shrugging him off and turning to the Empire's soldiers as they advanced slowly towards them.

"Batu, listen to me," Nugai said.

"No," Batu said. "Leaving people behind is what my father would've done. I'm not doing the same."

That was the end of the discussion. Cirina's eagle descended from above and landed on her shoulder. She took out a piece of paper.

"What should the message say?" Cirina said.

"Just write, 'Captured'. She'll know what it means," Batu said.

"Got it," she said. Before the Empire soldiers realized what they were doing, the eagle was gone, flying in the direction of the Steppe and the Harnda camps.

The Empire soldiers approached them, waving their spears in warning. Batu dropped his sword.

"Don't fight them," Batu whispered. "There's no point."

Nugai growled, the pained noise coming from deep in his throat. After a moment's hesitation, he and Cirina dropped their weapons as well. Batu breathed in and looked to the sky, feeling the sunlight beat down on him. He raised his hands in surrender.

"Good," one of them said. "The general will be glad to have some nomad captives for once."

The soldiers took away their weapons and forced them to their knees. They brought out rope and began binding Nugai's hands.

"I'm not letting you tie me up," Nugai said, raising his hand to strike the soldier holding the rope, but another soldier caught his arm then slammed a spear butt into his face.

Nugai grunted and fell to the ground, blood trickling from the side of his jaw.

"It will be easier on all of us if you cooperate," the soldier said, then he knelt beside Nugai and bound his hands.

Batu allowed them to bind his hands without incident and glanced upwards to give the Temple one last look. Then his eyes widened. For a moment, he couldn't believe what his eyes were seeing.

The Temple of Gaeon was in flames.

# 30
# Erroll

Erroll watched as the three nomads entered the clearing. He held up a hand and signaled his men to stay back. They had been waiting at the Temple for two days, ever since their scouts had detected the nomads moving across Omnu territory.

"Shouldn't we go in now?" Khalja whispered. "Isn't it better for us if we surprise them while they're inside?"

Erroll shook his head. "There's only one entrance into the Temple. If we go in one-by-one, the nomads will have the advantage. When they try to escape, that's when we'll get them."

Sure enough, the trio disappeared into the Temple, then Erroll gave the signal. His soldiers emerged into the clearing, weapons drawn, and began forming a perimeter around the Temple.

"Any moment now," Erroll said. The second he finished speaking, the three nomads emerged into the clearing again, this time with their own weapons drawn.

"You were right," Khalja said.

Erroll nodded, then called to the squad's captain. "Capture them, but be careful. You'll be rewarded if there is no bloodshed."

The captain nodded and directed his soldiers to advance. The nomads started arguing among themselves as the Empire soldiers advanced on them, but Erroll knew that there would be no contest. Even the best nomad fighters could not stand against a group of armored Empire soldiers without their horses. Then Erroll turned to the five soldiers that were gathered near him and Khalja.

"Come with me. We're going inside the Temple," Erroll said.

"Why do we need to? We have them already," Khalja said, though he followed Erroll as he led the small force into the Temple. One of the soldiers carried a small barrel with him that Erroll had specifically requested from Sandulf.

"Tying up loose ends," Erroll said.

"What does that mean? We already have manna supplies for the next six months." Khalja said, taking out his sword.

Erroll shook his head. "Exactly. Trust me, Khalja. I know what I'm doing."

They moved into the Temple's main room, inspecting each corner to make sure they did not miss anything important. Erroll looked at the statue that dominated the room and the spring at its feet. This was supposed to be Gaeon, god of the Steppe, but to Erroll, he wasn't impressed. Even General Sandulf had had a far more imposing presence. Compared to him, this god only seemed like a mildly frightening master-of-arms. He knelt down and dipped his finger into the spring. The manna had not been processed yet, so right now, it was just raw energy. Erroll felt nothing.

He got up again and shook his head. He did not know what he was expecting. He was standing in an old and weathered building. That was all. But Khalja seemed to hesitate as they walked into the room. He made sure not to disturb any of the slabs or decorations as he walked around, kneeling for a brief moment when they came to the statue.

Erroll turned to the soldier holding the barrel and gestured for him to advance. At that moment, Khalja seemed to realize what it was; his eyes widened and he tried to catch the soldier on the arm.

Before he could get there, however, Erroll stopped him, grabbing Khalja by the shoulders and forcing him to his knees.

"Don't interfere," Erroll hissed into Khalja's ear, but Khalja didn't listen. He thrashed against Erroll's grip. He managed to come free for a moment before two of Erroll's soldiers grabbed him by the arms and restrained him.

"What do you think you're doing? This is sacred ground," he

shouted as Erroll straightened his armor and joined the soldiers at the door. "This isn't right."

"Sandulf's orders. The Omnu cannot be allowed to retake the Temple of Gaeon. We're just opting for a more permanent solution," Erroll said, then he turned to the soldier with the barrel of oil. He was waiting for Erroll's command to pour it onto the ground surrounding the wooden supports.

"Please!" Khalja shouted. "Your father wouldn't have wanted this."

Erroll stopped. He turned back to Khalja, who was no longer struggling against his captors. There were tears in his eyes, and he was looking straight at Erroll.

Erroll hesitated for a moment, then he shook his head. "And why does that matter to me? I didn't know my father."

He turned to the soldier at the door and gave the order. He nodded and tipped the barrel, letting the oil spill into the Temple's main room and back rooms. The rooms were mostly made of stone, but there were enough wooden supports and flooring that the entire place would go up in flames. Just as Erroll wanted.

"No!" Khalja shouted.

One of his soldiers lit a match and threw it into the oil. Instantly, huge orange flames leapt up around it, washing them all in a wave of heat.

"Get back!" Erroll shouted. His soldiers ducked out of the way as flames began engulfing the wooden supports and singing the stone.

Erroll led his soldiers as they hurried out of the Temple's main room just as the flames began to spread. They were almost to the door when Erroll realized that not all of them were out. He looked behind him and saw Khalja kneeling where he had been earlier, the two soldiers desperately trying to pull him away from the flames. But he refused to budge.

"Don't be an idiot, Khalja," Erroll shouted as the two soldiers gave up and dashed out of the room. The wooden supports holding up the Temple were starting to crack, and the flames had almost engulfed the entire room. But Khalja did not move, even as the flames licked at his body.

Khalja turned slowly to face Erroll as the fire began to spread throughout his body. His face contorted in pain as Erroll's nose began to fill with the smell of burning flesh.

"This is your fault," Khalja screamed as the flames surrounded his body. He fell to the ground, writhing in pain as Erroll watched, unable to move as the Temple fell around him. The fire spread to the ceiling, which came crashing down as the supports could no longer hold it up.

But Erroll did not move. His eyes were fixed on Khalja's body, which had stopped moving by then. Something at the back of Erroll's mind screamed, and his limbs would not cooperate, as if they refused to let him live.

One of Erroll's soldiers reached inside and grabbed Erroll, yanking him outside right before a beam crushed him. When they got outside, the Temple finally collapsed, stone crushing wood as the flames consumed everything that was left. In a few hours, there would be nothing left except charred stone and the smell of smoke.

Erroll fell to his knees. He was surprised to find tears flowing down his face. He did not understand why he felt this way. The Temple was destroyed along with the manna spring. As he looked to the side, he found the three nomad captives bound and disarmed without any casualties from his own soldiers. They watched as the Temple collapsed right in front of their eyes.

His soldiers watched him with confused expressions on their faces. They were shaken, but otherwise unharmed.

And yet, he felt a massive weight pressing on his ribs from the inside, as though some beast within him was straining against his bones to escape. His chest heaved as new tears sprouted from behind his eyes and he vomited into the soil.

"What have I done?" he whispered.

# 31
# Sara

Astorm was brewing over the Steppe. The skies had been clear just hours before, but they were now filled with gray clouds. A few droplets pelted the ground as Sara rode to her destination. Thunder cracked in the distance and wind howled through the Steppe like the roar of a forgotten god.

Within minutes of receiving Batu's message, Sara was at the Harnda's northern gathering point. Soon, the Omnu hunters would receive her message and they would be with her. She prayed to Gaeon that it would be enough. Even from here, they could see the smoke coming from the Temple of Gaeon. They knew what it meant — the Temple was lost.

Kara and Khulan arrived, each with their own hunting groups. They were ready to go to battle, armor and weapons and all.

"How many more?" Sara asked Khulan as she approached.

"We have two more hunting groups on the way," Khulan said. "Two of them were part of the patrol tonight, so they're taking a little while longer."

"We can't waste any time," Sara said. "If they were captured today, there might still be a chance we'll catch them as they return to the camp."

Khulan nodded and began shouting orders to the messengers. The Omnu force stood at the gathering point as Sara eyed them. It had not been more than a month since the last battle, and Sara could tell that they were not eager to go into battle again. She had promised them that they wouldn not see fighting for a long while yet. Tonight, however, she would have to break that promise.

The crowd of hunters parted and Ibakha arrived on a horse. Sara thought for a second that she was going to join them, but she was not wearing any armor or weapons.

Ibakha approached Sara and got off her horse. She motioned to Sara to dismount. Though Sara was itching to go, she relented. Ibakha took her aside so that the other hunters were out of earshot.

"I heard about what happened," Ibakha said. "You know he's as good as dead now, right?"

Sara shook her head. "Not if we get there soon enough. I can still save him."

"Sara, listen to me. I had Zayaat send his eagle north towards the Temple. His eagle-eye didn't see much because of the storm, but he spotted a group of soldiers moving from the mountain to the Empire's camps. There weren't any others, so it must have been the group you're targeting."

"That means we can still catch them."

"They didn't have any prisoners. They were all Empire soldiers. You know what that means, right?"

"I won't believe it. He can't be dead," Sara said. Batu's message had said 'Captured', hadn't it? That meant that he still had a chance.

Sara shook her head, then she started to walk back towards her horse, but Ibakha caught her on the shoulder.

"I'm begging you," Ibakha said. "If you do this, you'll be caught in enemy territory without any hope of escape. You'll die, and so will your hunters."

Sara shook Ibakha's hand off and started to walk away.

"For Gaeon's sake, Sara, don't throw your life away like this."

Sara turned to her. Even though she tried to hide them, there were tears in her eyes and her voice caught in her throat as she spoke.

"If he's dead, then it's my fault," she said. "I can't have his blood on my hands without at least knowing that I tried to save him."

Ibakha's stern gaze faded away and she placed her hands on Sara's shoulder again, this time looking at her like a mother would. Sara remembered the gaze well. When she looked up, she realized that her face was wet with tears that were indistinguishable from the raindrops that fell from the sky.

"I know how you feel," Ibakha said. "I've been chief for long enough to know what it's like to lose people."

Sara shook her head, but she allowed Ibakha to pull her into an embrace.

"I don't want it to happen ever again."

"I know, child. I know," Ibakha said, stroking Sara's hair. Sara felt safe when they were standing like this. She didn't need to worry about being a leader or being chieftain. She could simply be Sara.

Then Sara pulled herself away, the sobs beginning to fade.

"But you're a leader now," Ibakha said. "That means that you need to protect everyone in your tribe, not just Batu. Your people put their trust in you, and so it's on you to protect them."

Ibakha pointed at the Omnu hunters, who had gathered in force and were waiting for her command.

"You're their leader too. Believe me, they would ride to their deaths in an instant if you asked them to."

Sara watched her hunters, who waited quietly and stood tall in the rain, ready to ride through the mud at a moment's notice. She gave a long sigh and nodded.

Sara got onto her horse and rode until she could see her hunters. She had not noticed how their gaze towards her had changed in the past few months. She remembered the uncertainty and confusion she had seen among them when she first led them.

"The mission's off," she said. "Thank you for coming, but we've just had word that Batu was killed by the Empire during his journey to the Temple."

An audible gasp came from the crowd when Sara made her announcement, but their eyes and ears remained on her.

"We will remember his sacrifice and pay it back tenfold when the Empire threatens us again. Thank you for your bravery and your trust. That's all."

Sara got off her horse. After a few seconds of stunned silence, the hunterss began to disperse. Ibakha too left after a few moments, passing Sara as she walked back to the camp.

"You did the right thing. I'm proud of you," Ibakha said. Sara nodded and whispered her thanks, but she found herself unable to look Ibakha in the eye.

"If the mission to the Temple failed, and if I'm right about what that smoke means, then the Temple and the spring are gone. Why would the Empire do such a thing to a sacred place?"

"I don't pretend to know what those godless fools are thinking, but I know that they don't care at all for sacred ground," Temulun said. "All they care about is destroying everything we hold dear."

"Then Gaeon has truly abandoned us."

Ibakha placed her hand on Sara's shoulder. "I'll tell you a secret. I never had much faith in the gods after the plague took my parents. But I do have faith in people. And out of everyone in this Steppe, I have the most faith in you."

Without a word, Ibakha left the clearing. And after the crowd had dispersed, only two people remained with Sara at the gathering point. Kara and Khulan approached her.

"I'm sorry, Sara," Khulan said.

"Batu saved all our lives," Sara said.

Khulan was quiet for a long time. "If it was up to me, I wouldn't risk any more lives for them."

"That's not…"

Khulan raised a hand, silencing Sara. "I know that your father taught you all about justice and goodness, but the reality is that it's not worth all of our lives to save Batu and Nugai. Especially since we're already guilty."

"I thought better of you, Khulan," Sara said, and the words tore through her like a spear.

Khulan shrugged. "I'm just not like you, Sara. I don't know what you want me to say."

She turned and walked away without asking Sara if she had any orders for her. Sara watched her go, feeling the wound in her chest grow each time Khulan took another step. But she took a deep breath and supressed her feelings. She still had to be a leader.

Sara turned to Kara. "I need you to do something for me," she said.

"Anything," Kara said.

"Sneak into the Empire's camps and find out if Batu's really dead. If they are holding him prisoner, report back immediately. Don't try to get him out on your own."

"Sara, are you sure that's wise?" Kara said. "The Empire camps are on high alert right now."

"I just need to make sure," Sara said. "Just be careful. If things get dangerous, get out of there immediately."

"Of course," Kara said.

"You can leave today at dusk. Tell Bataar if you need any supplies," Sara said.

Kara left in a moment, heading in the direction of Bataar's supply tent, leaving Sara alone in the clearing.

"I hope I didn't just send her to her death," Sara said to herself. She thought about Ibakha's words again and prayed to Gaeon that Kara's trust in her would not be wasted.


The rain began to let up as Sara stepped back into the camps, which were beginning to look like what they once were after being rebuilt over the past month. The rain was a symbol that the seasons were beginning to change. The camp would need to pack up and move again, but not for another two weeks or so.

Her fight with Khulan still weighed heavily on her mind, but Sara was beginning to feel as if normalcy wasn't so far away as she walked through the camps,. There was the laughter of children running between the tents, though it was quieter than it used to be.

They splashed puddles, jumped into the mud, and chased each other through the streets.

People nodded at her as she passed, but they mostly kept to themselves as they attended to their daily tasks, whether it was preparing food, repairing tents, polishing weapons, and so on.

Sara did not have anywhere in particular she wanted to go. She simply wanted to be alone, and part of her wished she could jump on her horse and ride out into the plains to get rid of the heaviness that clung to her stomach. But riding alone in the Steppe was dangerous these days, so walking through the Omnu section of the camp was the next best thing to do.

Sara found herself among the tents where most of the families were staying. She recognized most of them by face, but she did not know any of their names since none of them were hunters. Still, each family stopped their conversations as she drew near. Some even got to their feet.

"Chief Saragerel," one man said, his hand still on his wife's shoulder. "Thank you for all you've done for us."

Sara smiled and she took his hand in hers. "Call me Sara. And really, I should be thanking you. I've asked so much from all of you these past few months."

"It's nothing," the man's wife said. "We're happy to follow you."

"I'm grateful," Sara said, grasping the woman's hands next. She left them after ruffling their son's hair.

She continued walking through the camp. More families stood up to thank her as she did.

"You got us out before those horrible soldiers burned the camp down," Zhims said. "You saved all of our lives."

"Zhims! Focus on the meat and stop bothering our chief," Ergene snapped. She turned to Sara with a wide grin on her face. "The hunters say that you kept fighting after Chanar fled. I figured. No one ever trusted him to begin with. I knew we could count on you."

She smiled and thanked each of them in turn, but had to stop when she reached a tent where she found one of her hunters inside. She recognized him from Khulan's reserve force during the battle, and there was a huge gash along his arm. The wound was dressed with bandages and herbs, but it seemed as though he was in a lot of pain.

"I'm sorry this happened to you," Sara said, kneeling beside him. "I should have protected you during the battle."

"What? This old thing?" he said, glancing at his wound. "It's nothing. I already miss the battlefield. Make sure you don't ride to battle without me, you hear?"

Sara smiled. "Of course I'll wait. It would be an honor to fight by your side."

"Hey, tell me something, Chief."

"What do you want to know?"

"When do you think this'll all be over? The war, I mean. No disrespect, of course, but I'm just a hunter. I'm not meant to be fighting wars. My wife's helping make armor these days, but I think she misses making regular clothes. And my kid, well, he's too young to understand, but he misses the Omnu lands. Harnda is too cold for him, I think."

The question gave Sara pause. She had gotten so used to the war that she had not thought about how long it would be before it ended.

"We won the Battle of the Rivers, right?" the hunter continued. "That means it'll be over soon. The Empire will think twice about facing us again."

"I think so," Sara said. "But there are still so many of them left in the Steppe. I think it'll be a long time before we can even think about the war being over."

The hunter's face fell. "Oh. Of course. I see."

She took his hand. "But here's my promise. If there's anything I can do to make this war end, I'll do it."

He smiled. "You ask me, Chief, I think it's time for us to take the fight to them."

"What do you mean?"

"Again, I'm just a hunter, but if a pack of wolves attacks your hunting party, and you fight them off, the next thing you do isn't to wait for them to lick their wounds and attack again. You chase them down and finish them for good."

When Sara left the hunter's tent, she wondered if she had just made another promise that she could not keep. She mulled over his final words to him and realized that perhaps it was not such a bad idea after all.

Sara continued walking through the tents and found herself at the end of the encampment, with only the wide open plains in front of her. The drizzle had finally ended and patches of sunlight began to light up the grassland. With the sun shining, Sara allowed herself to dream of the war's end.

# 32

# Batu

They forced Batu to his knees before they removed his blindfold. He was pushed to the ground by hands that he could not see, and only then did they remove the helmet and blindfold that obscured his vision. He looked down and saw that he was dressed in the armor of an Empire scout, but his hands were not bound.

"Here we are," a voice said from in front of him. He looked up and saw an old, balding man standing in front of him alongside one of the soldiers that had captured Batu's group. As far as he could tell, there were only three of them in the room. They were in a tent and they were still in the Steppe, but Batu could tell that it was not a nomad tent.

"Your name is Batu, I'm guessing," the man said.

"What does it matter to you?" Batu said, but when he spoke, his voice came out sounding like gravel.

"The kid must be thirsty. Get him some water, Erroll," the man said.

"Of course, General," the soldier said, then he took a bowl from a table, filled it with water from a pitcher, and then walked over to where Batu was kneeling. He placed the bowl into Batu's mouth. Though Batu tried to resist, the cool water was too compelling to deny.

After he finished, Erroll was left to stand behind the general again.

"Is that better?" the general said. Batu felt the water running down inside of his throat, and he felt his head begin to clear. He took a few moments to think, then he spoke.

"Where are my hunters?" he asked.

"They're safe. For now," the general said. He took a chair from the back of the tent and placed it in front of Batu, then he took a seat.

"And I'm just supposed to believe you?"

"Batu, all things considered, you are not exactly in a position to doubt me. In any case, I would like to begin our conversation on a foundation of mutual trust. You trust that I have not harmed your friends, and I trust that you will answer my questions truthfully. Are we on the same page here?"

Batu considered for a few moments. He took another long look at the general sitting in front of him, then adjusted his position so that he was sitting cross-legged on the ground. He scoured through his memory of what Jochi had told him about the Jusordian generals.

"So you're the famous General Sandulf, then," he said. "I know you by your reputation, and I believe my father knew you from the battlefield."

When Batu was young, Chinua had taken every opportunity he could to call Sandulf a 'lesser general', since he had not been on the front lines during the battle. But Jochi and the other chiefs always used to whisper about Sandulf's genius, the way he could play a battlefield like an instrument. Sandulf was a brilliant commander, and Erroll knew better than to underestimate him.

"I suppose I didn't give enough credit to nomad intelligence," Sandulf said. "Yes, you have it right. And I did know your father. He was a good sparring partner during the First Expedition."

"From what I remember, you were little more than a punching bag to him back then," Batu said.

Sandulf chuckled. "I'm not some nomad chieftain that you can confront like a wild boar, Batu. If you want to distract me, you're going to have to do better than that. Now, I have some questions for you."

"I won't answer any of your questions."

Sandulf ignored him. At his command, two soldiers entered the tent, each of them armed with an iron club the size of Batu's arm. Batu felt his breathing quicken when he saw the clubs, but he struggled to maintain his composure. From the way Sandulf's grin grew, Batu could tell that the general had noticed. He was sitting so close that there was nowhere to hide when his eyes bored into him.

"I want details on where the nomad camps are. I understand that when the seasons change, the camps move to new positions, correct? Tell me their locations. I also want to know the composition and status of your armies. How many soldiers do you have in fighting condition? How many are being mobilized at this moment?"

"I don't know any of that," Batu said.

Sandulf motioned to one of his soldiers. The man stepped forward and swung his club so that it hit the side of Batu's torso. The blow was not at full strength, but it felt as though Batu was being slammed against a boulder. He collapsed to the ground and coughed, feeling the wind escape from his lungs.

"Answer the questions," Sandulf said. "I won't ask again."

"I'm sorry, I'm a little deaf. We savages aren't born with the best hearing. You'll have to repeat your questions," Batu said, getting shakily back to a sitting position again.

This time, both soldiers stepped forward, and they both delivered blows, one to the side of Batu's face, and the other to his leg. Batu's body seared with pain, and he felt as though he was being dragged across a river's rocky bottom.

They struck him again, and the pain was almost too much to bear. Batu's vision blurred and his mind started to fade. All he saw were the clubs being raised again. His body screamed with pain, and he was willing to do anything to make the pain stop. He opened his mouth to speak, but before he could say anything, Erroll stepped in between the two soldiers and Batu.

"That's enough. If you keep going, he'll fall unconscious," he said, and the two soldiers lowered their clubs.

Batu felt the pain begin to fade. The pause had saved him, and he was able to stagger back upright and clear his head. He did not want to think about what he might have said if they struck him again.

The two soldiers backed off. Sandulf said nothing, though he did look at Erroll with a confused look on his face. He looked as though he was assessing a damaged machine with a busted gears.

"General, we must be above this kind of brutality. Shouldn't we?" Erroll said.

"If the reports I heard were correct, your actions at the Temple were far more extreme than this," Sandulf said. "Why the sympathy for this one savage?"

Erroll seemed to hesitate for a moment. "I did what I needed to at the Temple to ensure the highest chance of success. But this nomad is our prisoner with nowhere to go."

Sandulf scowled. "I'd have thought better of you, Erroll. I assumed you were the kind of soldier that could get things done. You're off the mission."

"You can't do this to me, General," Erroll said. "I was the one who planned the destruction of the Temple of Gaeon. I burned it to the ground on your orders, and I was the one who captured these hunters alive."

Sandulf took a step towards Erroll and placed his hands on the man's collar. He raised Erroll a few inches off the ground, and Erroll could feel his armor strain against his neck.

"Do you remember how we first met? You begged me to spare your life," Sandulf said. "I don't care how much you think you've achieved, because I will always have the option of taking it all away."

Sandulf released Erroll and he stumbled to the ground. His legs could not support him any longer.

"Now, get out. Don't make me repeat my words," Sandulf said. Erroll looked away from Sandulf, then at Batu, who was still nursing his wounds.

"Of course, General," Erroll said, getting to his feet and dusting himself off. He left the tent.

Once he was out of earshot, one of the soldiers asked, "Should we eliminate him, sir?"

"Not yet. Let's give him some time to think," Sandulf said, then he turned back to Batu.

But he did not speak. Instead, he looked straight into Batu's eyes with an unreadable expression on his face, as if he was waiting for something. Batu stared back at him, but he realized he could not meet the general's eyes for more than a few seconds without wanting to flee the room.

He looked away. "I won't answer you," Batu said. "No matter how much you hurt me."

"Oh, Batu," Sandulf said. "I've heard that the nomads call you Flamewalker, but trust me, you don't know real pain. But I think young Erroll had a point. Physical torture will not work on you, so we'll have to try something a little more creative. Bring in his friend, the one with all the scars."

The soldiers left the room, and Batu felt the color drain out of his face.

"No. Leave Nugai out of this. Please," he said.

Sandulf shrugged. "I'm sorry, Batu, but you made that choice for him."

The tent flaps burst open, and the soldiers dragged Nugai inside. Nugai kicked and thrashed the whole way despite being bound, but they managed to get him inside. They tossed him onto ground in front of Batu. He noticed that the soldiers had swapped their clubs for swords.

"Nugai," Batu said. "Saenor's scales, if you hurt him, I'll kill all of you. I'll burn this entire place to the ground."

Sandulf laughed. "So now you're showing who you truly are."

Nugai raised his head from the floor and grinned at Batu, as though he just realized that he was there.

"Hey, Batu," he said, his voice nothing more than a croak. "Didn't think I'd bump into you here. I've got to say, that armor really isn't your style."

"Get him some water," Batu said, only then noticing that Nugai's lips were dry and cracked. His eyes looked sunken and he probably has not slept for days. "He's dehydrated."

"I'm afraid not, Batu," Sandulf said, leaning back in his seat. "He's not the one who needs his voice."

Sandulf motioned to his soldiers, who picked Nugai up by the arms and held a sword to his throat.

"You're going to have to work on your grip, pal. I could break out of this in a second," Nugai said, but it was clear from his pale skin that he barely had the strength to speak.

"To Saenor with you," Batu said to Sandulf, pounding his shaking fists on the ground. "I'll rip your fingers off and shove them down your throat. I'll drag your corpse along the depths of the ocean. I'll…"

Sandulf raised a hand, and Batu fell silent despite his anger. The soldier holding the sword tightened his grip and the blade drew blood from Nugai's neck.

"Are you ready to talk?" Sandulf said. "Or would you rather I give your smiling friend here a red smile?"

"Don't listen to him, Batu!" Nugai shouted. One of Sandulf's soldiers pulled the sword away from his throat and punched Nugai in the face with a mailed fist. Nugai stumbled to the ground and coughed blood. They then held him up by his arms again.

"It's going to be okay, Nugai," Batu said. "I'm going to get you out of here."

Nugai grinned. "I don't doubt that you will. But by Onoe's blood, if you tell him anything, I'll kill you myself."

Sandulf snapped his fingers and the soldier raised his blade to Nugai's throat again. Finally, Nugai fell silent.

"Enough. Make your choice, Batu," Sandulf said.

Batu looked away from Nugai's face and into Sandulf's.

Batu took a deep breath. "Okay, I'll tell you what you want to know."

Sandulf smiled, and it was like staring into the face of the Serpent itself. "Good. Go on."

Batu opened his mouth to speak, but Nugai interrupted him.

"No!" he shouted at the top of his lungs, and one of the soldiers punched him again, this time in the stomach. Though the wind was ripped from his lungs, Nugai still managed to croak his next words.

"I made my choice, Batu. It's my life. Let me live it the way I want."

Batu stared into his friend's eyes, and was surprised to see tears flowing from them. He had never seen his best friend cry before. He closed his eyes and whispered, "I'm sorry."

He turned to Sandulf, who was still looking straight at him. Then Batu shook his head. His hands were motionless now, and they hung from his side like the branches of a dead tree.

"I see," Sandulf said. He gestured to the soldiers, who exchanged a look before dropping Nugai and removing the blade from his neck.

Batu breathed a sigh of relief as Nugai began to get on his hands and knees, shaken but alive. Batu allowed his thoughts to flow back into his mind again. They had a chance.

Then Sandulf got to his feet, drew a dagger from his belt, and plunged it into Nugai's neck. Batu screamed as Nugai's blood spilled onto the soil.

# 33
# Erroll

Erroll left the interrogation tent and began walking out of the camp. He did not have a clear destination in mind, but he knew that he had to get away from Sandulf. He did not want to think about what the general might be doing to the nomads.

Several of the other soldiers nodded to him as he passed by. Sandulf's camp, right on the border between the Asjare and the Omnu lands, was a huge, sprawling complex. Despite this, people seemed to know who Erroll was wherever he went. They made sure to salute him or nod when he passed, and always gave him a wide berth.

Erroll's thoughts inevitably drifted back to his father.

"He was one of my closest friends," Temulun had told him. "He came from the Empire, so he was always a little strange, but everyone knew he had a good heart. He ran into some trouble with his superiors so he came to live with us, but I don't think he liked to talk about it much. But he did talk about you a lot. And your mother. He thought about how you were doing, if you were still in the smithing district or if your mother had found a way to get out of there."

"What happened to him?" Erroll had asked.

"The plague," Temulun had said. "I remember that day. Erwan announced that he had found a way to get back to Ruson. A merchant or something that could smuggle him in one of his carts. But when the day came for him to leave, he got sick. He said that he'd find another merchant the next time, but...but the time never came."

"So he failed," Erroll had said.

Temulun had surprised Erroll with what she did next. The master of hunters placed a hand on Erroll's shoulder. "The entire time I knew

Erwan, he was searching for a way to get back to you. He would have crossed the ocean to see you again."

Erroll had not had the time to think about what Temulun had told him. The week leading up to the battle and the two weeks after had kept him busy, and so he preferred not to think about things that might distract him from the job.

But now he had nothing but time. Erroll reached the end of the camp's neatly-arranged streets. Sandulf's camp was always filled with troops silently going about their tasks. Erroll wondered what the Asjare might have thought of Sandulf's camp. They would have called it boring and repetitive, but Erroll figured that the nomads did not really care all that much about the way the Jusordians lived.

He kept walking through the Steppe, traipsing over hills and through the damp grass until the camp was nearly out of sight. He took a seat and pulled a flask out of his jacket. He turned it over in his hands. It was the one Manvel had given him, in a time that felt so far away now. It had been so long since he had thought about Manvel, the first friend that did not abandon him the second things went south. He wondered if Manvel was still alive, or if Sandulf had turned on him as well.

He opened it and took a drink. He had filled the flask with some rum he found in Syra's tent, and the liquid burned his throat as it went down.

"Saenor's scales," he muttered to himself. "Syra has horrible taste."

He kept drinking it anyway, because it was something to do as he sat there and watched as the late night breeze swept through the Steppe. No matter how much he drank, he could not get Sandulf's words out of his head.

"I don't care how much you think you've achieved, because I will always have the option of taking it all away."

It was almost as if he could hear Sandulf's words, clear as day, as he walked through the camp. Erroll supposed that it was only a matter of time before Sandulf called for his execution, so he figured that he might as well enjoy his final night on the Steppe.

Something had felt wrong with him ever since the Temple. He tried to push the memory Khalja burning in the fire away from his mind and cast himself towards happier thoughts. He remembered the question that Khalja had asked him before they left for the Temple.

"So, where do you think you belong? Here or back in Ruson?" Khalja had asked him.

Erroll finally had his answer, but it was too late. He was sitting around the campfire in the Asjare's mountain camp the night before the battle. Geser had managed to steal some fresh venison from his friend that had arrived that day, and even though it was not allowed, Temulun had allowed them to have a meal on one of the ridges near the camp. That place overlooked the entire Arban Valley.

Erroll had seen the view countless times, and it still managed to take his breath away each time. The way the Steppe seemed to breathe as one, the way everything seemed to be part of this huge tapestry made Erroll feel as though there was a place for him within this grand machine.

It pained him to take his eyes away from the spectacle, but he finally turned back to his hunting group.

"Did you hear about Boal and Chambui?" Geser said.

"Not this again," Temulun said. "Geser, you need to stop with this gossiping. It isn't healthy."

Geser grinned. "I see myself as a connoisseur of information. No harm, in my opinion, if people know what's going on."

Temulun folded her arms, but this seemed like a conversation they had had before. She did not push it further.

"I thought that Chambui was with Taragai," Khalja said.

Erroll stroked his chin. "Taragai, that's the head of the hunting group nearest to ours, right?"

"Hey, you're actually starting to learn," Geser said. "Yes. Everyone knows how devoted he is to Chambui. I don't believe this story, but some people say that he saw a shooting star in the sky one night and took it as a sign from Gaeon that it was time to ask her to marry him."

"You must be joking," Erroll said. "Does Gaeon take interest in your romantic lives?"

"If he has, then he's playing the long game with me," Khalja said. One of the other hunters reached out and gave him a pat on the shoulder.

Geser laughed. "Well evidently not, because last night, while I was out on my patrol, I found Chambui and Boal sitting together underneath the moonlight."

"Perhaps they were just having a chat," Temulun said. "Men and women can be friends. Who's to say that that's not the case with those two?"

"Temulun, you're the master of hunters, but I'm the master of love," Geser said. "I know when two people are in love, and that's what I saw last night."

"Saenor's scales, Geser," Khalja said, laughing. "This is serious. Boal is the one leading our right flank. If Taragai hears about this…"

"What Taragai doesn't know won't hurt him," Geser said, holding up a finger to his lips. Temulun rolled her eyes before continuing with his story after another bout of laughter,.

Everyone in that group was either dead or held as prisoners by the enemy. Erroll was the only one left. He downed the last of the rum in his flask and placed it back into his jacket. The liquid burned his throat, but he was glad, for the feeling helped him forget the thoughts that occupied his mind. The alcohol made his thoughts hazy and his vision swim, but he had enough presence of mind to see movement on the hill just in front of him.

It was just for a moment, but he saw a flash of what looked like the nomads' leather armor. Erroll felt the drunkenness leave him and all his senses went into high alert. He picked up his spear and shield and prepared to fight.

Erroll knelt down and undid the hunter's bonds, but he left her gag on, for now. She had given him a tough fight, but he had eventually managed to capture her and bring her to his tent without anyone noticing. Luckily, no one else frequented the personal guard's section of the camp, so it had not be difficult for him to stay undetected.

"From your armor, you're an Omnu hunter. I'm guessing you were sent here to free your comrades."

She did not move to remove her gag, but neither did she look happy about what Erroll had said. That told him that he was on the right track.

"But why only you?" he wondered aloud. "Normally, a rescue mission would involve three, maybe four hunters. Your people are good, but you're not that good. You're here on a suicide mission."

Suddenly, the hunter could not meet his eyes. She looked down at her lap and knit her hands together.

"You're ashamed," Erroll realized. "Ah, I understand. You didn't come here to rescue them. You came to see if they were even alive. I see that our little ruse with the armor worked out quite well. Nevertheless, you went against your orders and tried to rescue them anyway."

From the look in her eyes, Erroll knew that he had guessed the truth. He did not need to ask her any more questions. He reached out and undid her gag.

"I still have one more question," he said. "What's your name?"

She looked confused. "K-Kara. My name is Kara. What are you going to do with me?"

"Kara. Well, Kara, I haven't decided yet," Erroll said. "It was that chief, Saragerel, that sent you? Is that correct?"

Kara nodded. Her eyes darted around the tent, searching for a way to escape. Her eyes lingered on the entrance to the tent located behind Erroll.

"I'm not like Sandulf, Kara," Erroll said. "I'm not going to torture or harm you in any way."

"That's a lie," Kara blurted. She then realized what she had said and her eyes widened. Instead of backtracking, she kept speaking. "All of you are ruthless killers."

Erroll sighed. "I suppose that's fair. We've done some horrible things to your people, haven't we? Some of them were directly caused by me."

He got up from his chair and began pacing through the room.

"If you're going to kill me, just be done with it already," Kara said. "I've made my peace."

Erroll looked at her again, his eyes widening when he saw the resolve in her eyes. He thought about the last time he had seen determination like that in the face of death. It was Khalja, watching him from across the Temple as it burned around him.

"How can you be so calm about your own death?" Erroll found himself asking.

"Everyone passes into the wind eventually," Kara said. "And maybe my time has come. I'm lucky that I will die in service of my chief and my tribe."

"But you'll be gone," Erroll said. "You won't even know if your sacrifice was worth it."

Kara shrugged. "I won't really be gone. I'll live on, in the wind, in the flowers, or in the grass. The Steppe claims us all in the end."

"And you're really okay with that?"

"I am. You Jusordians don't care about anyone besides yourselves, but that's not the way we nomads live. I lived as a proud nomad of the Steppe, and I'll die as one."

Erroll looked at her. Without missing a beat, she glared back at him. Erroll almost felt as though it was him who was held captive. He knew that he should turn her over to Sandulf. Sandulf would thank him, maybe even forgive him for his outburst at the interrogation tent earlier.

He considered binding Kara again and taking her to Sandulf's tent.

He would be finished with Batu and the rest by now, but Erroll could not imagine himself doing it. The thought felt poisonous to him, like walking through fire. He realized that he was done with being instructed of his place in the world. This time, he was going to do it right.

He turned back to Kara with his decision made. He found himself thinking of Manvel over in Asghar's camp, and he realized that there was no one he wanted to speak to more than him.

"You're here to save Batu and his hunters, correct?" he said.

"I thought that you already knew that," Kara said. "Yes I am, not that it matters now."

"It does," Erroll said. "I'm done playing Sandulf's games. I'm going to help you."

# 34
# Sara

"The first scout reports are back, and they seem promising," Bataar said. Since their discussion the other day, Khulan had been ignoring Sara, which meant that she had to receive most of her reports from Bataar. "The Asjare aren't ready for another assault. They're too busy trying to pool their hunters to keep their own people fed. I don't think they'll be launching any attacks against us anytime soon."

"Good," Sara said. "I want regular scouting missions to keep tabs on their camps. Send only half a patrol group to make sure they don't stand out too much. With any luck, we'll be able to figure out when their next attack will be."

"How about Yargai and the rest? Have they discovered any more Omnu hunters?"

"Yargai returned with his group yesterday. He found a group of ten hunters, all from Yegu's camp. They managed to get out when the Asjare betrayed us. Yegu himself fell in battle," Bataar said.

"That's a damn shame," Sara said. "I didn't know him well, but at least his hunters carry his memory now. What about the other scouts?"

"Yargai's is the only one back. That could mean that the other scouts have found larger groups and need to move slower."

"That seems promising," Sara said. "Good work. I should probably speak with the new hunters soon. They don't know me at all, so they must be rather confused."

"How do you feel about that?" Bataar said, cocking her head to the side. "Are you scared?"

Sara shrugged. "They don't have much choice, do they? And besides, I think my achievements speak for themselves. We shouldn't have much trouble."

Bataar smiled. "That's what I like to hear," he said, and then he sighed. Something was clearly on his mind.

"What is it?" Sara asked.

"You know, you really should work things out with Khulan. You two aren't meant to be fighting like this."

Sara shrugged. "I'm not the one who needs to apologize."

Before Bataar could reply, the tent flaps opened. Galeren, Herald of the Qhurin, stepped into the tent.

"Good evening," Galeren said, taking a seat next to a wide-eyed Bataar. "I'm sorry to interrupt such an intimate meeting, but I was getting impatient."

"Herald Galeren, what a pleasant surprise," Sara said. "This was a private meeting, so we weren't expecting you."

Galeren waved her hand dismissively. "You can do away with the pleasantries, Sara. I have no need for them."

"All right," Sara said, taking a deep breath. "What are you doing here? Are you spying on us?"

"A little bit," Galeren said. "But I don't believe you haven't been doing the same for all the other chiefs. We all just want to get to know each other a little better."

Sara ignored the accusation, though she had indeed sent a few hunters to mingle in the Qhurin section of the camps to make sure they were not doing anything drastic. She turned to Bataar.

"I think you should give us some privacy," she said.

Bataar got up immediately and left the tent. The moment they were left alone, Sara turned to Galeren, her arms folded.

"You still haven't answered my question," Sara said. "What are you doing here?"

Galeren smiled. "I'm here because I know what you're up to."

"I don't know what you're talking about, Herald," Sara said. "You'll have to be more specific."

"Again with the formalities, Sara. And here I was thinking that you were the kind of leader that got things done without all the nonsense. Okay, fine, I'll bite. I'm here because I know that you've found a secret passage to the Asjare camps. And don't even think about playing dumb. My sources are quite reliable."

Sara was silent for a few seconds before replying. "Do any of the other chieftains know?"

"By Gaeon, of course not. None of them have the brains. Chanar's too busy licking his wounds after the Battle of the Rivers and Thaube couldn't gather information even if it were staring him in the face. The Harnda already know, so that just leaves me."

Sara nodded. "Okay, you know that we've found the passage. What are you going to do? Blackmail us? It'll hurt you as much as it'll hurt us if Chanar and Thaube found out."

"So you're a suspicious one, then? Just like your father. No wonder you've survived this long. But you can rest easy, child. I just want to know what you intend to do with this information."

Sara folded her arms. "If you've been listening, you'd know we're only using it to keep tabs on the Asjare movements. To make sure they aren't organizing another assault."

"That's what I heard, but what's the real story?" Galeren said, raising an eyebrow. "You don't just discover a secret passage and then use it for scouting. If you're the leader I think you are, then you'll know better than that."

Sara considered Galeren's words. Before today, she had still been deciding whether or not she could trust Galeren. Although her people said she had been blessed by Gaeon, Sara had no doubt that her rise to power was the result of a series of careful, calculated moves. Thus, she would much rather have Galeren on her side instead.

"We're planning a raid," Sara said. "We're preparing the Omnu and Harnda hunters as we speak, and we'll invade the Asjare camps once we're ready. If we do it right, we'll be able to get rid of that threat entirely."

Galeren stroked her chin.

She laughed. "I didn't think you'd do something so bold. Some would say that it'd be unwise to commit all your hunters to a single assault."

"Some people don't see how dire our situation is. The Empire is rapidly recovering after that last battle and so are the Asjare. If we let them have enough time to rebuild their armies, it won't matter how united the rest of the Steppe is. We'll be crushed entirely. But if we act now while the Asjare are still weak, we've got a shot."

"And the Arban Valley would be an excellent place to face the Empire in a final battle," Galeren said. "That is, if you manage to take it."

"We will," Sara said. "I trust my hunters."

"You'll likely win the battle," Galeren said. "But have you considered anything about holding the territory once you've captured?"

Sara raised an eyebrow. "I don't follow."

Galeren gave her a sly smile. "From what I know about that old leopard Dayir, he's not one to just let you have the Valley. And neither will the Empire. They'll launch raids against you, disrupt your supply lines, kill your hunters while they sleep. Within a month, you'll be forced to pull out of the Valley and the Empire will proceed to occupy it. You'll be right back where you started."

"I hadn't considered that."

"Of course you didn't. Nomads aren't made to hold ground, are they? We're meant to be constantly on the move. But perhaps I'll be of help to you, just this once."

"What help can you offer?"

"My soldiers aren't like the other nomad hunters. You know this already. We know how to build fortifications, maintain patrols, keep the peace, and most importantly, hold ground. If we're in charge, you won't have to worry about anyone taking back the valley from you."

"What's in it for you?" Sara said.

"Ah, a smart one," Galeren said. "I like that. Okay, here's my price. After the war, if we happen to win, the Qhurin will take control of the Arban Valley."

Sara had to admit that the offer seemed enticing even though the price was steep,. If Galeren could keep the Arban Valley stable, they could focus all their energy on the remaining Empire forces in the area. They would have a real shot at winning the war. But there was just one thing that Sara needed to know.

"The Asjare people," she said. "There will still be many of them living in the Valley after we take over. Gatherers, tanners, butchers, and so on. What will you do with them?"

"Why does it matter to you?" Galeren said. "They aren't your people."

Sara folded her arms. "Think of it as a promise I'm keeping."

"Well, the Asjare definitely wouldn't be happy if we took control of their lands. So we'll need to enforce a little discipline, perhaps have some executions or demonstrations to quell dissent."

Sara shook her head. "You'll do no such thing. If we give you control of the Asjare camps, you must agree to treat the Asjare people with respect."

Galeren scowled. "This is war, Sara. Sacrifices need to be made. I thought you'd understand that better than anyone. Be glad that the sacrifices don't come from your own people."

"They're nomads, too, aren't they? It's not their fault that their chieftain chose the wrong side. We will not punish them for the sins of their leaders."

"It can't be done," Galeren said.

"Then we have nothing left to discuss. I'll carry out the raid on my own," Sara said, then she got up to leave. "Excuse me, Lady Herald. I have some business to check on."

She started to walk out of the tent. Galeren stopped her before she lifted one of the tent flaps,.

"Wait," the Herald said, and Sara stopped. She smiled to herself.

Galeren wasn't the only one who knew how to play this game.

Sara turned to face her. "Yes?"

"I'll do what you ask. But only if you lend me some of your hunters for peacekeeping."

Sara grinned. "We can do that. My hunters will make sure you keep your word."

"Fine," Galeren said, then she laughed. "You know, I've heard things about you, but I didn't think you'd be this fierce in person. Turns out, I was the one who underestimated you."

Sara felt the early morning breeze blow through her hair as she stood on the ridge overlooking the trail to the Asjare camps. It had taken them the better part of two weeks to get their hunters through the passage and into locations throughout Arban's Peaks where they could launch their assault. They had managed to do it without much incident, except for the occasional Asjare scout that they had to silence.

The assault on the Arban Valley was about to begin. She looked behind her and saw the hunters arrayed on the ridge alongside her. They had divided their forces into numerous groups to make sure they could attack each Asjare camp simultaneously, which meant that Sara was commanding a force only about as large as a hunting group. Alaqa and Yargai would be leading their own groups to attack the same camp she was, while the Harnda and Qhurin had their own assignments throughout the Valley.

Nonetheless, Sara felt uneasy. She remembered the last time she had led the Omnu into battle, and she did not want to think about how many lives she had cost them that day. She shook her head and turned to see Khulan waiting for her. She was surprised to see her there, as Khulan had given her no indication that she would actually show up despite orders for her to join the assault.

"Khulan, I…"

Khulan held up a hand. "Save it, Sara. We have a battle to focus on, so we shouldn't let our personal differences get in the way."

Sara frowned. "You mean, we're not even going to address what happened?"

"I'm still your master of hunters. You're still our chief. We'll just remain as that for today."

Sara gulped. She was not used to seeing Khulan like this, all uptight and cold.

"Fine," Sara said. "Chief and master of hunters. That's all."

"They're in position," Khulan said. "You ready?"

"Ready as I'll ever be," Sara said, then she took out her bow and signaled to the rest of the hunters, all of whom were ready to go. She looked out onto the valley and watched the peaks for their signal. Eventually, an eagle flew from one of the other hunting groups' positions. A few seconds later, another eagle emerged, then another. Sara closed her eyes and took Altan's eyes. She soared out into the valley on his wings, joining the other eagles to signal that they were ready to begin.

She allowed herself one last glance over the rest of the camps. There were four camps in total. Their numbers shrunk because they did not have enough hunters to support groups of six at a time. The camps were about a kilometer from each other, with a few groups of hunters patrolling the space between the camps.

There were no horns or war cries. Instead, Sara took her own eyes again and raised her bow. With the clattering of hooves and the sound of wind howling through the valley, they charged down the ridge and into Asjare territory.

As they made their way through the thick forest as quickly as they could, Sara noticed how different the Arban Valley felt. The air here was still about as cold as the Harnda lands, but it was thick with moisture. The trees were also denser here, as if they were closing in on Sara as she led her group through them.

They spotted their first Asjare patrol, a small group of five that was riding along the edges of the trees. Sara raised her hand to signal to her hunting group, and they sped up, spurring their horses into a gallop. Sara nocked her bow.

She took aim and fired, taking down the patrol's leader. Khulan shot down a second one, sending the group into disarray. Two of them tried to run while one of them drew his sword, but it was too late. Within moments, Sara's group had cut right through the patrol, their bodies knocked straight off their horses with blood gushing from their wounds.

They emerged onto the valley floor where the trees were sparser, but still provided some cover from the sun. Sara was glad to feel the sun on her back and the wind in her hair. It made her feel like she was back home, chasing a group of deer instead of a group of hunters.

Sara took her eagle's eyes again and surveyed the land before her. There were two more patrol groups and neither of them had noticed the raid. It would not be long before they did, but Sara wanted to delay them as much as she could.

She led her men towards the nearest group, intercepting them as they were riding around the base of a hill. Sara put away her bow and drew her sword, cutting off a woman's hand right as she reached for her horn to signal the rest of the Valley. Sara drew her sword back and finished the job with a thrust through the woman's chest.

By then, however, the third group had noticed them. Before Sara's group could stop them, they had managed to blow their horns, signaling their camp that they were under attack. Sara heard similar horns ringing out across the Valley. Within moments, their element of surprise was gone.

Sara raised her bow and charged towards the last group, but she held back, letting her own hunters finish the job as she took her eagle's eyes again, watching her assigned camp. Zayaat had decided to stay in the Harnda camps in case the Empire tried something, so he had sent Alaqa, his best hunter, to lead the Harnda forces in this battle. She saw Alaqa and Yargai's teams making their way steadily towards the camp, but Yargai's group was delayed by a small skirmish with a patrol group.

As for Sara's group, the way ahead was clear. The Asjare camp began to erupt with horns, and a force of hunters soon assembled at one of the camp's gathering points. It was the gathering point closest to Alaqa's group, which meant that they charged her first, meeting her forces in a small clearing northeast of the camp.

Sara snapped back to her own body before turning to Khulan.

"We'll go for the force attacking Alaqa," she said. "With any luck, that'll leave Yargai free to secure the camp."

Khulan nodded. Once they had dealt with the main force of hunters, the camp would be relatively easy to secure. They had brought torches just in case, but Sara hoped that they would not need them.

They advanced, ignoring the smaller groups of hunters that were leaving their patrols to join the main force. Alaqa had split her force into three groups. The first one led by her was keeping the main bulk of the force engaged, while the other two rained arrows on the enemy hunters.

Alaqa did manage to lead the Asjare hunters away from the camp, which made it easier for Yargai's group to charge through the tents and kill any straggling hunters. The camp was relatively large, so it would take a while for Yargai to secure the entire premises. Sara needed to buy him more time.

She led her hunters as they crashed into the rear of the Asjare force, taking them by surprise and leaving them surrounded on both sides. The Asjare stopped advancing towards Alaqa's group and stood their ground, trying to hold firm as Sara cut through line after line of their hunters, slashing through saddles and armor alike.

She allowed herself to focus on the fighting right in front of her. She parried a blow from a hunter on her right and pivoted to avoid a sword on her left. She then threw a knife at the first hunter, before charging forward and skewering the second hunter with her sword before she had a chance to react.

Her hunting group was having similar success. They had attacked right as the sun rose, with their hunters fresh and ready for battle. The Asjare were battle-weary and fatigued from a long night of patrols. None of them had been expecting a raid on this scale so soon after the last battle.

At that moment, Alaqa's group took the opportunity and advanced herself. Within a few moments, the Asjare force was scattering. All that remained was a small group of hunters that Alaqa's group had managed to surround. When Sara arrived, they were throwing their weapons onto the ground and getting off their horses.

"Any problems, Alaqa?" Sara said.

"None," Alaqa said, then she gestured towards the hunters that had surrendered. "And we managed to capture old Dayir, too."

"Great," Sara said. "Let me go have a word with him."

Sara got off her horse and approached the captive who looked most likely to be the chief. Dayir reminded her of Zayaat, only he did have nearly as many scars as the older hunter did. Still, Dayir kneeling on the ground with his hands behind his head looked more dignified than most of the hunters Sara knew . He was dressed in a tight black cloak and had a face that made him look much older than he was.

"You must be Dayir, I presume," she said, standing in front of him. "You may stand."

Dayir took a moment before getting to his feet, eyeing the hunters that were standing around them with their swords drawn.

"That's my name, yes," he said. "And you must be the Omnu chief, Saragerel. I've heard things about you, and I must say, I didn't expect you to be a wisp of a girl."

Sara grinned. "Well, this wisp of a girl just defeated your entire force of hunters in under an hour. I want you to order your camps to surrender. There will be no more bloodshed today."

Dayir laughed. "So you think you've won, is it? Think again, girl. I was only the diversion. The Empire will soon be here to kill all of you."

As if on cue, Khulan pushed through the crowd of hunters until she was standing next to Sara.

"Sara!" she said. Sara gestured to the other hunters to restrain Dayir as she listened to Khulan's report. "The Asjare camp was hiding Empire soldiers this entire time. They ambushed Yargai's hunters and have established a defensive perimeter around the camp."

Sara's stomach dropped to the floor. "And Yargai? Is he safe?"

Khulan shook her head. "He was trying to get the upper hand on the Empire, but there were just too many of them."

Dayir was laughing behind her, but Sara tried her best to ignore him until someone gagged him.

Sara bit her lip. "Well, we just need to make sure he didn't die in vain. Can we organize an offensive to break the Empire's lines?"

"We'll lose too many hunters in the process," Khulan said. "The Empire built some tough fortifications, and it seems like they're ready to resist a frontal assault."

"Saenor's scales," Sara said. "We didn't expect something like this."

"There is something we can do," Alaqa said, then Sara and Khulan turned to her. "We have our torches, don't we? If we set fire to the grass around the camp, it'll break the Empire's defenses."

"And kill everyone inside the camps as well," Sara said. "We won't do it."

"Sara, if we don't take the camps by today, we'll be in a worse position than when we started. They'll send for reinforcements and we'll be forced to retreat," Alaqa said.

"Sara, Alaqa has it right and you know it," Khulan said. "The Asjare betrayed us. Why do you still care about them?"

"I won't do it," Sara said. "The Asjare aren't their leaders, and I didn't come here to destroy the Asjare's homes. Do we know what's happening with the other camps?"

"It's a imilar situation," Alaqa said. "It seems like the Asjare were prepared for our raid."

"Send out riders," Sara said. "Tell them that they are not to burn the camps under any circumstances. I need to think about the best way to proceed."

Alaqa went off the deliver the order, but Khulan grabbed Sara by the shoulder. "This is ridiculous, Sara," she said. "You're willing to let all of us die just because you can't stomach a few deaths?"

"That's not…" Sara said, then she swatted Khulan's hands away. "I just need to think, okay? For Gaeon's sake, Khulan, give me some space."

She walked over to Dayir and ripped the gag from his mouth.

"Tell your people to stand down, now."

Dayir grinned, then he said only a single word. "No."

Sara punched him in the face, feeling a cheekbone crack as Dayir fell to the ground, blood seeping from a cut on his cheek.

"You'd rather have your people burn than surrender to us?" Sara said.

Dayir laughed, but it became hard for him to speak with his face pressed to the ground.

"I've already lost, haven't I? But now the decision falls on your shoulders, Saragerel. I know your reputation. How many of those principles are you willing to sacrifice in order to win?"

Sara put the gag back on him. She pushed past the line of hunters and watched the Asjare camps. The Empire had dug a few trenches and put up a few traps so that cavalry couldn't charge through the streets. Sara could not see a way around them.

She took the eyes of her eagle and watched the camp from above. There was no one on the streets anymore. Everyone was either hiding inside their tents or gathered in the central clearing, surrounded by a small group of soldiers for protection. Next to the clearing was the pen where they kept their horses. Sara noticed that there was a surprising number of horses still in the camp, almost three dozen. The pens built around the horses did not serve much of a purpose, and Sara knew from experience that a horse could easily jump that distance if it wanted to.

Then she snapped back to her own body.

"I know what to do," she said, turning to Khulan. "I need you to collect every bag of manna our hunters have, then get everyone that's got a soul bond with an eagle."

Khulan raised an eyebrow. "What are you planning, Sara?"

Sara grinned. "You remember what we did to throw Batu off our tail?"

Khulan's eyes widened. "You realize that we'll need a lot more manna for that than we have?"

"Well, I guess I'm going to have to owe Galeren a favor."


The Empire soldiers watched as Sara led a small group of hunters to a clearing near the edge of the enemy camps. They readied themselves to prepare for a charge, leveling their spears and raising their shields. But instead of advancing, they closed their eyes and took the wings of their eagles, soaring into the skies with bags clenched in between their talons.

The soldiers watched as the eagles soared high above the camps. While some of them tried to aim with their bows, their arrows fell out of reach.

The camp looked far more peaceful from this high up, and so did the rest of the Valley. The fighting had died down across the four camps, but Sara's instructions were being carried to the rest of the hunting groups, and they would soon erupt into chaos once again.

Sara sent her eagle forward. The flock of eagles followed as they circled the camp, finally coming to rest right above the pen of horses. After making sure that the rest of the eagles were in position, she released her load, letting the bag of manna drop onto the pen of horses below. The rest of the eagles followed her lead, and the horse pen soon glowed with azure light.

Sara snapped back into her own body and closed her eyes, casting her senses outwards until she could feel the herd of horses. She would not be able to take their eyes or give specific commands from this far away, but she could feel the wave of emotion erupting from the herd of horses.

She felt their fear, uncertainty, and the frustration of being caged, unable to go anywhere. She took that feeling and pushed until its breaking point, making each horse want nothing more than to break out of the camp and run wild in the plains.

The pen exploded with energy as the horses leapt over the fences and started galloping through the camp, barreling through the streets towards the edge of the camp.

Sara looked behind her and gestured to Alaqa, who had prepared the rest of the hunters for an assault. At her signal, Alaqa led the assembled hunters and charged the Empire's lines. Sara hoped that she had gotten the timing right as she watched the Empire prepare their defences.

As Alaqa's hunters got within a hundred meters of the enemy lines, Sara heard the sound of clattering hooves and angry whinnying. The Empire soldiers turned to find a herd of horses charging straight for them. Some of them dropped their weapons and ran, while others were torn between pointing their weapons at the herd or at the hunters charging at them.

The horses paid no attention. They barrelled through the Empire's defences, crashing through the soldiers and shattering traps in their desperate attempt to get out of the camp. Similar stampedes happened at various places throughout the camp's defensive lines, but the area where Sara directed Alaqa to charge was thought to be the hardest hit.

Alaqa led her hunters through the camp's boundary with almost no trouble, save for a few brave Empire soldiers that were still holding the line. Alaqa then entered the camp to secure it.

Sara sighed in relief as she watched Alaqa carry out her task. She sat at the base of a tree next and took a long drink from her waterskin.

"You did it," Khulan said after taking a seat next to her. "Without needing to burn the entire camp down. Maybe I was wrong."

"Khulan admitting that she's wrong? I never thought I'd see the day."

"Okay, you can lay off me now," Khulan said, placing her arm around Sara. "Hey, I'm sorry that we fought. I got in my own head again, and I made it your problem."

Sara looked into her friend's face, and she wanted to be angry, but the only thing she could feel was relief when she realized that she finally had her best friend back.

"Of course it's okay," Sara said, pulling Khulan into a hug. "What would I do without you?"

"I don't know, but I know you'd still do amazing. Just like you did today."

"I'm just relieved we didn't have do what Dayir wanted," Sara said.

"True," Khulan said. "But what would you have done if you had no choice?"

Sara raised an eyebrow. "What do you mean?"

"Well, you managed to find a way out of it today, but what will you do if there comes a time when you won't have the luxury of a clever plan or army to save you?"

Sara thought about that for a long moment. "I'll do what I think is right," she said.

"But how would you know what that is?"

Sara did not answer. Instead, she looked above her to where the flock of eagles was still soaring, not caring at all about the battle unfolding beneath them. The eagles formed a ring in the sky and Sara took her eagle's eyes, letting herself drift among the clouds.

# 35

# Batu

Batu sat in his cage wondering how long it would take for him to starve. Ever since Nugai passed into the wind, he'd refused to eat any meals and the Empire soldiers had been forced to pour water down his throat. It was the dead of night, and yet sleep eluded him. Every time he shut his eyes, all he could see was Nugai's blood spilling onto the soil and all he could hear was his father's voice howling in his mind.

Batu found himself wishing again and again that someone would just come into the cage and kill him. He could not get Nugai's final words out of his head.

"I made my choice, Batu. It's my life. Let me live it the way I want."

The guilt weighed on Batu like an unshakable chill. If Batu had not been able to do anything while being questioned by Sandulf, perhaps he had failed all the way back at the Temple of Gaeon. Batu should have told Nugai and Cirina to fight. The might have had a chance to escape. Or maybe he should have sacrificed himself to hold the Empire's soldiers off, giving Nugai and Cirina a fighting chance if they chose to run.

Or maybe Batu's fault lay even earlier than that. He should have asked for more hunters to accompany him to the Temple. They were heading into enemy territory, for Saenor's sake. He should have known better. Instead, he had paid the price with his own hunters' lives.

His thoughts began to spiral and Chinua's long dormant voice emerged.

"I never would have let them die," Chinua said.

Tears began streaming down Batu's face, though he tried as much as he could to stem the flow.

"I'm sorry," he repeated to himself as he imagined himself speaking to everyone that he had allowed die. "I'm sorry."

Their faces swam before him. The hunters he had lost in the Battle of Orange Sky. Khabichi. Nugai. His own father. He hadn't even had the strength to protect his own father.

"Apologies won't bring them back," Chinua's voice echoed.

Batu buried his head in his hands, but there was nothing he could do to stop the flow of tears. He wished that someone would kill him, because he could not find the strength to do it himself.

Then the cage door opened in front of him and Batu tried to pull himself together.

"You're here to kill me?" he said. Erroll was standing in front of the door, and he was dressed as if he were going to battle, complete with a spear and shield strapped to his back. "Get it over with already."

"Not today, Batu," he said, reaching forward and slicing through Batu's bonds with a knife. He stepped aside and revealed that Cirina was standing behind him, dressed in her hunter's armor. She was standing beside one of Sara's hunters. Her name was Kara, if Batu's memory was correct Beside her was a man he did not know, but he had the nose and build of the K'harini warriors who sometimes guarded merchant caravans that visited the Steppe.

His eyes widened, then he shook his head. "I won't go," he said.

"What?" Erroll said. "Don't you want to help your tribe?"

"Why should I? I'll just end up getting someone killed. Better for me to stay here and rot."

Erroll turned to Cirina. "Can you help him?"

"Let me handle this," she said.

"Make it quick. The guards will be back in five minutes."

Cirina pushed past him and entered the cage. He found that he couldn't meet her eyes. Instead, he turned away from her and leaned against the bars.

"Just get out of here, Cirina," Batu said. "Leave me. It's the rational thing to do. If you brought me with you, they'd chase you down. But if it's just you, they might let you give them the slip."

Cirina shook her head. She placed her hand on Batu's shoulder. "You know I'm not going to do that, Batu."

Batu took her hand and took a deep breath, finally finding the courage to look her in the eyes. "You remember what I told you, right? Before we began our journey."

Cirina nodded. "I told you that I trusted you to make the right decision for our people."

"This is the best decision," he said. "I saw...I let Nugai die. He depended on me, both of you did, and I failed. I'm clearly not fit to lead you. So, just go."

Cirina shook her head.

"Damn it, Cirina," Batu said, gripping the iron bar next to him. "Just listen to me. Please. Let me do something good for once. I can't handle failing again. I just can't."

By then, Batu's cheeks were streaked with tears that dripped silently onto his lap. He could not see the look on Cirina's face, but he imagined her disappointment. He expected her to curse and leave him to die like the mess he was. It was what he deserved.

Instead, she pulled him into an embrace. She held him tightly, and shushed him when he tried to protest. After a few moments, he allowed himself to exhale and sob into her shoulder.

"We all fail, Batu," she whispered. "But there are people depending on you now. They're depending on you to get back on your feet and try again. Myself included."

"I don't know if I'll have the strength," Batu said.

"Well, I believe that you do," Cirina said, releasing him and staring straight into his eyes. "And I think I have enough faith in the both of us."

"How could you still think that after all that's happened?"

Cirina chuckled. "How could I not? I saw you lead us into a burning camp to save your father. You burned a hill to the ground to get us out of the Asjare lands. And you saved the Steppe by bringing the Qhurin army to the front lines. No one else could have done what you did."

"I had help," Batu muttered.

"Give yourself some credit. For a long time, I didn't think I would find a leader I could believe in. They were all old and uninspiring. Then I was assigned to your group, and I ended up believing in you. "

Batu's eyes widened and he found himself smiling when he met Cirina's eyes again. He rubbed the back of his head, and the feeling in his chest was like a peace he had not known since... since he was a child and his mother was stroking his hair, singing him to sleep.

Batu remembered how Cirina had reached through the smoke to save him. And how she had helped him come home. He had to repay her somehow. He nodded.

"All right, all right," he said, staggering to his feet and wiping the tears from his cheek. "You've convinced me. Let's go save our people."

Cirina grinned as she helped him out of the cage and onto his feet. "That's better. Now get your ass out of that cage. We don't have a lot of time left."

Batu took the reins from Erroll and got on the horse that Erroll had found for him. The horse seemed reliable enough, though it was not the same as his own.

"I still don't understand," Batu said. They were standing on a hill near the borders of the camp, concealed in darkness. The guards would not be able to see. "Why are you doing this? You captured us and burned the Temple to the ground."

"It's a long story," Erroll said. "No time to get into it now. Let's just say I'm keeping a promise to an old friend. Is that good enough for you?"

"I still don't know if we should trust him," Kara said. She still had not gotten on her horse, despite the K'harini man offering her the reins.

"Manvel, will you talk to her?" Erroll said to him. Manvel wore the uniform of one of Asghar's men, even though they were standing in Sandulf's war camp. He carried himself like one of Batu's archery instructors and looked like he could wrestle an angry stallion if he wanted to.

"Sure," Manvel said. "Look at it this way. We're giving you horses and supplies when we could have killed you instead. You're on our territory right now, so it would have been quite easy. Doesn't that make our intentions clear?"

Kara shook her head. "You two could still be up to something. You're from the Empire, after all. I know what your kind are like."

"Kara, there's no need to look a gift horse in the mouth," Cirina said from the top of her horse as she checked its supplies. "Just get on the horse."

"Maybe they're trying to get us to show them where our camps are," Kara said. "Or they're going to follow us to find our camps."

"The plains are large and there's almost nowhere to hide. We know how good your tracking abilities are. We wouldn't be able to follow you even if we tried," Erroll said. "And besides, I suspect we have a better idea where your camps are than you do."

"And why is that?" Kara said.

Manvel pointed towards the camp where a small group of tents were pitched near the neatly-defined rows. Those tents were wide and circular, instead of the tall and pointed Empire tents.

"Those aren't Empire tents," Batu said. "They look like they're from Asjare. What are they doing here?"

"They're refugees," Manvel said. "A week ago, the nomads led a raid into the Arban Valley. As far as we could tell, their victory was decisive. The Arban Valley is theirs, and the Asjare army will no longer be of use to us."

"She actually did it," Batu said. "Sara took the Valley right underneath their noses."

"Why are there so few of them?" Cirina said. "It must have been a slaughter."

Erroll shook his head. "Most of them chose to stay. With Chief Dayir dead, there was almost no reason for most of them to stick with the Empire."

"So we're just supposed to walk into the Arban Valley and trust what you're saying?" Kara said.

Manvel shrugged. "No need to take our word for it. But you'll see the patrols long before you reach the valley. They'll be all the proof you need."

Kara crossed her arms. Batu could tell that she did not like it, but they were right. They had to trust Erroll and Manvel for now. As far as he could gather, Sara had sent her here to see if he was alive, but she had gotten ambitious and tried to free him. Obviously, she was not too happy about two Empire soldiers doing her job for her.

"One last thing," Erroll said. He walked up to Batu and handed him two scrolls. Batu opened it and saw that it was a map of the Steppe filled with complicated diagrams and plans. Upon closer inspection, he realized that it was a plan to invade the Arban Valley. He unrolled the second scroll and saw that it was a similar plan, only with different tactics.

"Is this what I think it is?" Batu said.

Erroll nodded. "The Empire isn't happy about losing the Valley. In particular, General Asghar sees it as General Sandulf's failure, so they're both planning to retake it. The first scroll is Sandulf's plan and the second is Asghar's. Use them well."

"They're separate? Why?"

"It's a long story, and those plans are bound to change," Erroll said, exchanging a look with Manvel, who grinned. "Sandulf and Asghar together still have enough troops to destroy all of you, so the two of us have a plan to make things a little easier for the nomad armies."

"If we play our cards right, that is," Manvel said. "But in any case, you need to warn them. The Empire's legions are on the move, and they won't take any prisoners."

Batu looked over at Cirina, who had heard everything but still hadn't said anything. Then he tightened his grip around the scrolls.

"I'll get these to Sara," Batu said. "And the two generals will regret the day they set foot in the Steppe."

"Good man," Erroll said. He looked like he was about to leave, but he turned back to Batu all of a sudden. "And for what it's worth, I'm sorry for taking you prisoner. It's my fault your friend died."

Batu shook his head and managed to maintain his composure, but his fists were shaking at his sides. "The only one at fault is Sandulf. Holding a grudge will do nothing but poison me. Someone very wise told me that some time ago."

Erroll nodded. "I'm grateful. Every day, your people continue to surprise me."

"What's that supposed to mean?" Batu said.

Erroll laughed. "Never mind. Go ahead. I think the both of us have some work to do."

Batu smiled, then he reached out and clasped Erroll's outstretched hand. "Thank you," he said. "For giving me a second chance."

Erroll gripped his hand. "Tonight is a good night for second chances, Batu. For both you and me."

# 36
# Erroll

Erroll signed the letter with a flourish, approximating Sandulf's handwriting to the best of his efforts. He blew on the ink to make sure it was dry before looking over the letter. All things considered, he thought that he had done a pretty good job with it. It was the best version of Sandulf's signature he had managed to forge in the last hour.

He placed the letter on the desk alongside five versions of the same letter, addressed to Sandulf's captains. Each letter contained a slightly different version of the plan, as was Sandulf's style, and there was a cipher in the letter's content that would tell the reader if it was the correct letter.

"Finished, I think," he said, looking up from his desk. He looked around the small cave that Manvel and he had turned into their temporary headquarters. As far as they could tell, this was the hiding place of some surviving Omnu hunters while the Empire occupied their lands. It was larger than they had expected since the Omnu hunters had brought their horses inside, but that also meant that it emanated the distinct smell of horse dung.

"Good," Manvel said, picking up the latest letter and examining it. "This one's supposed to be the genuine copy, right?"

"It is," Erroll said. "Sandulf's cipher is in every fifth word, not counting verbs. That last part is the one that has confused Asghar's people thus far. Until you pass him the information, of course."

"Got it. I've just heard the news from Sandulf's personal guard."

"And?"

"They aren't happy, to say the least. I heard that Sandulf broke someone's leg when he found out that you defected. He broke other things, of course, but I think the leg was most notable."

"Fantastic," Erroll said. "Not for the poor sod who had his leg broken, of course. But Sandulf had it coming."

Manvel nodded. "Hopefully this will make him angry enough to launch his attack early."

"He will," Erroll said. "I know the man well enough. This will make him itch for a fight. In his mind, this will be his way to reclaim all the glory he's lost."

"Will it be enough?" Manvel asked. "I mean, I know the nomads fight well, but is having Asghar and Sandulf attack at different times going to be enough to secure them victory?"

Erroll shrugged. "Well, it's all we can do. It's not like we can get one of the legions to leave the Steppe. They'll just have to make do."

"Fair enough," Manvel said, taking a seat next to Erroll. He pulled out some rations from his pack and passed a meal to him, who took it gratefully. He had not realized how hungry he was until he saw the food.

"I didn't think I'd ever enjoy these rations," Erroll said. "Do you remember the first time we had them? Back at the outpost."

Manvel laughed. "I remember we started missing the dining hall in the training camps."

"Those were the days," Erroll said. "Though, of course, Jarlen would eat anything they gave him."

"Quince would, too. He'd just complain about it the entire time."

Erroll laughed. For a moment, he felt as though he was back in the camps, sneaking out from their barracks in the middle of the night because Manvel had heard that the stars looked amazing in the Steppe. "I wonder what happened to those two," he said. "I never got a chance to say goodbye, since they were supposed to think that I'm dead and all."

Manvel's face fell. "Oh. You didn't hear?"

"What?"

"Both of them were killed during the Battle of Harnda," Manvel said. "I didn't hear the details, but they were placed on the front lines when the nomads first charged. They didn't stand a chance."

Erroll pounded his fist on the table. "By Saenor, this is exactly the kind of thing Sandulf would do. That bastard must've put them on the front lines to get to us. Just so we'd have nowhere to go but work for him."

Manvel sighed, then he placed a hand on Erroll's shoulder. "I don't know about that, Erroll. It might have just been a terrible coincidence."

"Really, Manvel?" Erroll said, looking up at Manvel. He was surprised at the hostility in his voice, but he did not back down. "After all you've done for Sandulf, you don't think that he considered doing such a thing? The man doesn't let any stone go unturned with these things."

Manvel's expression grew somber. "Even so, there was nothing we could have done."

"That doesn't make me feel any better."

"I know that. But I didn't know you cared about Jarlen and Quince so much."

"Yeah, well, I didn't either. I guess I've changed since we last saw each other."

"You have. Though I have to say, I wasn't surprised at all when you showed me this plan."

Erroll looked over at Manvel. He was surprised to see that his friend was smiling. "What do you mean? Manvel, if you had told me two weeks ago that I was going to betray Sandulf and help the nomads, I'd have called you an idiot."

"Guess you don't know yourself as well as I thought," Manvel said. "You remember what I asked you back when Sandulf first caught us?"

"You asked me what our next play would be."

"Exactly," Manvel said. "I knew you'd eventually cook something up to get the better of Sandulf. Took you a little while, but you got there. I never believed you for a moment when you said you'd given up. And I have to say, I'm more than a little impressed with the scale of your plans. This scheme is probably your best one yet."

Erroll smiled. "We're trying to end a war, Manvel. It has to be."

Manvel chucked. "You never were one for following orders, Erroll. That's probably what drew me to you in the first place."

"Is that the same reason you're here now?"

Manvel shook his head. "Nah. Not anymore. I've changed, too, since you last saw me. I was confused for a while, but now I've realized that it's time to walk my own path. Not my father's, not Sandulf's, but my own."

"Thank you for coming, Manvel. It really means a lot," Erroll said.

Manvel chuckled. "Sure. After Sandulf had me teach recruit after recruit how to wipe their own ass, I was dying for a chance to get out of that camp. So your letter was just what I was waiting for."

Erroll thought for a moment. He didn't think he'd ever seen Manvel this sure of himself. "I don't think I could have done it on my own."

"Don't mention it, Erroll. Now that we're both traitors, we're in the same boat."

Erroll shook his head. "I appreciate the sentiment, but not really. Sandulf still thinks you're working for Asghar. You could walk away at the end of this and return to the Empire. I don't have that option."

Manvel frowned. "So where will you go after this?"

"I don't know. I doubt the nomads will take me in, so I'll have to find somewhere else. Outside the Empire and the Steppe. Which reminds me, I need you do to something for me after this is all over."

"Anything."

Erroll picked up a piece of paper from the desk and looked it over. It was the letter to his mother that he had been planning to send for months now. After all these months, he realized he finally had the words to tell her. The first few lines were the same as when he'd written it back in the camps, but his eyes rested on the final sentence.

"I'm out looking for new horizons, Mother. I can't wait to tell you all about it."

Erroll placed the letter into a sealed envelope and handed it to Manvel. "This letter is for my mother. She lives in the smithing district in Ruson. Look for the jewelry store with the red sign. I want you to deliver it for me."

"You should be the one to deliver this," Manvel said. "In person."

"It's just in case. Take it, Manvel. And don't worry, I don't have any intention of dying."

Manvel took the envelope gingerly, as though he was handling a precious gem. "Fine. But only if this war ends in our favor. And only if you aren't able to deliver it yourself."

Erroll nodded. "Thank you. I have one more thing to ask of you."

"Something else you need delivered?" Manvel said, raising an eyebrow. "An old friend? Or a lover?"

"Nothing like that," he said, reaching into his jacket to pull out the flask that Manvel had given him. "I was wondering if you had any rum. I seem to have run out."

Manvel laughed, then he gestured to a barrel in the corner of the cave. "Fortunately for you, I came prepared."

Erroll laughed, then he walked over to the barrel and filled his flask to the brim. When he returned to the table, Manvel already had his flask out.

Erroll raised his drink. "To second chances," he said.

Manvel grinned. "Second chances," he agreed. They toasted and each of them took a long drink from the flask. The liquid burned the inside of Erroll's throat, but he was familiar with the feeling by now.

Erroll settled into his seat and allowed himself to relax. He had no idea when was the next time that he would be able to let his worries float away. He tried to enjoy the moment while it lasted.

# 37

# Sara

Horns blared throughout the Arban Valley to signal the arrival of riders. The sound caused a commotion throughout the camps, but the blasts did not signal a large-scale assault, even though they had been expecting one for days.

When she heard the news, Sara left her tent, jumped on her horse, and started riding towards the Valley's mouth, where the patrols would be watching for new arrivals. She joined the patrol group a few hundred meters away from the entrance. They were standing with their weapons at the ready in case it was a threat. Since the Battle of the Camps, Sara had instructed all of her hunters to carry weapons with them at all times, in case of any unrest.

"Is that who I think it is?" Sara said as she watched three riders enter the Arban Valley. Behind her, the patrols that were watching the valley's mouth with their hunting eagles had given her the signal that it was safe. She saw them emerge on the horizon, and had no doubt in her mind who it was.

Khulan came riding up, her face red with excitement. "You'll never guess who it is," she said.

"It's Batu, isn't it?" Sara said.

Khulan blinked. "Okay, good guess."

Sara grinned. "I knew it."

Without waiting another second, Sara and Khulan rode to meet them. Sara noticed that they were wearing the armor of the Empire's scouts, and the horses they were riding were of a different breed and build. She would have thought that they were enemies if she had not noticed the distinctive way they rode, with their hands on the backs of their necks so that they would not arouse suspicion. Sara was glad that Kara remembered the signal they had agreed upon before sending hunters behind enemy lines.

When they spotted Sara and Khulan approaching them, they got off their horses, handing them to a few hunters that had come from the border patrols. Batu in particular seemed glad to finally be rid of the horse. She noticed that someone was missing from their group.

"There are only three of you. Where's Nugai?" she asked. Batu's face dropped to the ground immediately. Sara knew what that meant — she had seen that look before, even carried it herself on some days.

"Oh," she said. "I'm sorry, Batu."

Batu shook his head. "I know what you thought of him. He did some horrible things. But I think you should know that he sacrificed himself to save our tribe. He was a good man."

Sara exchanged a look with Khulan, whom she expected to jump at the mention of Nugai's name, but Khulan looked uncertain for once. She was fiddling with the straps on her armor and was making every effort not to make eye contact with Batu.

"He deserved better," Sara agreed, then she looked over at Khulan.

"I'm sorry for your loss," Khulan muttered under her breath, then she walked away, got on her horse, and rode off. Kara looked between Sara and Batu and then followed Khulan.

Before Kara left, Sara said, "You'll explain yourself to me later. I only told you to see if Batu was alive. I didn't ask you break him out."

Kara flinched, but she relaxed as Sara patted her on the shoulder. When she was gone, Sara turned to Batu.

"Sorry about that. Khulan will come around," Sara said.

Batu shook his head. "It's fine. Nugai's death doesn't make up for the things he did for my father. I just hope that the way he lived towards the end meant something."

Sara nodded. "We'll give him a proper burial."

"There's no time for that," Cirina said. "We have some bad news. The Empire isn't happy about us taking the Arban Valley. They'll be here to take it back, and soon."

"We've prepared for that," Sara said. "How soon?"

"Within the week," Batu said. "They might be on their way already."

Sara took a deep breath, pressing her hands to her cheeks to calm herself down. "That's earlier than we expected. I'll need to send riders to all the head chiefs to muster all the forces we have. And then we need a war council with all the head chiefs. They'll be throwing everything they have at us, and we have to be ready to meet them."

Sara turned around and started walking towards her horse. Batu remained in her place for a second before following her, as did Cirina.

Just as she was about to get on her horse, however, she turned to face Batu. "I'm glad you're alive, by the way. You'll have to tell me about how you got out."

Batu smiled. "It's a long story, but the short version is that we had some help. From an unlikely source."

Sara wished that she could ask him for more details, but there was no time. She nodded and said, "Well, we're going to need all the help we can get if we want to live to next week. Get your hunters ready. I'll send you a messenger to let you know about the war council."

Without another word, she was on her horse, riding off into the distance. For a second, she regretted not taking enough rides into the Steppe when she could. It seemed as though this might be one of her last.

The war council was shorter than Sara had expected. Chanar and Thaube had arrived within the day, so they held the meeting just before sundown. They finished discussing by dinner time. They moved through their agenda quickly, as though all of them could feel the looming threat on their shoulders. Whatever happened, this might be the last time all of them could gather like this alive.

"If we send our forces together, it may work," Thaube said to Galeren. "I have some of the best riders in the Steppe, and your infantry can hold strong against any charge. You've taught me that quite a few times during our battles."

Galeren folded her arms. "I don't mind lending you some of my troops. But I would much rather they be given the freedom to move through the battlefield without having to follow your hunters around."

"You're being unreasonable," Thaube said. "The Empire's soldiers will be arranged in large, organized ranks. We don't have a chance of stopping the Empire if all we do is mimic their formation."

"Ridiculous," Galeren said. "I am no Jusordian imitator, Thaube. My soldiers fight in the way our tribe has done for generations."

"Galeren's captains are some of the most skilled in the Steppe," Sara said. "If Thaube can lend you some of his riders, your captains should know how to command those units, won't they?"

Galeren considered for a moment. "That seems reasonable. But will this old stag let me have control of his hunters?"

Thaube's eyebrow quivered at the insult, but he managed to hide his anger. "I think Sara's right. It's a good plan, provided your soldiers can pull their weight in battle."

Galeren laughed. "Never in my life did I think I would see Qhurin soldiers fighting alongside Gur hunters. So be it, then. We'll ride this tide together."

Thaube had surprised Sara. After the last battle, she had realized that he had become one of her most trusted allies. He had even convinced Chanar to back down when he threatened to walk away from the alliance.

The council was over before long. Every member went off, presumably to give the news to their hunters, herders, and their respective families. Everyone had their own promises to keep before the final battle.

Before Sara could leave the tent, however, Ibakha pulled her aside. Zayaat was standing next to her, but there seemed to be a weight on his shoulders. Even in his huge coat, he looked small.

"Is there something you need?" Sara asked.

Ibakha merely shook her head. Sara thought she could see tears in her eyes.

"I never thought I'd see it again," Zayaat said. "The tribes brought together. You really did it, Sara, against all odds."

Sara shrugged. "Let's just see if we'll live through the week. If not, it'll be all for nothing."

"Nonsense," Ibakha said, placing her hand on Sara's shoulder. "I've told you this before, but I have all the faith in the world in your leadership, Sara. You'll see us through."

Sara smiled. "Do you remember when we sat on that hill together before the Battle of the Rivers?"

"I do," Ibakha said, cocking her head to the side. "What about it?"

"You told me that being a leader isn't about being a general or a tactician. That it takes more than that."

"Ah, yes, I remember. I was half joking, but I wonder if you've come up with an answer for me."

"It's simple. It takes trust," Sara said. "And right now, I trust that we'll all live to see the dawn."

Ibakha grinned. "I can't think of a better way to put it."

She and Zayaat left the tent to coordinate their hunters. After a few moments, Sara left as well, accompanied by Khulan and Bataar who were waiting for her near the entrance of the tent. The task ahead would require the work of everyone in the Omnu tribe, and Sara did not want to make any decisions without her masters of hunters and herders present.

"So," Khulan said once they were out of earshot of the other chieftains. "Might be the end of the tribe as we know it. How are you going to spend the week?"

"Don't say things like that, Khulan," Sara said. "We still have a chance."

Khulan laughed. "Of course we do. Just humor me, Sara. You can lighten up every once in a while. This chieftain business is really dampening your mood."

"You know, she might be right," Bataar said. "When was the last time the three of us had time to hang out like this?"

"We have preparations to make tonight. Maybe we shouldn't even be hanging out," Sara said, but when the other two raised their eyebrows, she sighed. "Okay, fine. Bataar, why don't you go first?"

"Easy," Bataar said. "I'm finally going to tell her how I feel."

Khulan laughed. "At long last, Bataar. I thought you'd never drum up the courage."

Sara frowned. "Wait, who are you talking about? I didn't know you had feelings for someone."

Bataar wrung his hands together. "Well, that's because I didn't tell you. It's, uh…it's…"

"Kara," Khulan said. "He's had a crush on Kara for, what, two years now?"

"Two years is a perfectly reasonable amount of time to have a crush on someone," Bataar said.

"I suppose after spending five years crushing on Sara, two years is an improvement, isn't it?" Khulan said, laughing when she saw the look on Bataar's face. "What? Everyone knows he did. No point in hiding it. You remember the time your father took the four of us up to the Temple of Gaeon? I don't think he talked to me the entire way there."

"Well, did you know that I liked you, Sara?" Bataar said.

Sara winked at him. "So, Kara, huh? What do you like about her?"

"You're really going to make me answer that?" Bataar said. He knew that she was serious when he saw Sara raise her eyebrow,. "Okay, fine. She started coming by while I was watching the animals and would help out sometimes. She said that she always wanted to be a herder, but she felt obliged to become a hunter when she lost her dad,. And I don't know, I guess, she's just so…assertive. She doesn't take anything from anyone, you know? One time, Ganbold tried to use her as a decoy and she came back and punched him right in the gut. She's the kind of person I wish I could be."

Khulan laughed. "So, in short, you're into women that can kick your ass."

"Basically," Bataar said, shrugging. "Wish me luck."

"Of course," Khulan said. "As for me, I'm going to spend as much time outdoors as I can. We're on the Steppe, but we don't get enough sunlight in the valley. It's ridiculous. First thing tomorrow, I'll go see if the patrols need any extra hunters."

The chieftain part of Sara wanted to tell Khulan that it might be dangerous, but she held herself back for a moment. "That sounds like a great plan. I'd love to join you."

Khulan grinned. "I've always got great plans. How about you, Sara? What are your plans for the end of the world?"

Sara chuckled. "You know, I've never really had the chance to think about that." She looked away to think about her answer. Out of the corner of her eye, she saw Batu walking alone from the meeting, heading towards the Omnu section of the camp.

"Do you think Batu's going to be okay?" Sara asked suddenly. "He didn't seem to talk much during the council meeting."

Khulan folded her arms. "If you ask me, he just seemed happy to be there."

"It was good that you invited him, I think," Bataar said. "He's had his ups and downs, but people still look up to him as the son of Chinua. There's talk that he received Gaeon's blessing when the Temple burned."

Sara nodded. "He's not Chinua's son at all, though. In the same way that I'm more than just Julian's daughter."

Bataar blinked. "Of course. Sorry, that's not what I meant."

"Don't worry about it," Sara said. "I'll catch up with you two later. I think the both of you have things to do anyway."

Bataar left immediately, but Khulan stayed with Sara, her hand on her shoulder.

"Yes, Khulan? What do you need?" Sara said.

Without hesitation, Khulan pulled Sara into a hug, which surprised

Sara at first. With Khulan's steady arms around her, she felt the fear being squeezed out of her body.

"Be safe, Sara," Khulan whispered in her ear. "You're holding up the world, but first, you have to hold yourself together."

Then Khulan released Sara and left before Sara could say anything, leaving Sara blinking in disbelief. She sighed, her lips curling into private smile that only she could see, and started walking towards Batu.

Batu walked with his eyes on the ground and did not seem to notice when heads turned to watch him as he passed.

She tapped him on the shoulder. "You can't keep walking around like that, you know."

Batu turned and raised an eyebrow. He didn't seem that surprised to see her here. "What's that supposed to mean?"

"I mean, look around you," Sara said. "You saved them at the Battle of the Rivers. You emerged from a burning temple alive. They call you Flamewalker, blessed by Gaeon. Even the Asjare seem a little in awe of you. If you want to inspire them, you can't walk around looking like you just lost a battle."

Batu looked around him, and noticed that a few circles of people seated around campfires were sneaking looks at the two of them. He straightened his posture and did his best to make his clothing look a little more presentable.

Sara took him by the arm and began pulling him away from the camp. "Okay, come on. I'll take you somewhere."

"Where?"

"It's a place I go when I want to stop being the chief for a little while."

She led him through the trees until the camp was no longer in sight, then they started walking up the slope of one of Arban's Peaks. They hiked up one of the paths until they were seated on one of the ridges overlooking the camp.

"Why is no one up here?" Batu asked.

"This is the pass to the Asjare's mountain camps," Sara said, pointing at the trail leading higher into the mountains. "Since we hold the Harnda lands, there's no real reason to guard them, so they're empty most of the time."

"But why did you bring me here?"

Sara laughed and gestured in front of them, where they had a view of the entire valley floor, including the four Asjare camps and the field camps of each of the other tribes. The view was made of a huge tapestry of orange lights, flickering and wavering as winds blew through the Valley. "The scenery, of course."

Batu finally looked at the view and he was speechless for a few moments. He took a deep breath and closed his eyes. "I wish Nugai were here to see this," he said, then he saw Sara next to him and winced. "I mean…"

Sara shook her head. "It's fine. You're allowed to grieve for your friend."

"Thank you. It's just strange. He was at my side the whole way. I wouldn't have made the choices I did if not for him. And it just feels wrong that I'm here, able to dream of a future that he doesn't share with me."

"I feel the same way about my brother. Well, him and everyone else I've lost. Doesn't seem fair that I've made it this far and they didn't. I don't think I deserve it."

"You know, I think you give yourself less credit than you deserve. What you did here is nothing short of incredible," he said, gesturing towards the camps of hunters from across the Steppe.

Sara smiled. "Galeren told me what you said to her. About me."

Batu's eyes widened, and Sara thought she could see him blush. "And? What did you think?"

"I'm grateful, though I think you exaggerated a little bit. I spoke to your hunters while you were gone, and from what they told me, I realized something about the future of our tribe."

"And what's that?"

"That after all this is all over, it can't just be me that leads us. It's going to take both of us to rebuild our tribe."

Batu stared down at his lap. "Do you think I have any right to lead the Omnu? After all the mistakes I've made?"

"I think you've paid the price for those mistakes many times over," Sara said. "And it's exactly someone like you, who has made those mistakes and learned from them, that we need to restore the glory of our tribe."

"What do you mean? What will change after this war's over?" Batu said.

"I don't know," Sara said. "But we can't go back to the way things were."

"I guess you're right," Batu said. "My father had big dreams. He wanted to tear down the barriers between the tribes and create a united Steppe. But he did horrible things in pursuit of that dream. He would have built his vision out of the ashe of every tribe that stood in his way. I don't want to force my vision for the Steppe onto its people, but I think I owe it to my father to carry his dream with me."

"I can get on board with that," Sara said, then she got up and stretched.

"Where are you going?" Batu asked.

Sara grinned. "You've inspired me, Flamewalker, so I think I'd like to get some work done tonight. We can't realize our vision for the Steppe if we're dead, can we?"

Batu nodded and got to his feet as well. Sara took one last look at the view in front of them. Omnu, Qhurin, Harnda, Chenkah, Asjare, and Gur. Somehow, as she looked at the huge, sprawling camp with all the tribes preparing for battle together, her dreams for the Steppe did not seem so far away.

"It takes trust," she said, repeating the words she had said to Ibakha and Zayaat. Back then, they had seemed like platitudes, but for this brief moment, she believed it.

# 38

# Batu

Batu stood at the head of the Omnu and Harnda force as a thousand thoughts swirled through his head. He heard the horns of the approaching army as he turned and saw the hunters yell and cheer, raising their weapons and preparing themselves for battle. He felt like he was about to explode.

He watched as the enemy legion began to swarm through the mouth of the Arban Valley, forming ranks that spread across the valley floor. He took a deep breath. Chinua's voice reminded him that he would fail, that the strategy that they had prepared would not work, but he did his best to push the voice to the back of his mind. There was work that he had to do, and he was not going to let Chinua hold him back this time.

"There are fewer of them than we expected," Cirina said. "I wonder if Erroll and Manvel actually pulled through for us."

"This looks like it's just one legion," Batu said. "Sandulf's, if the scouts are right. Asghar's is taking a little longer to mobilize, but he'll be here soon."

Cirina nodded. "Then we'll just need to take Sandulf down as quickly as we can."

"Exactly what I was thinking. We can't afford to get overwhelmed," Batu said, then he turned to Gerelma. "I want your hunters to charge in first. Don't bother with each individual infantry square. I want your hunters to weave in between them, harrying them the entire way with arrows. My hunters will follow as best as we can."

Gerelma nodded, then she turned to give the orders to each hunting group leader.

"Are you ready?" Cirina said. "From being a prisoner in the Empire camps to leading an army against them. All in one week."

Batu shrugged. "I've had bigger jumps in shorter amounts of time. I'm glad you're here, though."

Someone cleared his throat behind him, and Batu turned to find Bala, Dorgene, and Jochi assembled and mounted.

Jochi folded his arms. "Chief Flamewalker, back from another dance with death. I doubt you even remembered us the second time you returned."

Batu laughed. "Of course I remember the three of you. There's a reason you're all here now. I wouldn't face this battle with anyone else."

For the first time since Batu had met him, Bala smiled. "It is a shame what happened with Nugai. But now we will avenge him. I am with you, Chieftain Batu. You ride with Gaeon's blessing, after all."

Batu's eyes fell on Dorgene, who was busy adjusting her quiver and bow. She looked up and noticed that everyone was staring at her. "What? You want me to say something too? Don't worry, kid. You'll do fine."

Then she turned back to her quiver. Batu turned away from them to face the Empire's army, which was advancing slowly through the Valley. They were taking their time. It was clear that they expected the nomads to make the first move.

Batu looked to his side and saw that the central army, commanded by Sara, was lining up into neat rows. The front lines were not filled with cavalry but with infantry and backed up by archers. There were hunters on horseback patrolling behind the lines, ready to jump in at the first sign of trouble. On the left flank, which was led by Galeren's captains, the mixed infantry and cavalry units were ready for battle. They began to slowly advance, taking the signal from Sara's group.

Batu turned to his hunters. He could not quite tell what they were thinking, and he wondered if they were used to facing death after so many battles. The monster that raged inside of him made him feel as though the fear never really went away. Nevertheless, he raised his sword and turned to his hunters.

"Thank you all for standing with me today. They say that I am blessed by Gaeon. They say that I walked through fire and lived. I don't know if any of that's true, but if you follow me, we'll walk through the inferno together. Gaeon ride with us all," he said, and the hunters cheered after him. He turned to Cirina and whispered only loud enough so that she and the other three hunters could hear. "This one's for Nugai."

He patted his horse on the neck, spreading manna across its mane, and spurred it onwards. They spilled into the valley towards the enemy.

Batu swept through the enemies like a hurricane. He was running low on arrows, so he took out his sword and used it to sweep through the Empire's soldiers.. Behind him, his hunters followed as they crashed through the Empire's flank.

He thrust his sword through a man's head and trampled two more under his horse, leaving them for his hunters to finish off while he engaged two more soldiers. Batu threw himself into the battle, allowing his instincts to take over as he let his sword arm do the thinking, the blade itself becoming nothing more than a blur as it moved from enemy to enemy.

"Show no mercy," a voice said in his head.

They encountered little resistance as they charged through the enemies. The Empire's ranks were built to sustain a long, drawn out offensive, with soldiers ready to move up to the front line when the soldiers at the front got exhausted, but it was not designed to withstand a dedicated cavalry charge.

Soon, Batu knew that the Empire would catch on and begin their counterattack, especially with the sea of enemies spread before them. He found that he did not care. Each Empire soldier that he managed to kill took on the face of Sandulf. Each time he faced the Empire, he had someone to protect. This time, he felt months of pent-up-anger rushing forth, like he could not hold it back any longer.

"You'll make a river from their blood," the voice said. "You'll drag them through the sea and strangle them with their guts."

He screamed as he fought, each strike punctuated with a howl until his throat felt raw. The enemy soldiers did not stand a chance. He had to stop and look behind him to make sure he did not get too far ahead of his hunters several times, when he had enough clarity to think through the crimson, pulsating anger. He did not give pay it much attention, however. They were not much more than fleeting thoughts at the back of his mind as he hacked through the Empire's soldiers, as though they were nothing more than sacks of meat.

"KILL EVERY LAST ONE OF THEM!"

One soldier managed to score a hit on Batu's arm and drew some blood, but he did not even feel it. He stabbed the man through the chest and pulled the sword out of his arm, grunting with the effort. Otherwise, he felt nothing as blood ran down his armor.

Another soldier charged at him, but Batu easily swept his sword aside and grabbed the man's head, yanking his helmet off before sinking his fist into the man's face. He felt his own blood splash against the soldier, and he heard teeth and bones come loose as the man crumpled underfoot. Batu roared, feeling his anger course through him.

"Avenge the dead. This is your chance to pay your debt."

Each time he swung his blade, he imagined he was saving his father from the flames. He imagined their faces swimming among the enemy. Killing Jusordian soldiers allowed him to imagine the faces of the dead finding peace as they were finally able to pass into the wind. But the faces were endless. So many had died in this war, and he was just one man. He could not save all of them.

"You useless excuse for a son," the voice said, seeming oddly familiar to Batu. "You're too spineless to be head chieftain. It seems that I've failed as a father."

Batu blinked, and his sword arm dropped as he recognized the voice. The red on the edges of his vision finally faded away, and he looked around him, seeing a sea of dead Empire soldiers piled around him, with the rest of the enemies too scared to approach him.

His father's voice raged on. "What are you doing? Why have you stopped? Kill them all! Do your duty, Batu."

"No," Batu muttered, cursing himself. He thought that he had managed to push Chinua's voice away, but he had not. He looked behind him, realizing that his entire arm and most of his chest were covered with blood. He saw that his hunters were struggling to follow along, and their line was a few meters behind him. They were tiring fast. Each time they faced a new wave of enemies, they cut through them at a slower pace.

Batu realized that the hunters on the front lines had changed a few times by rotating with the hunters behind them, but he had not noticed that till now. He had fought through so many rotations that when he finally felt the fatigue, his sword dropped to the ground. He did not have the strength to pick it up again.

Finally, he heard Cirina's voice calling from behind the lines, "Batu! Batu, you have to stop."

Her voice brought him back to reality. He turned his horse and disappeared into the approaching wave of hunters, letting them take his place in front. Directly behind the lines, which parted to let him pass, he found his group of hunters. Batu got off his horse and joined them, catching a glimpse of Gerelma and a group of Harnda hunters riding past him to fend off an advance from the Empire's main army.

"What in Saenor's name were you thinking?" Jochi said. "The other hunters were convinced that you were on a suicide mission. They had half a mind to let you die, seeing the way you were pushing us harder and harder."

"Where's Bala?" Batu asked, looking around him.

"He's wounded," Jochi said. "He tried to follow you into the enemy ranks but ended up taking an arrow to the shoulder."

"You're being too hard on Batu," Cirina said. "The plan was clear. We're meant to push the Empire as hard as we can to surround them."

"No, Cirina, it's okay. I got a little carried away," Batu said. He sighed in relief. At least Bala had not died from his foolishness. He could still feel the monster inside of him strain against its bonds, spurring him to leap back on his horse and punish the Empire's soldiers. He managed to bite down the feeling. He took a deep breath, and his vision cleared.

"You're wounded," Cirina said, noticing the cut on his arm. Batu looked at it and saw that it was bleeding profusely, and only then did he feel the sting of the wound. He winced as Cirina inspected it, pulling his sleeve away to reveal a cut about ten centimeters long.

She pulled out a bandage and cloth and began to clean the wound with herbs. The medicine stung, but Batu gritted his teeth and tried to speak through the pain. "It looks worse than it feels," he assured her, but Cirina did not seem to listen.

"I swear to Gaeon," she muttered under her breath. "Making me worry like that. Totally irresponsible."

"I'm sorry," Batu said. "It won't happen again."

"It better not," she said. She pressed the cloth to the wound, making him wince. She smiled when he did, even humming a song to herself as she worked.

Batu turned to Jochi. He still looked irritated, but seemed willing to listen when Batu called his name.

"Jochi, I'm going to need a report. What's going on with the other flanks?" he said, scanning the battlefield. He only saw the Empire's flank engaging their advance, with most of the main army moving deeper into the valley to engage Sara's force. But he could not see past the enemy's massive army, so he had no idea how Thaube and Galeren's force was faring.

"We had a messenger about ten minutes ago," Jochi said. "Galeren's force is faring well, though their progress has slowed because of the terrain. And Sara's army is holding strong."

"At least the plan seems to be working. Send a messenger to Gerelma to send the archers forward. With any luck, the enemy will be shaken enough by our initial charge that we can surround them," Batu said. He could feel the gears in his mind start to click, and he shifted back into thinking about tactics and battle strategies.

Jochi nodded, then he moved away to deliver Batu's orders.

"I didn't think I'd end up relying on him this much," Batu said to no one in particular. Cirina did not look up to respond.

"Your father trusted him," Cirina said. "Say what you will about Chinua, but at the very least, he knew how to choose the right people to lead."

"Then it makes sense why he didn't choose me," Batu said. Cirina finished bandaging his arm and he pulled it away from her, running his hand absentmindedly over the bandaged area.

"Batu, I won't have this from you again," Cirina said. "You're a good commander, even though your father never saw it."

"He thought I was soft. That I cared too much about our hunters."

"That's your greatest strength."

Batu did not respond. Instead, he got to his feet, though the loss of blood was making him queasy. "I want to go see Bala. Where are the wounded?"

Cirina looked shocked for a moment, but smiled and took him by the hand. "I'll take you there."

# 39

# Erroll

Erroll's spear was dripping with blood when he approached Sandulf's center of command. Manvel followed after him with two daggers glinting in his hands.

Some soldiers came forward to stop them, but Erroll dispatched them both with thrusts to the chest. They crumpled immediately, and so did the two others that approached from Manvel's side. Erroll and Manvel stepped over their bodies to approach Sandulf, who was standing with Syra and some of his other officers.

Sandulf did not notice them approaching. He was busy giving orders to his captains, watching the battlefield unfold before them.

"Asghar's force will be focused on capturing the center of the valley," Sandulf said.

"Shouldn't we cooperate with him, General?" one of his captains said. "We're all on the same side, after all."

"Are you an idiot?" Sandulf snapped. "If we let that upstart take control of the valley, he'll win all the glory again. And I'll be stuck fighting bandits on the coasts until the end of my days. Push the forces harder. Send word to the fourth, fifth, and sixth squadrons to reinforce the main army."

"The captains of the fifth and sixth are dead, sir," Syra said. "Perhaps it will be wise to keep them as our rear guard, just in case we need to pull out."

"I don't care," Sandulf said. "Send them all now. I will be the one to raise the empress's standard in the valley's center, or you will all die trying."

"Of course, General Sandulf," the captains said, and they all left to deliver his orders. Syra, however, remained and he whispered in Sandulf's ear.

Sandulf turned to face Syra, and it was then that he finally noticed that Erroll and Manvel standing there. He did not look surprised. Instead, he pulled out his sword, a huge two-handed weapon that was nearly as tall as the general was. Erroll had never seen the general wield it before, but it seemed almost natural to see the general dressed in full plate armor.

"Ah, Erroll, I suppose that I have you to thank for killing my captains. I wondered when I'd see you again," Sandulf said. "Originally, I'd assumed that you'd turned tail and ran, just like your father."

"Don't you speak about my father," Erroll said.

"I see you share his love for the savages. Filth, both of you. And you, too, Manvel? Duke Marcel will not be happy to hear about this."

Manvel grit his teeth, but he did not back away. "You won't live to tell him."

Sandulf laughed. Syra pulled out his sword and stepped forward.

"I thought better of you, Erroll," Syra said. "I wouldn't have imagined you as a traitor."

Erroll shrugged. "I guess you taught me a little too well."

Syra turned to Sandulf. "Shall I call for reinforcements, General? It appears that they have killed all your bodyguards. We should get you out of here," he said.

"No need," Sandulf said, standing next to him in a battle stance. "The army is busy enough as it is. The two of us will be enough to handle a couple of traitors."

"As you wish, General," Syra said, and they both advanced on Erroll and Manvel.

"I'll take Sandulf. You can have Syra," Erroll said to Manvel.

And so the battle begun.

Sandulf went for an overhead blow first, which Erroll blocked by raising his shield. Erroll could feel the shock travel down his arm as the blow came crashing down. He grunted from the strength of the blow, and Sandulf raised his sword again, hammering it down before Erroll had a chance to recover.

Erroll rolled aside this time, letting Sandulf's sword bite into the ground beneath him. Erroll tried for a thrust, but Sandulf let the blow glance off of his gauntlet, barely even wincing as he knocked the strike aside. The general yanked his sword out of the ground and went after Erroll again. Each strike Sandulf launched was like a crack of thunder, and the sound of metal biting into Erroll's shield resembled lightning scorching a hill in a storm.

Sandulf refused to give Erroll any room to attack. He stepped forward with each strike, barely even noticing as Erroll's spear glanced off his armor, even drawing blood at one point when it grazed his arm. Erroll kept his stance steady, parrying each blow and feeling his heels bite into the ground with each crash of Sandulf's sword.

"You knew what would happen if you betrayed me," Sandulf said, hammering in his words with another swing of his sword. Erroll could feel his legs buckle underneath him with the strain. He found himself pushed backwards, almost to the edge of the hill.

Sandulf pounded him again with another blow. Erroll could tell that he was not tired from the way the general's face stiffened up like a cliff face in the dead of night. Each blow felt savage and wild, but Erroll knew that they were calculated, each of them perfectly placed to collapse Erroll's defences. Erroll knew the general well, because Syra had taught him to fight the same way.

Erroll blocked another blow, gritting his teeth as the shock traveled through his entire body, making his vision spin and his muscles ache. He stepped forward with his shield in front of him, catching Sandulf off guard for a moment.

His shield connected with Sandulf's elbow, breaking his stance for a moment. Sandulf's sword dropped to the ground, and he took a few steps back, his torso exposed. The general raised one hand from his sword to his chest to block any incoming blows.

Erroll saw his chance. It was just for a brief moment, but it would be enough. He raised his spear above his head and brought it crashing down on Sandulf's head, ready to splinter his skull.

Sandulf caught the spear. His gauntleted hand flew upwards with impossible speed as he clasped the spear's shaft between his fingers. Sandulf grinned when he saw Erroll's wide-eyed. He yanked the spear out of Erroll's hand.

Erroll's stance came apart. Sandulf stabbed him with the spear, piercing Erroll's left shoulder. Erroll cried out in pain and felt hot blood run down his arm. His shield crumpled to the ground as Erroll stumbled backwards, clutching his arm and trying to get away from Sandulf.

The general struck Erroll in the face with the handle of his spear, the wooden shaft snapping across Erroll's cheek with a loud crack. Erroll stumbled. From the blood flowing down the side of his face, he could tell that something was definitely broken.

Sandulf threw Erroll's spear aside and came at him with his sword again. Erroll just managed to dodge in time, but he could feel his vision blur as the pain and blood loss set in, making him wish he could let Sandulf kill him to get it over with.

"Erroll! Catch this!" a voice called. Erroll looked up to see one of Manvel's daggers spinning towards him. Erroll grabbed the weapon out of midair. He felt his mind click into place as his fingers closed around its hilt,.

He watched as Sandulf came at him, swinging his blade again. This time, however, he saw a pattern to the general's strikes. He would not win this battle if he fought like a Jusordian. He had to try something else.

Erroll danced around Sandulf, ducking under his strikes and letting Sandulf's sword come within inches from his face before leaping away again. Sandulf raised an eyebrow as Erroll feinted at Sandulf's neck, making him raise his gauntlet in defense to block a blow that never came.

Erroll smiled as he saw Sandulf's brow furrow. He continued to tease the general, letting him get the upper hand for a few minutes before dodging Sandulf's attacks once again.

"Damn coward," Sandulf growled, raising his sword again. It came crashing down and Erroll charged straight into it, his dagger raised. The sword dove towards Erroll like a flash of lightning, as Erroll dodged to the side at the last moment, letting the sword slam into the stone underneath his feet.

Erroll saw Sandulf's eyes grow unfocused as the sword shook with the force of the blow. The general could only watch wide-eyed as Erroll came at him with the dagger, scoring cuts on Sandulf's cheek, torso, and arms. Erroll refused to give Sandulf any time to recover and pressed on with the attack, drawing blood in a dozen different places.

Sandulf's grip finally gave way. The huge blade clattered to the ground as Sandulf stumbled backwards, but he did not fall. He planted his feet into the soil and raised his fists.

"I'll beat you into the ground like I did with your father," Sandulf said. His teeth and fists were bloody, but they looked nonetheless deadly.

Erroll laughed. "You think I don't know? My father didn't die under your command. He died where he belonged. In the Steppe."

Sandulf didn't answer. Instead, he charged at Erroll with his fists raised, roaring like a leopard. Erroll charged to meet him, but dodged when Sandulf got close enough to throw a punch, sweeping Sandulf's arm aside to catch him off balance. When Sandulf swiped in retaliation, Erroll ducked, feeling the armored blow narrowly miss him,. He then drove his dagger straight into Sandulf's thigh, piercing through the chain mail and tearing through the general's skin.

Sandulf howled in pain and tried to grab at Erroll, but he was already gone, making his way through Sandulf's attacks to emerge behind the general. Erroll slammed his knee into the back of the general's legs, making him topple with the weight of his armor. Sandulf was on the ground, with Erroll's foot on his back and his dagger right above his neck.

"Any last words?" Erroll asked. "It's more than you would have given my father."

"No...no...." Sandulf said. "Please...please don't kill me."

Erroll paused. Six months ago, Erroll would not have hesitated, but now, it felt wrong to plunge his dagger into the neck of a man pleading for his life. Erroll looked up to check on Manvel, then he gasped.

Manvel was on his knees before Syra, who was holding his sword above Manvel's head. His friend's dagger was long gone and he seemed to have lost the strength to fight. Manvel's head was bowed and his arms fell limp at his side. This time, Erroll didn't hesitate. He took aim and threw his dagger straight at Syra.

The dagger spun in the air before burying itself into Syra's neck. The captain sputtered for a moment, blood flying from his mouth. He collapsed to the ground, the sword clattering to the ground beside him.

Erroll was about to smile, but then he felt the ground underneath him shift. He fell down, only just managing to catch himself before his head slammed onto the stone. Sandulf had pulled himself out of Erroll's grasp and was now standing above him.

Erroll recognized the look on the general's face. It was that of a wild deer at the end of a long chase. His eyes were wide and his cheeks sagged. Sandulf gave Erroll one last haunted look before fleeing, throwing off pieces of his armor as he went.

"So, the great general Sandulf was a coward in the end," Manvel said, appearing next to Erroll.

Erroll nodded. "Thanks for the dagger."

"Don't mention it," he said, then his eyes saw that Erroll was still bleeding. "You're hurt."

Erroll shrugged. "It's nothing. I told you, I don't intend on dying."

Manvel pulled out a bandage from his satchel and began wrapping it around Erroll's shoulder while Erroll dabbed at the wound on his cheek.

"Aren't we going to chase after him?" Manvel said, pointing as

Sandulf got on a horse and rode straight out of the valley, his captains calling after him.

"Let him go," Erroll said. "I think he's learned his lesson."

They were on the edge of the hill, where they watched as the battle unfolded before them. Sandulf's legion, which had lost many of their captains, was faltering, and the nomads had managed to surround the main bulk of the force while routing its flanks.

"The battle isn't over yet," Manvel said. "There's still Asghar to worry about."

"I wonder which way he's coming from," Erroll said. He spotted commotion on the far side of the battlefield, near the mountain pass that he had ascended with the Asjare long ago. Asghar's force emerged from the mountain pass, right behind the nomad forces that were just beginning to notice their approach.

"Gaeon's staff, are you seeing this, Manvel?" Erroll said.

"Yup. I had no idea that Asghar even knew about the mountain pass. He must have marched his soldiers through the night to get there on time."

"He's going to catch the nomads entirely by surprise. We need to do something about it," Erroll said.

Erroll paused for a moment. They were both wounded, and Asghar's force was all the way on the other side of the battlefield. They would have to find a way past both Empire and nomad forces to reach them.

Erroll watched the valley before him. Even though it was filled with death and chaos, it still breathed; winds swept through it and swayed the trees without paying any attention to the battle unfolding. When Erroll thought about the prospect of letting Asghar wipe the nomads off the Steppe and turn the valley's forests to ash, he found that the thought of fleeing was even more repulsive than that of dying. He owed the nomads a debt, and though they would never know it, he was determined to repay it.

"What are we going to do, Erroll?" Manvel said.

Erroll grinned. "Help me find my spear. We're going to pay Asghar's legion a visit. It's time to make my father proud."

# 40

# Sara

Sara rode up and down their line, watching as her hunters faced another wave of Empire soldiers. They braced as the Empire crashed into their line. They planted their feet and felled soldier after soldier, their swords flashing as their arrows pelted the enemies from behind. And once again, the Empire was forced backwards.

But each time they were sent back, another rotation of soldiers replaced them and they hsf to ready themselves for another assault. It seemed endless, and her hunters were tiring quickly. There were not enough of them to replace the wounded and exhausted hunters, so all they could do was grit their teeth and dig their feet into the soil.

"Hold strong, everyone!" she cried, pulling out her bow and nocking an arrow. She loosed it into the crowd and an Empire soldier crumpled to the ground. "Archers, I want another volley. Keep them on their toes."

The archers nocked arrows and launched them, sending the Empire's soldiers scrambling. Then the nomads' line parted and a group of hunters charged towards the enemy, all of them mounted on horses. Before the Empire's soldiers could react, the hunters cut a swathe through their ranks, disrupting their formation and sending them into chaos. The Empire tried to tighten their formation, but they were too slow. The hunters were gone before they could even react.

Sara saw that Khulan was the leader of this group. She directed her hunters to disperse as soon as they crossed the line, riding off to the other parts of their army to support the defense. Once Khulan was sure that her hunters knew where they were going, she approached Sara.

"Doing all right, Khulan?" Sara asked.

"As well as I can be," Khulan said. "They're disorganized today. Their formations are sloppy, and they react far too slowly. They're not used to fighting in the mud. It's almost too easy."

"Still, be on your guard," Sara said. "This is Sandulf we're dealing with."

"Of course," Khulan said. "Where do you need me to go next? I can muster another raid within ten minutes."

Sara sat up on her horse, scanning the line. The hunters in front were switching places with hunters behind them and were finally allowed to rest. The new hunters would need another cavalry charge to gain their footing.

Before Sara could decide on a place to send Khulan, Bataar emerged from the back of the army and approached them. Sara and Khulan got off their horses to listen to his report.

"Bataar, good to see you," Sara said. "Has Chanar sent the reserve troops I asked for?"

Bataar shook his head. "Bad news, Sara. It's Asghar. He's marched through the Harnda territory and is attacking us from the mountain pass."

"Saenor's scales," Sara said. "We should have posted guards there."

"It wouldn't have done any good," Bataar said. "He's attacking in force, and even the patrols we left in Harnda weren't enough to stop him."

Sara took a few deep breaths, clutching the saddle of her horse. She didn't have time to lose her cool during a battle like this. "Okay, what's he doing now?"

"They've attacked right in between Batu's force and ours, so we're cut off from them," Bataar said. "We've sent word to Batu to stick to the plan, but we haven't heard anything from him. Chanar sent his entire reserve force to intercept them, and they're holding on for now."

Sara considered for a moment. "Asghar's legion is as large as

Sandulf's. If they're in advantageous terrain, which they are, Chanar won't stand a chance, no matter how well-trained his hunters are. We need to help him."

"Sara, wait," Khulan said, catching her on the arm. She pointed towards Sandulf's force, which was preparing another attack. They raised their spears and advanced, shields ready to block any arrows that came their way. "If you ride to help Chanar, you'll leave our backs exposed. Sandulf and Asghar will crush us like two boulders."

"Galeren and Batu are in position," Sara said. "They'll be able to handle Sandulf's legion."

Bataar frowned. "That won't be enough. Sara, you know the plan. It would be unwise to abandon it now."

"I'm not going to leave Chanar to die, if that's what you're asking," Sara said.

"Sara, just listen," Khulan said. "Why do you care so much about Chanar? He was happy to abandon you at the Battle of the Rivers."

"No," Sara said, removing Khulan's hand from her arm. "It's final. We're not leaving any one of our own behind."

"You'll have to," Khulan said quietly. "Don't sacrifice your entire people to save a few lives."

"What are you talking about, Khulan? Don't you trust me?" Sara said.

"Sara, of course I trust you. I'll follow you to the end," Khulan said. "But please, don't lose the war to win one battle. It's not worth it."

Sara suddenly remembered Ibakha's words to her when she was about to ride to Batu's aid. Batu had survived without her help, but even Sara had to admit that she had been right. Back then, they had not even been sure if Batu was alive. Things are different this time.

"But he's right in front of me," Sara said. "And we're sure he's alive. How am I supposed to be a leader if I can't protect the people who trusted me with their lives?"

"This is part of the job too," Bataar said. "I'm sorry, Sara, but Khulan's right. It's a tough choice, and you're the only one here with the strength to make it."

Sara closed her eyes. "What would my father have done?"

"He's not here right now, is he?" Khulan said, taking her hand. "Sara, we don't have time. You need to decide right now. What are you going to do? What kind of leader are you going to be?"

Sara opened her eyes and saw her friends staring at her. It seemed like the sky was bearing down on her, pushing onto her a burden that she had never asked for.

"What word do we have from Batu and Galeren?" she asked quietly.

"They're ready to attack," Bataar said. "The flanks are routed and Sandulf isn't ready to face an attack on three sides. They're just waiting for your signal."

Sara took a deep breath. The weight of the sky pressed down on her, and she wanted nothing more than to curl up into a ball and let Khulan make the decision for her. But her hunters had given her their trust, and in return, she had to trust them as well.

"Gaeon, forgive me for this," Sara said. "Give the order. We're taking Sandulf down."

Bataar nodded, then left to instruct the other hunters. He seemed unsure of what else to say. Khulan moved to leave, too, but Sara caught her on the arm.

When Sara met Khulan's eyes, her own started filling with tears. Khulan took Sara's head into her hands and pulled her into an embrace.

"I'm sorry," Khulan said, and allowed Sara to sob into her shirt.

"I didn't ask to be chief. I didn't ask for this duty."

"I know," Khulan said. "I know."

Sara took a few deep breaths and pulled away from Khulan. She looked around, making sure that no one had noticed them. "You should go now," she said.

Khulan hesitated for a moment, but Sara shook her head.

"I'm still a chief," Sara said. "Regardless of whether or not I asked for it. So I have to figure this out on my own. Go."

But Khulan stayed. She stepped closer to Sara and placed a hand on Sara's cheek.

"You're carrying so much on your shoulders, Sara," Khulan said. "I wish I could help you."

Sara sighed and placed her hand on Khulan's. "You already have, in so many ways. You fought for me even when I didn't believe in myself."

Khulan smiled. "That's what friends do, right?"

"Really? After all this, we're only just friends?" Sara said.

Khulan shook her head. Instead of answering her, she took Sara's head in her hands, and kissed her. Sara's eyes widened when their lips met, but she did not want to pull away. She took in Khulan's scent and the shape of her lips. She felt like she could do anything. Khulan's touch felt like the wind in her hair and sunlight on her back. It felt like home.

"I love you," Khulan whispered into Sara's ear. The world raged around them, but where they were standing, everything seemed to fall silent.

Without a moment's hesitation, Sara replied, her cheeks wet with tears. "I love you too."

Then the cloudy sky above seemed to clear. The wind blew stronger around them, rushing through Sara's hair in a whirlwind.

They parted, and Khulan smiled. "Your tears got on my face," Khulan said, wiping her cheeks with her sleeve.

"I'm sorry," Sara said, chuckling despite herself. "But I didn't ask you to kiss me, did I?"

"I guess you didn't," Khulan said, then she got on her horse. "You don't need to do everything, Sara. Your friends are here to share the load."

She rode off, and Sara repeated Khulan's words to herself. "Share the load," she whispered, then she got on her own horse.

Sara closed her eyes and took on the vision of her eagle, which had been circling the front line. Instead flying straight towards the valley's mouth, she changed its direction. The eagle shot through the sky; the crimson streak it made would be bright enough for both Batu and Galeren to see. She saw an eagle emerge from both sides of the battlefield. Together, the three eagles met and flew towards the edge of the valley.

# 41
# Batu

Bala was sitting alone in the middle of their small medical camp. The arrow had not struck too deeply, but the medical corps had declared him unfit to go back into battle because of how close it had come to his artery, despite his angry protests.

"How dare they keep me away from the front line," he said, fuming, as the hunter assigned to take care of him shrunk before the hulking man. "I can fight. I will lend my power to our victory."

Batu laughed, then he patted Bala on his good shoulder. He turned to the medic. "You can move on, now. I'll make sure he doesn't do anything dangerous."

The medic nodded and moved on to the next wounded hunter, who had a sword wound in his thigh.

"Excellent. Thank you for sending him away. Now help me find my horse and sword."

"The medic is right, Bala," Batu said, raising an eyebrow. "I don't want you out on the battlefield right now."

"Preposterous. I am more ready to fight than ever," Bala said, raising his arms, but he winced and clutched his wound.

Batu laughed. "I don't think I've ever seen you this riled up, Bala."

"It is only natural. I finally found a chief who deserves my loyalty, so now I am willing to follow him wherever he goes. Even if it means going into the depths of the sea."

Batu flushed at the compliment. As he turned to Cirina, she grinned and pretended to inspect another wounded hunter.

"I'm grateful," Batu said. "But the best thing for you to do right now is to stay alive. I don't want to lose any more people."

Bala nodded. "If that is your command, then I will follow gladly."

Batu turned to Cirina. "I need your help. Send riders to the front lines. I want them to send some of our forces back to help escort the wounded off the battlefield. Make sure they're our finest hunters—Alaqa's group will do fine, I think."

"Don't we need those hunters for the front line?" Cirina said. "We've almost broken through the enemy."

"Getting these hunters to safety is our priority," Batu said. "If the plan doesn't work and we need to retreat, they'll be the first ones to die. I won't have that."

Chinua's voice emerged in Batu's mind. "They'll die anyway if the battle doesn't go your way. You'll waste your own resources." Batu did his best to ignore him.

Cirina nodded. "I'll send riders immediately."

"Rest well, Bala," Batu said. "I'll need to speak with more of the wounded, then I'll be back on the front line. I'll fight those bastards on your behalf."

Bala nodded. "Gaeon ride with you, Flamewalker."

Batu gave Bala a smile, then he started to speak with some of the other wounded hunters. He recognized many of their faces from the training ground, but he had yet to learn their names. Batu knelt down next to each of them and spoke to them if they were conscious, asking them to tell him their name.

Husun, Boal, Togene, Hongorzul, Khashi, Jamukha, Chimbai, and so many more. Batu knew that he would never remember all of these names at once, but he repeated each of them and tried his best to see them as more than hunters. They were his people, and he needed to see them as such.

"You're the Flamewalker, right? The one blessed by Gaeon's flame?" one of them, Togene, had said to him.

"I don't really like all the fancy titles," Batu said, and Togene laughed. Her laughter was pained as she had taken an arrow to the chest. Her armor had stopped it from piercing her flesh, but it still left a nasty bruise and a few broken ribs that had taken her out of combat.

"Fine. So what should I call you then? Chief Batu?"

"Just Batu is fine. So, tell me, Togene. What are you looking forward to the most about returning to Omnu?"

"I haven't thought about that, really," she said, and a far-off look in her eyes emerged. "I can't wait to go to the flower fields and pick some for my wife. She likes the purple ones that only grow in this one field to the northeast."

"I know the place," Batu said. "My mother Oyuun used to take me there when she was mad at my father."

Togene laughed as she coughed, but she seemed to enjoy it anyway. "Ah, your mother was something else. Did you know that she used to join my wife and I for dinner? It was only once every year or so, but we loved her company."

"I miss her," Batu said. Suddenly, he felt like a child again, sitting in front of his mother's grave, wishing that she would get up and give him a hug.

Togene reached out and took his hand. "She's still with us, you know. In the wind, the flowers, and the grass. And I know that she would be so, so proud of you."

Batu smiled, looking up at her with tears in his eyes. Before he could respond, someone tapped him on the shoulder. It was Cirina, back from delivering his orders to Alaqa and the rest.

"Batu, you're needed on the front," Cirina said, and then when she noticed Togene, she gave her a nod. "Sorry to interrupt."

"No problem," Togene said. "I was just thinking that I need a nap anyway." She turned to Batu. "Go, Batu. Go make us all proud."

Batu reached the front line just as they sent the bulk of the enemy's flank into a rout. The archers had pulled through, and their hunters had managed to take control of the southern edge of Arban's Valley.

He watched with satisfaction as the Empire's broken ranks, fled before their advance. A few hunting groups chased after them. He looked at the main army, hoping that the retreat of the flank would be enough to trigger a more general rout, but it did not appear so.

Jochi rode up to Batu, followed by a few hunters that he had picked up from the Harnda forces.

"The Empire are in full retreat, Batu. The southern edge of the Valley is ours," he said, a huge smile on his face. "Gerelma is sending some of her horse archers to harass them. I can send some of our own people to pursue them."

Batu shook his head. "Let Gerelma finish the job. I only want her to make sure that the Empire retreats out of the mouth. Go no further than that. The objective of today is to protect the Arban Valley, nothing more."

Jochi nodded, then he turned to one of the hunters at his side. "Got that? Good. Now, go."

As he rode off, Jochi continued his report. "The main army is still holding strong, though they seem spooked by our quick victory. They're setting up some ranks to defend themselves, but most of them are still pressing against Sara."

"Make sure our hunters are ready to engage the main army, though hold off until we get word from Galeren. And Sara? How is she doing?" Batu asked.

"Fine," Jochi said. "According to the last report, they're holding up well enough. That Saragerel's tough as stone, and so is her master of hunters. I'm expecting another message from them soon."

As soon as Jochi finished speaking, Cirina emerged from the back of the army, pushing past many of the hunters. She approached Jochi and Batu.

"What is it?" Batu said.

"General Asghar," she said. "He's here."

Batu looked about him, but from what he could see, there was no new army emerging at the mouth of the Valley. The mouth remained empty, save for the soldiers that were now retreating through it.

"Where?" Batu asked. "We must intercept them. They can't be allowed to link up with Sandulf."

"They're not trying to link up with Sandulf," Cirina said. "They broke through our patrols in Harnda and marched through the mountain passes. They took us by surprise, and now we're cut off from Sara."

Chinua cackled in Batu's mind. "This is where your arrogance got to you. Soon, everything will crumble because of your mistakes."

Batu felt his breathing quicken. "That bastard Asghar. Of course he had something up his sleeve. Never mind, then. We'll ride to support Sara. If we combine our forces, we should be able to break through the enemy. Jochi, send word to the front line. We'll need every hunter we can muster."

Jochi moved to deliver the order, but Cirina caught him by the arm.

"No, stop!" she said. "Batu, if you stop the assault on the main army, you lose our grip on the battle. The entire plan will be in flames."

"I didn't think the plan was going to work anyway," Batu said. "Look, Sara needs us right now, and that's what we're going to do."

"She'll die because of you. They'll all die because of you," Chinua's voice said.

"Sara can handle herself," Cirina said. "She trusted you to see this through, Batu."

Jochi turned back to them after listening to a report from one of his hunters. "Galeren's force is in position, Batu. They had heavy casualties, but they should have enough hunters if we can support them from the other side. What's it going to be, Flamewalker?"

"We can win this battle, Batu. We believe in you," Cirina said.

"But I don't," Batu said, turning away from her. He looked at the main army arrayed before them. They were setting up shield walls and their formation seemed impregnable. He tried to get a glimpse of Asghar's force flooding into the Steppe, but he could not see past the trees. The Empire's army organized their ranks, and he saw his hunters behind him watching him decide, ready to follow him wherever he went.

Batu found that he could not meet their eyes. They would find out that he was a fraud, like every other force he had commanded thus far. He was not fooling anyone. He turned away from them and walked to a clearing, leaving Jochi and Cirina to argue.

He closed his eyes, but all he could see were the flames encasing his father's camp, burning Chinua and everything he had known into the ground. He gasped and his eyes fluttered open. Suddenly, his father was standing in front of him. a pale shadow formed from the wind. Batu recognized the look in his eyes, the same one his father had whenever Batu missed a shot with his bow or fell off his horse.

"I've never been enough for you, have I?" Batu said. "No matter what I did, I was never good enough to be your son."

"Everything I did, I did for you, Batu," Chinua said.

Batu scoffed. "I hated myself for so long because of you. But all I wanted was your support, and you never gave it to me. How could you even call yourself my father?"

"I knew you could be better. I don't regret it."

"And what would you do? You're the greatest general the Omnu have ever known. How would you win this battle?"

Chinua took a moment, scanning the battlefield, then he turned back to Batu. "I'd burn it all to the ground. The Arban Valley is filled with trees. If you start a fire, the Empire's soldiers will burn, and you will be victorious. But of course, you're too cowardly to try something like that."

Batu looked at the valley with new eyes, feeling blood burn the inside of his bones, screaming at him to act. He wanted so badly to prove his father wrong, to burn down the entire Steppe and claim victory, just so his father could never call him a coward again.

But then he thought about the night he spent with Sara on that ridge, dreaming of a new world together. It was not only his world, but hers too. The stars had seemed so much closer then, as if he could reach up and claim them. He knew then, that he was to be a builder and not a burner.

He laughed, and for once, Chinua looked confused. "That was all I needed to hear, Father. You were always a coward. You burned every tree that crossed your path, and that's why you'll always be alone."

Chinua gave him a sly smile. "Ah, my foolish son. It will be a pleasure to watch you lose."

"I'm not your son. You said so yourself," Batu said. At his words, his father disappeared into the wind. He turned back to Cirina and Jochi.

"I was afraid you'd gone into a trance again," Jochi said. "We need an answer."

Batu did not answer. Instead, he got on his horse and faced the center of the valley. "The plan stays the same. Sara can handle herself, but she's counting on us to rout Sandulf's force."

"I knew it," Cirina said. She got on her own horse, and so did Jochi. Both of them took out their weapons.

The hunters assembled behind them began to gather into their ranks again. He scanned their ranks again, and this time, he was no longer gripped with fear. He saw them grasp their weapons, steady their horses, and cast their eyes towards the sky.

"Come with me! We'll ride to victory, and to the new dawn!"

# 42

# Erroll

Erroll watched as the nomads made their final stand and approached from the peaks of the Arban Valley. His spear rested on the grass next to him, dripping with the blood of Asghar's officers. Manvel sat next to him. His friend was a little worse for wear. He had several cuts across his face and arms, but he was pressing a damp cloth to the biggest wounds and had bandaged the rest of them.

"So," Erroll said.

"So," Manvel said.

They both started howling with laughter. Manvel doubled over in laughter while Erroll had to grip the sides of the mountain to keep himself from falling over. In front of them, the battle was still raging.

"We just betrayed the entire damned Empire," Manvel said, still on the ground.

"Best day of my life. How about you?" Erroll said.

"Oh, of course," Manvel said. "I'm just imagining the look on my dad's face when they tell him."

"I bet they won't even tell him," Erroll said. "They'll drum up some lie about your heroic death in battle. Who knows, maybe the news of your betrayal will be enough for your dad to pick up a sword against the Empress."

Manvel chuckled. "Now, wouldn't that be a sight. Maybe we should go tell him ourselves, just to see how he reacts."

Erroll clapped his friend on the shoulder. Up until now, he had not realized how far they had come together. All this time, Erroll had thought he was alone, Manvel was with him the entire time. It had taken him far too long to realize that.

"You know, I do have to go back to the Empire anyway. I have a letter to deliver," Erroll said, holding up the letter to his mother.

"Ah, everyone's favorite pair of idiots, now fugitives from the Empire, sneaking back into the capital city," Manvel said. "Seems like we've got an exciting future ahead of us."

"We did just kill a bunch of the Empire's finest soldiers and sent Tomyris's second favorite general running," Erroll said. "I think we can handle it."

"Sure we can. And how about after that? What do you want to do then?"

"Might come back here," Erroll said, gesturing broadly to the Arban Valley and the Steppe that lay beyond. Right now, the main nomad force was standing their ground, with enemies on every side. If it were any regular Empire force, they would have been routed ages ago, but the nomads were fighting more ferociously than ever. And if Erroll's hunch was right, he thought they had a shot at winning.

"What's left for you here?" Manvel said.

"Ah, I think I have a few debts to pay," Erroll said, waving a hand. "And in any case, the view isn't bad."

He pointed towards the Arban Valley. It was filled with death and gore, but, the hills, the grass, and the trees were still the same. He remembered climbing up here a few months ago with Geser, Khalja, and the rest. That was when he saw the Steppe in all its glory for the first time.

He was used to the view now, having seen it so many times while he stayed with the Asjare. The mess of snaking rivers, trees, and camps spread out like a few specks of dust on a vast sheet of green. Eagles soared through the skies and trees swayed in the wind. A grand tapestry, the likes of which not even the best weavers in the Empire could ever hope to replicate.

Sitting on the side of a mountain watching all of it with him was Erroll. Here he was.

# 43

# Sara

Sara raised her sword and let out a war cry. Her hunters answered her. They let out the loudest cheer that Sara had ever heard, ready to fight and defend their home. She turned and saw Khulan mounted on her horse next to her, sprinkling a pinch of manna onto its mane to keep it calm.

She smiled at Khulan and he smiled back. Sara felt something warm turn in her stomach, pressing against her sides. She had to look away, hearing Khulan cackle with laughter when she did.

"Hunters of the Steppe," she said. "You trusted me during the Battle of the Rivers, the Battle of the Camps, and countless times before. Trust me again, and we'll throw these bondless fools out of the Steppe once and for all!"

The hunters roared their approval, and Sara raised her sword again.

"Gaeon ride with you all," she said. Without waiting for their reply, she kicked her horse into motion. As she charged forward, Sara did not have to look behind her to see if her hunters were following her. She only needed to hear the thunder of hooves and the cacophony of war cries to know that her hunters were with her all the way.

They charged into the line of Empire soldiers assembled before them. They held up their shields and pikes in defiance, but scattered as soon as they saw a line of screaming nomads barrelling towards them.

Their pikes pointed towards the ground and their shields crumpled underneath the horses. A few hunters fell when the Empire fired a volley of arrows against them, but most were able to dodge out of the way, sprinkling manna onto their horses' manes when they saw the arrows being loaded. Sara herself weaved out of the way of a squadron of Empire soldiers that were trying to group up against her.

She looked behind her and saw that Khulan and a few other hunters were following her. It reminded her of that day all those months ago when they were out on the Steppe, the wide open sky right above them.

"Just another day on the hunt," she whispered to herself, and gestured to her hunters. They obeyed instantly, firing arrows into the crowd of Empire soldiers, punching past their defences as they watched a few of them crumple to the ground.

The moment their defences faltered, Sara leapt into the fray with Khulan. The squadron broke and the surviving soldiers dropped their weapons and began running as fast as they could. Most of them were felled by the horse archers, and those that survived would soon be out of the battle completely.

"How are the flanks?" Sara said, riding up next to Khulan as she took reports from a few messengers that wore the markings of Galeren and Batu's forces.

"Wonderful," Khulan said, nodding to the messengers, who left to deliver messages down the line. "The attack is going as planned. Galeren got held up for a moment, but she mobilized immediately when she saw the signal. Batu apparently didn't hesitate."

"Well, they call him the Flamewalker for a reason," Sara said. "And how about the rear flank?"

Khulan shook her head. "No word from Chanar yet. Asghar seems to be taking all of his attention."

"I don't like the sound of that."

"Sara, you're not thinking of running to his aid, are you?"

Sara took a deep breath. "No, I'm not. I've made my choice. I can only hope that Gaeon blesses him and his hunters."

"That's the spirit," Khulan said. She pointed towards the rest of Sandulf's force, which was scattering, though there were still quite a few of them left. "Now, you let me handle the reports. You need to be on the front line. Keep our hunters energized, okay?"

"Yes, ma'am," Sara said, winking. Before Khulan could reply, she drew her sword and led the rest of their hunting group towards the front line. They followed her without question, and cut a bloody swathe through the Empire's forces together.

Sara found Batu at the valley's mouth watching the enemy retreat. His sword lay bent and bloody on the ground next to him. His quiver was empty, and his arm was bandaged, but he was alive. Sara herself was out of arrows as well, and she had lost her sword while fighting one of the Jusordian officers. Sara got off her horse and joined him as the rest of her hunters joined his and chased the last of Sandulf's legion out of the valley.

"You're a little late," Batu said.

"My hunters were on foot," Sara said, taking a long drink from her waterskin. "And your force left several pockets of enemies behind. I had to clean up after you."

Batu shrugged. "Well, they've been defeated, haven't they? Let's not get too hung up on the details."

"We haven't won yet," Sara said. Bataar approached them to deliver his report. "What's the news of Asghar's legion, Bataar? I'm ready, whatever it is."

"Asghar's force has been sent back," Bataar said, and immediately, both Sara and Batu turned to face him.

"Are you serious?" Batu said. "Chanar's tiny force managed to send back an entire legion?"

Sara laughed. "That crazy bastard actually managed to do it."

Bataar nodded. "Chanar's force contained most of the Asjare hunters that surrendered after the Battle of the Camps. They knew the territory and played it to their advantage. And I haven't confirmed the reports yet, but I've heard rumors that two Jusordian deserters killed many of Asghar's captains, sending them into disarray. But I have some grave news, as well."

"What is it?" Sara asked.

"Chanar held back Asghar's force, but he did it at the cost of his own life. Most of the Chenkah hunters died in battle as well."

"Oh," Batu said, his face darkening. "I'm sorry."

Sara nodded. "May Gaeon ride with them. Send every hunter we have to spare to reinforce them. Khulan's in command."

Bataar nodded and got back on his horse, but before he left, he said, "This was the right thing to do, Sara."

"I know," Sara said. "It just took me a while to realize that."

She stood with Batu in silence as the hunters finished their work with Sandulf's troops and moved to assault Asghar's legion. With each hunter that passed them, Sara realized that the long battle was finally ending. She thought that she would feel triumphant and excited at the thought of rebuilding, but she only felt tired.

"So, what now?" Batu finally said.

"What?" Sara asked.

"You told me before the battle that things needed to change. Well, the war's over. So, what's going to change?"

Sara grinned. "Everything. Now that it's all over, we have a duty."

"A duty to do what?"

"To rebuild. The Steppe divided itself into smaller and smaller pieces after the first war, and that was nearly the end of us. We can't let that happen again. And I hope that I'll have your help."

Batu nodded. "Of course. I still owe you a debt for saving my life. We need to make sure that something like this never happens again. I still have my father's—no, my own dream to carry out."

"Agreed," Sara said. At that moment, Altan descended from the sky to land on her shoulder. She fought the temptation to take its eyes and soar into the skies. For once, she did not want to know how the situation was going. She would have things to do, for sure. They had to tend to the wounded, hunt down the last of the Empire's soldiers, and eventually, reclaim the Omnu lands. But all of that could wait for now.

Around her, the hunters began to clear away the carnage of battle. The valley seemed to breathe again when the bodies were cleared from its hills. She took a long, deep breath through her nostrils, letting the air flow through her lungs, The air still smelled of metal and blood. Sara exhaled and allowed the air to leave her. The wind seemed to clear as it did.

The task in front of her seemed large and daunting, but she allowed herself to be still and listen for now. She listened to the wind howling through the Arban Valley, to the trees swaying in the wind, and to the soil crunching underneath her boots. When she listened hard enough, she could hear Od's voice echo in her mind, though she could not make out what he was saying. It did not matter.

Sara looked up at the clouds that were tinged orange from the setting sun. Above her, the sky opened up.

# 44

# Epilogue

The nomad chieftains gathered where the Temple of Gaeon once stood. It was a solemn occasion, and the mountaintop was filled with chieftains, hunters, and herders from from every tribe across the Steppe, all of them clad in thick wool coats to protect them against the biting cold.

A single figure, dressed in ceremonial robes, ascended a small wooden stage to address the crowd. The clearing was small enough to allow her voice could carry throughout it, and the crowd fell to silence immediately as they saw her,.

Saragerel, daughter of Julian, head chieftain of the Omnu and hero of the Second Grand Alliance, addressed the crowd. "Thank you all for coming today," she said. "We are gathered here in the spirit of remembrance, in the hope for new beginnings, and most importantly, yo express our wish for unity. We are here today to remember those we lost in the Second War with the Empire over a year ago. They bled for the Steppe, for the grass, the wind, and the flowers beneath their feet. Without them, we would not have the freedom we celebrate today. Gaeon ride with them."

"Gaeon ride with them," the crowd repeated. Sara looked into the crowd and made eye contact with Khulan, her wife, who gave her a thumbs up and a smirk. Sara had to hold back her own smile as she continued.

"I will now speak their names. We hope that Gaeon will grace the winds with their memory," Sara said. She began rattling off the list of names that she had painstakingly memorized in the months following the Second War. Most of them were hunters that she did not know or only had heard of, but she took pains to remember all of their names as if they were her closest friends. In a way, they were.

Out of all of them, there were several names that stood out to her. She had to hold back the bite in her throat and the tears in her eyes.

Mide. Yargai. Orda. Ganbold. Dagun. Yegu. Chanar. Khasar. Nugai. Odgerel.

"Od," she whispered under her breath after she said his full name, and no one seemed to notice except for Bataar, who was standing next to the stage, arm-in-arm with Kara.

When she finished listing the names, there was no applause or acknowledgement from the crowd. She knew that all of them had lost people close to them. She looked out into the crowd and saw so many familiar faces: Ibakha, Zayaat, Galeren, Alaqa, Gerelma. The losses still stung as much as they did a year ago, but at least she did not have to deal with them alone. Without another word, she descended the steps. Taking her place on the stage was Batu, one of her chieftains.

Batu ascended the stage, wearing robes that were completely different from the ones his father had worn in the past. Instead of the embroidered wolf-skin robes that Chinua had once used to dominate council meetings, Batu wore a simple hunter's armor, the one that he put on when preparing to ride into the Steppe with his hunting group.

Everyone fell to silence immediately as he ascended the stage. They watched as Batu, son of Oyuun, the Flamewalker, blessed by Gaeon himself, ascended the stage to speak to them. Batu felt his palms sweat, but he pushed the doubts deep inside of him. He had come so far in the past few years, and he was not going to let anxiety get the better of him today. He locked eyes with Cirina, who was standing near the front of the crowd, and she gave him a knowing smile. She was standing alongside Jochi, Bala, and Dorgene, all of whom had made the long journey up the mountain to be here for him. Batu relaxed immediately.

"This one's for you, Mother," he whispered.

Then Batu took a deep breath. "Thank you, Sara. For the first time in two years, we are holding the ceremony to receive Gaeon's blessing at the Temple. We've endured many losses in the Second War with the Empire. One of the biggest was the Temple of Gaeon, burned to the ground in another one of the Empire's attempts to break our spirits. But we did not falter, not even for a second."

Near the back of the crowd, a man dressed in hunter's clothing shifted nervously on his feet. His complexion was different from the rest of the nomads, and he looked like he was from the Empire. It had been a year since Erroll burned down the Temple of Gaeon, and though many had forgiven him for it, he still felt pangs of guilt whenever it was brought up in conversation.

"Today, we restore the Temple to its former glory," Batu said, and he gestured behind him. The blackened, burned ruin of the Temple of Gaeon had been painstakingly cleaned, repaired, and newly polished, looking like when it was first erected a thousand years ago. A former Empire soldier, Erroll had led many of the restoration efforts, traveling all over the Steppe to collect testimonies on what the statue of Gaeon looked like so that another former Jusordian, Manvel, could get it exactly right when he carved it.

"The Temple of Gaeon used to be a place where nomads from all the tribes across the Steppe could come and receive Gaeon's blessings," Batu said, and then he took a deep breath. "My father disrespected that tradition when he closed the Temple after the First War with the Empire. As his son, it's only right that I reopen the Temple. This place used to be a place of unity and equality, where there were no tribes or conflicts, only proud nomads of the Steppe. So it shall be again."

Finally, the somber mood of the ceremony began to lift and the nomads in the crowd applauded. Batu looked out and saw people from across the Steppe: Qhurin, Gur, Chenkah, Harnda, Omnu, and even Asjare. He had traveled all across the Steppe after the First War, living with each of the tribes for a period of time, and he saw first-hand the deep divides created by his father.

He had hoped dearly that today would be a step in mending those bridges, and the crowd watching him made him believe that his dream might become true.

Erroll watched Batu's speech from the back as he stood next to Manvel, who crossed his arms. He thought about his father. He wondered whether or not his father had ever felt truly at home among the nomads or if he had always thought that there was a distance he could not cross. Erroll still felt that way, even after all this time.

Erroll sighed and Geser, one of his first friends from the Asjare, clapped him on the back. He did not say anything, and his eyes remained fixed on Batu. Erroll finally stopped shifting from foot to foot. He did his best to stand up straight in his hunter's armor that finally felt as though it fit correctly. Batu spoke again.

"The Steppe does not belong to one person or tribe," Batu said. "It belongs to everyone who believes in our way of life, and in the lives that dwell in the flowers, in the grass, and in the wind. Gaeon rides with all of us."

As he said those words, a bright azure light began to glow in the small pool of water that had for so long sat empty.

# Author's Note

This novel has been in the works since December 2018, nearly three years ago now, and at times, working on it felt impossible. It felt like scaling an impassable peak or getting out of a warm bed on a rainy day. I am here now because of the countless people that lent a helping hand along the way, all of whom I hope to thank here.

First, I'm grateful to Balestier Press, who took a chance on a first-time author from the Philippines and believed in my project. Asian and Asia-inspired literature owes so much to Balestier Press, who paved the way for so many Asian stories to be told on a world stage. I'm also deeply grateful to Yale-NUS College and the team at the Dean of Students office for their generous support of this novel. I would not be the writer I am today if not for the guidance, challenge, and learning I received at Yale-NUS.

When I was a bright-eyed first-year at Yale-NUS, I never imagined how wonderful the writing community I'd discover here would be. To the Literary Collective, helmed by the amazing Phoebe, Lee Ann, Sean, and Wern Hao and populated by too many terrific writers to name, thank you for inspiring me to write better, kinder, and braver. The late night crit sessions were the home that I had always dreamed of as a young writer. I hope that it will remain a home for many years to come.

I owe so much to the mentors that found the hidden gems in my writing, even when I didn't see them yet. Thank you to Larry Ypil, whose early morning writing spaces were the first place I learned to share my writing. Thank you to Prof Balli Kaur, whose Intro to Fiction Writing class provided all the laughter, critique, and community I needed as a new fiction writer. Thank you to Roshan Singh, whose playwriting workshops taught me to approach creative work with structure, care, and wonder.

Thanks to my summer writing group: Hong Jin, Nicole, and Vi, who helped peer pressure me into getting through the last stretches of this novel. I owe special thanks to Wisha Jamal, my former debate partner and current best friend who, at times, was more invested in this story and its characters than I was. The stories of Sara, Batu, and Erroll owe so much to her honesty, humor, and attention to detail.

To the friends who give me a reason to keep getting up every morning, simply by being them: Avneesh, Alex, Runchen, Chitvan, Vanessa, Mato, Prayog, Eva, Shani, Marc, Josh, Raj, Charis, Miguel, Betina, and Kalla. I owe all of you the world.

Thank you to my parents, Steve and Julie, who saw the stories I scribbled on my bedroom wall, handed me a pen, and told me to get to work. And of course, to my little sister, Kaitlyn, who I hope can pull her nose out of K-pop videos for long enough to read this novel.

Finally, to my self-appointed literary agent and partner-in-crime, Kanako, who holds the frayed strings inside me together when they're close to snapping. Thank you for being the wind in my hair and the sunlight on my back. I could write for a thousand years and never run out of words to describe how much you mean to me. Here's to us.

I have a final message for every new author out there that's just getting started and isn't sure if their writing is good enough for the world. I was in your shoes a very short time ago, and I still have many of the same doubts. I wrote for nine years and threw four full-length novels in the trash before one was finally picked up by a publisher. But I wrote anyway, because I believe that my writing is part of something bigger than me. If you feel the same, then I guarantee that the world is waiting to hear your story. Gaeon ride with you.

STEVEN SY was born and raised in Quezon City, Philippines, but traded in one sunny, tropical country for another, moving to Singapore to study anthropology at Yale-NUS College. His fascination with epic fantasy began with *The Lord of the Rings* and *The Elder Scrolls* series, and he continues to be obsessed with how made-up worlds can make people see the real one in new ways. He also dabbles in playwriting and is the co-creator of *Tiwala*, a musical about faith and community set in provincial Philippines. He dreams of being a creative writing teacher one day in an apartment with many dogs and his partner. *Vacant Steppes* is his first novel.

You can visit him at his various social media accounts.

Facebook: https://www.facebook.com/stevenjustintsy
Twitter: https://twitter.com/stevenjustintsy
Instagram: https://www.instagram.com/systevenjustin/
Tiwala Productions: https://www.facebook.com/tiwala.productions

Lightning Source UK Ltd.
Milton Keynes UK
UKHW011035100921
390347UK00004B/536